THE
LOCUST
EVENT

THE
LOCUST
EVENT

GENE BRYANT

authorHOUSE®

AuthorHouse™ LLC
1663 Liberty Drive
Bloomington, IN 47403
www.authorhouse.com
Phone: 1-800-839-8640

This is a work of fiction. All of the characters, names, incidents, organizations, and dialogue in this novel are either the products of the author's imagination or are used fictitiously.

Published by AuthorHouse   12/12/2013

ISBN: 978-1-4918-4165-5 (sc)
ISBN: 978-1-4918-4164-8 (e)

Library of Congress Control Number: 2013922376

Any people depicted in stock imagery provided by Thinkstock are models, and such images are being used for illustrative purposes only. Certain stock imagery © Thinkstock.

This book is printed on acid-free paper.

I dedicate this book to my family and friends.
A group of genuine and wonderfully real people
that make every day better than the last.

You have always been there for me and I am humbled
by your love, support, guidance and patience.

To those that assisted me during the writing
of The Locust Event, I give a special thank
you. Your insights and knowledge proved
invaluable and are very much appreciated.

Cheers, the first beer is on me, and yes,
I'll probably be running a tab . . .

The music was deep and rich as it flowed across the Mayflower Hotels main ballroom, the sweetness of the string section slowly fading as the orchestra leader brought another classic to a close. He had always enjoyed live orchestral music and even though the acoustics here were somewhat spotty, it did bring him back to the many nights he had spent at the Teatro Dell'Opera in Rome. Sensing a presence beside him, he started to turn around.

"Pirates . . . really?" she sneered with as much disdain as possible while trying not to laugh.

Shing Shen, better known as Slinky, looked up at what was truly the most stunning woman he had ever seen. Rising from his chair they gave each other a crushing hug. "It's so nice to see you Jaime, you look fantastic," he said as he held her at arm's length.

"Thank you sweetie," she replied, dropping into the empty chair beside him. "I have to sit down, my feet are killing me." She raised a foot to show him her new Brian Atwood designed heels. They were the most expensive shoes she had ever bought but like most things, you get what you pay for and with shoes, unless they are broken in, you pay for it big time.

"Well, that's a first, I've never seen you in shoes like that or a dress like that either." Looking at her as not only a close and trusted friend but as any man would look at such a remarkably attractive woman, Slinky had always had somewhat of a crush on Jaime but it was as much intellectual as physical. He could only imagine how many in the room were looking at them. The men and especially the women were all taking sideways glances, trying not to notice her, but being drawn to her nonetheless. He had seen it many times before. Slinky had learned to appreciate her beauty and elegance as normal, whether she was in the lab, library or out on the town.

Jaime propped her hand on her hip and slightly cocked her head and said, "Well Dr. Shen, you clean up pretty good too, so I guess we just need to get out more." Her smile was as bright and infectious as always. "What does a girl need to do to get a drink around here?" Her dark eyes sparkled in the low level lighting of the cavernous ballroom.

Slinky slowly stood, grinning and shaking his head. "I'll be right back."

"I know," was the mocking reply.

Jaime wasn't sure if she would enjoy tonight. She knew Slinky would be here and had always enjoyed his company but she didn't really like getting all dressed up and having to spend half an hour on her hair and makeup. Most days, she didn't even wear makeup, but that was because she knew she didn't have to. When she first walked into the ballroom, she saw the reactions and the number of heads that turned her way. She knew it also wasn't just because of her new heels, which caused her to tower over almost everyone in the room. Coming to grips with her beauty during her senior year in high school had been difficult, but she had never let what she knew was just a genetic fluke get in the way of her accomplishing her goals. Her good looks had actually been a detriment throughout much of her adult life, a good problem to have as one of her friends used to say.

By the time Slinky returned, Jaime was surrounded by a group of fawning men, he recognized one of them as Luke Adams, a former Harvard classmate and basketball player. As he stood there with a wine glass in each hand, Jaime rose from her chair, actually welcoming the interruption. Taking the offered glass from Slinky she quickly said, "Luke, you remember Dr. Shing Shen from school?"

Luke took a step back, looking Slinky up and down, somewhat disturbed that his conversation with Jaime had been interrupted. "Yes, yes I do." Extending his hand, he looked over at Jaime for a reaction. "What did we call you back then, wasn't it Stinky?"

"It was Slinky actually." The response controlled but the handshake became firmer as he continued, "But most people now call me Dr. Shen." That was a purposeful shot at Luke's flunking out of medical school, or as his Facebook page stated *leaving school to pursue my lifelong dream of playing professional basketball in Europe'*. The frosty stares were broken only when Jaime slid between the two tall athletic men and grabbing Slinky's arm she escorted him to the dance floor.

As they both came from privileged backgrounds, they were excellent dancers and that did nothing except increase the attention that they were receiving from the other guests. They made safe, comfortable small talk as another waltz began and they reminisced about their time in college.

Slinky recalled his first few semesters at Harvard and how they were filled with awkwardness and frustration until he met Jaime. He had no friends and stood out like a sore thumb and for good reason. Firstly, there were not a lot of Chinese guys that stood a little over six and a half feet tall and in a school known for over achievers; he had received nearly perfect marks in every class he took. Barely nineteen, he had not yet really grown into his body, especially his legs which comically to everyone except him, seemed to sometimes have a mind of their own. No matter how hard he tried he still had that bouncing rhythmic gait, especially when he was walking down the stairs. One day, a group of his biology peers were watching him and one of the comments was that he looked like a slinky going down the stairs. The name stuck and to everyone except his family, Shing Wei Shen became Slinky.

"I have never seen so many people out at a National Geographic fundraiser," Jaime said. "There must be over a thousand people here. The Mayflower always does such a good job with these things."

"It is a good turn out for them and I'm glad to see some of the diplomatic core here. My father says that it has become one of the go to events here in Washington. The politicians are encouraged to come but are not allowed to speak, so that's probably why it's so popular." Slinky noticed for the first time that Jaime was almost as tall as him in her heels and as they effortlessly made their way around the dance floor they made for an imposing couple. His tuxedo was a rental and it fit him perfectly. The shoes, also rentals, were another matter and he could already feel the blisters forming.

It had been some time since Jaime and Slinky had been able to spend any time together as he was now back in Beijing and she was working with her father in San Diego. They regularly emailed and occasionally chatted on the phone but hadn't had any face time since they were able to grab a lunch together while they both waited for connecting flights out of LAX almost six months ago.

"You didn't laugh like you usually do when I mentioned your pirate story." Jaime couldn't stifle a huge grin as the music came to a close and the orchestra took another break.

"I tried but your never ending beauty left me speechless." Grabbing her hand, he kissed it and made a little bow.

Jaime actually felt a little colour rising in her cheeks. Wow that hasn't happened in a long time she thought to herself.

"I think it will always be our private little joke," Slinky said, taking her arm and leading her back to the table as he recalled the first time they had met.

They had been in a second year class at Harvard when the entire class was randomly matched up in pairs to complete an assignment. Jaime was the star soccer player, a straight A student, drop dead gorgeous and very popular. Slinky, or Shing as he was known then, was just the abnormally tall Chinese guy. To the chagrin of every male classmate, Slinky was paired together with Jaime and that was the beginning of their friendship.

"When we were first matched up, I remember how I said to myself I hope he speaks English," Jaime snorted, a story Slinky had heard many times. "Boy was I surprised, how many languages did you speak then?"

"The same as now, only six," he replied with a smile. His father was not only a high ranking official in the communist party but a career Chinese government diplomat. Slinky had spent considerable time in Geneva, Rome and New York when he was growing up, always attending the best schools while receiving additional tutoring at the Chinese consulate. Slinky was identified early as having an extremely high IQ so he was someone that the communist party took an immediate interest in.

That first assignment that they did together consisted of performing an interview and writing a paper about the others family ancestry. Slinky went first and had Jaime recount her family history. Interestingly enough one of her ancestors had served as ships doctor for Captain George Vancouver, the British explorer. They laughed at the memories of Slinky furiously questioning her on Captain Vancouver's explorations of the South Pacific and North American west coast. When it was Jaime's turn, she heard Slinky's story of his ancestors who had been one of the ruling families of what is now Fujian Province on the southern coast of China. They had been forced out of Macau by the Portuguese when they had taken over and Slinky was also descended from a famous explorer, although of a slightly different kind. Dao Shen was a thorn in the side of China's ruling class as he controlled the South China Sea with an iron fist. His fleet of large trading ships and huge war junks dwarfed the Chinese Emperors naval fleet and he had free rein to ply his trade throughout the region. They both doubled over in laughter as they remembered Slinky trying to convince Jaime that his famous ancestor, Dao Shen, had discovered the south pacific long before the Europeans did and that he was essentially a pirate.

Jaime was as quick as always, her smart aleck comments rolling off her tongue as they laughed at length about how they had met and how their friendship had blossomed and continued to grow since they had graduated almost ten years ago. She always felt so happy, and safe, when they were together.

The laughter was broken when Jaime's father found them. "I've been looking all over for you." Giving Jaime a big hug he held her at arm's length. "You are quite the hit tonight honey—any marriage proposals?"

"Just a few dad, nothing to get excited about."

"Nice to see you again Dr. Shen, I see you are keeping my girl laughing as usual." Riley Jones, founder, president and chairman of the board of Cleanetics Biomedical Research reached over and shook Slinky's hand. "You know I am still holding that job for you at Cleanetics."

"Nice to see you as well Dr. Jones, thank you, always a pleasure."

As Slinky was once again forming the words to graciously decline Dr. Jones offer, he looked over Dr. Jones' shoulder and could see two Chinese men in dark ill-fitting suits rapidly approaching through the crowd. He didn't recognize them but they had all the trappings of Chinese consulate attaches.

Without even an excuse me, the smaller of the two men grabbed Slinky's elbow and started to lead him away, all the time speaking to him in rapid fire Mandarin. Slinky's shoulders noticeably sagged and then he broke free and returned to Jaime and her father.

"My mother is very ill. I have to go." All the good humour had drained from his face which now painfully serious.

Jaime had never seen him look that way; he was always happy and carefree even when they used to cram for exams. While Jaime had been completely freaking out, Slinky was always calm and cool, never flustered. Suddenly nervous, she felt his pain, deep inside her, as she remembered her own feelings when she was told her mother was dying. Almost feeling feint, she stood there like a statue, looking at him.

As he turned to leave, Jaime reached out and grabbed his arm. Turning him around she reached up and put her arms around his neck. "I hope that everything will be OK," she whispered. She then kissed him, for the first time on the lips, and it lasted long enough to raise her father's eyebrows.

Slinky couldn't even muster a goodbye as he was quickly ushered out of the room. Neither of them knew it at the time but both their worlds were about to change forever. Actually, everyone's world was about to change.

Jaime just couldn't shake the image of Slinky's face and it haunted her for the entire flight home to San Diego. She had never seen Slinky look that way and for some reason, it bothered her tremendously. He looked so hurt, so vulnerable, but it was nothing she hadn't seen on hundreds of other faces before. Why was this different? Why did it bother her? She was an analytical thinker but the answer was not coming to her. Even the flight attendant noticed that Jaime was at the very least pre-occupied and at the worst very distraught.

"Is everything all right Ms. Jones, would you like something from the bar?"

"No, no thank you. Actually, if I could, just an ice water please, thanks." Jaime made eye contact with Riley across the aisle.

"Hi honey, lots on your mind?" He had noticed how restless and unsettled Jaime appeared.

"Ya, I just keep seeing that look on Slinky's face, he looked absolutely devastated when he was told his mother was sick. He looked so hurt, I just don't have a very good feeling about it." Feeling the emotion rising in her throat she said, "I guess I'm just worried for him."

Riley hadn't planned on bringing it up but, after all, he was her father and that familial attachment always takes precedence over logic. "Well, I did notice how close you both have become and if you guys are now a couple, I think that's great."

Jaime looked over at him and shook her head slightly and then, without warning, a single tear rolled down her cheek and dropped onto her sleeve. "It's not like that Dad. I don't know, it just upset me for some reason, I'll be fine."

"I know you will honey," he replied, thinking back to the times when Jaime was a pre-teen, struggling with first crushes and that whole girl-boy thing. Smiling he remembered his attempts at trying to be both mother and father and how truly hopeless he was in dealing with the typical young girls angst. Her teen age years went surprisingly smoothly even as she matured into a beautiful woman long before she should have. He did occasionally wonder how she had been able to stay single so long and hoped it wasn't somehow his fault. Thinking back to that meathead hockey player that she had dated at university, he could sure do far worse for a son in law than Dr. Shing Shen.

After arriving they made their way through the terminal and as they waited for their luggage they chatted about Cleanetics and the upcoming special board meeting. Riley had founded the biomedical research company fifteen years ago and it grew from a three person shop to one of the world leaders in medical research. The company had recently gone public which had made Riley extremely wealthy but what they feared would happen by taking the company public was happening. Powerful shareholders and mutual fund managers were pressuring the Cleanetics board to drop some unprofitable programs and concentrate on quick wins and easy profits. That went against how Riley and Jaime thought the direction of the company should be and there was a deepening division within the board of directors.

As a surgeon, Riley had seen the need to try and heal people earlier in the process. Tired of trying to fix something that was already damaged, his vision was to not only understand how diseases worked but where they came from. He hoped to eventually be able to answer the question *'why me?'* and identify and cure the disease before it manifested itself, wanting to take positive actions before the pain and suffering that he knew all too well had taken hold.

Following a long standing family tradition of medical service, Jaime was hooked at an early age, captivated by her father's zeal in what he saw even then as the future of medicine. Like everything she does, Jaime threw herself into medicine and science with a controlled fury. She had become one of the world's leading microbiologists by the age of thirty, which had earned her a seat on the board of Cleanetics. Her very rapid rise to prominence was well documented which had led her to receive considerable criticism as she had to deal with the constant accusations of nepotism. Jaime didn't care as she could hold her own with anyone in her field, in the laboratory, on the lecture circuit or in the board room.

Cleanetics was far ahead of the curve in looking at genetic markers and the human genome as it relates to disease. Almost all biomedical researchers now incorporate genetics into their work. Cleanetics and specifically Riley Jones recognized early on that genetics were the key to not only identifying those with disease potential, but genetics also offered the ability to fight and cure disease's at the most fundamental cellular layer. Their initial successes with lupus and spina bifida rocketed them into the limelight and allowed them to attract the best scientists and researchers from around the globe.

As usual Darnell Drummond was waiting to pick up Riley and was waving furiously at them as they exited the baggage area after claiming their luggage. Jaime saw him first and asked, "Does Darnell always do that dad, like how can you miss him?"

They both laughed as Darnell hurried over looking to take their bags. "Good afternoon Mr. Riley, Miss Jaime," Darnell boomed out. "Let me take those bags for you." He reached down with amazing quickness for such a big man and picked up their bags like they were filled with feathers.

"You know Darnell, you don't have to carry them, they do have wheels." Riley teased him as they had had this conversation many times. "Makes me feel like I'm earning my money Mr. Riley," replied Darnell as he led them outside towards the waiting car.

Riley had met Darnell through working with one of the charities Cleanetics supports. He is a massive man, as big if not bigger than a professional football lineman and although he looks thirty, he was close to sixty years old. At an Easter charity dinner in Los Angeles many years ago Riley introduced himself thinking Darnell was one of the visiting San Diego Chargers. He learned that Darnell volunteered at the sponsored church and did odd jobs in the neighbourhood to support his ageing mother. They kept in touch and when Darnell's mother passed away,

Riley arranged through Darnell's minister to ensure that there was enough money to have a proper service and funeral. Their friendship blossomed after Darnell wrote the most amazing thank you letter that Riley had ever read. Riley offered Darnell a job at Cleanetics as a driver and odd job specialist—a job that he excelled at. He had become an instant favorite with staff and his popularity was assured shortly after he brought in his first batch of corn bread. Riley often teased him that he was going to sell everything and go into the corn bread business with Darnell a la Bubba Gump Shrimp.

"Got some corn bread waiting for y'all in the car Mr. Riley," Darnell proudly proclaimed. "Just made it up this morning."

"Yum, can't wait," said Jaime. "How is Dr. Sandecker treating you Darnell?" Dr. Eric Sandecker was one of the new board appointees and he was developing a bad reputation among staff for being extremely rude. Riley had found out through the grapevine that Sandecker had belittled Darnell on many occasions. He had even tried to get him fired and Riley had mentioned it in passing to Jaime on the plane. Jaime thought Sandecker was a pompous ass from the first time that they had met.

"Well Miss Jaime, Dr. Sandecker ain't too easy to please but he can't hurt me so pay it no mind. I haven't been talked to like that since I was a child, but I've got big shoulders if y'all know what I mean."

"Yes, you do Darnell but no one expects you to take any abuse," replied Riley. "Board members are no different than employees, we are all covered by the same code of conduct. If there is any abuse towards you Darnell, I want to hear about it. You know how I feel about things like that."

"Yes sir, I do," Darnell said, but all three of them knew he would never say a thing.

Darnell loaded the bags into the trunk and they made their way out of the airport into the early afternoon traffic, headed towards the office.

3

S linky was able to briefly speak with his father while on a short layover in Los Angeles. His mother Li was now bordering on critical condition and the prognosis was not good. Quizzing his father at length about her condition and symptoms all he could really glean was that she had what they initially thought was a cold but it turned out to be the flu. His mother was now hospitalized and currently semi-conscious with waves of delirium and fever sweeping over her regularly. Slinky's optimism was starting to fade.

He could hear the emotion in his father's voice. "We are in The People's Hospital, government wing and there will be a car waiting for you at the airport. I have already cleared you through customs but if you have any difficulties, ask for Waotung Feng, he is an old friend."

Slinky's father, Lin Ji Shen, was one of the most senior and experienced Chinese diplomats and held considerable influence and power. Strong, reserved and stoic, Slinky had never heard such weakness in his father's voice until now.

"I can't believe it's just the flu," said Slinky, holding his cellphone closer to his ear to try and hear through the cacophony that is LAX. "She is only sixty five and in wonderful shape, there needs to be another explanation for the fever, who is the doctor in charge?"

"It doesn't matter Shing, she has the best medical care in the world here," Lin said, knowing that was a lie. "I have told her you are coming but I don't know if she understood me. I will see you when you arrive."

Lin and Li Shen gave birth to Slinky later in life than most Chinese parents as they had aggressively pursued their careers into their mid-thirties. Lin was a senior policy maker within the communist party before he transitioned into the diplomatic core shortly before Slinky was born. Li was a chemistry professor and gave up her career to become a mother and support her husband's career. Lin had risen quickly through what was arguably the most complicated political system in the world and it was rumoured that he was now being groomed for a politburo seat. The Chinese political system rules by a collective leadership model so if that were to happen, it would make Lin one of the most powerful men in China.

The preparation for landing announcement from the cabins overhead speaker jolted Slinky out of an uneasy sleep. Having been awake for over twenty four hours he needed that few hours of sleep as his Cathay Pacific flight was now on final approach to Beijing. His legs were cramped and his neck was sore even in the comfort of the first class cabin.

He didn't know if it was the lack of sleep or the lack of food but Slinky felt very weak and barely noticed being whisked through the airport and out into the chaotic traffic of Beijing. There was no conversation in the car as they darted their way through, what had become in less than two decades, one of the most traffic congested cities in the world.

Slinky approached the anteroom on the ninth floor of the Peoples Hospital, government wing and saw his father speaking in low tones to three other men, none of which he recognized and none of which looked like a doctor. Lin broke away and took Slinky by the arm, leading him out of the anteroom and into the attached hospital ward. Entering the darkened room the first thing he noticed was the lack of activity, the room was essentially empty except for a bed. He quickly approached and saw his mother, her skin already turning to a grey pallor. He never had the chance to say goodbye.

Slinky met his father for an early lunch the next day in the lobby of his hotel. His parents were renovating their Beijing home and had been staying in a small one bedroom apartment just outside of the financial centre of downtown Beijing. His father had arranged for Slinky to stay at this hotel as it was close to his temporary apartment. The conversation was strained, somehow too formal and lacked the emotion they both felt. Slinky had finally cried himself to sleep the night before and although he yearned to be more emotive he maintained that cultural rigidity. It reminded him so much of his rebellious phase as a teenager when he struggled with the dichotomy of trying to live in both eastern and western cultures and to deal with one of the most difficult Chinese customs, the concepts around saving face. Recalling one particular argument with his mother on how a person should never point out that someone is wrong as that causes both people to lose face; Slinky at the time thought that was utterly ridiculous. As a young boy the concepts were maddeningly difficult to master and as he matured he learned to understand how the concept plays out on a daily basis in the Chinese culture. Slinky never had issues with the multiple aspects and the intricate layers of showing respect but he still fundamentally disapproved of what he called cultural game playing. The concepts around face were always just a little phony for him. It wasn't that he couldn't do it, it was an integral part of his personal and business life but he detested it all the same.

They spoke in hushed tones so as to not alert those around them or even their servers as to what had just occurred. Chinese culture, for all its thousands of years of history and growth, continued to stigmatize those who were surrounded by a recent death. It is considered extremely bad luck to be in close proximity to someone who had just had a death in the family and although Slinky again thought that was ridiculous, he went along with it out of respect for his father.

Lin was trying to make small talk when he noticed an embassy staffer, a junior diplomatic assistant, standing against the far wall looking right at him, holding an envelope in his hands. When they made eye contact, the assistant had bowed slightly. They continued to stare at each other for a moment and then Lin motioned him to approach. A sense of relief washed over the courier as he walked over and placed the envelope on the table in front of Lin.

"Excuse me sir, I have a message from the politburo for you." Lowering his voice he added, "We are very sorry to hear that Madam Shen has passed on. The entire diplomatic service sends you and Dr. Shen our deepest sympathies." Turning, he left without another word.

I guess the rumours are true Slinky thought, watching his father slowly open the ornate envelope. As Lin began to read the message, Slinky studied his face. His father had always been a serious and studious man, someone who was in complete control of his emotions. He could read nothing on his face but his eyes betrayed him. They noticeably softened, an almost imperceptible line of moisture formed just above his lower eyelid. Blinking it away he handed the letter to Slinky, not saying a word.

The funeral arrangements were all in place. The Party would be looking after everything. Travel arrangements had already been made and every living relative would be attending, all paid for by the Party. What came as a shock to Slinky was that the president will be attending. It would take place on Saturday, three days from now in the Great Hall. A tremendous honour was being paid to them, far beyond what would have normally been appropriate. He had a feeling that he would find out more as the letter also contained an invitation for both of them to attend a private meeting with the president, the premier and the general secretary of the communist party at the presidential palace the day after the funeral.

Slinky had never been a supporter of the Chinese government or their policies. Out of respect for his father, they never openly discussed politics. Slinky felt somewhat nervous about being asked to attend a meeting with arguably the three most powerful men in China. Convincing himself that being invited was nothing more than a sign of respect to his family and his father, he tried to accept it just for what it was, just a way for everyone to save face. If the rumours were true, it may also have something to do with the potential of his father joining the politburo. It really didn't matter, it wasn't like he had a choice, so he quickly put it out of his mind.

Jaime returned to her cluttered but spacious office eager to get back to work. She loved her office, it was on the northwest corner of the building giving it just the right amount of sunshine and it overlooked a small park. It was decorated simply for an executive's office, there were no bookshelves filled with never read books or over-stuffed leather couches. A large desk for paperwork and a smaller desk over in the corner where her computers were located blended easily into the large room. What dominated the room was a five hundred gallon circular aquarium located in the alcove where traditionally a meeting table would exist. Jaime had surrounded the aquarium with soft Art Moderne chairs designed and built by the famed Josef Urban in 1934. She loved these chairs and so did her staff. They were bold and bright, luxurious to sit in with their rounded forms and simplistic but beautiful designs. It was not by any means a traditional meeting space but everyone loved *'the pit'* as they called it. No one knew that these beautiful chairs should probably have been in a museum. They had cost Jaime almost $60,000 at auction in New York but when she saw them, she had to have them.

Jaime had hoped to sneak away later in the day to have a workout and a walk along the beach to clear her head before the board meeting tonight but she realized that was not going to happen. Her voicemail was full and she had numerous progress reports on her desk.

"Soooo . . . how was Washington?" her assistant Angie asked, waving a piece of paper in the air as she made her way to Jamie's desk.

"Hello to you too, ok, what's going on?" Jaime replied, trying not to sound sharp but she knew something was up by the way Angie was acting and she didn't have the time for office gossip. Angie had been her assistant and Girl Friday from the first day she started at Cleanetics. Loyal, hardworking with an exuberant personality, Jaime loved her like the older sister she never had.

"Well, I know you're busy and I should just leave this for you to read but that would take all the fun out of it." Angie sat down on the front corner of Jaime's desk. "I'll skip all the mumbo jumbo and go straight to the good stuff." Angie could barely contain herself as she started to read from the piece of paper. "One noticeable hook up was with the stunning Jaime Jones who looks more like a super model than a scientist and a tall dark stranger from the east. They were inseparable all night and by the way they were dancing you could tell there was going to be a little Cha Cha Cha later on."

Angie had done everything she could to try and get Jaime to date more often. It drove her crazy that such a smart and beautiful young woman spent over sixty hours a week working. Angie was a former cocktail hostess in Las Vegas during the 1970's. She worked hard and played hard and even though she was approaching sixty five years old, she still turned heads on the street.

"Jesus Angie, what is that, give it to me." Jaime reached out her hand as she rose from her chair.

"Not until you spill the beans," Angie mockingly replied, holding the paper over her head.

Jaime snatched it out of her hands and saw that it was a printout of some kind of online gossip column from Washington D.C. called *'What comes out of the Wash'* penned by the yet to be discovered literary master Madame de Kink.

"So," Angie purred, "Was it a cha cha cha or a slow tango."

Jaime read the story and looked at Angie with disdain. "They are talking about me and Slinky. And that reminds me, I need to call him. He was pulled away apparently his mother is very sick." Jaime instantly felt guilty for not calling him earlier.

Angie was noticeably disappointed. She had met Slinky a few times and although he was obviously cultured, intelligent, extremely polite and professional, she could tell there wouldn't be any cha cha cha between the two of them. Too many good friendships are ruined by the cha cha cha she thought; she was living proof of that. Angie mockingly said her goodbyes and told Jaime she'd hold any calls till she was told otherwise as she sashayed her way out of the room.

Geez, I do feel guilty Jaime thought to herself. She didn't quite know what to say to Slinky and although she wanted to talk, in another way she didn't, remembering how he looked that night. It somehow didn't feel right, with his mother being sick and him being so upset. Realizing how awful that thought was, Jaime was now even more confused, her mind grinding through why this was so difficult all of a sudden. It was just Slinky and his mother is sick so give him a call and wish him the best. Staring at her phone for the longest time she finally realized that she was just upset at seeing him upset. Deciding it would be best to put it off for another few days, Jaime got to work.

Jaime tried to knock off as many of the voicemails as she could knowing she didn't have time to go through all the progress reports. To save time she had Angie arrange a meeting with her team for the end of the day to get a verbal update from her team leads. Another item on her to do list was to sit down and go over her presentation about the lupus findings with her dad but he didn't really seem that interested, which she thought was odd. Something was bothering him and it seemed to be connected to tonight's board meeting but she brushed it off as she knew she didn't have time to deal with it now. Actually, he has been acting a little strange for the past month. They were going sailing on Sunday so she planned to clear the air with him then.

When Cleanetics went public there was a need to have a formal board of directors. Prior to that, Riley made all the decisions. The board now consisted of Riley as chairman, Jaime and one of Riley's old friends Christoper Higgins, Dr. Raj Chouhan who was relatively new to Cleanetics but had worked with Riley previously and the new appointees, Dr. Eric Sandecker and two financial types, Margeret Blake and Joseph McDonald. There was some animosity early on and some of the voting went to the natural 4-3 split but with the exception of Sandecker, the other two new board members seem to be coming around to Riley's way of thinking. Riley had always said that good science and fundamental medical breakthroughs to help people were more important than profits. Unfortunately that was an anomaly in the biomedical research industry, as well as just about everywhere else.

Jaime had let time get away from her and was the last to arrive for the board meeting. Riley waited for her to settle in and opened the meeting, handling the first few agenda items quickly and then he handed the floor over to Jamie for her progress report on their lupus project. Cleanetics had become a world leader in lupus research after developing a new drug that replaced previous medications that were essentially just cancer fighting drugs that were not specific to the symptoms or fundamental makeup of lupus. Their superior knowledge in identification and treatment of lupus right from the molecular level had them all hoping it would lead to bigger and better breakthroughs, especially around certain cancers.

The real exciting news is that there had been some dramatic advances within their venom research department. Compounds from snake and scorpion venom have been used for decades all over the world in heart and blood related diseases and recent clinical trials showed a number of new venom related products would be making it to market soon. The researchers at Cleanetics had always taken the road less travelled so they had concentrated on the molecular makeup of the venom of sea creatures, specifically cone shells and sea anemones.

"Everything is contained in the report in front of you and I remind you that it is confidential and for your eyes only." Jaime started to quickly run through her PowerPoint presentation. "For the last five years we have been working on Systemic Lupus Erythematosus commonly referred to as SLE which is the most damaging form of the autoimmune disease known as lupus. Most lupus sufferer's deal with skin and joint irritation but those with SLE also have considerable internal organ dysfunction which can also lead to death. As you know, we commercially launched our lupus medication Imoxofene late last year which has been very well accepted within the medical community. Pfizer who were contracted to manufacture the drug under license from us will be ramping up production at a second facility in the Boston area to keep up with the demand."

"Isn't it cheaper to make these drugs in India or China?" Joseph asked. "The ten year profitability chart indicates outstanding returns but if we outsourced it, couldn't we double our profits?"

Irritated by the constant boardroom talk about profitability, Jaime said, "Someone can always make an argument for cheaper outsourcing in Asia but as you are aware there are significant quality control issues and security risks associated with overseas production. We are actually protecting our profits by working with a trusted partner like Pfizer here in North America."

Continuing, Jaime gave a brief and simplified explanation of the autoimmune system and how the drug works by acting as an alkylating agent that causes a cross-linking of the DNA. This prevents new cell growth and is most effective in diseases that multiply rapidly, like lupus and cancer.

"We have had some significant successes in the last quarter with targeting an improved version of the drug, which is linked to specific tracers within the DNA. Early results indicate a minimum 95% success rate in disrupting cellular growth in infected cells with a less than 2% disruption in normal cells. This equates to a dramatic increase, an almost doubling of the effectiveness over the original version of Imoxofene. We have found one of the peptides contained in the venom of a particular species of deep water anemone blocks a basic protein that feeds the cellular inflammation process. This massively inhibits cellular growth in the infected cells. This indicates a potentially significant shift in the treatment of the disease, what I mean by that is that we don't necessarily have to eradicate the disease itself. What we can do is just stop the disease from progressing and if it's caught early enough it would not become a health issue. We hope to move to clinical trials within three months and if everything pans out, we may have a very significant discovery, not only a cure for lupus, but potentially other autoimmune disease as well."

Riley sat back, enjoying watching his daughter work. Immensely proud of both his children, he marvelled at Jaime, a leader in her field at such a young age. He didn't care if either of his kids followed him into medicine but was so glad when they did. For as driven and complicated as Jaime was, his son Jeremy was laid back and driven by another purpose. As soon as Jeremy had finished his residency he immediately went to Africa to work with Doctors Without Borders. He had been there ever since, only coming home for one Christmas. Driven and absolutely committed to helping the poor and needy he had no interest in the modern world or its conveniences. Living most of the year in a mud brick hut in the jungle of the Congo, he only moved into town during the rainy season. Both his kids were so different, but in a way—they were exactly the same. They had both been changed by their mother's death. Both committing themselves to helping others, both never asking for help and never quitting on anything.

"After not getting the courtesy of receiving your report ahead of today's meeting," Dr. Eric Sandecker interrupted, not even attempting to hide his displeasure, "Am I reading page thirty two correctly. You initially had similar results with the improved version of Imoxofene on cancer cells in mice?"

"That is correct and once we start our lupus clinical trials we will be dedicating half the team to start looking into the cancer angle," Jaime said as she was again cut off by Sandecker.

"I don't know and don't really care who taught you about priorities young lady but who gives a crap about lupus when we have a potential cancer drug in the works." Sandecker, with his voice rising and face reddening, he became even more belligerent. "Drop the lupus and get started on the cancer, pronto."

Jaime took a deep breath trying to calm herself as she didn't want to fall into Sandeckers trap. Dr. Eric Sandecker was the kind of doctor everybody loved to hate. He was loud, brash and truly did not care what others thought of him. Convinced he was the best and brightest and that he knew it all, his own opinion was the only one he cared about.

Jaime levelled her gaze and with the hint of a forced smile said, "Well Doctor I'm not sure who taught you about priorities but that's not the way it works. We have been working on lupus for years and are less than a year away from a possible and I'm actually willing to say a probable cure. There are over five million people around the world with lupus and I'm not willing to push them aside for the next four years while we look into the cancer angle. We are too close and it would seem to me to be a poor business decision to stop working on an already identified revenue stream whereas the potential of profitability for the cancer side may be many years distant."

"Bullshit," Sandecker snorted. "You are just trying to justify your altruistic values which don't mean anything to me or the shareholders. There are twenty times more people with cancer and finding a cure would make this company the number one medical research firm in the world."

"Enough," shouted Riley in a rare show of emotion. "I told you before Sandecker that your bullying crap wouldn't be tolerated around this table. I've known about the cancer opportunity for a month and I agree with Jaime, the lupus work has come too far to drop it now. The last item on the agenda is about growth and expansion and that's directly related to the cancer opportunity. I'm talking to Kent the CEO at Pfizer about the possibility of a partnership to start working on the cancer angle right away."

Both Sandecker and Joseph McDonald almost jumped out of their chairs. Joseph shouted, "You don't own this company any more Riley, you don't have the authority to do that without Board approval!" Sandecker as usual, talked over everyone else. "I'll have your ass Riley if you leaked anything about this cancer work."

It took a few minutes but Riley was able to get everyone settled down although there was no more business to be done this night. With Raj Chouhan acting as the peacemaker they all agreed on an extraordinary board meeting to be held the following night to learn more about the opportunity with Pfizer and to have a vote to see what direction Cleanetics would take.

Slinky had no idea he had so many relatives as he slowly made his way through the crowded family reception area shaking the hands of dozens of people he didn't even know. The funeral lasted less than an hour and was all too contrived and impersonal for his liking. He thought to himself that he must have become more accustomed to western style funerals. They felt more personal and gave you the opportunity to release the grief and sorrow that hung in your chest. His mother's funeral was antiseptic, filled with political doctrine and was nothing more than a regurgitation of his mother's accomplishments. It was all about what she was, not who she was and that angered him. So typically Chinese he thought.

Slinky had spent the night at his father's apartment. Fully intending to go back to his own hotel but they had been up most of the night talking and he decided just to stay. They both spoke openly about their loss and how much they loved her, reminiscing about their travels and adventures all around the world. It was the first time in Slinky's life that he had seen his father seem vulnerable.

Like most strong men, there was usually an equally strong woman behind them that helped them keep up, what for most was, just a façade. Slinky made a mental note to keep closer contact with his father as he no longer had the support that his mother provided.

The car arrived exactly on time to take then to the presidential palace. The ride was mostly in silence as they had already spoken about what the most likely scenarios of the meeting were. They were in agreement that the probability is that Lin would be offered a seat on the politburo and that Slinky was invited to witness the event.

The palace was not as ornate as Slinky thought it would be but it was still very impressive, filled with ancient artwork and treasures. Assuming that it would be rich and opulent, showing the decadence of the highest levels of government, Slinky was impressed and somewhat embarrassed in finding it was rather sterile and functional. They were first met in a small anteroom by president Wei Pi Tan where tea and dim sum was served. President Tan apologized for the delay but an unexpected event had delayed the Secretary General but he shouldn't be long. The Premier was tied up on other business and would not be joining them today.

Between bites of hargow and crispy duck skin, President Tan said, "It is unfortunate that such a significant day for both of you cannot be witnessed by your beloved Li."

Lin noticed the look on Slinkys face as he absorbed that comment. He already knew what lay ahead, it had been in the works for months. Li's unexpected death almost delayed the plan but as President Tan respectfully pointed out to Lin, the timing now, although unfortunate was perfect. Lin knew, as did his political masters, that Slinky would never agree to work for the Chinese government. This was their one chance to convince him to work for them, by not only leveraging his father's politburo seat, but also sadly, his mother's death. Although Lin found it initially distasteful, he could not argue with the practicality. They needed Slinky, he was one of the leading viral researchers in the world and they were so close to having the LOCUST plan as a viable option. The future of their new world order depended upon it.

Lin thought that he should feel bad for misleading and essentially betraying his son but he didn't. His relationship with his son was overshadowed by China's needs. The fact that he would finally be in the inner circle and so close to the reins of power was intoxicating. What was good for China was good for his son, although he knew Slinky would never agree to that statement.

Should the LOCUST plan even prove marginally effective, he like the other Chinese leaders would be preparing China for its destiny. They would take over the world economically and become the preeminent state on the planet, forever. LOCUST could make that happen sooner than later.

The three of them continued to make small talk until the Secretary General arrived. It was immediately evident that Slinkys father did not have the same close relationship with him as he did with President Tan and Slinky could see why. Secretary General Jung was blunt and officious, obviously a man accustomed to being in charge and getting his way. After curtly ordering the various aides and assistants out of the room, he sat down and got down to business. It took him less than five minutes to outline the offer of the politburo seat to Lin and to Slinkys absolute amazement, the Secretary General then requested that he join the Army's bio-medical research team.

"General Han is a tough task master but I am told you would be up to the challenge Dr. Shen." Taking a long drag on his cigarette, the Secretary General let the smoke slowly roll out of his mouth before he continued. "You come highly regarded and are apparently someone we desperately need."

Slinky sat stunned, knowing his shock and surprise was written all over his face. Wanting to look over at his father he resisted that urge and sat stone faced, looking back at the most powerful man in China.

"You both have heard the offers and I am sure you understand the consequences for both of your positions." Partially hidden by another pall of acrid cigarette smoke, the Secretary General's eyes never left Slinky as he slowly sat back in his chair.

Lin cleared his throat as if preparing to speak and Slinky instinctively reacted, for which he would later regret. "Excuse me sir, I mean no disrespect, but you must agree that your offer appears to me as blackmail as I do not see what my father's politburo seat has to do with a job offer to me?"

"I'll give you one warning Dr. Shen, I do not accept being spoken to in that tone." Secretary General Jung said, leaning forward looking menacingly over the top of his reading glasses. There were not many men who ever angered the Secretary General twice. "What I see doctor is someone who either never learned or has forgotten how this country operates." The Secretary General straightened up in his chair, sticking to the plan. "We know how westernized you are, how you may not agree with how we run this country and I understand that. At a certain level, I even appreciate it and that is why Dr. Shen, you are being offered this position. We need free thinkers, we need men of action, leaders in their fields who will shape the worlds future. We know you have turned down offers from leading research labs all over the world but this is more than a job. This offer will allow you to move China forward, to help us take our rightful place." Leaning back, he folded his fingers over his ample belly, thinking the first part of the trap is about to be sprung. "We have developed the most modern bio-medical research lab in the world and our vaccine research, especially around newly emerging flu's needs your expert assistance. We are very close, and we are hoping that with your help there will not be any more needless deaths from the influenza virus." He let that sink in knowing the grief from his mother's flu death was still raw and visceral for Slinky. Looking over at Lin, the Secretary General waited for him to deliver the coup de grace.

"Thank you Secretary General, your offer to both me and my son is very generous," Lin said, taking a deep breath as he prepared himself to set the trap. "I very much enjoy diplomatic service and leaving it would be very difficult for me. I will serve you, the party and the country in any way I can but to be honest, a politburo seat was always more of my wife's dream for me. I am humbled by your offer."

Slinky was now blankly staring at his father as he recalled a dinner he had with his parents for Chinese New Year in New York last year. He remembered his mother specifically saying that his father needed to start playing political hardball now if he was to get what he deserved and what she had given up her career for, a politburo seat.

Lin continued, looking over at Slinky, "We come from different generations my son. Your mother and I always wanted you to be more supportive of the work that we did and to be honest, to be more understanding of the Party and our government. But what we wanted more was for you to be happy and successful and to achieve greatness, in whatever way you choose. You have done that. We are both very proud of you."

Lin now looked directly at the Secretary General and said, "With all due respect, we decline your offer."

It was like a crushing weight suddenly appeared on Slinky's chest. The grief over losing his mother was now compounded by the embarrassment of his father giving up his career, for him. For just a fleeting second he felt so proud of his father and then he was racked by a wave of almost unbearable sorrow. He felt like he was going to burst into tears. What kind of son would take this away from his father, he asked himself. The shame was almost unbearable and he reached over and placed his hand on his father's shoulder.

"No. Thank you father but I disagree." Slinky's mind was blank but the words just came out. "I would be immensely proud to serve my country and I accept the offer of working with General Han and the Army's bio-medical research team. I am also immensely proud to see my father's lifetime of work and dedication to the party be acknowledged by him receiving a seat on the politburo. It is a fitting reward for one who has served the country for so long."

Both the President and the Secretary General sat back in their chairs, with an undeniable look of satisfaction in their eyes. This was too easy. He truly is westernized they thought.

I t had been months since they had been out sailing and Jaime knew they both needed a break from the office. The special board meeting had been a disaster. The board had accomplished nothing except for worsening their relationships and they couldn't even agree on the date for the next meeting. Sandecker had brutally attacked Riley's character and business acumen and she felt like she was the only one who backed her dad. She had been almost hiding out down in the lab for the last couple of days, avoiding the entire management floor. Rumours were swirling and staff morale was starting to be affected as stories of takeovers and board revolts increased daily. Jaime was comfortable in both the scientific and management worlds, or so she thought. The selfishness and egotism of the board room was sickening and she had heard it many times from her dad that the potential of great wealth and power is the biggest corrupting influence in business and in the world today. Riley had often said every moment affecting great change in mankind had started with an individual who just won't put up with some injustice any longer. Jokingly, he said he would be that man. That was why he always ran the company with the interests of patients and science first, but he doesn't run the company anymore. Jaime would never say so but she wondered if taking the company public was a mistake.

As Jaime walked down the floating dock toward the slip where their Hunter45 sailboat named Brandy was docked, she could see a flurry of activity and realized that Brandy wasn't there. Looking around she approached a knot of people, not recognizing any of them and that's when Riley arrived and stepped off one of the marinas small Boston Whaler tenders.

Riley could see the look on Jaime's face and before she said anything he called out to her, "Don't worry honey, we are still going sailing."

Something was going on and she essentially ignored the half dozen men standing around and said, "Where is Brandy? What's going on dad?"

It was then she noticed that Riley had his old smile back. He looked tanned and vigorous, like he used to years ago. More importantly, he looked happy and she hadn't seen that in months.

Riley came over and gave her one of the hugs he was famous for, grabbed her duffle bag and said, "Sorry gentlemen, introductions will have to wait, I have to show my daughter the new boat. Miguel, can you shuttle us out please? This way honey." Grabbing Jaime's arm he helped her step into the Whaler.

Jaime quickly took a seat as they reversed out of the slip and headed out into Mission Bay. Riley was standing beside Miguel holding onto the center console as the small tender came up onto plane. He looked back at Jaime as the wind whipped his hair across his face and held out his hand in a *just give me a minute* gesture. Again about to ask him what was going on she hesitated as they powered through a small boat wake, watching him effortlessly absorb the small rollers with his legs. Standing there looking all nautical, made her think of the sailing trips he used to take her and her brother on after their mother had died. Jaime kept quiet as she probably wouldn't have been heard over the noise of the outboard anyways. Riley was looking out ahead of them and he pointed towards a pair of large and beautiful emerald green yachts riding easily at anchor.

They powered around the first yacht which was absolutely huge. Both the white superstructure and the deep emerald green hull were reflected in the calm waters of the bay. Jaime looked up and was in awe of not only the size but the beauty of her lines, it must be 150 feet long she thought. The tender started to slow as they rounded the stern of the second, much smaller but still impressive yacht and she could see the freshly painted name on the stern, *JayJay*.

As Miguel brought the tender alongside he expertly nudged them softly into the yachts protective fenders. Quickly tying them off, he grabbed a large cooler and leapt into the larger boat. He offered Riley a hand up and as he reached out to assist Jaime he said, "Let me be the first to welcome you aboard your new yacht."

Jaime nimbly came aboard as she tried to absorb what Miguel had just said. Miguel jumped back into the tender and started to manoeuver away. "Adios, Mr. Jones, I'll be watching for your return." Miguel slowly peeled off away from JayJay and powered up, heading back to the marina.

"Dad, what the frick is going on?" Jaime asked as Riley plopped himself down in the newly upholstered cockpit.

"Well, it's a bit of a long story and as I promised that we would go sailing today, let's get started and I'll fill you in as we go."

Riley asked Jaime to deal with the food in the cooler and to start a pot of coffee. Going forward he released them from the anchoring buoy and from the inside pilothouse he deftly maneuvered JayJay forward and motored towards the harbor mouth and the open Pacific.

Jaime quickly found the coffee pot and had a quick look around. This wasn't a new boat, but it sure looked like it. Everything seemed new and it was spotless, freshly painted, all the teak had been refinished, new furniture and a brand new gleaming stainless steel galley. She took a minute to have a quick tour, she passed through the main salon and dining area, down the hallway popping her head into the two guest cabins amidships. The forward master stateroom was huge and she saw her old comforter from Brandy was folded neatly on the king sized bed.

When Jaime returned to the main salon Riley was setting the navigation equipment while he was talking to the harbourmaster on the radio. She knew that they had known each other for years and had been on a number of fishing trips to Panama together, so they would be a few minutes. The throbbing of the engine was barely perceptible under her feet as she headed outside into the aft cockpit and plunked herself down on one of the newly upholstered side seats. Looking around she realized just how much bigger JayJay was than Brandy. She was dying to know what was going on but decided just to sit back and enjoy the view as they started to clear the harbour.

Riley was an accomplished sailor and had crewed in America's Cup qualifying races back in the 1980's. Both Jaime and her brother Jeremy had grown up sailing and after their mothers death, Riley had made a point of having a family sailing adventure every summer, just the three of them, touring around the Bahamas' and western Caribbean. As Jaime relaxed she could feel the small swells and knew they were now in the open ocean. As the sun warmed her back she recalled one of those family trips when they had come across about fifty Haitian refugees crammed on a small sailboat trying to make it to the United States. Jeremy spoke some French courtesy of a school exchange program and acted as translator. They had given them almost all of their food and water and Riley had administered to a few of the children as they were sunburnt and quite seasick. That experience seemed to change Jeremy. Jaime recalled how shocked he was at their level of poverty and desperation, willing to risk their lives for just the opportunity for success. That experience could very well have been the pivotal point for Jeremy in deciding to dedicate himself to helping some of the world's most desperate people. It's not that their relationship was bad, but it wasn't good and she realized that she hadn't seen her brother in almost three years.

Riley came aft and took control of JayJay from the rear sailing station. He called Jaime over, asked her to just hold on for another few minutes, flashed her a huge smile and started to show her the controls and explain how automated everything is.

"This was all designed to be sailed by one person," Riley exclaimed. "It is fully automatic and amazingly simple for this size of vessel."

Jaime could see how happy he was and even though she had a million questions, she kept quiet as Riley continued the tutorial and brought JayJay under full sail. In no time they were cutting through the rising early morning chop on a strong northwest tack.

I t had taken Riley almost two hours to explain what was going on.

The first hour was spent explaining how six months ago, Riley had bought this Baltic Custom 76 yacht and had her completely refitted. Everything had been upgraded, retrofitted or replaced. It was truly a one of a kind vessel. From its extensive offshore range and capabilities to its desalination plant, there wasn't another vessel like it. This was to be Riley's future retirement boat, something he could enjoy for a leisurely afternoon sail or a trip around the world. Then he saw the writing on the wall at Cleanetics and knew that it wasn't all going according to plan.

Riley had delayed re-christening and naming the boat and he was glad he did. Explaining proudly that this boat was now for her and her brother, the name JayJay being representative of both of their initials. Riley then admitted he had been in regular contact with Jeremy lately, which was a big shock to Jaime. Jeremy knew about JayJay and Riley had even emailed him some pictures. They both laughed when Riley recounted Jeremy's normal objection to spending that kind of money on possessions when there are so many sick and starving people in the world. Riley handed Jaime an email that Jeremy had asked him to pass along.

In it, Jeremy had finally admitted that he did need some time away from Africa and that he really did miss his family. He was doing good work but it wasn't bringing him the satisfaction it once did. He pledged to take a leave after August and try something new which Riley would explain. The note contained none of his usual laments about the rot of corporate America, global warming and rising sea levels or the soon to be unsustainable population of the world. Jeremy was ashamed that most of the world lived in poverty and sickness and was one of the rare complainers who actually did something about it. Jeremy's only possessions were the clothes on his back and his medical equipment, his wages were spent on food and medicines. Explaining to Jaime that he was truly sorry, he gave a heartfelt admission that he was solely responsible for the dysfunctional relationship with both Jaime and their father and it was time that he fixed it. He also admitted that the work that they do at Cleanetics probably helps more people and saves more lives than the work that he does in Africa and apologized for his years of not supporting them. Jaime was truly surprised that her brother had such a dramatic turnaround and assumed that was going to be the biggest shock of the day, but she was wrong.

"So what's the news dad? What is Jeremy going to do?"

"Well honey, it's more like what both of us are going to do," Riley said as he reached over and grabbed his daughter's hand. "I know I didn't consult with you and I hope you'll understand after you hear me out but I am leaving Cleanetics."

It was like a jolt of electricity went through her body.

"What? What are you talking about? Dad, it's your company, we need you." But before she could say anymore Riley lifted up her hand and kissed it.

"Just hear me out, no questions till I'm finished, ok?"

Riley talked for twenty minutes straight. He talked about his great pride in what Cleanetics had become and what it stood for but had increasing frustrations with both the political and business worlds. It troubled him deeply that most leaders and influencers in society barely paid lip service to the important and fundamental sustainability issues all the while chasing the next easy dollar. Although not a zealot like Jeremy, Riley couldn't help but agree with what his son had been saying for years. The world couldn't wait for the next generation to fix things, it would be too late. Melting ice caps, growing carbon emissions, depleted oceans and huge population increases were serious and needed attention now. A quarter of the world's population is under nourished and almost half do not have access to adequate health care. Jaime had never seen her father so serious as he explained that it had all started to affect his outlook, not only on the business, but on his life. Riley quietly commented on how truly proud he was of Jaime and Jeremy and how proud their mother would be. Lushly praising their coworkers and friends at Cleanetics he explained the company was now poised for even greater success as Jaime's team was at the cusp of a lupus cure and heading towards some significant cancer breakthroughs. Riley thoughtfully told her how much he trusted and respected her and how he is at complete peace with his decision.

Before Jaime could ask, Riley said his major issue was with his family. Concerned that he was losing his son and that he may never get the chance to work with him and interact with him on a daily basis like they had done these last few years, he needed to change it up. Bottom line he said, he wanted to become close to his son, like he is to his daughter.

"You know honey, how you've always said things happen for a reason." Jamie nodded as she knew that was one of her favourite sayings. "Well, listen to this."

Riley continued the story and told her how he just happened to meet an amazing man at the shipyards in Florida where JayJay was being retrofitted. They literally bumped into one another as they rounded a corner. Bryan Silky was also a surgeon, about Riley's age and was a widower like Riley. Becoming fed up with the politics of corporate medicine he had decided to leave it all behind and try and make a personal difference in the world. Bryan and his son, who was a dentist and his daughter in law who was a nurse, sailed all over Micronesia in their beautiful 164 foot Benetti yacht. It had been modified to contain a small medical operating room and a combined medical/ dental office. They had provided health and dental care to remote villages and islands throughout the south Pacific for the last three years. Bryan's health was failing due to a genetic heart condition and his son and daughter in law wanted to start a family so it was time for them to turn the page. He was at the shipyard to get an estimate of the cost of having all the medical equipment removed and the boat retrofitted and returned to its original state.

Riley was now guiding JayJay back towards the harbour and kept talking as he changed tack upwind to bring them well clear of a large naval vessel. "You know it was funny how we, Bryan and I, were so similar. We were both waiting to talk to the same estimator, our situations were almost identical and we both needed a change."

Looking hard into his daughter's eyes he said, "You know honey, I have had it all. A great wife, bless her soul. A great career. I built Cleanetics from scratch and am so proud of that. I have you, so accomplished at such an early age. We have worked together, very successfully and you, well both of us, have grown so much. The only thing I haven't done in my life is have a real relationship with Jeremy."

Jaime didn't need to hear the rest, she knew what they were going to do. All of the arguments Jaime had been formulating to try and change her dads mind just disappeared. It just wasn't Riley that was sick of what the world had become, Jaime too felt saddened about the absolute dysfunction of the political system and how big corporations were taking over everything for their own benefit. She knew the present system wasn't sustainable and that the cracks appearing in Europe and the Middle East were just the beginning. Things were getting really messed up and we were forgetting those basic tenets that made us who we were. It had appeared to her that most people would rather be rich than happy.

Jaime worked against that system every day and she knew her dad did too. Turning, she took a deep breath and started to speak but then had to look away. San Diego was off in the distance, the sun was now high in the sky and it muted the colors but it was still the most beautiful city in the world to her. Looking back at her dad just as the tears started to stream down her cheeks all she could say was, "I love you dad."

As they headed back to the harbour they put JayJay through her paces in the freshening afternoon wind. Under full sail she was amazingly fast and handled like a dream. They were soon joined by a pod of pacific white sided dolphins that slashed and darted through their bow wake and seemed to effortlessly hang beside the boat as they looked up at them, blankly staring with their mischievous little grins. Jaime and Riley just looked at each other, they both knew what the other was thinking. Dolphins had always brought them good luck.

Shortly after JayJay was anchored and secure Miguel arrived to ferry them back to the marina. Jaime had been admiring the huge sailboat anchored just a hundred yards off their stern.

"What's her name dad?" she asked.

"Unfinished Business, which I thought was appropriate," Riley replied with a grin.

They took their time as Riley toured both Jaime and Miguel through the massive steel hulled vessel. It was more than twice as long as JayJay, 164 feet with a thirty foot beam and two huge masts. Jaime saw right away that all the rigging and sails were new but that it didn't have the same kind of retrofit as Jay Jay but everything was functional and clean.

"She's a beauty dad. Very comfortable, not too over the top, well, except for how big she is."

"Ya, it'll hardly be roughing it, that's for sure. And you should see the holds, they are massive. She can carry over three tons of extra supplies and she has the same desalination system as on JayJay, oh, that reminds me, I forgot to mention someone."

Jaime didn't know why but she immediately thought that her dad had met a woman.

"Have you heard of Javier Catalina?"

"Umm, sure, he is one of those big ethical fund guys. Super green environmentalist but still very well respected by Wall Street. How does he fit in with this?"

"Well, I also met him at the shipyards and that's where the desalination plants came from. His foundation provided start-up capital for this Israeli inventor who came up with this upgraded desalination system. I showed you the unit, it is very small and uses half the energy of the traditional desalination system while producing almost twice the fresh water. It is a really unique process and I bought a couple of them from their first commercial production run. Javier and I have kept in touch and I hope to nominate him for the board at Cleanetics."

Jaime was jolted back to reality as she started to consider what Cleanetics would be like without her dad.

"You know, I totally get it," she said, "But do you really have to quit? Can't you just take a leave of absence and see how it all works out with Jeremy?"

"I know honey, I've thought all that through," Riley countered as he led her to the gangway. "I can't have a fallback position. To make it work, you have to be all in and that's what I am doing. It's like your mom always used to tell me whenever I doubted a decision or struggled to make one. She would say be true to yourself, and that's what I am doing."

"But Jeremy is just taking a leave." Jaime's reply came a little too quickly but she couldn't help it. Starting to feel a little panic set in, she started to plead with her father not to leave.

Riley let her talk without interruption.

Jaime suddenly stopped mid-sentence and hesitated. "Oh my God, I'm being so selfish."

She covered her eyes with her hands and started to cry. She sobbed throughout the trip back to the marina.

There was a tremendous amount of work completed prior to Riley's planned announcement. Everyone in the entire company knew something big was brewing but no leaks had occurred, which was surprising. Both Jaime and Riley had concerns about Sandecker but he somehow managed to not spill the beans about what was going on.

The new joint venture between Pfizer and Cleanetics had been assembled in record time. An amazing team was formed to follow up on the cancer opportunities that arose from their Imoxofene research. Once Jaime had brought the board at Pfizer up to speed on the most recent data, they wasted no time in agreeing to join forces and partner up with Cleanetics. What really surprised Jaime was that after only two weeks of due diligence, they also agreed completely to the original terms offered by Cleanetics. Pfizer would directly fund the start-up with a $60 million dollar cash contribution and provide a $25 million dollar interest free loan for a 25% equity stake in the new company. Cleanetics was to provide $20 million in start-up capital and would retain control of the board of directors.

Pfizer obviously saw the potential and moved quickly to ensure their involvement.

Rumours were swirling in the media that something was going on at Cleanetics so they made the announcement the day after the deal with Pfizer was completed. A press conference was hastily arranged and it was another beautiful San Diego morning when Riley Jones, President and CEO of Cleanetics stepped up to the dais in the flower filled courtyard. Almost all the staff at Cleanetics were present and those that were still in the building had their noses pressed up against the windows.

"Good morning everyone, thank you all for coming at such short notice." Riley spoke firmly and confidently into the microphone as he was inundated with the camera flashes of the assembled media. "It seems like yesterday when I stood before many of you in this exact same spot to open the Cleanetics building that you see behind me. I have an equally satisfying task today." Pausing he looked out over the crowd seeing a wide range of emotions from his staff. As he broke into a broad smile, he was hit with another round of camera flashes. He thanked the assembled dignitaries which included Mayor Sylvie de Santos, who had just returned to work after her latest round of chemotherapy. Sylvie was a very much loved and respected mayor whom the electorate could not get enough of. Short and round with a smile the size of Texas she really resonated with the working class voter as they appreciated that like most of them, she had come from humble beginnings. Working hard in what previously was a massively dysfunctional City Hall, she was now the most popular mayor that the city had ever had and her illness had rocked everyone.

"I am here to announce the formation of a new company." That was the cue for a couple of his community relations people to start handing out their press release to the media and invited guests. "With our trusted partners Pfizer, we are launching a new bio-medical research company that will concentrate specifically on the successes that Cleanetics has had in fighting autoimmune disease. All the background is contained in the press release that is currently being circulated." Riley paused, taking a sip of water before continuing. "We have had tremendous success with our drug Imoxofene. It has shown amazing abilities to combat diseased cell growth in a number of high profile autoimmune diseases like lupus. It has been so successful that we have decided to form a new company called IMARCO, which is short for Imoxofene Advanced Research Company."

Riley again paused, this time for effect. "To help facilitate the creation and start-up of the new company, I will be leaving Cleanetics immediately to take a leadership role at IMARCO." An audible gasp emerged from the crowd, which were mostly Cleanetics staffers. Riley was very active within the company and was tremendously well respected, which was somewhat unusual for a senior executive in this day and age. A number of reporters called out questions which Riley ignored. "Raj Chouhan will temporarily take over as president and CEO of Cleanetics until a full time replacement can be found and approved by the board of directors." Riley looked over at the assembled senior management team and board members and added, "But they shouldn't have to look too far."

The crowd was still murmuring about Riley's departure as he sang the praises of Cleanetics and its staff. He congratulated all the employee's for their dedication and hard work and even mentioned a few by name, including two of Jaime's team leads who had been instrumental in the advancements of Imoxofene. Jaime looked on and felt so proud of him. Looking at him smiling and thinking he looked ten years younger, even though she knew he was going to be leading IMARCO in name only, she felt the same enthusiasm and admiration that was coming from the assembled staff.

"I will be having a meeting with all Cleanetics staff at 11:30 this morning in the atrium to personally provide you with more information and to answer any of your questions. I also sense there are some members of the media who may have questions and we'll open it up to questions after I make my first statement as chairman of IMARCO." Riley paused again and took a sip of water. "IMARCO will have one purpose and one purpose only; to build upon Cleanetics successful research with Imoxofene into blocking diseased cell growth. Our target is specific and it will be our primary focus. The target is cancer."

The applause temporarily drowned out the questions being shouted by the media and that led to a bit of a scene as the cameramen and print reporters scrummed in front of the podium. Although Riley answered questions for over twenty minutes, one moment was captured that assured the announcement received international media coverage.

Mayor de Santos was asked by a reporter whether the city had encouraged IMARCO to locate within the city limits in the hopes of providing jobs or at the very least increasing the faltering commercial tax base. She hesitated for what seemed like an eternity before answering.

"As many of you know, I am once again, fighting cancer." Everyone could see the emotion in her face as she tried her best to control what those around her knew was inevitable. She turned towards Riley and gestured for him to join her at the podium. As he approached, the tears started to flow and she reached out and grasped Riley by the shoulders. With her wig slightly askew and with camera flashes erupting all around she looked up at him and with a significant treble in her voice said, "The only thing I encourage Mr. Jones to do is to find a cure for this horrible disease."

S linky had been part of General Han's team for over a month but this was his first week of actually working at the Army research facility. It was a large and impressive five story concrete structure with an adjoining three story windowless building that was jokingly referred to as Mao's tomb. Both facilities were tucked away in the centre of what anyone would assume was a typical industrial park containing various manufacturing and industrial enterprises. In actuality, it was a closely guarded government compound, for use exclusively by various government and military agencies and was made to look like a typical commercial operation. Being a completely fenced and guarded industrial compound wasn't unusual for China and only the most astute observer would notice the increased levels of security and surveillance. What unnerved Slinky somewhat was yesterday's dramatic increase in armed military personnel and the fact that there were numerous armored military vehicles now patrolling the property. He understood there was growing unrest within the country with some isolated rioting reported in the western news media, but he thought all this increased security was an over-reaction to what he viewed as the general public's normal reaction to such an overbearing and authoritative government.

General Han had promised Slinky a complete tour of not only their facility but of the entire compound and that had not yet happened. Slinky was continually irked at the fact that he was the Director of Vaccine Research, yet he was restricted from entering more than half of their own building and was not even allowed to walk around the compound. He made a mental note to bring his security clearance up with the General when they next met.

Slinky was sitting in his somewhat nondescript office when he was surprised to receive a letter from Dr. Xiang Bo welcoming him to the team. Dr. Bo also requested a meeting and asked him to call ahead to make sure he was in the building. Dr. Bo had been the senior statesman of Chinese genetic research and he was China's equivalent to American Craig Venter who was the first to sequence the human genome. When genetic research was just starting to blossom, Dr. Bo made a number of significant breakthroughs in sequencing viral and bacterial genomes. He had spent a few years at the Pasteur Institute in France before returning to China and what appeared to most to be scientific obscurity. Slinky had read every word of what he had published and considered him one of his scientific heroes. Reading the letter over and over he couldn't believe he was right here, inside the very building where he now worked. For the first time since reluctantly accepting this position, Slinky was excited.

Slinkys team seemed competent and their labs were some of the most modern he had ever seen. Splitting his people into two separate groups, Slinky had them working on the same problem of identifying viral mutations and then making vaccines specific to those mutations. Attacking the problem from two completely different directions at first raised some concern from his staff as it was not normally the way research was done in China. Typically one direction was identified and all resources were applied but these were all extremely smart and dedicated researchers and they soon threw themselves at what was purposefully designed to be somewhat of a competitive process.

It was a hot and muggy morning with the air pollution hanging like a horizontal curtain over Beijing when Slinky picked up the telephone and dialed Dr. Bo's office. After being on hold for a number of minutes, Slinky was about to hang up when the receptionist returned to the line and told him that security was on their way and would escort him to meet with Dr. Bo.

As he made his way to Dr. Bo's office, Slinky was now thinking this security stuff was becoming more comical than irritating. He was being escorted by two guards to the top floor of the facility and had now already received two temporary clearances which hung from his neck. The elevator door opened and they exited to yet another security checkpoint.

After the customary scanning of his clearance and a phone call to someone, Slinky was allowed to pass and was led through what appeared to be a more traditional office environment. There were no laboratories here but he passed by rooms of very high end computer equipment and a beautifully appointed research library. He was led to the end of the hall where a very slight balding man with white hair ushered him into a spacious office and closed the door.

Dr. Xiang Bo appeared to be quite frail with a noticeable stoop which made his head tilt at a funny angle as he looked up at Slinky. He extended his hand, "Very pleased to meet you Dr. Shen."

"It is truly my pleasure Dr. Bo. I have followed your work for years and I had no idea you worked here."

"Well, I wouldn't really call it work anymore." Dr. Bo smiled and lit a cigarette as he motioned for Slinky to take a seat. "I oversee some parts of the initial research I did years ago. I haven't been in the lab for quite some time."

He took a long drag on his cigarette and asked Slinky, "Why did you come here Dr. Shen? I have read your file and you do not seem to be the type that would want to do research here."

Slinky took a moment to choose his words carefully. "I see it as an opportunity Dr. Bo. As General Han has explained to me, this facility is in the top three in the world for vaccine research and that excites me."

Dr. Bo leaned forward and said, "Yes, that racist dog fucker Han can be convincing can't he." Dr. Bo grinned as he started to laugh. He then started to cough, a deep throaty cough that was out of place for such a small wizened old man. As he reached into his top desk drawer and grabbed a pack of cigarettes he said, "Just so you know Dr. Shen, Han can see everything you do and hear everything you say. As you can see, I don't care, but it is something you should be aware of."

Dr. Bo started coughing again and Slinky could see the strain building in his face. It went on for a full minute before Dr. Bo leaned over and spit into his waste basket. Slinky started to speak but Dr. Bo waved him off and stood up. Leading Slinky to the door they shook hands and Slinky could feel a piece of paper being pressed into his palm. Their eyes locked as the door was opened and Slinky was passed over to the security detail. "Thank you for coming Dr. Shen, I apologize for not having more time for you today. We will meet again soon."

Slinky kept the scrap of paper in his hand as he was escorted back down the hallway, slipping it into his jacket pocket only when they were momentarily held up behind a technician wheeling a dolly out of one of the computer rooms.

Slinky stepped off the elevator and entered the first floor and made his way back to his office recalling a conversation he had had with his father just after his mother's funeral. They were talking about the potential of his father being granted a politburo seat and discussing politics, specifically Chinese politics. It was one of the rare political discussions they had ever had but there was one thing that had made a big impression. Slinky was very proud of his heritage and the thousands of years of history behind it. His issues were more with what had occurred during the Cultural Revolution firstly with Mao's rule and then with the communist regimes that followed. His difficulty had always been in accepting the oppression and scientific censorship of his youth, but currently it was with the corruption that came with the drastic change to a market economy, which to him was really a change to a fake market economy. The biggest divide between him and his father had always been the underhanded tactics of the government, the oppression that they imposed, the ongoing spying and from his point of view the unnecessary censorship that took place. His father had always denied it in the past but it was different this time as in what could only be described as a moment of weakness, he did acknowledge the problems which existed in his beloved China. Slinky's father confirmed most everything of what he suspected but gave him a dire warning. The government had eyes and ears everywhere, both inside the country and out. He pleaded with him not to take any radicalized views and to keep his feelings to himself. He, like Dr. Bo warned him that no phone or computer was secure. What surprised him is when his father said *'anywhere in the world'*. What was memorable about that conversation was that his father's admission made him look somewhat vulnerable and Slinky later regretted even bringing it all up.

As Slinky sat at his desk reviewing some lab reports the piece of paper that Dr. Bo had slipped him finally got the better of him. He had reached for it once but stopped himself just in case he was being watched, later laughing at his paranoia. The new plan had been to look at it during his drive home at the end of the day but he couldn't wait so he told the administrative assistant that he was leaving for the day and headed for the parking lot.

Traffic had become insufferable in Beijing and it was getting worse every day. When he was a couple of blocks away from the compound he reached into his pocket and retrieved the neatly folded square of paper. Opening it he and read it quickly.

Written in small dainty characters it instructed him to go to a small noodle house near his home tonight between 8:00 and 9:00 o'clock and he would be contacted by Dr. Bo's granddaughter who had a message for him. He knew the noodle house as he had eaten there a few times this past month.

10

Slinky opened the door of the small restaurant at a little after 8:00 o'clock and was immediately assaulted by the humidity from the cauldrons of boiling water and the hot and spicy smells of northern Chinese cuisine. One of his favourite foods was noodles made from mung bean starch and he could feel his mouth start to water as he thought of his last dinner here. Looking around and not seeing any available tables, he just stood there in front of the door which elicited a lot of staring by the diners. As he scanned the room again he noticed a young woman at a small table near the back give him a little wave. She was sitting by herself but an old Mao jacket was hanging off of the chair opposite her.

As Slinky approached she smiled and poured him a cup of tea. Dressed in very basic and dated clothing, which was very out of style in today's fashion conscious China, she watched as he took off his jacket and sat down. Noticing most of the customers were dressed plainly this night he was the odd man out with an open necked dress shirt and expensive Italian blazer.

"Hello Dr. Shen, thanks for coming, my name is Rosy," she said in near perfect English.

The use of English caused a number of people close by to stare even harder but she snapped at them immediately in Mandarin saying they are English students and to mind your own business.

"Hi Rosy, you can call me Shing. Your English is very good, did you study overseas?"

"Yes, for a time," she replied as Slinky made himself comfortable. "I have been back for a couple of years now studying business. I was hoping to return to the United States but that has now become difficult."

"And Dr. Bo is your grandfather?"

"Yes, he is such a great man." Rosy smiled slightly as she sipped her tea.

Something still didn't look right to him, it must be the clothes as they did not match her stylish makeup and hair. Sipping his own tea, he estimated Rosy to be probably late-twenties, was obviously educated and carried herself with a great deal of confidence. Her statement about travelling also seemed a little out of place. This was becoming interesting.

"I understand there is a message for me?"

Rosy met his gaze, sat back in her chair and asked, "Have you eaten yet Shing?"

"Well, no, but . . ." and before he could finish she continued.

"I am very hungry and I would prefer we eat first, business later." She waved the waitress over and ordered an appetizer of pickled jellyfish and spicy shrimp rolls followed by buckwheat lo mein. Slinky ordered his favourite mung bean noodles with pork and vegetables.

Once the waitress filled up their tea pot and departed with their order, Rosy asked, "Why do they call you Slinky?"

"Who is they?" Slinky replied, leaning forward with interest.

The faintest trace of a smile again creased her face and her eyes sparkled intensely. "I just thought if I am using my western name, maybe you should too and was wondering where such a name came from."

"It was a nickname given to me at college in the United States and it just stuck." Slinky could see she knew more about him than he realized. "It appears I am at a disadvantage Rosy. You seem to know a lot more about me than I know about you."

Rosy flicked her hair dismissively and asked, "What do you want to know?"

They talked casually for the next few minutes and both shared the appetizer that Rosy had ordered. The conversation was somewhat forced but that was natural under the circumstances. The small talk carried on through dinner and Slinky did find out a little more about her, but not anywhere near enough to level the playing field.

After they had both finished eating Rosy excused herself and instead of heading to the bathroom as Slinky expected, she made her way through the rapidly emptying restaurant and paid the bill. She returned quickly, grabbed the jacket that was draped across Slinky's chair and said, "Let's go for a walk."

There were a few blocks full of restaurants and shops and they strolled casually, just like many of the other couples out this night. The sights, sounds and smells were typical for any Chinese city. Merchants were aggressively calling out to potential customers and that just added to the sometimes unbearable irritation of the many extremely loud conversations. Living both in Europe and the U.S. had made Slinky aware of just how loud Chinese people talk. The exotic smells from the small specialty spice and herb vendors wafted over them as they rounded a corner and entered a street market. Children ran around with abandon as their parents shopped, the crowds became more intense, the noise even louder now.

To Slinky, the never ending small talk was maddening. He grew tired of talking about his travels and how he viewed certain things. Rosy seemed to be a master at asking questions and getting him to talk about his opinions and feelings. He finally came to the conclusion that she was really interrogating him.

They stopped at a motorcycle dealership and were standing looking in at this year's models when Slinky asked, "Have you found what you are looking for?"

"I don't like motor cycles," she replied.

"I'm not talking about the bikes. You are interrogating me and you are looking for something. Did you find it?" The words came out a little blunter than Slinky had intended.

Rosy turned and looked up at him and said, "I think so."

As they walked back towards the restaurant Slinky asked again about the message.

"I really don't have a message for you Slinky." She was looking down, for the first time not studying him. "My grandfather asked me to, well, I guess the easiest way to say it is to check you out."

"Check me out for what?" Slinky replied.

Rosy stopped and now looked directly up into Slinky's eyes. "He very much trusts my judgement. He wanted my opinions of you. What I thought of your character, whether

I thought you were a good and honest person. He mostly wanted to know if you could be trusted."

"Trusted? Trusted for what?"

Looking down again she said, "I don't know." Rosy started walking again and Slinky had to hurry to catch up.

"If I didn't trust you, as a ruse, I was to essentially ask to see you again, umm, socially." Hesitating slightly she turned away and picked up her pace once again. "If I did trust you, I was to tell you that my grandfather has something to tell you that is very important."

Slinky reached out and gently grabbed her arm. She stopped and made eye contact with him. "You aren't a business student are you?"

Almost sheepishly she said, "No, I'm actually a psychiatrist."

Slinky asked, "Are you really Dr. Bo's granddaughter?"

"Yes. I love him very much and would do anything for him." A little grin appeared as she said, "Even getting dressed up in these ridiculous clothes."

"Well, they are a bit out of style for someone your age. Were you trying to change your appearance?"

Rosy looked away again, somewhat embarrassed by the whole thing. "He told me to watch my back. That people might be following me and to not talk about anything about this to anyone and to not talk to him on my cell phone. He told me not to drive my own car and to try and hide my appearance for this meeting."

At somewhat of a loss for words, Slinky asked her in a pleading and hushed tone, "Can you please tell me what's going on."

"No, I don't really know, sorry." Rosy replied embarrassingly. "I do know grandfather isn't well and he has been at odds with his superiors for quite some time. I think they want him gone but he refuses to leave. He can be very stubborn. I also know that my travel visa to return to the States was not approved. Grandfather is sure that it has something to do with my relationship with him."

Slinky now realized this is the most Rosy had talked all night. "So all you know is that Dr. Bo wants to tell me something."

"Yes, that's really it, I don't know any more." Rosy sheepishly replied.

"Well," Slinky said, somewhat disappointedly," I guess at this point, all that I really know is that you won't be asking me out."

After his meeting with Rosy, Slinky didn't have to wait long for Dr. Bo to contact him again. The next day he was invited to take a walk through the labs by a senior employee and was then unceremoniously left standing alone just outside one the biohazard labs. He was watching the employees inside the lab, in full biohazard containment suits, placing some drops of liquid in various racks of test tubes when a lab technician that he had never seen before, appeared from nowhere. As the lab tech briskly walked by Slinky he discreetly dropped a piece of paper onto the floor. Slinky slowly moved towards the paper and stepped on it. Waiting a few minutes to ensure he was not observed, Slinky bent down and re-tied his shoe and then quickly picked up the folded piece of paper. Walking out of the lab he scanned the paper and read the instructions to meet Dr. Bo for lunch on Saturday at the same noodle house where he had met Rosy. He was to park his car in the alley at the back of the restaurant and meet Dr. Bo there at noon. When Saturday arrived Slinky drove to the restaurant and parked as instructed. Walking out of the alley and around to the front he entered the restaurant and was almost immediately ushered into a back room where Dr. Bo was waiting, sipping on a cup of tea. They quickly left out the back door and had been now driving and talking for well over an hour.

It had been a longer drive than expected as they had the misfortune of getting caught in a traffic jam caused by a head on collision between two trucks on a small secondary road just outside of Beijing. Once they cleared the accident scene they made good time and arrived at the temple compound just a few minutes later than expected.

Dr. Bo had tried to brief Slinky on what to expect on their clandestine trip, but wasn't able to say much between his numerous coughing fits. Seeming to be weaker each time they met, Slinky noticed that he wasn't chain smoking as much, which suited him just fine. All Slinky was really able to grasp was that there was some important information in a book that he needed to read.

He was completely astonished when Dr. Bo told him that his older brother had been a Shao Lin monk for close to seventy years. Like most young Chinese boys, Slinky had dreamed about becoming a Shao Lin monk. He had seen their demonstrations many times and like so many others was in awe of their athleticism and spirituality.

They parked outside the gates of the temple as motorized vehicles were not allowed within the high mud brick walled compound. As they approached, Dr. Bo ground out his cigarette and said, "This is the only part I don't like about coming here, they won't let me smoke."

As they entered Slinky marvelled at the huge flowering shade trees that dominated the grounds and he could see some imposing and intricately decorated brick and stone buildings within. Immaculate gardens stretched out towards the rear of the property and the distant beige smudge of the rear wall indicated how large the compound really was. Chickens and goats wandered happily about within their enclosures as they were led past another smaller set of what must have been old fortifications. Slinky could now see the various inner defensible walls within the compound that protected the buildings and allowed for fall back positions should the outer walls be breached. Slinky wondered how many battles had been waged on this very ground hundreds if not thousands of years ago. Passing a small and very old stone building he stopped to read an ornate sign with an inscription written in red and gold characters. It identified this property as the Bei or North Monastery. There was no mention of this having any connections to the Shao Lin but that became evident soon enough.

Two young monks dressed in the typical orange robes opened the beautifully carved gate that lead to the inner compound. Walking along a flagstone path, Slinky was surprised when they were directed away from the buildings and headed towards a small courtyard shaded by one of the most beautiful flowered arbours that he had ever seen. As he approached the fragrance was almost overpowering and he could feel a calmness settle over him. Marvelling at the serenity of this spot, slinky realized it wasn't just here, looking around, the entire area had a feeling of serenity to it.

An older monk rose from a bench and came forward with his arms extended towards Dr. Bo. Slinky held back as they embraced and spoke in low tones to each other. Slinky could see that there was some resemblance in the brothers.

Introductions were made and Slinky was amazed at how mentally sharp and seemingly physically fit the ninety year old monk was. Dr. Bo had said his brother had been the Abbot here for over twenty years.

They made small talk for a few minutes and during one of Dr. Bo's coughing fits, the Abbot asked Slinky if he would like a tour of the facility. Before he could even answer there were two monks beside him and they were leading him away.

Slinky was gone for over an hour as he toured the main temple and the grounds. He was amazed at the cleanliness and intricacies of the buildings, the architecture and stone work was obviously ancient but that made it even more fascinating. Asking one of the monks how old a particular building was the reply was simply *'very old'*. He estimated the age of the compound itself must be well over a thousand years with many of the buildings not much newer. The fact that such a place, so close to Beijing, survived the Cultural Revolution shocked Slinky as he was well versed on how many ancient sites were destroyed during that time.

After his tour he was reunited with Dr. Bo on a small raised dais that overlooked what looked like a parade ground. The hard packed clay surface was a stark contrast to the rich darkness of the loamy soil of the nearby vegetable gardens.

Slinky leaned over and commented to Dr. Bo that this was an amazing place when he saw the monks approach. Six rows, six men deep, they walked silently by and formed up in ranks in front of them. What followed was truly the most fantastic display of martial arts that Slinky had ever witnessed. It became clear that this was not only a demonstration but an actual training exercise as a few of the monks received minor injuries, their cut lips or bleeding noses completely ignored as they finished their rituals.

Slinky was startled as Abbot Bo seemingly appeared from thin air and asked him what he thought of the exercise.

"I am amazed sir. Your monks are fabulous, these fighting skills . . . well, I have never seen such intensity and ability."

"Yes, they work hard but they all have much more work to do." Abbot Bo looked over the monks, smiling to himself at the high praise which was to be expected from an outsider. "We have some archery practice that you might find interesting, please, come."

Abbot Bo led both of them to a small field covered in knee high grass just a short walk from the main practice facility. In the distance, a young monk was placing a pumpkin about the size of a basketball on a spike about five feet off the ground.

A gentle breeze swayed the grass and birdsong was everywhere. Slinky was just admiring the beauty of the area when he saw something out of the corner of his eye. Again, about thirty monks were standing just behind them with a few younger apprentices holding oil skinned covered bundles. Slinky just couldn't grasp how so many people could approach so closely without making a sound. He asked Abbot Bo about it.

"One of the main jobs of a monk is to meditate Dr. Shen. We live in close quarters here and at all of our temples. We learn from a very early age to be quiet, to move silently so as not to disturb another's meditation."

"And I assume," Slinky said, "That also has helped the Shao Lin during combat."

A small grin appeared on Abbot Bo's wrinkled face. "As you know Dr. Shen, we are not only monks, but warriors. Throughout history, many emperors have used our services. We have served for over fifteen hundred years." The Abbot momentarily paused as he appeared to be lost in time, thinking. "Yes, many of the vanquished never heard us coming. But we know, their last thought before they pass over the great divide is that of the Shao Lin." The grin remained on his face.

Chairs had appeared and they sat facing away from the staked pumpkin as the monks, in complete silence, strung their bows and they each grabbed two arrows. A bow and one arrow were gently placed at the feet of Abbot Bo.

"A small demonstration for you Dr. Shen." The Abbot quickly gave some instructions and the monks silently took up positions behind the three men.

"You saw the pumpkin, which is our target. Our monks will demonstrate their abilities to you. Please continue to face this way and count from one to twenty."

The three of them sat in the chairs, facing away from the staked pumpkin as Slinky counted out loud.

When Slinky had finished the Abbot said, "Now please, turn around."

They all rose up and turned around and all they saw were a couple of the young monks standing off to the side each holding a pile of orange robes. Dr. Bo started to laugh which amazingly did not turn into a coughing fit. Slinky couldn't believe it. They had just disappeared. The birds still sang. The grass still swayed, but where were all the monks?

The Abbot reached into his robes and pulled out a little wooden device that looked like a cricket.

"There are twenty eight monks hidden here, in groups of two's and three's. On my signal, each group will lose their arrows towards the target." The Abbot held up the little wooden cricket and clicked it once.

Off to their left, three monks popped up out of the grass and shot their arrows in rapid succession. Slinky followed their flight and all six hit the pumpkin. Another click and two monks just thirty feet in front of them came to their knees and shot. Again, all the arrows found the mark. Another click, but Slinky saw no one, but saw four arrows strike the target.

Dr. Bo was excitedly pointing. "They are in the trees, over there, in the trees!"

Another click and the same result.

Abbot Bo spoke again. "For the last group, may I suggest you duck down a little bit Dr. Shen."

Just as Slinky ducked down, he looked behind him as he heard the click. Not twenty feet from where they had sat, two monks rose from the grass and loosed their arrows just over his head. He quickly turned to see all four strike the pumpkin which was now much the worse for wear.

The monks all stood in their spots, unmoving as the sunlight glistened off their bare backs.

"Amazing, simply amazing," was all Slinky could say.

Dr. Bo reached over and grabbed Slinky's arm and with a rare twinkle in his eye said, "Now you know why I keep the book here." He laughed but this time couldn't avoid the coughing.

Slinky was about to thank Abbot Bo when he saw him reach down and pick up the bow that was previously placed at his feet. "Would you like to try?" He held the well-worn wooden bow out to Slinky.

"No, no thank you Abbot." Slinky said without any remorse. "My memories of this day should not include any failed archery attempts by me."

"As you wish." The Abbot said as he carefully nocked the arrow, pulled back the bowstring and sighted on the target.

Slinky was amazed at his strength. The bow was nearly as tall as the Abbot and the target was at least eighty metres away. The Abbot then pulled his head back, looking up and making direct eye contact with Slinky. The bow still taut in his hands, as solid as granite, never wavering.

"A Shao Lin monk becomes his weapon." Abbot Bo was still holding the bowstring at full draw. "This arrow becomes part of me, no different than my arm or finger."

Slinky was transfixed as the Abbot held the bow and he held his stare. The Abbot then slowly closed his eyes. He took an almost imperceptible breath and then let the arrow fly without even looking back at the target.

It struck the middle of the pumpkin, delivering the final coup de grace as the arrow riddled gourd finally disintegrated and fell to the ground.

Abbot Bo had already turned away, he didn't need to see the arrow hit. He knew it would and he knew it did. The monks ever so quietly grabbed their robes and dispersed as the Abbot led them away.

Dr. Bo grasped Slinky's arm as they followed the Abbot back towards the main grouping of buildings. "Time for you to see the book," he said.

Abbot Bo led them to a small room down the hallway from his office in the largest building of the monastery. For the most part, the majority of the temple complex could best be described as functional with few amenities. Monastic life after all was not one of comforts or pleasure but it became quickly evident that this area was different. The slate floors were covered in ancient silk and wool carpets hand stitched generations ago in the Middle Eastern and Asian steppes. Some of the wooden panelled walls contained intricately carved scenes and was the colour of dark chocolate. What fascinated Slinky more than anything was the more formal artwork that ran down the length of the hallway. Some very old and delicate three dimensional scenes, masterfully carved, hung from the walls. Small alcoves held magnificent jade statuettes that depicted warriors in battle. Slinky stopped to admire an old seemingly faded watercolour in a bamboo frame. It depicted a number of monks encircling an old and gnarled tree, fighting off a large number of men on horseback. Although the characters in the inscription were faint it indicated it was from the very beginning of the Ming Dynasty. Slinky was not a Chinese history buff but he knew enough to know that was around 650 years ago.

"Abbot Bo, excuse me," Slinky said, almost embarrassed to ask. "Is this painting really from the Ming Dynasty?"

The Abbot returned down the hall and stood in silence, admiring not only the painting but the intricacies of the frame, which was a work of art all on its own.

"Yes Dr. Shen, this depicts a somewhat famous battle between the Shao Lin and a number of Mongols from the northern steppes." The Abbot leaned in closer to read the inscription and then stood back smiling slightly. "Based upon the modern calendar, in April 1370, thirteen monks were attacked by sixty men on horseback. All the Mongols were killed except for one which was sent away with the message to never again threaten the Shao Lin."

The Abbot looked up at Slinky, now smiling broadly. "Knowing that you are an educated man Dr. Shen you might be interested to know that it was this very battle that also introduced the Shao Lin to horses." Abbot Bo went on to explain that previously, the Shao Lin never used beasts of burden but after this battle, they were the reluctant caretakers of over fifty horses. The Abbot vividly recounted the tales of how the monks had tried to turn the horses loose, only to have them return, day after day. Ultimately, they turned it into a very profitable enterprise and actually bred and trained horses for royalty and noblemen for the next four hundred years.

"We have many works of ancient art here Dr. Shen. Not anywhere near the amount that our first temple at Mount Song has though." The Abbot reached up and grabbed Slinky's arm and led him down the hallway and into a small but well-appointed library. "Now doctor, I will leave you and my brother alone."

As the Abbot left the room and closed the magnificently carved door behind him, Slinky couldn't help but notice the floor to ceiling bookcase. Without a close inspection he could see many of the books were very old if not ancient, many had what appeared to be faded and cracked leather bindings but most of those covers turned out to be wood. Dozens of scrolls, probably made of bamboo paper were rolled and stored in intricately decorated wooden tubes. He had never seen so many old and ancient writings in one place. Dr. Bo walked over and to Slinky's surprise approached the wall besides the single small window. The panelling was carved with scenes of ducks and geese and he reached up and grabbed two of the ducks in flight and turned them vertically. Slinky heard a small click and a secret compartment opened just below the carved relief.

Slinky was holding his breath, not knowing what to expect. The single biggest threat that the world has ever known, according to Dr. Bo, was about to be shared. Slinky knew he was about to view over twenty five years of Dr. Bo's research but what frightened him was his warning. "If I have read you right, once you see the book there will be no going back. You will be like me, trapped forever."

"I will leave you alone until dinnertime." Dr. Bo said as he placed the book on the table in front of Slinky, holding his hand over his mouth to stifle a cough. "You cannot read nor will you be able to absorb everything. Please just read the monthly reports from 2004 to the present." Dr. Bo was again wracked by coughing and he quickly left the room.

Slinky looked down, somewhat disappointedly at a large red vinyl three ring binder. Laughing at himself and his imagination, for his surroundings had led him to expect he would be reading some ancient text or fabulously detailed manuscript like the ones that graced the bookshelves behind him.

The binder was tabbed into years, and then months. At the end of each monthly section was a short one to two page synopsis. The early years, which started in 1987, were all typed reports but since late in 2006, Dr. Bo had written everything in long hand.

Slinky had always known that Dr. Bo was a very intelligent man, a brilliant geneticist and researcher. After a half hour of reading it was immediately apparent that he had made some amazing genetic breakthroughs. Things that Slinky had never even heard about were chronicled here, results and breakthroughs a decade old that had never been made public or published. Even more amazing was the fact that his research had been subverted and he had been forced to work on a government plan called LOCUST. Reading on he could feel the perspiration starting to soak into his clothing as the horror of what he was reading started to sink in. Never one to be accused of being a slow reader, Slinky was deliberate, ensuring he didn't miss a character that may change the meaning of what he was reading. Nothing did. A sense of dread and foreboding came over him as he learned all there was to know about LOCUST. The only thing that was not surprising was that General Han was involved from the very beginning.

As Dr. Bo had expected, Slinky had passed on dinner. Finally he convinced Slinky that they needed to go and return to Beijing so as to not arouse any suspicions. The binder was placed back into its secret compartment and with a quick goodbye and thank you to the Abbot, they were in the car and heading out into the rapidly failing light.

After another serious multi-minute long coughing fit, Dr. Bo was exhausted.

Slinky said, "I am sorry to ask so many questions Doctor." He passed him another bottle of water and the last of the tissues as he braked hard to avoid a small herd of goats standing in the middle of the road. "But, I just cannot believe what I have just read."

The binder's monthly entries contained not only the scientific data but also the innermost thoughts and feelings of Dr. Bo, it was almost a diary of his last twenty years. The information on this LOCUST plan bordered on unbelievable, it was like bad science fiction on steroids. LOCUST had been in development for close to three decades, originally designed to be a weapon of mass destruction, a fearsome biological agent. It had slowly morphed into, what was now considered by the ruling elite, to be a weapon of economic opportunity.

The LOCUST virus was initially developed from genetically similar strains of H5N1 influenza and influenza from the 1968 Hong Kong flu outbreak. Both flu strains had been formed when genes somehow swapped between the human and avian flu. Once General Han's research scientists had determined how that happened they were eventually able to genetically manipulate the virus and finally introduce a genetic immunity variant into what was to become LOCUST. The information that Slinky had read was disjointed and in some cases incomplete but the inference was clear.

LOCUST was a virus that could be used to diminish or eliminate other ethnicities to ensure enough space, land, food or whatever is available on the planet for the ethnic Chinese. What truly frightened him, right to his core, were some references about overpopulation and birthrates, essentially maintaining the Chinese identity into the future as the world became 'browner'. Slinky couldn't argue with the science behind the differences in ethnic birthrates but the message was clear. It was 1939 Germany all over again. This was crazy. Shockingly, the information on using LOCUST for economic gain, to cripple competing economies and to ensure China becomes and remains the world's economic kingpin was completely current. It wasn't a plan for the future; it was a plan for the present.

The silence didn't last long as Slinky asked the Doctor not to speak but to just shake his head yes or no in response to his questions.

"Does this LOCUST plan have the backing of senior leadership within government?" A nod confirms a yes.

"So it goes much higher than General Han?" Another confirming nod.

Slinky struggled with how to ask this question. "Do you think my father knows about it?" Yes again.

With so many questions and possibilities running through his mind it was hard to focus. Unknowingly he was racing along at a very high rate of speed for the small country road and suddenly headlights appeared directly in front of him. He braked hard and steered as close to the ditch as he could and barely avoided a collision with a small mini-bus. The questioning continued.

"The racial DNA variants that have been isolated can actually be injected into the virus?" Yes.

"The racial variant is used as a negative, meaning those carrying the variant will be immune from the virus, is that correct?" Yes.

"There are four intensity strains of the virus ranging from typical flu like symptoms to the LOCUST strain, which is 100% lethal?" Yes again.

Slinky thought back to what he had read in the book about General Han and government conceding that typical warfare had now become obsolete. There would be no winners, only losers. They had embarked on a strategy of economic warfare, being able to cripple or even eliminate specific populations through the genetic profiling of disease. The flu was just the start and although Dr. Bo was not privy to the command structure he was confident that General Han's group were working on even more sinister opportunities for their genetic variants. It was a plan decades in the making and it would take many more decades for it to bear fruit. There is one thing that the Chinese culture teaches and that is patience and the virtue of taking the long term view, Slinky thought.

"You are sure there is no cure or possibility of a vaccine?" Yes.

"You say it has been tested but are you convinced that it will really work?" Yes.

"I'm not sure if this is right but the infection is immediate and then the carrier becomes massively contagious for a week to ten days, spreading the virus unknowingly? Another yes.

"Once LOCUST manifests itself, death then comes quickly from fever and organ failure, in about a week? Again Dr. Bo shook his head yes.

"Jesus Christ, I can't believe this." Slinky drove on for a bit in silence, just trying to absorb everything.

"Because it is based on the influenza virus, you are most afraid of mutations which might occur if the virus was to transfer to swine or birds and then back to humans again, like the normal flu occasionally does, is that right?" Yes.

"If it does, it would probably lose the genetic variant, right?" Another shake of the head yes.

"General Han doesn't believe you and thinks you are just stalling?" Yes.

"Enhanced mutations were built into LOCUST to ensure a vaccine could never be produced?" Dr. Bo waved his hand and nodded both yes and no.

Slinky tried a different tact. "The mutations will always keep ahead of any vaccine, ensuring that the lethality of the virus remains active and contagious within the infected population?" Yes.

"And the virus has been adapted to survive much longer than a traditional influenza virus." Slinky again hesitated, running his hand through his hair, feeling the perspiration on his scalp. "Did you say the virus can live

outside its host for up to three weeks and still be viable?"
Yes again.

"And if it does get into swine or birds, you think even
one of the less intense strains, let alone LOCUST could
mutate and potentially transfer back to humans and cause
a catastrophic worldwide pandemic?" The answer again was
yes.

"Although the chance of that happening is
infinitesimally small?" Another nod yes.

As they left the countryside and entered the highway
system they started making good time. Holy shit Slinky
said to himself. This was the real deal. The possibility of
our very own Andromeda Strain made the hair on his
arms stand up. Although he didn't really want to know, he
needed to ask.

"You are sure General Han had your son in law killed?"
Yes.

"He faked your daughter and one of your
granddaughters death and they are being held in a prison?"
Up to this point Dr. Bo had just been looking out the
window, but he turned to face Slinky and shook his head
yes.

"Your other granddaughter, Rosy, the one that met me,
she thinks her mother and twin sister are dead?" Yes again.

"Han has blackmailed you and forced you to cooperate
to complete Locust for over a decade now, all the while
threatening your family?" Yes.

"And my father knows about this?" No.

"So he just knows about the existence of LOCUST
then?" Yes.

"But you think that Han might be having second
thoughts about your human to animal to human mutation
theory and that's why he wants me here, to work on flu

vaccines that can mutate along with the virus?" Dr. Bo, holding a number of soiled tissues to his mouth, shook his head vigorously yes.

"Last month's entry says that you think General Han is getting ready to use LOCUST against the growing insurrection in the North?" Yes.

"Do you really think he would do that, the risk of mutation is slight but the ramifications could be unimaginable?"

Without any hesitation Dr. Bo looked at Slinky and spoke for the first time, his voice was unsteady and he reached across and put his hand on Slinky's arm. Squeezing it he said, "Yes."

He had not ever been one who lacked the ability to make decisions, but Slinky was in the unusual position of having no idea what he was going to do now.

I t didn't take as long as Riley thought it would to say goodbye to everyone at Cleanetics. There was to be no party, cake or celebration because for most, Riley's leaving was not anything to celebrate. He wanted to look each and every one of his employees in the eye, shake their hand and thank them for their contribution to both the company and his own personal success. It was his way, he never compartmentalized people or judged people on their position within the hierarchy's of either business or society. Riley fundamentally and at a very deep personal level appreciated and respected the work of every single one of his employees. Often saying to Jamie that he would rather have a coffee break or a lunch with the ladies from accounts payable than the governor or the elite at his country club, she knew he meant it.

Earlier via email he had requested that everyone at Cleanetics either be at their desks or in their labs on this, his last morning. Starting in the parking garage the first person he said goodbye to was Darnell. That first goodbye proved to be one of the toughest of the morning as he then worked his way around the building. There were congratulations and hugs along the way with lots of tears from his employees, many still somewhat in shock from his announcement. Riley Jones was truly respected and loved by everyone at Cleanetics. They all considered him more than the boss. He was a friend, a colleague and in some cases a confidant. There are far too few companies in corporate America that would have elicited such emotion from staff when their chief executive was leaving. It was one of the reasons that Cleanetics was successful. It was about respect, it was genuine and everyone knew it worked both ways.

When he finished, Riley made his way to Jaime's office. Sitting in the pit, she was looking at her newest aquarium resident, a large purple hermit crab. It was window shopping a number of shells that she had dropped onto the sand, sizing them up seeing if he would like to change his ever-mobile home. Jaime turned to see Riley standing in the doorway silently watching her. It was hard to keep the look of disappointment off of her face.

"Well, I'm all done honey." Riley walked over to his daughter and gave her a big hug. Jaime didn't say anything, she wished he wasn't leaving but she loved him even more because he was.

Riley spoke softly into Jaime's ear. "I just spoke to Captain Frederich and all the crew is aboard. Unfinished Business is ready to sail as soon as I get there.

Jaime promised no more tears but her voice cracked with emotion. "It's going to be so different without you here dad." She just couldn't bring herself to talk anymore about the business or their exciting new discoveries and what that meant down the road. She just said, "I love you so much."

They had spent most of the last two days together. Jaime helped Riley pack his things for the voyage and helped Darnell move some of his things in. Darnell was housesitting until Riley returned and both of them knew the house was safer now than it ever was.

"How long before you reach Oahu dad?" Jaime asked as they started to walk out to the elevators.

"I'm not exactly sure sweetie but it won't be long. With a full crew we will be sailing full out 24/7." Riley quickly ran through the itinerary that had them using the trip to Hawaii as a shakedown cruise and then with a smaller crew, heading off to Papua New Guinea where he was to meet up with Jeremy who had just taken a one month Doctors Without Borders assignment. They would take on a full load of supplies and provisions there and then they would head off, first to Micronesia and then to French Polynesia.

"So what do you make of Jeremy asking to bring along his new friend?" Jaime didn't mean for it to sound like she didn't approve, but it still came out that way.

"You know as well as I do that Jeremy was never going to be a eunuch." Riley laughed as he remembered his many talks with his son about his overt promiscuity which started in high school. "He says she is a wonderful girl and a very capable nurse. The fact that she is not formally educated doesn't seem to make any technical difference. He says that she has worked in so many African conflict zones that she could outdo most doctors in an emergency room setting."

Jaime piped in as they rode the elevator down to the ground floor. "Well I guess someone needs to look after you two." Squeezing his hand as they exited the building they walked out towards Darnell and the waiting car. "I can't see two male doctors ever being organized enough to keep things clean or to schedule patients, or to cook anything edible for themselves."

Riley stopped and turning towards her he grabbed her by the shoulders and looked her straight in the eye. "And the best thing is, apparently she makes a mean curried rat." Jaime giggled as she let her father envelop her in his arms. Riley pulled away but still held Jamie at arm's length. "Everything is in good hands here, great hands actually." Being his honest and truthful self he felt that, actually it was more than that, he knew that he was now a minor player in what his company had become. Evolution isn't a bad thing. Trying to add some levity to the tension that was building, Riley smiled, "With all this unrest in China, it appears I am escaping civilization just at the right time."

Although they had said their formal goodbyes last night, Jamie searched for words to match the moment. None came. Somehow Jaime had kept her promise not to cry as they walked out of the main doors and stopped. Riley looked back up at the building, the building he helped design and build. Dozens of people were standing at the windows, some started waving, others just stared unbelieving that this day had come.

Riley kissed Jaime on the forehead and gave the employees looking down at them a half wave-half salute. Smirking at himself for making that kind of gesture, he thanked Darnell and climbed in the back seat of the car. Although Jaime had kept her promise not to cry, Darnell hadn't made one. His tears streamed down both cheeks as he gently closed the car door.

N ot even one of the most authoritarian regimes on the planet can control everyone and everything in a country as large as China. The democracy uprisings throughout the country were met with swift and brutal reactions by not only local police but the military. The government was quick to limit media coverage in any areas where demonstrations and rioting were occurring, but stories continued to appear on a daily basis around the world, which was a constant irritant for the government. Many political pundits in the west predicted the downfall of the ruling Chinese communist party due to this *'Chinese Spring'* movement. They said it would be just like what had occurred in the Middle East years before during the Arab Spring democracy uprisings.

Hundreds of protesters had been killed, many more than what was reported in the western news. Their bodies immediately removed, never to be returned to their families. Many thousands more were arrested and placed into the vast Chinese penal system and some just simply disappeared. The seeds of discontent had been sown and what was a slow boil had started to intensify within the general Chinese population. Many saw an opportunity to oust a corrupt authoritarian regime, even though the thought of how true democracy would work in China was terrifying to most people. The government knew that it could not allow this movement to get any more momentum or it could reach the tipping point and threaten their privileged way of life.

The nine members of the Politburo Standing Committee were discussing the latest reports out of Heilongjiang Province. The city of Mudanjiang continued to be in almost constant turmoil. A full Red Army division had been dispatched from Harbin to reinforce the small local military base and stamp out the insurrection. There was a great deal of tension in the room and almost everyone was losing patience. There had not been this amount of concern and worry at the top echelon of the Chinese government in decades.

Quishan Li, a former army general was one of the most vocal. "This needs to be stopped now!" he shouted. "They must be neutralized before this disease spreads any further. I say we use all the force necessary to bring those half-breed dogs under control."

As the discussion raged one of the telephones on the conference table rang which stopped everyone immediately. A Standing Committee meeting was never to be interrupted unless it was an extreme emergency. All heads turned towards the Secretary General who slowly reached for the phone.

After listening for a few moments he said, "Send him in."

They all recognized General Junqi Han immediately and an interruption from the director of the Central

Military Commission and de facto leader of the secret police brought them to full attention.

"My apologies comrades but this information could not wait." General Han started handing out a small file folder to all of the nine members. "The military base in Mudanjiang has been overrun. The regiment has retreated and has suffered significant casualties. They are down to less than two hundred men. Local police seem to have disappeared and the remaining portions of the regiment have regrouped on Highway G10 to the west of Mudanjiang on the outskirts of Hailin City. The rebels are in control of both Mudanjiang and the base. They now have access to the remaining armaments which include small arms, surface to air missiles, artillery and approximately twenty tanks."

"When did this happen?" asked the Secretary General.

"Less than two hours ago, sir," replied General Han. "If you turn to the photographs you'll see a satellite shot of the rebels within the base."

Secretary General Jung slowly shook his head while trying to remain calm. "Do we know who is behind this?"

"No sir, but there are thousands of them and they seem to be very well organized. I suspect there must be some military expertise involved." General Han's mind worked furiously as he anticipated the question he knew was coming.

"This is not just a riot by disgruntled farm labourers or unhappy factory workers General, how could this happen without your elite group catching wind of it?" The Secretary General was well known for his biting sarcasm, which was now in full throat.

General Han knew he needed to play hard ball now or he would spend the rest of his life in a prison cell. "Trust me comrades, I will get to the bottom of that, but here is my plan on how to deal with this problem." He started handing out another folder with just one word on the cover, LOCUST.

Spending almost an hour General Han explained all the broader details of the plan which included his thoughts about Mudanjiang specifically and the Chinese Spring uprising in general. He provided intricate details about the abilities of the American spy satellites that were just now coming into range. Explaining that it was standard Chinese military policy to do most troop and equipment moves at night he was hopeful that any further activity on the base would not arouse any suspicions.

"Nonsense." The Secretary General hadn't intended to shout but he saw the effect it had on the room. "The Americans have just as many abilities and spies as we do. I would expect their president is receiving a briefing now, just as we are."

General Han waited a moment before he continued to explain that the previous orders from the standing committee, which was that any area of insurrection was to be immediately cut off from the rest of the world, no telephone or internet services and all media, domestic or foreign were to be arrested, had been carried out.

"We can isolate the city by having the air force paratroopers secure all the bridges and also isolate highways G10, G201 and G301. Troops currently on route can secure all other roads, rail lines and escape routes and enforce the quarantine area needed for LOCUST deployment. Evacuation preparation has already begun in the rural areas and we have cut off all electricity to the city.

They all knew of the LOCUST plan and what it entailed, not one of them ever thought it would be initiated in this manner. Although there was little if any formal discussion about it, most felt that it was a sacrifice the few had to make to ensure the many survived and prospered. It wouldn't be the first time that had occurred in Chinese history.

Not that he really cared but Quishan Li asked "How many people in Mudanjiang, General Han?"

"A little over 800,000 in the urban area and approximately 2.75 million total if you include Hailin City and the surrounding suburbs.

"And what about the genetic infusion process that we have been pumping nothing but money into for the last decade general?" The Secretary General asked, "Who are we targeting here?"

"As you know sir, we are dealing with a general insurrection in Mudanjiang. The population is of considerable mixed race. Those with true Han Chinese genetic markers are estimated to be less than 25% of the overall population. We had never really anticipated the need for a LOCUST event against our own people, however we can genetically infuse LOCUST to isolate the Han Chinese marker and only eliminate those without that genetic marker. That is my recommendation."

Like most Han Chinese the Secretary General considered his racial background to be the one true and pure Chinese bloodline. Over the centuries, long before the invasions of Genghis Khan there were multiple conquests of what is now China. Dozens of ethnic groups, hundreds of different tribes and ethnicities had inter-bred over millenniums to form what is now China. It was estimated that approximately 70% of China's population currently contained the Han Chinese genetic marker with the remaining 30% being other differing but identifiable ethnicities.

General Han reviewed his notes carefully to ensure an accurate number. "If we can set up a quarantine perimeter to the east of Hailin City, and target only Mudanjiang, I anticipate casualties after a LOCUST event to be approximately 600,000 people. If we are unable to set up between the two cities and set the perimeter to the west of Hailin and target both Hailin and Mudanjiang, casualties are expected to be a little over two million."

"It is the only viable plan that allows us to save face and gives us the time needed to eliminate the leaders of the Chinese Spring movement." General Han knew it was now all or nothing. "It is my opinion that we can successfully use the cover of a bio-medical emergency to isolate Mudanjiang while LOCUST runs its course. We will naturally ask the Americans and Russians to help us with this outbreak and that is contained in the plan in front of you. I have just conscripted Dr. Shing Shen, a world renowned virologist, to lead the bio-medical division of the Central Military Commission and his reputation will help immensely with the worldwide scientific community. The effects of a killer flu epidemic will slow down the insurrection long enough for us to locate the leaders and cut off the head of the serpent."

General Han was speaking a little louder and a little more forcefully now as he explained the final intricacies of the plan. "The flu outbreak will allow our military to roll out all over the country to deal with the insurrection under the guise of controlling movements within multiple quarantine zones. Any pockets of resistance can immediately be deemed hot and isolated while we crush those that threaten us. The Americans and the United

Nations will praise us for taking quick and decisive action to control a killer flu. They will never know it was all a deception."

General Han looked around the table at each and every one of the standing committee members, most were deep in thought, staring at nothing. The newest politburo member, Lin Shen, sat passively, his face did not reflect the fear he felt deep within his heart. Only the Secretary General continued to stare directly into General Han's disfigured face. As an instructor in military school, Han had been a ruthless bully. One of his students had finally had enough of the abuse and threw acid in his face. Han had grabbed his young student and had choked him to death as the skin on the left side of his face literally burned off. He was never charged for the killing and none of the other students present ever spoke out against him. In fact, many of them continued their military careers and now dutifully serve under him. That one act had begun the fearsome reputation of Junqi Han.

"The full Red Army division from Harbin won't reach the area for another fifteen hours but paratroopers and helicopter assault teams are now standing by. I have also been in contact with the commanding officer of the remaining regiment in Mudanjiang and expect a report about the feasibility of setting up the quarantine zone between Hailin and Mudanjiang as soon as we are done here."

"Well General Han," the Secretary General said, while standing to stretch. "I must admit that you have thought of everything, but I wonder if it's really the best solution or are you just covering for your initial failures?"

"My loyalties are only to the Party and to China." Han turned to face the majority of the standing committee, not even attempting to hide his disfigurement from them. "I have made significant personal sacrifices and I am willing to do so again. I am certain that this is the only way to save ourselves, our culture, the communist party and China. May I remind everyone that all we need to do is look at what happened in Syria, and consider those consequences. Bashar al-Assad killed over 200,000 of his own people, one out of a hundred of the general population before that conflict ended. The more people he killed the more powerful the resistance became. A military intervention here could backfire on us as well and that is why LOCUST is the answer."

There was now considerable discussion amongst the standing committee but the final answer became clear in everyone's mind. An awkward silence hung in the room as everyone waited for the Secretary General to make the announcement.

"Institute the LOCUST plan immediately General Han," he said as he slammed the LOCUST folder down onto the table and grabbed his solid gold cigarette case from his pocket. "And have the Red Army division set the quarantine perimeter to the west of Hailin City."

Once the order was given, Mudanjiang and Hailin City were isolated by the elite paratroopers of the Red Army Special Forces unit. They immediately secured all egress routes from the area and within hours, ten thousand soldiers had spread throughout the countryside to ensure no one entered or left the quarantine zone. The military propaganda machine was out in full force dropping leaflets informing people of an infectious disease outbreak and that they were now quarantined. Few, if any, believed the message.

Every radio and television channel in the area was interrupted with a looping message that Mudanjiang and Hailin was now were under a complete quarantine and asking people to remain calm, stay in their homes and await further instructions. All television and radio stations throughout China started playing a similar message about an infectious disease outbreak in Mudanjiang, but the government assured its citizens that it had successfully quarantined the area and everything was under control. The western news media immediately picked up on the story and started sending their Beijing correspondents to the front lines, all surreptitiously tracked, as usual, by those that had been watching them since they had first stepped into China.

Mandatory evacuation areas were identified and being enforced by the military around Mudanjiang and Hailin City. All inhabitants within fifty kilometres were being readied for evacuation. The Chinese Military Infectious Disease Centre had already started to mobilize, setting up field laboratories and decontamination areas. Press conferences were being arranged in Beijing and contact had been made with both the White House and the Kremlin, all of this was accomplished within twenty hours of the Secretary General's decision to initiate LOCUST.

Qing Shial, the leader of the local insurgents didn't believe a word of the announcement about a disease outbreak. He knew that it was being used as a ruse to isolate them until more troops could arrive to wipe them out. He was meeting with his lieutenants to plan an exit strategy when they started to hear the reports of the paratroopers. All communications had been cut early on, but they had been able to get some video footage of the initial fighting posted on the internet, which was a strategic win for them.

"My ancestors ruled the steppes for three hundred years," Qing boasted, knowing full well they all knew his families rich Mongol history. "We have won this battle and we will win the war, but not today or tomorrow. China will be divided, just like the Soviet Union was, but in time my friends, in time. We will regain our autonomy and we will throw the oppressors out!" he announced to massive cheers. Almost all of the insurgents were of mixed race with the leadership group being almost exclusively Khalkha

Mongols who had been displaced from their homeland areas and resettled in Heilongjiang Province.

"Now is not the time to shed our blood needlessly." Qing spoke quickly to his brother. "Buyat will disable whatever captured equipment that cannot be destroyed. It is time to disappear, time to melt back into the everyday workings of Mudanjiang. We have inflicted a huge wound on the Chinese and the entire world has seen it. Give the orders, my friends." Standing up he started shaking hands and slapping backs, "It will be light soon, let us all go back to our homes and our wives and girlfriends, but go to your wife first!" he said as they all laughed at the old Khalkha proverb.

Two specially outfitted JL9 fighter/trainer jets were readied in Beijing to deliver LOCUST to an army base just outside the city of Harbin. Two SnowOwl drones had already been delivered there by helicopter and awaited their payload.

General Han had overseen the initial design and development of the SnowOwl virus delivery drone system himself. Typically, when chemical or other biological weapons were delivered by air, a pod was attached to an aircraft that flew over a target, slowly releasing its cargo. General Han had been fascinated with drone technology ever since he first saw it in action. Early on he had petitioned his government to use its vast worldwide web of industrial and military espionage agents to steal the technology as soon as possible. Within six months, they had obtained ninety percent of the guidance and control systems from an American civilian contractor who they had been blackmailing for years.

Han had immediately recognized the practicality of using drones as the delivery vehicle for LOCUST. They were virtually invisible to radar, had a long range and were remotely guided. The Chinese drone program was bigger than anyone realized and as usual, they were using stolen technology which they had improved upon and had now surpassed both the Israeli's and Americans in autonomous drone technology. These new generations of surveillance drones could think and act on their own and could be designed to even mimic birds in flight. Having the ability of using high definition cameras and directional microphones they could surreptitiously spy on anyone, anywhere.

When they were building the first prototypes they had scaled back on the size and weapon carrying abilities of the standard military drone to build the smaller and lighter SnowOwl. The new design was now easily transportable and weighed less than 250 kilograms fully loaded with fuel. It could be assembled in under an hour, had a range of over 1400 kilometres and was whisper quiet. Han hadn't become one of the most powerful military leaders in China by being timid. He had explained to the politburo that the Americans had thousands of drones armed with advanced electronics and hellfire missiles but they were all dwarfed by the killing power of one SnowOwl. Every time the Americans used a drone strike to blow up a house in Pakistan or Yemen, there was evidence for the entire world to see. With a SnowOwl and LOCUST, China could use racial and genetic profiling to kill thousands if not millions of people and everyone would just think it was a flu outbreak. It was the biggest military breakthrough since the atomic bomb and it left no fingerprints. However there was one problem that persisted and that was the contamination of the drone during delivery of the virus. They had not perfected a way to ensure the drone did not return with the virus still present so the current practice was to direct the drone to the open ocean or a deep lake. It was then powered down and slowly parachuted into deep water, sinking to the bottom to be lost forever. Ballistic destruction was initially attempted but that still left some evidence of the drone itself so this method had been perfected and it ensured no wreckage remained.

Shortly after leaving the meeting with the politburo General Han had sent his staff to every LOCUST team members home to escort them into the laboratory. Once they arrived, he met with the managing directors and immediately told them that they needed to prepare four kilograms of Locust with the Han immunity variant immediately.

"That's not possible General," complained Gianli Wang, one of the longest serving biologists on the team. He was still irritated at being woken up in the middle of the night and as he started to explain the handling protocol for LOCUST production, General Han reached inside his jacket and withdrew his pistol.

"You will do this and do it right now or I will blow your brains all over this room!" General Han shouted, his face contorted into a rage. He grabbed Wang by the hair and jammed the pistol into his temple, forcing his head down onto the table. The general was known for his temper but not even his aides had seen him this angry.

"I have put up with your whining and complaining for years Wang." His voice had become laboured and even more sinister as he continued to grind the pistol into Wang's temple. A small rivulet of blood started to run under Wang's eye and drip off the end of his nose onto the conference room table.

"Nothing would give me more pleasure than to kill you." General Han could feel his finger tightening on the trigger, the bloodlust growing by the second. "But I need you." He relaxed and slowly removed the pistol and noticed Wang's blood for the first time. He wiped the barrel of the pistol down the front of Wangs lab coat and holstered his weapon.

The other directors were wide eyed, each too afraid to move as General Han stepped back to the head of the table, slowly regaining his self-control. His disfigured face was flushed red and he looked at them all with a menacing scowl.

"Four kilograms of LOCUST with the negative Han variant, prepared for aerial dispersal immediately," the General said to no one in particular. "Use two SnowOwl pods, two kilograms in each. When they are loaded and decontaminated, load them onto a truck and notify me immediately as I will be accompanying them to the airport. I'll be in my office."

The room cleared out immediately as each team sprinted to their labs and started their protocols for infusing the genetic variant into LOCUST and loading the aerial pods. The manuals indicated it would take two and a half hours to complete the infusion, load and decontaminate the pods. They did it in an hour and fifty minutes.

G eneral Han stepped out of the military commissions newly acquired 45XR Lear Jet in Harbin. It's not that he didn't like the Chinese military jets, it was just that this jet was so much more comfortable. His second in command of the LOCUST delivery team met him on the tarmac as he was walking towards their mobile command centre. "The SnowOwls are fully loaded, tested and operational sir."

"Thank you Captain. Have both dispersal and disposal plots been programmed?"

"Yes General, programmed according to coordinates you provided." Captain Yun was nervous with anticipation to see if they had passed what he assumed was to be yet another drill. Yun thought they were years away from a real LOCUST deployment and he also couldn't believe that they would deploy LOCUST against their own citizens so he was just following standard operational protocols until the drill was declared.

General Han double checked the programming and identified drone one as primary dispersal and drone two strictly as surveillance. He asked a few questions of the five staff within the command centre then asked Captain Yun to step outside.

"Is everything to your satisfaction sir?" Yun was still extremely nervous and had always been intimidated by General Han.

The General looked over the Captains shoulder at the two drones receiving their final field checks. "Yes it is. I was expecting a call from the Secretary General, have you heard anything?"

Captain Yun was caught a little off guard by that question. "No sir."

Just then an aide appeared and said that there was an important call for the General.

Just as General Han turned to return to the command centre, he said to Captain Yun, "This isn't a drill. This is the real thing Yun. No screw ups or all our careers are finished."

Captain Yun watched with his mouth agape as the General entered the command centre. A strange feeling pulsed through his body and he instantly started to perspire. Swallowing hard, he followed the General into the large camouflaged tent.

Han grabbed the secure telephone and wasted no time in getting to the point. "Everything is ready Secretary General, am I cleared to proceed?" General Han didn't have to wait long for a reply.

"Yes, yes you are. One more thing Han, I want to tell you, I never liked you, but I've always trusted you. All of China is in the balance here. Once we start this it must be seen through to the end. I'm just getting word of rioting throughout the Southern provinces and demonstrations are being organized as we speak for Tiananmen Square. This needs to work."

"It will work Secretary General, I guarantee it." With that, General Han hung up the telephone and looked around the room. Everyone was looking at him as Captain Yun had just finished briefing most of them. The General relished these moments, being in total control and seeing the fear in the eyes of those that he controlled. How I love this feeling he thought. "This is not a drill. We are in full operational mode. Takeoff in three minutes." The assembled staff busied themselves with their checklists, all hoping and praying that this was just another drill and that it would be called off soon. No one spoke but the looks they exchanged across their monitors were ones of abject fear. They had all been schooled from a very early age to follow orders and not question authority. No one would speak out as they all knew the consequences would be immediate and significant. The tension in the command centre rose and one technician on the telemetry and guidance team not so quietly threw up into a waste basket. This was not a drill. LOCUST was being unleashed.

General Han watched as both drones climbed quietly into the sky heading east. Their specially designed pusher propellers lifting them effortlessly through the late afternoon sun and onto what General Han thought would be his defining moment. Captain Yun stood as still as a statue just a step behind General Han, hoping the silence continued for some time because at this moment, he was speechless.

The drones lazily circled just to the north of Hailin City awaiting complete darkness. The entire area had been locked down and secured. Everything contained in the hastily prepared plan to deliver LOCUST onto their own people had gone according to plan. Drone one received its command to drop to five hundred feet and begin its delivery run while drone two recorded the action from two thousand feet above. Three passes through Hailin City delivered more than enough of the LOCUST virus. A short hop to Mudanjiang and four more passes emptied the drones payload of LOCUST. Just like the insect it was named for, the virus silently swept into the two cities, voracious and unstoppable.

Both drones now followed their disposal coordinates, they headed southeast staying just above treetop level. SnowOwls employed stealth technology, their carbon fibre shells virtually invisible to radar but there was no point in taking unnecessary chances so they stayed well clear of Russian territory. Quickly passing over Sonbong North Korea they headed out into the Sea of Japan. Thirty kilometres out drone two climbed to an altitude of two thousand feet and circled while drone one slowly bled off speed in what was to be a slow death spiral. Just before stalling the nose of drone one was brought up to vertical and the engine turned off. The explosively launched parachute blasted out of the nose cone and the chute opened quickly as the drone started to slide backwards towards the sea. It only took about twenty seconds before the drone gently splashed into sea and sank to the bottom in two thousand feet of water. Drone two had also now fulfilled its purpose immediately turned and headed for its first waypoint on its way back to Harbin.

General Han had already contacted the Secretary General to inform him of the successful deployment of LOCUST, he had never taken his eyes off of the monitors for the entire mission. Every SnowOwl drone had conventional, low light and infrared cameras. Both their video and navigational communication systems were encrypted with the latest coding and were completely immune to hacking. In the darkness, the video wasn't the best but they had seen enough to know all aspects of the mission had been successful.

As the LOCUST team were completing their post deployment checks and preparing to debrief their specific aspects of the mission, General Han stood up to thank them all for a job well done. Ever since his face was disfigured, he had taught himself not to smile. Having lost portions of his lips and some facial muscles, what was a smile for most turned into chilling cartoonish sneer for him. Now, looking over his team, he was smiling broadly, immensely proud of their achievements and fully confident that his plan would work. Most of his team busied themselves with their work, either afraid or ashamed to make eye contact.

17

Just like his grandfather and his grandfather's grandfather, Xiang Tan raised fowl. For generations his family had lived on a lightly forested plot in a small depression of land just west of Mudanjiang. Two shallow but productive spring fed ponds kept Xiang's ducks and geese happy and well fed. His ten acre parcel also contained numerous fields of grain and vegetables, all nourished by the algae rich water from the springs. His family would never be rich but they had always prospered as most Chinese farmers do. Xiang lived on the farm with his wife Ping, his eighteen year old daughter Linzou and two farm hands. Linzou's name was a play on words meaning 'to make beautiful jade' and although she was cursed with the darker skin and coarser hair that occasionally appeared in his family, Xiang still hoped that his awkward and somewhat unattractive teenager daughter would turn into a beautiful young woman. And if not, she would stay and work on the farm and that wasn't a bad thing either.

It had been well over a week since the government had announced the quarantine. Xiang like most people didn't believe the stories of a sickness, he was convinced as were most others that it had something to do with the democracy movement. He had been told the quarantine could last for months and this was good news to him as he was one of the biggest suppliers of ducks and geese in Mudanjiang. Selling only forty or fifty birds a week would limit the supply and drive up prices. Every farmer in the world understands the economics of supply and demand. With luck, he could make enough money to buy a truck.

The next day both of Xiang's farmhands and his wife became ill. It had come on suddenly and by the following day they were all bed-ridden with high fevers. Xiang had sent Linzou into town earlier in the morning to bring an herbalist or better yet a doctor to the farm. Looking down towards the road he could see her riding her bicycle, pedalling furiously back up the driveway. Even at this distance he could see she looked upset.

"Are they coming? Did you see the doctor?" Xiang asked before she had even come to a stop.

"No father," she said breathlessly and then quietly buried her face in her hands. What she had witnessed terrified her. "This is not a government trick. The sickness is everywhere. People have closed their shops and refuse to answer." The tears now started to flow as she trembled with fear, thinking of her mother lying sick and feverish inside their house. "The army is piling dead bodies in the middle of the road and burning them."

Linzou was sobbing but relayed as best she could what she had witnessed. They stood silently for a number of minutes and Xiang asked Linzou to check on her mother and then make tea. It was time to herd one of the flocks of geese back into their pen and walking away, Xiang felt a little weak. Now perspiring, he wiped the sweat from his forehead as he slowly headed down the path towards the pond. A pounding headache, seemingly synchronized to his heartbeat, had started as he again wiped the sweat from his brow.

As fate would have it, Linzou's parents and the farmhands weren't the only things that became sick on the farm. Along with ducks and geese they also kept a few chickens mostly for their own personal use. A number of the birds were exhibiting signs of disorientation and lethargy.

By the end of the week Linzou's mother and both farmhands had died. Linzou's father was struggling with a fever but he was still herding the various flocks to the ponds and back every morning and afternoon. A friend from school had visited Linzou shortly after her mother had died and reported that Mudanjiang was in chaos. There was death everywhere but it appeared that not everybody that catches the disease dies. Her friend said it seemed that only about one in five people survive. Linzou continued to feel fine but she was really worried about her father.

Linzou fell asleep that night completely exhausted. She woke feeling better but that did not last as she found her father completely incapacitated by fever. It took him another day to die. Afraid to leave the farm she worked day and night and tried to manage as best she could. After burying her father beside her mother in a shallow grave behind their house she tried to figure out what to do next. She knew there was no way she could maintain the farm on her own. It appeared that she wasn't going to catch the sickness but she didn't really know why or what to do next. Overcome with grief and stressed to her breaking point Linzou tried to formulate a plan.

The next morning a local government official arrived at the farm. He wanted to check on their ability to continue to provide geese and ducks to the survivors in Mudanjiang. After explaining she was the only one left, the man asked Linzou some questions then quickly left with a promise to return later in the day. Just a few hours later a number of men in a large truck appeared, slowly making their way up the rutted driveway from the road. They unloaded bags of rice, cooking oil and pre-packaged food which really surprised Linzou. The official told her that they needed her to maintain the farm and continue to provide geese and ducks to the newly formed government market in town. Three of the men would stay to help her run the farm and she was to bring ten geese and twenty ducks every second day to the market. The price she was quoted was more than double what they were paid before the sickness.

Linzou now did very little of the actual farm work. Her days were spent supervising and preparing the meals and she was amazed at how smooth everything was running. The new helpers caught on quickly which pleased her but she was getting worried as she had noticed more deaths among the flocks than what was normal. A couple of the chickens had died as well.

A little over seven weeks later, the outbreak was deemed to be contained and the quarantine was to be lifted soon. Linzou had heard that almost three quarters of the local population had died but there had been no deaths for the last week or so. Government workers, doctors and army personnel were now everywhere in town. She was stopped at a checkpoint and required to fill out a number of forms before being interviewed and requested to come in for a meeting with the resettlement committee early the next week. She was told that the government would probably buy her family's farm and use it for the re-settling refugees that would be coming from other areas. Linzou was still in a state of shock about everything that had happened but she quickly realized that this was an opportunity of a lifetime. She knew she didn't want to be a farmer all her life and now with her parents gone, she had no real ties to Mudanjiang.

One thing Linzou did notice was that almost all of the survivors looked like what they called locally as 'Pekinese'. It was a somewhat derogatory term referring to the rich seemingly perfect people from Beijing with the classical Chinese good looks. There didn't appear to be anyone of mixed heritage, and no one with a flatter face and darker skin like her.

After her meeting in town with the government officials she returned to her farm and started to think about preparing dinner. Going out to the henhouse to get a chicken, she was surprised to see they were all in their pen, not roaming around in the gardens like they did most days. Surmising the farm hands must have forgotten to let them out she gave them some grain and then reached down to grab a hen. Getting one on her first try put a smile on her face. Normally it took a few minutes of chasing them around before she could corner and grab a hen. Linzou tucked the chicken under her arm as she walked back towards the house. She killed it outside and started boiling water so that she could start to pluck the feathers.

No one knew but what Dr. Bo had always feared had happened. This chicken, already weakened by avian flu, had been infected by LOCUST. It had been mixing and mutating with the avian flu inside this chicken for weeks. LOCUST was trying to do what all viruses want to do, to survive. It was a one in a million chance, probably one in a trillion, but Dr. Bo had recognized that possibility. General Han and most others had dismissed it as too remote to be significant.

While Linzou was handling or possibly butchering this one chicken, the mutated LOCUST virus entered Linzou's system. It did what it was designed to do, it infected her lungs and began to grow. This was a new form of LOCUST and it still maintained many of its original traits, most importantly it was still 100% lethal to humans. When LOCUST crossed into that chicken and mutated with the avian flu, it only lost the Han Chinese DNA immunity component. Viruses are both simple and complex organisms, but first and foremost they fulfill their basic needs, their basic programming. This new form of LOCUST just wanted to survive. It was programmed to mutate and that's what it did, from its original form, into this one chicken and now back into humans through Linzou.

Buried deep within Linzou's DNA was an almost infinitesimally small piece of ancient DNA that predated modern humans by tens of thousands of years. A thousand generations before modern humans walked the earth there was other hominid like species that populated the world. There were many branches on the evolutionary tree, some still yet to be discovered.

Some of those branches were somewhat successful like the Neanderthals but they eventually died out. Like the others, they were unable to adapt to their environment or compete with what was to become modern humans. Strangely enough there was interbreeding amongst these hominid relatives and the proof of that interbreeding is that billions of people in the world today carry significant portions of DNA from Neanderthals and other archaic human ancestors. Most DNA is simply passed from mother to child through mitosis. For reasons unknown, particular pieces of ancient DNA could bypass hundreds of generations, sitting idle and undiscovered in modern humans. Through some genetic quirk or mutation, these hidden pieces of DNA would occasionally become active again and that is what had happened to Linzou. This ancient DNA, from a long extinct hominid species, that had been passed along in her family for generations had become active. It has provided her with immunity from almost all human illness and disease her entire life. That's why she originally survived LOCUST and why she would survive it again.

As scheduled, Linzou appeared before the resettlement committee the next week and was offered a great deal of money for the farm. She immediately accepted and couldn't help but smile, all her problems seemed to be over. During her appearance before the committee a tickle in her chest made her cough and she politely covered her mouth with her hands.

Linzou proudly shook everyone's hand as she left.

Later that day two members of the resettlement committee flew out to Beijing to report back to the government on the new resettlement program. The next day those same committee members were giving a lecture on the resettlement program to over a thousand representatives from aid agencies from around the world and then, later that night, to an assembly of United Nations delegations. Once the educational component was completed, a media tour of Southeast Asia was planned.

The perfect storm had begun.

18

The world's last pandemic was the Hong Kong flu outbreak of 1968 that claimed 750 thousand lives. It took almost a full year for that virus to spread around the world and the CDC in Atlanta and most other's involved in infectious disease research, including the World Health Organization, agreed that the next pandemic would spread twice as fast. That prediction wasn't even close.

From a small poultry farm near Mudanjiang LOCUST lived up to its name and spread around the world like a never ending wave of destruction, just like its namesake, it devoured everything in its path. It was the ultimate virus, infecting people quickly but staying dormant while it was unknowingly spread further and further. Finally, with the infected host's job done, LOCUST manifested itself and death soon followed.

Besides Linzou, who was infected but immune, the next people to carry the LOCUST virus were the members of the resettlement committee. They quickly spread it to everyone they came into contact with and what some people in the infectious disease community really feared, happened. They called it the neutron bomb effect and it was made possible by our insatiable need to get to where we want to go fast. The airline industry can only make money if they keep their planes flying for as many hours of the day as they can as it is a very competitive business. Basically whenever a plane is on the ground the airline is losing money so it is not uncommon for the same plane to fly from Los Angeles, to New York, back to Los Angeles, then to Dallas, a short hop to Houston and then again back to Los Angeles all in the same twenty four hour period. The plane that started the unstoppable march of LOCUST across the planet left Mudanjiang with the two infected members of the resettlement committee and flew to Beijing, then onto Shanghai and Hong Kong where there was a crew change. It then carried on to Tokyo and then back to Beijing. LOCUST was now active and spreading through passengers and flight crews at four international airports which have thousands of international flights a day. The passengers and flight crew members interacted with hundreds of others who then spread the virus into thousands. In less than forty eight hours LOCUST had reached every continent except Antarctica. It was over before anyone really knew it had started.

LOCUST had already infected millions of people before the first carriers started to fall ill. It started amazingly fast and it continued to gain momentum, never stopping, the spread of infection grew exponentially. It was relentless, its purposefully manufactured virulence unmatched by anything ever seen before. Each day the virus continued to spread, mankind was one day closer to extinction.

The World Health Organization proved to be as useless as most overly bureaucratic institutions are. Completely fragmented with politics and insidious inefficiency, it soon became a non-entity in the fight against this new threat. The Pasteur Institute in France and the Centres for Disease Control in Atlanta quickly became the world leader for both research and information dissemination for governments around the world. Infighting between the academics at both those institutions soon reached a boiling point as once deaths from the virus reached 100,000 casualties the CDC wanted to declare it a pandemic. Those at the Pasteur Institute waffled and soon worldwide deaths were in the millions. Not too long after that the CDC, on its own, issued a proclamation that this virus that appeared to be just a new strain of flu was classified as a possible Extinction Event. It received the highest classification of danger from the CDC, something that no one had ever really thought would happen, had happened. This new seemingly simplistic but deadly virus was given the name that everyone that worked in infectious disease research hoped they would never hear. They named it Andromeda.

Slinky couldn't stay outside for long, the stench of rotting corpses filled his nostrils with the gagging realism of a world gone mad. He was running for his life and had to find a vehicle and somehow escape from the compound. He didn't know why he wasn't infected, all he knew was that unless he escaped General Han was going to put a bullet in his head.

By the time Slinky had figured out what was going on and he realized it was actually LOCUST that had started the pandemic, he had been already been cut off from the outside world for close to a month. Over a hundred scientists and researchers had been quarantined inside their building and forcibly held against their will as they were ordered to work on a series of new and previously unknown vaccines. It had now become clear that they had been kept completely in the dark about what was going on in the rest of the world. When the evidence was unmistakeable and some of them became ill and started to die, the researchers realized what they were dealing with. Some had known and had even worked on LOCUST in the past. Chaos quickly followed as those in the know, knew, there was no vaccine.

Slinky resorted to the only thing he could think of, he immediately hacked into the buildings computer system from an IT techs computer. He was able to break through the firewall and send an email to Jaime Jones outlining all he knew about LOCUST. That email had obviously been intercepted and the computer he was sending the email from had been immediately shut down and his access card was deactivated. Slinky knew General Han was in the building and was now probably searching for him. After stealing an access card from an unattended security station, Slinky had stealthily made his way through the building and had noticed only a few staff remained at their posts. Most were dead or dying.

Having now escaped the building he needed to get back into the parkade without being seen. Once inside, it took him just a few minutes to find a small military truck with the keys inside. Slinky slowly drove out of the parkade and seeing no one he matted the accelerator and roared across the parking lot and through the closed gate of the complex, smashing through the aluminum barricade. Now outside the compound, he drove through the mostly deserted streets of the industrial area running for his life. He was free but knowing the general, he wouldn't be far behind. Corpses littered the streets, thousands and thousands of them. Slinky knew if there was one chance to beat LOCUST it was with Dr. Bo's book. Unfortunately, he figured, so did Han. He was so mad at himself for describing the book and even mentioning where it was in his email to Jaime. It was unbelievably stupid but these were stressful times. He just hoped he would get there first.

The military vehicle that Slinky was driving drew far too much attention. Those that were still alive gestured wildly at him, some throwing stones and debris, their hatred directed appropriately towards the regime that was killing them. Shortly after leaving the compound a bullet shattered the windshield spraying him with glass. Speeding along the streets eerily empty of traffic, Slinky wanted to try and find another vehicle before he started his drive to the monastery. Taking an onramp littered with debris from an overturned truck, he made his way onto the expressway and quickly brought the aging truck up to its top speed. Up ahead he saw a large BMW sedan stopped along the shoulder under an overpass. It was wedged up against the concrete barrier and its brake lights were on.

Skidding to a stop he got out of the truck and opened the car door. A middle aged woman was in the driver's seat, her head was slumped lifelessly forward. He quickly put the idling car into park and pulled the woman out. She was a small woman and the seat was fully forward and there wasn't enough room for his long legs so Slinky fumbled with the multiple control buttons on the side of the seat until he was finally able to position the seat as far back as it would go. Climbing in he could hear a vehicle approaching and slammed the high powered BMW into drive and fishtailed out onto the multi-lane expressway. The old truck that had been approaching was soon just a speck in his rear view mirror as he drove away, the speedometer showed his speed approaching two hundred kilometres an hour. A quick check of the fuel gauge revealed an almost full tank, easily enough gas to make it to the monastery.

There was no one working in the fields or in the adjacent small village as he approached the monastery and Slinky had only seen a couple of other people during his entire drive. Goats and sheep wandered amongst the neatly planted rows of vegetables, eating their fill. There were no other vehicles parked at the gates and his calls and knocks went unanswered.

Slinky was tall enough to jump up and grab the top of the gate and pull himself over, which he did. The compound was as tranquil and peaceful as he remembered, then he saw the graves. Dozens and dozens of them neatly aligned in a grassy area next to a small outbuilding, a well-used shovel protruding from the ground beside them.

He just stood there looking at the graves and didn't hear or sense anything until he felt the touch of a hand on his elbow. If it was possible to jump out of your skin, that's what would have happened.

"I'm sorry if I startled you Dr. Shen, my name is Jun," the young monk said with a slight bow of his head. "I was not sure if you were real or an apparition."

Slinky could feel his heart pounding and the rush of blood in his ears. He was bent over, hands on knees, looking up at the young monk, his eyes trying to focus, now understanding even from a clinical scientific perspective, how a person could literally be scared to death. It took Slinky almost a minute to regain his composure and be able to speak. Jun stood passively, looking down at the ground in front of where Slinky was crouched, regretting that he had caused Slinky's obvious discomfort.

"Are you the only one?" Slinky finally asked as he looked around the grounds and buildings of the compound.

"Yes. All the others have passed on as have all the local villagers." Jun's voice belied no emotion, he was just stating the facts. "But I still live."

"I have come for a book of Dr. Bo's, the Abbot keeps it for him." Slinky was still breathing heavily but was finally able to stand up straight as he tried to calm himself.

"I know of no such book Dr. Shen." The young monk's demeanor changed slightly as the many ancient treasures of the monastery came to mind. A Shao Lin would defend the monastery until his dying breath.

"Dr. Bo and the Abbot showed it to me the last time I was here, I know where it is." Slinky started walking towards the main building complex silently followed by Jun.

Moving quickly through the building the scent of incense was almost overpowering as Slinky made his way down the hallway and into the small library. His hands shaking, he manipulated the secret compartment and accessed the binder, placing it on the ancient desk that dominated the room. A slender ray of light from the single window illuminated the dust particles that had swirled up from the desktop.

Looking at the binder stuffed with writing paper Jun was perplexed. This was obviously not something that belonged to the monastery and he doubted very much it even belonged to Abbot Bo. Jun would never have let an outsider take anything from the monastery but he felt he could trust this tall outsider. "If you knew of the book and how to open the compartment then you were obviously intended to have it, is it yours?"

"No. It belonged to Dr. Bo. I worked with him." Slinky stopped and stared at the binder, wondering, hoping that there was something in there that could help him bring a stop to the madness. Recalling his questioning of Dr. Bo after he first saw the information about LOCUST he remembered the look on his face when he confirmed that there was no possibility of producing a vaccine. A feeling of desperation swept over Slinky. "I had hoped the information contained here could help me find a cure and make a vaccine for the disease."

Jun just stood back watching, his face expressionless but his heart rate increased slightly when he heard of the chance of a cure.

Close to a month of being forced to work non-stop for reasons unknown and he now had all of the research and background material on LOCUST in his hands, but what now? Slinky was thinking about what to do and where to go. He couldn't go back to the lab, he was sure he would be killed if he did. He didn't have any information at all about what was going on around the world, but what he had seen today told him all he needed to know. The infectious disease protocol was to limit all travel so escaping somewhere would be impossible. So having the definitive pieces of the LOCUST information at his fingertips meant nothing.

Slinky was jolted out of his thoughts by Jun asking, "Why do we live Dr. Shen when all the others have died?" It was a question that Slinky couldn't answer.

Just then, Jun cocked his head slightly looking back towards the door and the gloomy hallway. He put a finger to his lips and directed Slinky to move off to the side. As Jun turned around a figure emerged from the hallway holding a menacingly large revolver.

A Shao Lin monk was always a formidable adversary but was no match for a man with a gun in an enclosed space. General Han moved further into the room and motioned them both against the wall. His facial disfigurement seemed to be intensified by his obvious sickness. Dried mucus was smeared across his cheek and he grabbed the edge of the desk for balance.

"So this is the book from the traitor Bo?" The General coughed slightly, gesturing at the large binder on the desk. His skin had lost all of its colour, he looked like a walking corpse.

"You crazy fool." Slinky yelled. "Your power hungry arrogance created LOCUST. We have to try and find a vaccine and stop this."

"You have been working on a vaccine for a month . . . Slinky." The sickened general spat his nickname out, exaggerating the pronunciation for effect. "LOCUST was designed to be impossible to stop. You didn't even come close. You aren't as good as we thought."

Jun imperceptibly moved slightly away from Slinky as General Han spoke again. "There is no hope now you idiot. Someone sabotaged our plans and now the world is over." He coughed again and spit onto the carpeted floor which made Jun bristle with anger. Spitting was common in the Chinese culture but it was absolutely forbidden for any Shao Lin to spit. For them, it was the ultimate insult.

"The virus has probably mutated. You didn't listen to him. Dr. Bo was right. You and only you are to blame." Slinky venomously hurled the last words out in utter disdain for the architect of what now appeared to be the end of the world.

The gun was now wavering in his hand but he kept it pointed at Slinkys chest. "Bo was an old fool and hadn't done any good work in years. It's too bad his heart gave out before he could experience LOCUST and feel what we feel."

A strange look came over the general's face as he stared at them with his watery bloodshot eyes. What he had just realized is that neither of them looked sick.

Jun had now moved a full three feet away from Slinky and had withdrawn his throwing knife from his robe. He was staring at its planned point of entry, a pulsing piece of flesh in the general's neck. In an instant he would flick his wrist with immense speed and power, driving the blade through the artery killing him instantly.

Han was very sick and close to death but he was also a trained soldier and expert martial artist. He saw the movement and anticipated what was to come. Adjusting his aim as quickly as he could he pulled the trigger.

Jun could almost see the bullet exit the barrel. He continued his throwing motion while turning his head quickly to the side. The bullet entered the corner of his left eye and plowed a deep trench through the flesh of his face and exiting out the corner of his right eye. A spray of bloody material splattered against the wall as the monk fell to the floor. His knife, just missing the general's ear, sank deeply into the wooden panelling behind him.

Slinky immediately bent down to help the stricken monk and almost as quickly General Han ordered him to stand up. Han slowly approached, holding on to the edge of the desk and put the pistols barrel into Slinkys chest.

Looking up he sneered, "You have never appreciated China and all that we have done for you. You would be nothing without us."

Slinky could feel the barrel being pushed farther into him, his back now pinned against the wall.

"You too are a traitor. Just like Bo." General Han slowly squeezed the trigger until he felt that satisfying little click that preceded the explosion of the cartridge.

Slinky didn't hear a thing.

20

The panic and chaos had now reached every level of society. From homes to schools and from business to government, every country on the planet was feeling the effect. Economies, food production, transportation and the basic functions of business all were quickly forgotten as people tried to survive against what only a few knew, was LOCUST. Death rates were now virtually incalculable and the fabric of society started to unravel quickly. Although there were far more instances of love and compassion, the darker underbelly of the human psyche now ruled the streets.

Since the declaration of a pandemic was made by the CDC, Jamie and the entire Cleanetics organization had been put on notice that at any time, their facility and resources could be essentially conscripted into the governments fight against the virus. A series of sweeping acts had been rushed through both the House and Senate giving immense power to both the President the newly formed Infectious Disease Command Centre. All national security issues concerning the pandemic were managed through the Command Centre and the CDC. Jamie was unceremoniously drafted into the employ of the federal government yesterday when she and a number of her colleagues at Cleanetics were escorted by heavily armed Army officers to a briefing at the local campus of the University of California. They were interviewed, briefed and then sworn in under these new laws as Army officers. There was no turning back now, the death toll from what they called Andromeda was estimated at ten to twenty five percent of the American population. It was a race for survival and it appeared that they were about to be lapped.

Once Jamie was fully briefed, the spread of this virus and its absolute lethality chilled her to the bone. Jaime was as scared as she had ever been and wished Riley was here but he had already left Hawaii and was on his way to New Guinea and she hadn't been able to reach him. Now they were under a complete lockdown unable to leave or to make contact with anyone outside their research lab on the campus of the San Diego State University. It was a prison that few if any thought they would walk away from.

Arriving early for her second fifteen hour shift, Jamie was drinking a cup of disgusting coffee from a stryofoam cup when she tried to enter the lab. She was blocked by the ever present armed guards and was almost run over as a man on a stretcher was being carried out. Many of the soldiers were now wearing gas masks and that look just added to the tension that was already palpable within the facility.

Jaime saw Ariel Rodenstern being forcibly restrained in the hallway by one of the masked soldiers. "Hey! Back off," Jamie yelled as she grabbed Ariel's arm and tried to pull her away and into the lab. Ariel was screaming that she wanted to go home and see her kids, her bloodshot eyes were bulging and she looked right through Jamie with a look of total desperation. As Jamie was roughly pushed aside, Ariel was handcuffed by two other soldiers and strapped onto a stretcher.

A weapon was raised and pointed at Jaime; the words were muffled but understandable, "Get to work."

Standing numbly, looking down the business end of a rifle, Jaime felt helpless. There was no point in resisting, no point in complaining. Turning around she could feel her nails digging into the flesh of her palms as she entered the lab. The conscripted research staff was doing the normal shift change debriefing, one man who Jaime had never even seen before was reading from the most recent twelve hour update that came in on the secure link from the CDC. The news was the same. No progress on stopping the mutations within the virus and no progress on a vaccine. The rest of the transmission was filled with brief reports from other agencies around the world. It took another five minutes to go through more weasel words than Jamie had ever heard in her life to say that they were no farther ahead. Bottom line, no progress is no progress but she guessed someone was just trying to make it sound better than it actually was. Two more staff had died last night and that didn't include any of the Army personnel who seemed to dwindle in number every day.

"The numbers don't lie. We have already reached the extinction point in just twenty five days from the declaration of the pandemic." Jamie didn't know the man's name but she watched him ball up a computer printout and throw it onto the floor. He walked to the window, his shoulders hunched as he looked outside, to a place they were no longer allowed to go.

Jamie looked around the room and could see it in the blank, exhausted faces. Everyone was past being scared, they were professionals, highly educated researchers, scientists and doctors, the tops in their fields. They like hundreds of other labs around the world had worked day and night for weeks to get a handle on this virus aptly named Andromeda. Most were already sick, flushed and with high fevers and debilitating headaches. No words needed to be spoken. It was in their faces. They all knew it was just about over.

It hadn't taken long. Jamie couldn't even remember how many days she had been here before there were just two of them left, Jamie and Dr. Kobus Hill, a virologist from South Africa. Dr. Hill was trapped in San Diego once all air travel was suspended shortly after the pandemic declaration and he had found his way, somehow, to this lab. They had watched as all the rest of the team had died over the last week. The lab was now as quiet as the campus outside.

Numbed with the pain of what was happening all around them, many of the remaining soldiers that had fallen ill choose suicide rather than the slow, feverish death from the virus. The last gunshot was yesterday and for the first time there were no guards in or around the lab. When Jamie walked outside for the first time in a month she saw thousands of bodies were now littered around the campus. The smell was overpowering and it was mixed with the haze and smoke from multiple fires burning throughout the city. Jaime remembered her childhood and the fiery sermons delivered every Sunday in church. Her mind brought her back to a family dinner when she was around seven years old and how she had proudly proclaimed to her family that she would never see hell and would only see heaven. Jamie now saw how wrong that proclamation was.

Barely functioning, Jamie re-entered the lab and placed a cool cloth over Dr. Hill's forehead as he lay incoherent in the cot. Checking her watch, she almost had to count the hours on her fingers to determine that the twelve hour bulletin from the CDC was now four hours late. No one had answered the phone when Jamie had called the CDC hotline just an hour ago. It was now sometime after midnight and the lab's emergency generator finally went out, plunging them into darkness. Jamie sat down on the floor beside the cot and crossed her arms over her chest. Staring into the darkness, she started to shiver.

It could have been minutes or it could have been hours but Jamie was roused from her stupor by a reverberating growl from her stomach. There really was no thought process or plan, her mind was barely functioning, seemingly following her bodies actions instead of directing them. Jaime followed the wall out into the hallway and to a set of hastily built lockers that held their personal possessions. Rooting around in the lockers she was able to locate a large duffel bag and a small flashlight. Moving down the line of lockers she found hers and grabbed her purse and the few personal possessions she had been allowed to bring. The yellowish beam of the flashlight revealed her two laptops and she lethargically placed them into the duffel. They had not been allowed to access any personal emails since they had come and she hoped with all her heart that there was something there from her dad. Collecting as much food and water as she could carry she walked back to her station in the lab for the final time. She had barely slept this last week, just waiting for the fever and headaches that signalled the flu's onset. When was it to be her turn? It had never come as one by one her colleagues had fallen. Now Jaime was the only one left, and she was tired of asking herself why. Surprisingly the decision didn't take very long to make, she needed to get away, as far away as she could, from everything and everybody. Being a doctor it wasn't difficult for her to recognize the signs of a pending breakdown in herself, her only question was why had it taken so long. The whole world had disintegrated around her, everyone was dead or dying. Was she really alive? Why? Was all this really happening? Am I already dead?

There was only one thing left to do as she reached down and put her fingers on Dr. Hill's neck. Blinking back tears that were long overdue, she reached down and gently pulled his eyelids down over his vacant milky eyes. There was no one else. It was time for her to go.

Taking the keys to an Army Humvee from a hook on the wall, she hefted the duffel onto her shoulder and headed downstairs towards the darkened streets.

21

Small rivulets of sweat slowly made their way down Jaime's back even though the night was quite cool. Her hands were shaking and her breathing was shallow and forced. For the millionth time she wondered if now was the time. Had her luck run out, was she finally getting sick?

Back-tracking a number of times due to impassable streets she was now within blocks of the marina. Driving quickly and aggressively in the big Humvee, Jaime tried not to notice the destruction and the multitudes of bodies. There was no other traffic on the roads, her headlights were the only light she could see.

Jaime slowed as what looked like a man was standing in the street facing her. His hand slowly rose from his side and she saw a flash. The bullet thudded against the shatterproof glass of the windshield, two more flashes erupted as Jaime momentarily ducked down below the dashboard.

The bump was barely noticeable as the big Humvee slammed into the shooter. Glancing off of a parked truck while she tried to regain control, the Humvee continued down the street and now Jaime's breaths were coming in rushed gulps. Surprisingly she felt little remorse for what had just happened, she was already too numb to care much about anything. Accelerating through an intersection, for the first time in a long time she saw the ocean.

The last road to the marina was blocked by a partially collapsed burnt out building that was still smoldering with some small fiery hotspots flaring up within the rubble. Jaime carefully pulled the large vehicle into an empty parking spot, the big tires just barely fitting between the lines. The irony of that was not lost on her as she made her way through numerous abandoned vehicles littering the street and sidewalks.

The marina gate was closed but a large hole had been cut in the chain link. Only a partial moon illuminated a mostly empty and very dark marina as she threw the duffel bag through the hole and climbed through after it. She could see a number of larger boats still at anchor just past the last float, she hoped JayJay was one of them.

The slight creaking of the floats was the only noise until a huge explosion rocked the marina. A gigantic fireball slowly rose into the sky from the south, masses of fire churning within its mushroom shaped cloud. It appeared to have come from the naval base south of Mission Bay.

Although her ears were still ringing, Jaime heard a high pitched whining and spun around to see a medium sized dog running towards her. It collapsed at her feet, whining and nuzzling her shoes. Jaime remembered when she was eight, their dog Max had run off during a thunderstorm and she assumed this dog had been frightened by the explosion. Reaching down she ran her hands over the dog's head and patted it vigorously. Re-adjusting the duffel bag, Jaime continued down the float.

Just past the spot where they had previously tied up their sailboat Brandy, Jamie saw a small marina tender floating just a few feet off the float. Its outboard engine was raised and she could see a docking line tangled in the propeller. It was just within her reach and she guided it back towards her with her foot. Throwing the duffel inside she climbed in and opened the deck compartment where she knew the paddles would be. Not having noticed that the dog had followed her, she now looked back and could see that it was now trying to decide whether or not it could make the leap into the small boat, the dog's small cropped tail was wagging furiously.

Under normal circumstances Jaime would have helped but these circumstances were not normal. She turned and started to paddle out and then she heard the splash. The dog quickly swam to the boat and was making its way around, looking for a way onboard. As it swam around the transom, Jaime reached down and unceremoniously hauled it in. Jamie reached down for the paddle as the dog gave itself a long shake, the cold water felt good on her face. The dog licked her hand and then ran and jumped up onto the bow seat as Jaime started to paddle, both of them looking forward in hopeful anticipation of something different than what was behind them.

It didn't take long for Jamie to see that JayJay was at anchor. Jaime didn't know what emotion she was feeling as she paddled up to the small boarding ladder, after the last few weeks, there weren't many emotions left. It took all she had to try and hold everything together, to focus and concentrate, she had never experienced survival mode before. Another huge explosion from the south echoed through the bay as she tied off the small tender and quickly climbed the ladder up onto JayJay.

It was obvious that someone had been on board. The cockpit had been ransacked and the lock area around the cockpit door had been damaged but they had not been able to gain entry. She recalled her father had told her that during JayJay's retrofit that they had significantly reinforced all the access points in anticipation of Riley's travels around the world. For some reason she also thought of the guns that were hidden in a secret compartment on board, two semi-automatic rifles, a shotgun and two pistols. Jaime hated guns.

Quickly realizing her keys were in her purse which was in the duffel bag Jaime swung her foot over the side to head back down to the tender and almost stepped on the dog's head. It had climbed up a couple of rungs on the ladder but was now stuck, its nails curled around the teak rungs, holding it tenuously vertical above the tender. Jaime reached down and grabbed the dog by the scruff of the neck and hauled it onboard.

"Well then, is that better?" Jamie's words were met by a slight cocking of the dog's head, its amber eyes lightly reflective in the limited moonlight.

Quickly grabbing the keys, Jaime opened the door and entered the main salon. Everything was as she remembered it or that was her impression as it was completely dark. Making her way to the couch, she fell onto it with a resounding thud.

She could physically feel the emotions rising within her. Her diaphragm constricted and her skin became clammy. Her breathing coming in small gasps was ragged and uneven. An overall feeling of wetness surrounded her as the perspiration was rising through her skin and starting to soak into her clothes.

"Get control of yourself," she whispered, fearing she was just seconds away from going into shock. Just breathe she thought, just breathe.

It might have been minutes or it might have been hours. It really didn't matter. Jaime lay on that couch and tried to rationally absorb what had happened. She couldn't do it. There was nothing rational about an unstoppable virus that was killing everyone . . . . except for her.

Either the wind or the tide had changed as she felt JayJay move slightly against the anchored buoy. The sky was still dark but she knew dawn was coming. She let her arm fall off the couch and to her surprise it was immediately met by the moist warm nose of her new companion. Both of them took comfort in the touch.

Jaime didn't know how long she had been asleep but it was light out when she awoke. A quick check of her watch revealed it was 9:25 a.m. A quick trip to the bathroom confirmed her first impression, JayJay was in perfect shape. After downing a bottle of water and pouring some into a small bowl for the dog, she went out onto the aft cockpit.

A huge pall of smoke still rose in the sky from the south. Small fires burned towards downtown and to the east of Mission Bay. The only noise was that of the seabirds.

Following the checklists it took less than an hour to do a complete safety check and bring JayJay to life. The generator hummed as Jaime made coffee and a bowl of oatmeal with dried fruit. Both of them were obviously very hungry and finished their portions very quickly. Jamie opened one of the Army MRE's, scrambled eggs, breakfast sausage and a biscuit. It didn't look very appetizing but smelled good. Jaime ate the eggs while the dog ate the sausage. They split the biscuit.

JayJay was fully stocked with food, although none of it fresh. Fuel tanks were full and she was fully prepped to sail. Fresh water was below ten percent of capacity but she could see that the desalination plant was working as the gauge indicated they had already gained a couple percentage points in the last half hour.

"Well girl, you need to have a name." The dog, a cinnamon and white Brittany Spaniel thumped her short little tail enthusiastically into the carpet as she sat at Jaime's feet. "We met where we used to moor our old boat Brandy so how about Brandy?" That response was met by an almost imperceptible woof and a round of serious hand licking.

It was approaching mid-day now and each time Jaime went outside, she felt the dread and despair start to creep back into her body. The blower light changed from red to green and she started the engine, the low rumbling could be felt through the soles of her deck shoes. Barely able to look landward, she went forward and disengaged JayJay from the anchored buoy. Heading back to the aft cockpit she untied the tender, hesitating slightly before throwing the bow rope from the little boat over the side.

As she climbed up into the captain's chair in the forward steering station Brandy jumped up onto an adjoining chair to get a better view and Jaime slowly pushed the throttle forward. JayJay responded immediately as they slowly picked up speed and entered the channel out of Mission Bay heading towards the open ocean.

Jamie could not look back. There was nothing there for her. All her answers lay ahead.

J aime and Brandy have been at sea for almost six weeks now. Initially they had sailed directly out into the Pacific and they were now over 200 miles off the coast of central California. The weather had been good with light prevailing winds and nothing more than a moderate six to eight foot swell. Jaime had sailed hard at first, getting to know the intricacies of JayJay but recently she had essentially sailed in a large circle, decompressing and just trying to escape the mayhem of what used to be her world.

She was tired of crying and knew she needed to get herself together and try and figure out what to do. Brandy had never really left her side for the entire time and she had become a much needed companion. Jaime absentmindedly stroked Brandy's head as she sat in the main salon. Her coffee was starting to taste like coffee again.

It had been another fitful night of sleep and the stars were now slowly disappearing as the eastern sky started to brighten. Jaime had always found the sunrise to be much more interesting than a sunset as she watched the sun methodically burst forward, up over the horizon. Quickly rising in the sky to bathe them and everything else in warmth and light, she knew it was an optical illusion but she could almost see the sunlight streaking over the ocean to envelope them. It was the start of a new day, a day she knew she needed to stop feeling sorry for herself and to try and make sense of what had happened to not only her world, but everyone else's too.

Brandy started to whine a little and Jaime realised she probably needed to do her business. At the beginning of their voyage Jaime had found a heavy piece of canvas and had zap-strapped a piece of carpeting to it. She laid it down and Brandy immediately squatted to pee. There was a strong grommet in the canvas and Jaime had tied a short rope to it and to the side rail. When Brandy was finished she just picked up the canvas and attached carpet and threw it overboard. She would give it a couple of minutes then retrieve it before laying it out to dry. This would soon become a ritual, done morning and evening and it provided the only routine in their new lives.

The batteries needed to be recharged today and she was thinking about going forward to uncover the solar cells when she heard a disturbance on the ocean's surface. Looking out in the ever-increasing sunlight she saw what she assumed was some kind of pilot whale beside the boat. It looked to be about twenty feet long, its skin was as black as ink. Brandy had heard it now too and was stretching up to have a look over the rail. Suddenly a small shape appeared followed by a cloud of blood and other material. A newborn whale, with its umbilical cord still attached, struggled to surface, hoping to take its first breath. The mother whale slowly rotated and gently pushed its baby towards the surface but at the same time, she was pushing it towards JayJay.

The baby, the size of a porpoise, broke the surface and Jaime saw its tiny blowhole open. She was then showered with a wet mist that smelled of low tide on a hot day as the baby exhaled and then audibly inhaled, taking its first breath. Both mother and baby seemed to look up at Jaime before they gently sank below the surface and slowly started to swim away.

Birth. Life. She had certainly seen enough death. Maybe this was some kind of sign. She busied herself with the preparations needed to open and connect the solar cells and for the first time in a long time, a slight smile creased her lips.

There had been some talk on the radio for the first few days at sea but that had diminished rapidly. Jaime had even made radio contact with a freighter captain that was heading to San Francisco. He had lost most of his crew and was sick himself and was just trying to get his ship into port. She had asked him if he knew how she could use the radio to try and contact her father who was somewhere around New Guinea. His deep and scratchy voice matter-of-factly said it didn't matter. Everyone was either already dead or dying. Before signing off the freighter captain had said that this was Gods way of punishing us for our sins and that simple comment made more sense than anything to her with one exception. Why was she still here?

Two weeks ago, she only heard one radio transmission and that appeared to be in Japanese. Since then, she hadn't heard anything and put little if any hope into thinking she may hear anything more. The radio had rarely been on this last week as it just reminded her that there might be some hope out there and realistically she knew there wasn't.

After tidying up the galley she wondered if that freighter captain was right. Was everyone dead or dying?

But that same question came up, the same question over and over that had haunted her since San Diego. The one that made her crazy to think about because she had no clue how to answer it, why wasn't she sick? It certainly wasn't because she hadn't sinned.

When Jaime was initially drafted into the military by the CDC and forcibly moved to the campus of San Diego State University she was not, to her knowledge, yet exposed to the virus. When the pandemic was declared and in full force, she had probably been exposed every single day. As her co-workers and fellow scientists fell ill and dropped all around her, and tens if not hundreds of thousands of people in California alone were dying every day, she carried on, unaffected. Why?

Jaime felt the pressure on her leg as Brandy leaned against her. Dogs were the best therapy she thought as she scratched Brandy's skull. They offer no judgement and they only listen. Staring out the window into the seemingly endless blue of the ocean she thought of her eighteenth birthday party and that serious talk that she had with her dad. It wasn't really a talk because she just needed to get some things out one of them being she just needed someone to listen once in a while. She wasn't looking for opinions, judgements or someone to fix something. Once she had explained that to her dad, their relationship had finally matured. He had completely understood what she needed. Maybe that's why he has such great rapport with women she thought. For the first time in a very long time, Jaime felt normal as she visualized her father's face. It was almost like a weight had been lifted off of her. For the first time since escaping San Diego, Jaime felt a little bit like her old self.

"Let's go forward Brandy," she said, opening the small gate to the starboard walkway topside. Brandy anxiously trotted ahead, stretching her legs, her nose lifted into the wind no doubt hoping to capture the scent of something familiar. Jaime unlatched and spread open the two solar cells located in front of the cabin and she also engaged the small wind turbine and saw it slowly start to spin in the freshening morning breeze.

"Enough running away," Jaime proclaimed to no one in particular although Brandy was the only one within earshot.

To say Jaime had been struggling would be an understatement of epic proportions and in an attempt to normalize an anything but normal situation, she had decided to get into her laptops and read her emails.

The last time she had even looked at her emails was a few days before she was taken to the lab at San Diego State University. While at the lab, they were completely sequestered and couldn't communicate to anyone not involved in trying to stop Andromeda. No family, no friends, no internet, nothing. It made jury duty seem like a picnic. Ever since what she called her escape she just hadn't been in the right frame of mind to look at anything that reminded her of what she had been through. That wasn't the case anymore.

Jaime checked the status of JayJay's power supply. Batteries were at about thirty percent and that would improve quickly with both the solar cells and wind turbine operational. She engaged the autopilot, set a course east-northeast and then raised the mainsail to about ten percent of its normal size. The automatic systems took over and she saw the wheel adjust hard to starboard and heard the ping when the proper heading was achieved. Although winds were light as they normally were in the morning she could feel JayJay start to move, picking up just that little bit of speed to break away from its drift. It reminded her off the sailing adventures that she used to have every summer with her dad and brother. When you spend a lot of time on the water, you eventually become in tune with your vessel, feeling every shift of the wind or change in currents. Moving into the salon she opened one of the storage closets and grabbed both her laptops.

She had purposefully avoided her laptops until now. Her mental state was too fragile and she knew it would have been impossible for her to concentrate. The living nightmare was far too vivid, the pain too real. What she witnessed was beyond any horror imaginable but that was then and this was now. Jaime knew it was time to get to work.

"C'mon Brandy, let's spend some time and see if we can figure anything out." If it's the one thing she had plenty of, it was time.

Brandy lay down under the table as Jaime plugged in the laptops and turned them on. As she normally did, Brandy maintained a physical touch with Jaime, lightly resting her paw on Jaime's bare foot. It comforted them both. Her heart rate quickened as she logged on to both her business and personal emails. She entered her password, PeLuvBy. It was an abbreviation for peace, love and beauty. Not much of that left in the world now she thought to herself.

Jaime had over four hundred unread messages on her personal and business emails. This was going to take some time. For how truly messed up she still was, Jaime quickly returned to professional mode. Knowing she couldn't make sense of so many emails on so many different subjects, she started organizing and making up folders and dropping the emails into them, unread. Think critically, avoid all the normal roadblocks and be organized she said to herself, always her own biggest critic.

The tally was now about a dozen folders, mostly dealing with aspects of the virus and the work that took place around developing a vaccine. There were a few emails from friends on her business account and she dropped them into the FRIENDS folder. When she saw a couple of emails from her old colleague Jill Barber she didn't even think they could be related to Andromeda and dropped them into the FRIENDS folder.

The sorting of the business emails took about an hour. Most of them were received early during the time she had been at the university and they had slowly diminished, like everything else, until there were no more. Different thoughts and emotions started to run through her head. "C'mon Jaime focus, we need business mode here," she whispered. When she started in on the personal emails she actually started to feel a little better. Knowing the demons and thoughts she could no longer afford to have were always right at the door it would take determination and tremendous focus to look forward and not backwards. There really was no past now. Thinking about what she had seen and had been through over these last few months was simply a hindrance to feeling better and moving forward.

Just like the business emails, she organized the personal emails into folders and she noticed right away that there appeared to be many duplicates of emails in both her accounts. People just trying to ensure I got it at work or at home she thought. Not wanting to slow down and lose momentum, she continued to just organize her emails and fought off the urges to read them.

There was one email that did slow her down though, it was from Slinky. It was dated just when things started to go bad and it was titled 'One of my best jokes for you'. That was weird as Slinky had never emailed her jokes before. The mouse icon hovered over that email until she decided that the same rules should apply to all. Carrying on she was going to put his email into the FRIENDS folder but decided, for reasons unknown, to make a folder up specifically for him. Then for some reason, everything started to come rushing back. Feeling the tears starting to well up she tried with all she had to stop the images from appearing. It always followed the same pattern, the death and destruction followed by the upset and fear for what had happened to her friends and family. Gently closing both laptops she placed her hands flat on the table and tried to control her breathing. No matter how hard she tried she couldn't get the images of her dad and brother out of her mind. This routine which haunted her sometimes day and night was really starting to take its toll.

Brandy had now sat up and Jaime could feel the weight of Brandy leaning against her leg, inexplicably drawn to her by her pain and discomfort. I tried so hard this time she thought, I almost did it. Just as the tears started to come she went out on deck for some fresh air.

Sitting outside now, she faced the growing breeze and it started to dry the tear tracks down her cheeks. Gripping the rich teak of the cockpits moulding she barked, "Jesus Jaime, snap out of this." Although she had been through the proverbial roller coaster ride of emotion since all this had happened, she started to feel an emotion she hadn't felt in a long time. It was anger.

Jaime had very high expectations of not only herself but those around here. A tough task master from an early age, her meteoric rise in the business world soon made her realize she could still be tough on herself but she needed to chill it out quite a bit for most of those around her. It was one of the things that made her a great colleague and an even better leader. When there was a problem she fixed it, even if the problem was herself.

Looking at her hands the skin around her knuckles had gone white as she was gripping the railing so hard. Shaking her hands out she willed this episode to be over and after a quick check of all the equipment topside Jaime walked as confidently as she could back into the main salon.

J amie was sitting back in the salon and had arranged both laptops in front of her. A large pad of writing paper, a number of coloured pens, post-it notes and a roll of scotch tape sat just off to the side. Her old school style of breaking down a problem was routinely panned at Cleanetics but it was the way her brain worked. Soon she would have all the information broken down into bits and pieces with papers taped up all around her. Her second go through would consist of trying to tie things together, using her own version of shorthand which she first used in college. Breaking it down, then building it up she would slowly start to form conclusions and whittle away until she hopefully, had her answer. Knowing that the answer to what had happened probably wasn't here, she still needed to try and at the very least it kept her mind occupied. Although it looked messy and disorganized there was a method in her madness although it made no sense to anyone but Jaime. Starting in to read the emails she began her note taking and slowly the disorganization grew. Finally engrossed in something other than the boat or feeling sorry for herself, she felt energized and involved for the first time since leaving San Diego.

There were hundreds if not thousands of academics that had been conscripted, just like her, all around the world. All their information was compiled by the various governments and agencies and funnelled through either the CDC in Atlanta or the Pasteur Institute in France. Reading the reports she could see no one was even close to developing a vaccine or getting a handle on anything about Andromeda except it was a flu that had the same similarities as the Hong Kong flu pandemic from the sixties. It appears all the standard processes had been followed multiple times by multiple labs and nothing worked. The virus mutated amazingly quickly, far quicker than normal but it always retained its lethality. Jaime knew that with successive mutations that lethality should eventually weaken, but it never did. Fascinated by the viruses' ability to survive outside of a host for long periods of time, she took on that problem in the hopes of seeing something, anything, that could possibly lead her to understand it. Until it was understood, you were just chasing your tail in trying to create a vaccine. Although realistically, she knew it was probably too late for that.

As darkness was falling Jaime reviewed some of the last reports to come out of the Centres for Disease Control. She read the entire reports, not just the summary and synopsis' and one recommendation surprised her. Some thought that all work should immediately stop and the CDC should institute an isolation order. That was a last gasp attempt for survival, to direct anyone still alive away from anyone else, into isolation, with the hope that anyone not yet infected could possibly outlive the virus and survive. Although the order was never given it was obvious that some were prepared to give up, to essentially run away and hide. Working in collaboration, the most brilliant minds in the entire world couldn't even understand Andromeda, let alone develop a vaccine. It appeared to be just a simple flu. What were they all missing? Sitting in a sailboat in the middle of the ocean, what kind of chance did she have to do anything? The doubts started to creep in and Jaime wondered if this was all a monumental waste of time. That weight started to return to her chest and all the feelings that she had hoped to cast aside started to come back. Closing her eyes Jaime tried to regulate her breathing and focus. When she finally opened her eyes, it was starting to get dark and Jaime started to methodically prepared JayJay for nighttime.

Falling into her bed, miraculously sleep came easy but her final thoughts were of those few remaining Army guards in San Diego who had committed suicide rather than slowly dying. She now understood it and even could appreciate it. You have to hit rock bottom to do that and that's where she was now.

The next morning Jaime forced herself to exercise and afterwards she felt better. Sipping her coffee the sun warmed her face and she watched Brandy as she sniffed a dead flying fish. These fish would often end up in the cockpit in the morning and Brandy was always intrigued by them. Picking it up Brandy daintily walked over to Jaime and placed it at her feet. Jaime couldn't help but laugh.

"Thank you Brandy. That is the nicest thing anyone has done for me in a long time." Patting her they both headed back inside and Jaime saw the laptops, still open, sitting on the table. As she was preparing to put them away she remembered the emails she had yet to read, those that she placed into the 'friends' folder. The laptops were still plugged in and Jamie plunked herself down into the chair and opened the folder. The first email was from Jill Barber.

Jill Barber was one of the leading viral epidemiologists in the world and her speciality was retroviruses and the symbiotic relationship of RNA and DNA. Just under a year ago she had published a paper about endogenous retroviruses and how they are imprinted into the human genome. That research had won her a large grant from the Max Planck Institute and that's where she now worked.

Jamie read the first email.

> Hey Jamie, you know me, can't keep a secret so I have to tell you we have made an amazing discovery—and you are part of it!!!
>
> Remember back in the summer of 2012 when the group at Planck finished sequencing the Denisovan genome??? If you didn't hear or haven't caught up with it yet, Denisovans are an extinct hominid group and they lived at the same time as the Neanderthals. I never worked on the project as I wasn't here yet but I have access to all the information.
>
> I won't bore you with all the technical research but the genome analysis shows that the Denisovan ancestors split with modern human ancestors approximately 7-800,000 years ago. But, we (sorry, they . . .) confirmed that there was inter-breeding with human ancestors and some humans still have Denisovan DNA. If this is old news, sorry . . .
>
> What I have been working on these last few months is amazing, it appears that the Denisovans had very little genetic diversity

(hence the extinct part—haha) but they carried little if any genetic markers for illness or disease!!! Less than .01% of homo sapiens!!! There was no evidence whatsoever of any viral traces within their DNA. There is no other multi-celled species in existence that is immune to viruses.

We know about 4% of the modern human genome comes from prehistoric interbreeding and have been looking at how that ancient DNA relates to the human immune system, specifically retroviruses and the HLA (human leucocyte antigen) family of genes. If we can isolate and extract any specific 'anti-viral' nucleotides, we are looking at the potential of genetic viral resistance. Sooooo excited . . . we have all been putting in 16 hour days.

I know, I know—I am dragging the YOU part of this out . . .

I can't tell you any of the specifics or what alleles we have identified in the genome, but we also did some quick and dirty research on the Perry-Benoit super computer. We ran all DNA that we had from the Cleanetics research that you provided last year (over 18,000 individuals) and guess what—YOU HAVE IT!!! You have the Denisovan nucleotide!!!

Here is the kicker, the Denisovan material appears on different chromosomes!! Weird huh?

Still working to tie it all together. Super excited.

Hope you and your dad are well. Get back to ya soon.

Love, Jill.

"Wow," Jamie said. That weight slowly started to ease in her chest and she quickly opened Jill's next email.

Hey, me again.

> *Boy that sounds like a nasty flu that's popped up huh? I'm trying to get more info on that.*
>
> *Just wanted to keep you in the loop. We ran over a million samples through the computer and we have found only one other person with that specific Denisovan material in their DNA. A Tessa Henry from Tofino, BC, Canada. Still trying to get permission to run bigger samples.*
>
> *We have been on this day and night and have come up with a theory. Some of what we thought was just junk DNA and RNA in us actually served a purpose in our ancient ancestors. Like endogenous retroviruses, this new material was integrated throughout the genome and it may have lain dormant until it was needed. Then something triggered it into action. We think some of it must be a key to activate the rest.*
>
> *More info coming in tonight. Will email you later in the week.*
>
> *Ciao for now.*

Jill

Jamie's pulse quickened as she opened the next email.

Hey Jamie.

We've been put on six hour shutdown notice. Looks like all hands on deck re this new flu outbreak. Doesn't look good. Yikes.

Here is the latest. Research shows between 3-6% of pacific islanders, Australian Aborigines and New Guineans have some Denisovan DNA. No Denisovan DNA has been found in people of African or Middle Eastern descent and the samples are too small to be statistically significant for other ethnicities.

What we are now calling the 'healthy gene' (creative huh . . .) seems to be active in only a few carriers. We did some tests on all of our samples identified as Australian Aboriginal and 5% showed Denisovan DNA—but no one had the healthy gene??

We don't know why you have it, or even how you inherited it—you have a British background, right? Tessa Henry is identified as aboriginal and both of you have most of the Denisovan DNA on your X chromosomes. The entire test group of Aborigines with confirmed Denisovan DNA had more on their autosomes . . . so there might be something there.

We haven't been able to ID anything more.

Gotta run. Stay safe.

Love, Jill

24

It had now been ten days since she had first read her emails and Jill Barber's notes still haunted her. Not only that, she was sick and tired of being sick and tired. No closer to satisfying her need to try and understand what had happened to her world, Jaime had fallen back into a deep funk. No appetite, unfulfilling sleep and a major lack of energy couldn't have come at a worse time as the last week of sailing had been the physically toughest so far. Looking in the mirror this morning she saw just a shell of her former self.

Two storms, four days riding the sea anchor and a bout of food poisoning had brought Jaime to the brink. For the first time since fleeing San Diego, she thought about giving up, surrendering to whatever it was that had just happened. It was by far the lowest point of her life.

Spending day after day and night after night going through the scientific reports and updates in her mind had her no further ahead. She had gone through every single email, looked at every possible angle. This appeared as the classic Andromeda event. A virus that slowly builds within your lungs, all the while being extremely contagious. It then manifests itself and then builds to high fever and respiratory failure within a week. It is completely lethal and continually mutates so that any vaccine is always one step behind. The apocalypse, armageddon, the end of the world. Call it what you want.

Being immensely frustrated was an understatement but she was smart enough to know that every brilliant mind, every research and medical institute, every country in the world tried to stop this but they couldn't. Jamie started to rip down all the papers and post-it notes stuck all around the cabin and she came across one that made her hesitate. She didn't recall writing it but it read *'Never EVER give up'*. Sticking that note above the sink in the galley she collected all the others and placed them in a large bag.

Was Jill right? Did she have the so called healthy gene? Is that why she was alive? And if she had it, who else did?

"Thank God for GPS," Jaime said as Brandy looked up at her, her tail thumping against the carpet in the forward cockpit. She had no idea how long all the satellites in orbit would stay aloft, knowing they occasionally needed adjustment, but she hoped for as long as she was on this boat that she had GPS. Manual navigation was something she did not look forward to. What she saw breaking through the clouds confirmed what the GPS said, that they were heading for the Golden Gate Bridge.

It was still cold with low cloud and fog but she had made good time since yesterday when she finally decided to stop feeling sorry for herself. Having a long luxurious shower, which she knew was a no-no on a boat, had been the turning point. You can be the bug or you can be the windshield. Jaime had chosen to be the windshield.

A stiff breeze and a following sea carried them quickly through the narrows and under the Golden Gate where everything seemed bathed in a coat of misty grey stillness. The only noise was that of the wind which constantly gusted and swirled. A huge container ship had run aground on Fort Point and had broken up on the rocks, scattering shipping containers all along the shoreline. Jaime could see the sheen of oil on the rocks and got her first smell of land in quite some time as they rounded the point. It wasn't what she remembered. Even with the salty ocean breeze it still smelled of oil and decay with tinges of acrid smoke.

Jaime kept well offshore watching for hazards, there were numerous boats and barges that had run aground and although the tidal flow in this part of the bay was strong, there was still a lot of debris in the water. The oil sheen was now thicker, giving the waves a shining green hue. What she saw as she headed south towards the financial district and Fishermen's Wharf surprised her. Huge sections of the city had burned, street after street contained the scarred remains of buildings and homes. Whole neighbourhoods reduced to nothing more than rubble and ash. Diminishing her sails again to cut her speed, she watched and listened, not quite knowing what she was looking for or wanting to hear.

Manoeuvering closer to shore and using the binoculars, the horror only became more evident. The only movement she could see were the birds and the occasional dog. Skeletal corpses were everywhere, thousands of them. The birds feasted at will, their squawks and calls were the only sounds coming from this once vibrant city.

Jaime searched for any sign of human life. There was none. The further south she went the more damage she could see. Burned out buildings littered the shoreline and the dusky grey light just seemed to enhance the bleakness of what stood silently before her. It was worse than any war zone she had ever seen on TV and she remembered how San Diego had fallen into chaos just as she had left. It no doubt had happened here and probably happened all over as a dying society ran out of options.

They sailed on and now approached the airport. The taxiways were full of planes of all shapes and sizes. Jaime consulted her charts and decided to keep moving south towards San Mateo. Her plan now was to search for other survivors and be able to find some food and top up with diesel fuel. What she had seen made her shudder at the thought of going ashore. The charts indicated there was a marina in San Mateo and that's where they would make landfall.

The marina looked only half full and there were many easily accessible berths but there was a narrow entrance and there didn't appear to be any boats the size of JayJay berthed there. Jaime furled the mainsail, started the engine and was now motoring slowly towards the marina. Scanning the area with the binoculars, looking for anyone or anything her heart started to race and a trace of moisture formed on her skin. It was a reaction she hadn't felt in quite some time. Jaime was scared.

Even though it was high tide, she didn't want to risk being grounded so she dropped anchor just outside the marina channel entrance. As she reversed and waited to ensure the anchor set, she scanned the area again and saw a brightly painted sign that indicated this was the Coyote Point Yacht Club.

It didn't take long to unlatch the small plastic tender from its mounts and slide it over the side. It was only six feet long and it didn't weigh much but it was stable and seaworthy. Being at sea so long she couldn't deny Brandy the chance to feel the dirt beneath her feet so they both delicately dropped into the tender. As Jaime was about to release the rope connecting them to JayJay she paused and took a deep breath. This was it. Knowing it was time and moving quickly so she didn't change her mind she sank the oars into the water and rowed into the channel and towards the first set of floating docks.

As the little boat approached the first dock Jaime heard them before she saw them. The drumming of multiple feet running upon the aluminum dock surface reverberated easily around the silent marina. She quickly spun the little boat around and saw them coming full speed. There was no barking, just some very low, almost imperceptible growls. A pack of about ten dogs, all larger breeds, were barrelling towards them. A large husky that appeared to have only one ear was in the lead and it was clear that its intentions were not friendly.

Jaime started rowing away as fast as she could but one dog never stopped running and leapt through the air, falling half in and half out of the tender. It was snarling and gnashing its teeth as it started to pull itself in, the rest of the pack had stopped on the dock and were now barking and baying in some sort of canine encouragement.

Brandy immediately leapt to their defence providing enough distraction to allow Jaime to unhook one of the oars. Just as the dog sank its teeth into Brandy's neck, Jaime hit it on the side of its head with the short wooden oar. It slid back out of the stern semi-conscious, pulling Brandy with it.

Brandy paddled furiously but she couldn't seem loosen the grip of the much larger dog. Jaime was trying to reach her when she finally broke free and was quickly pulled in, seemingly no worse for wear. The attacking dog floated nearby, slowly regaining consciousness.

Shaking and somewhat stunned by what had just occurred, Jaime rowed back out into the channel under a slowly diminishing chorus of barks and howls from the assorted dogs on the dock. The husky was now slowly swimming back towards the shore, holding its one ear tall and alert.

Brandy's wounds were not too severe and Jaime cleaned them then applied some antibiotic ointment from the medical kit. Luckily she would not be able to bite at the site so there was no need to bandage it up. It had taken her close to an hour to settle down and decompress from what had just happened. It's not that she didn't expect to find dogs but she hadn't thought about what that interaction might be like. All if not most of the people have died, but what about all the animals? Many people had pets and that's what those dogs would have been, someone's pets. There were millions and millions of farm animals across the country and tens of millions more across the world. It was an unsettling thought to think of all those domesticated animals that no longer had anyone to care for them. Most were probably now gone but some would survive and return to their primordial instincts, just like those dogs.

Scanning the marina with her binoculars there was no sign of the dogs but they weren't going back there. Jaime raised anchor and started to head over to the eastern shore of San Francisco Bay. It was now mid-afternoon and the puffy white clouds were moving rapidly across the sky. It looked like it was going to turn into a nice day. Although she had calmed down from the dog attack there was an important lesson to learn from it. The world was a completely different place now. If she were to find anyone else, how would that go? Sitting on deck she let the emerging sun warm her as she thought about all that. All the fears and unknowns were replayed again and again. This time it didn't dull her enthusiasm but her exploring was done for the day.

Charts of San Francisco Bay showed many good anchorages so they continued east and anchored off of a marshy area in fifty feet of water. Although JayJay was initially stocked with a great deal of food, it was all dried, processed or dehydrated. Jaime had caught a few mackerel and one small tuna during their trip, which provided a welcome change to their diet, but she knew it was time to locate more food and fuel. After what had happened earlier she knew that it was safer for her to stay on JayJay and quickly forgot about her plans to spend some time onshore. Breaking out the fishing gear she brought out some of the frozen tuna scraps from the small freezer to use as bait. While she was waiting for the bait to thaw, she noticed all the birds in the marsh. After so long out on the ocean all she was accustomed to seeing were gulls and gannets but she had never seen so many ducks and geese in one place in her life. They all looked healthy and happy, the honking and quacking was relentless as they fed and splashed in the shallows. There was no oil sheen on the water here so that's why there were probably such a huge number of them. Baiting a hook, she sent it to the bottom and put her feet up to try and enjoy the warmth of what had become a beautiful afternoon.

Brandy's bark awoke Jaime from her nap and set her heart racing. She initially didn't know what was going on, her head still foggy from sleep. Brandy rarely if ever barked and Jaime spun around, searching for what could have caused it. Spotting her fishing rod, she could see it was bent over deeply, its tip bouncing furiously as it came desperately close to bouncing out of the rod holder. Jaime grabbed the rod and started to reel in what appeared to be a decent size fish.

"Oh c'mon, please don't be a shark," Jaime said as she pumped the rod and tried to gain some line. Jaime had campaigned against the finning of sharks for shark fin soup but had never really liked them since she saw the movie Jaws as a youngster. Brandy seemed somewhat agitated beside her, watching her every move.

What broke the surface was a pleasant surprise, it was a flounder and a big one. Jaime hadn't thought ahead and didn't bring out a net or a gaff but the fish appeared to be well hooked. Taking a chance once the fish had exhausted itself, she grabbed the line and lifted it into the boat. Brandy was very excited and Jaime had a hard time keeping her away. The big flounder smacked itself rapidly on the deck, flipping back and forth as Jaime tried to remove the hook. It was a beautiful fish, close to two feet long and over two inches thick.

The small propane barbeque bolted to the back rail of the cockpit had only been used once before and that was when she quickly seared the tuna she had caught a couple of weeks ago. Jaime made a mental note to try and find another propane tank when she eventually went ashore and started to clean the fish. It was big enough that she didn't need to be delicate and there were soon four big glistening filets sitting on the cutting board. One would be enough for both of them so she wrapped the remaining three in plastic wrap and placed them in the small refrigerator. Fresh fish for dinner tonight and tomorrow, but as she often did, Jamie lamented on how she missed her fresh vegetables.

Jaime stayed up later than normal as their anchorage was actually somewhat exposed and she had considered moving to a better protected location. The clouds had returned and the winds remained light with the occasional star poking through as she sat outside, wearing an old windbreaker, scanning the far shoreline for any signs of life. It was deathly quiet and pitch black. The earlier cacophony of the ducks and geese had died down with the only noise now being the lap of the small waves against the hull.

Brandy had already fallen asleep at her feet and she could feel her own eyes getting heavy. Using an old trick taught to her family by a wizened old sailor in the Bahamas, Jaime mounted a now rusty set of wind chimes in the open salon door. They had used this many times in the Caribbean when they were not completely comfortable and didn't trust their anchorage. If the wind came up in the night, the wind chimes would wake her before they were potentially blown off of their anchorage and into any danger.

The night was uneventful and morning came quickly. After a light breakfast and coffee, Jaime decided to head north up the bay and set out for the Berkeley Marina. It wasn't really raining but everything was wet. A low misty cloud seemed to hang over the bay and it looked like some sheeting rain squalls were heading in slowly in from the west. The winds remained light and the waters of the bay were flat and calm. With minimal wind for sailing, Jaime decided to use the engine knowing she could find some diesel here and top up her fuel reserves.

The clouds soon parted and the sun shone through highlighting this side of the bay. It was still amazingly quiet with only the far off sounds of the gulls and the slight thrumming of the engine. You expect the quiet out on the ocean but it was difficult to get used to essentially being in this large city and having it dead silent. Jaime had sometimes wished for this kind of peace and quiet, but not at this cost.

Jaime manoeuvered out into deeper water and went around the long Berkeley pier, motoring slowly into the channel leading to the adjacent marina. Choosing a dock with just a small sportfisher tied up to it, she expertly guided JayJay into position and quickly jumped off to tie her off. Although she had wanted to leave Brandy behind, the anxious dog had already climbed up and off JayJay and was now madly running at full speed up and down the floating dock.

Remembering the last time, Jaime had a big can of pepper spray in a holster on her hip and carried a large filet knife in the pocket of her bright yellow raincoat. Jamie also grabbed an eight foot pike pole from a storage locker for protection. There were guns locked up aboard JayJay but Jaime detested guns and felt safer without them.

It was raining heavily now, the raindrops bouncing back up at them as they made their way up the dock to the locked marina gate. As with most marinas, you can get out but can't get back in without a key. Jaime opened the gate and had to restrain Brandy who for the first time in a long time was in sight of solid ground. Brandy was obviously well trained as she stayed on command until Jaime had tied the gate open with her scarf.

Jaime was on high alert, looking and listening but Brandy just wanted to get to the grass. Once they passed through the gate she bolted and once reaching the grass she immediately started rolling and rubbing her face into it. One long pee later and she was back at Jaime's side, her tail wagging fiercely. The pounding of the rain muffled any sounds as they made their way up to the sidewalk. A three storey hotel was spread out on the grounds to their right and Jaime knew from previous trips here that if they walked past the hotel they would reach University Avenue. If they walked about three miles up the hill from there they would be right at the University of California Berkeley campus.

Jaime's heart started to pound again and she started to feel clammy under her raincoat fearing a visit from another pack of dogs. Her head was on a swivel as they made their way to the front of the hotel.

To her complete surprise there was a dog's leash and collar tied to a bench in front of the hotel. Jaime untied it and called Brandy over. Jaime couldn't help laughing out loud when she saw Brandy's reaction to what she held in her hand. The twinkle went out of her eyes as she sat down and Jaime slipped the collar over her head and adjusted the buckle. The front door of the hotel was being held open by a chair and they slowly entered. What hit her first was the smell. It was stale and smelled a little earthy, like old mushrooms.

She didn't know why but Jaime yelled out, "Hello, is anyone here?" There was no response.

They explored just a bit and made their way into the restaurant. It was messy and disorganized, moldy and rotting food still sitting on plates at dirty tables. They went into the kitchen and for some reason Jaime opened one of the large refrigerators. That was a mistake that she wouldn't make again. It was then Jaime noticed the flies, hundreds and hundreds of them on the walls and countertops. No surprise she thought, lots for them to eat.

Jaime felt uneasy but did load her backpack up with some canned goods and three bottles of wine from the bar. The thought crossed her mind whether that was stealing or not but she had the feeling that it wouldn't be the last time she would be doing this.

As they made their way back through the restaurant, both Jaime and Brandy saw it at the same time. A huge black rat was making its way across the floor partially dragging what looked like a shriveled apple. It stopped and stared back, seemingly unafraid as Brandy strained at the end of her leash. Jaime stomped her foot and the rat nonchalantly made its way under the counter.

"I guess it's now a world of the survival of the fittest," Jaime said as they walked out.

26

Back aboard JayJay, Jaime just couldn't get comfortable. She was continually going outside to look around and when she was in the cabin, she couldn't stop herself from looking out the windows. The sense of unease and discomfort of being back into what was supposed to be civilization, was getting to her. There was about another hour of light left and she knew she wasn't going to be able to sleep here tied up in the marina so she started up the engine and prepared to leave the dock. Her plan was to anchor just outside the marina and then she would come back in tomorrow to do some exploring and try and top up her supplies.

Brandy was exhausted from her exercise and was asleep until Jaime started the engine. As Jaime ever so slowly backed JayJay off the dock and brought her around she could feel the reassuring throbbing of the big diesel engine beneath her bare feet. They headed out of the marina, the Golden Gate framing the setting sun far off in the distance across the bay. After a quick circle around the area in front of the marina she found an area suitable for anchoring. Her electronics showed the bottom was relatively flat and soft so as she prepared to anchor Jaime happened to look over at the Berkeley Pier and her heart skipped a beat. Someone was walking out on the pier and they were pushing a shopping cart.

The moment she had been thinking about was here and now she was seemingly frozen, not knowing what to do. Not sure if it was caused by her trepidation or excitement but Brandy was now in her feet, looking up at her almost asking what is going on. Scared and hesitant, Jaime immediately turned to port and headed towards the first person she had seen since Dr. Hill had died in San Diego.

The person stopped at the end of the pier and was methodically rummaging around in the shopping cart when Jaime turned Jayjay back into the westerly wind and swung in parallel to the structure, double checking the depth sounder to make sure she had enough water under her.

Jaime yelled out loudly, "Hey! Hello!"

The man stopped what he was doing and in a very deliberate fashion raised his head, looking back up the dock towards shore. His motions were slow and precise, almost robotic.

Jaime again yelled. "Over here, out in the water. Hello!"

The man slowly turned to face in her direction and lethargically walked over to the weathered wooden railing. He stood motionless then put his hands out almost to steady himself and then pulled himself closer, appearing to be straining to see. His features were gaunt, his face expressionless as he looked out at Jaime. He appeared to be Samoan or possibly Fijian, maybe fifty years old, but it was hard to tell. His hair was matted and disheveled, his clothes were filthy. His expression was nonchalant and completely devoid of emotion. The appearance was almost that of someone under the influence of a strong narcotic.

"Hello! I'm Jaime Jones from San Diego." Spoken now with a little less exuberance, Jaime waved but there was no response.

The man slowly turned around and took a few steps back. Reaching into the shopping cart he pulled out what looked like a heavy, round, cylindrical object. Coming back to the railing he brought the object up and rested it on the railing, his expression never changed. It was a shotgun.

Jaime sunk down in the rear cockpit, not really knowing what to do. Raising her hands up, she called out, "I won't hurt you, please don't shoot." She then stood up, not knowing why, and held her hands out towards him, palms up, in the most non-threatening way she could think of. "I want to help, what's your name?"

JayJay was turning slightly with the wind and wave action and Jaime corrected for that, she knew she couldn't hold the position long. Another quick depth check showed they were still safe but she knew she needed to pay attention or they could become grounded.

Brandy had now jumped up onto the cushioned seats of the cockpit and she was watching the man on the pier intently. The man's head moved slightly and then he lifted the shotgun off the railing and gestured with it in a way that could only be interpreted as he wanted them to move away.

Jaime slightly increased the engines RPM's to hold their position and began to call out, "My name is Jaime and I . . ."

The man had slightly adjusted his aim and pulled the trigger. Just thirty feet away from JayJay the water erupted into dozens of little geysers as the shot gun pellets blasted into the water's surface. The noise of the discharge was amazingly loud.

Jaime let out a little scream and ducked down into the cockpit. She applied full throttle and JayJay started to pull out and away from the pier. When she was at a safe distance she looked back at the man as he deliberately placed the shotgun back into the shopping cart and started to rummage around inside it again. Pulling out what appeared to be a bottle of dark liquor he made his way back to the railing and stood there, looking out at them, his bearded face as wooden as the railing he leaned against. Jaime watched as he put the bottle to his lips and took a long pull.

Turning away, Jamie motored out into the bay and then shut off the engine. Looking back at the shoreline she could still see him on the pier, standing and staring. Her initial excitement had now rebounded back to disappointment. Someone else had survived. The man was obviously severely traumatized, possibly sick or injured. If there was one, there could be more. Her mind returned to Jill Barbers email and how they had found one other person in their study that had the same genetic anomaly as her, Tessa Henry in Tofino, British Columbia.

It was obvious the big cities suffered greatly. San Diego was chaotic when she left and San Francisco looked like a war zone. It must have been awful here at the end. Maybe a small town like Tofino would be better.

They floated for a while as Jamie developed her thoughts. After anchoring in one hundred feet of water offshore of what looked like a state park to the north of the

Berkeley pier, she now had developed a plan. With a little bounce in her step Jaime made a list of needed supplies. It had only taken a few minutes to go through the galley and the storage lockers to see what was lacking and Jaime now folded the list and put it into her backpack. The next morning she would find somewhere to stock up on supplies, find some diesel fuel and top off her tanks and then head off to Tofino and try and find Tessa Henry. After double checking the anchor line, Jaime went to bed, feeling that she now had a purpose.

N ever one to stay up late or sleep in, Jaime was up before dawn. Preparing a cup of coffee and some oatmeal, she went topside to watch the sunrise. It looked like it was going to be a beautiful day, winds were light with just a few wispy clouds dotting the brightening sky.

Not feeling entirely safe going back to the Berkeley marina, Jaime motored north, under the San Rafael Bridge and into San Pablo Bay. There was a large naval base on Mare Island and Jaime thought that would be a good place to find some provisions and fuel. Recalling those army guards in San Diego she knew the military hung on right to the bitter end. They were the only constant in a suddenly chaotic world and she hoped all the military installations had survived the carnage. It was also a logical place to possibly find other survivors. She anchored just offshore in a small bay on the south side of the island alongside an older model sailboat, a Catalina 30. Jaime decided not to take Brandy until she checked things out but she did take the pepper spray and pike pole. Locking Brandy inside the cabin, Jamie unlatched the small tender and dropped it over the side. The slap off it hitting the water echoed off the large buildings in the distance, the sound slowly fading into the stillness of the morning.

As Jaime was about half way to the gently sloping rocky beach she was startled when a couple of harbour seals surfaced just behind her, their huge black eyes staring as the water ran off their mottled skin. Seeing nothing of interest, they both slowly sank back into the water leaving only a smooth patch of water above them. Starting to row again, Jamie could still feel her rapid heartbeat, a result of being startled by the seals. That is a good lesson to learn she reminded herself. There are many possible dangers, not that she was worried about harbour seals but there were other animals out there too. As the boat nosed up onto the beach she just said to herself to be vigilant and careful.

Jaime spent an hour exploring this end of the base. She found a number of potentially useful items including a garden hose and an empty five gallon jerry can. Knowing it would be impossible to get any fuel pumps working, she needed to find a vehicle or another boat with a diesel engine and siphon off some fuel, confidant that she didn't need much, probably fifteen gallons tops. Goose bumps appeared on her arms as she continued to walk amongst the well maintained buildings. It was the lack of any noise that was unnerving. It just went against everything that her eyes were telling her brain, there should be some noise here. It reminded her of a cheesy science fiction movie she saw as a kid where some guy was the only person left on the planet. Most of the buildings were unlocked so she would have no trouble getting into them and then she saw the large brightly painted base commissary or PX store.

"Hello, anybody here?" she called out, her voice echoing in the high ceilinged building. The only response was the squeak of a rat somewhere in amongst the shelves. Although there was a lot of natural light streaming in through the big windows, Jaime decided to grab a flashlight from one of the cashier stations. This was quite a big PX and she wouldn't have any trouble finding as much food and equipment as she wanted. The rows of shelves were orderly and well stocked, it had the feel of a small Costco. Seeing a door marked manager Jaime opened it and started to step inside.

The stench was overwhelming. It hit her like a warm wind and she brought her hand up to cover her nose as she quickly backed out coughing. There was no doubt a body or bodies in there. Standing back away from the door she wondered if she was somehow becoming immune to the smells as she now realized the PX itself stunk to high heaven. A large rat scurried across the floor and along the far wall, disappearing behind a stacked display of electronics.

Standing well back from the door she used the flashlight to peer in and saw a corpse lying on a cot against the far wall of the large office. In her opinion, the sailor had been dead for at least a month. The sight of cadavers never bothered her in medical school and now they had just become part of the landscape. On the floor were a writing pad and a pen and she could see that there was writing on the paper. Lying beside what was left of his head was a large caliber pistol. Taking a deep breath she quickly ran in, snatched the writing pad and ran back out shutting the door behind her.

Randall Samuels was only twenty two years old. When the viral event fully took hold, he was ordered from his clerical job to a security detail here at Mare Island Naval Station. His writings covered his last six days. He poignantly described first the city, then the base break down to what he described as *'complete chaos'* as both the structure of the base and society in general fell apart. His writing described arsons and indiscriminate gunfire rocking the surrounding suburbs and they had to defend the base by blocking off the bridge with vehicles. He was originally posted along with a number of other armed sailors in quickly constructed sandbagged stations at the base end of the bridge. Randall reported that huge fires had swept first through Oakland then San Francisco before heading out into the suburbs. On the base itself the military structure finally broke down with people unlawfully leaving the island but what seemed to bother him the most were the murders and rapes. He wrote very poignantly of how he was very disappointed in his fellow servicemen and women.

The handwriting was neat and concise at first but on this second page it had become messy. Jaime continued to read on and was very surprised at what came next. Randall had written that only a few sailors remained alive but his best buddy Arnie wasn't sick at all. They had a plan to steal a boat and they were both going to try and sail back to Arnie's family's home in Samoa.

Randall wrote that he was getting sicker and knew he wasn't going to make it. He talked about this being the end and wondered what man had finally done to deserve this. He had pleaded with Arnie for him to just go without him. Randall had lost both his parents in a car crash when he was eighteen and had no siblings and that's when he joined the Navy. All he had was Arnie and he didn't want to risk infecting him or slowing him down at all so he shot himself. His last comments were that Arnie was the family he no longer had and that he loved him like a brother. The last line simply read, *'Go home brother'.*

Jaime sat stunned. Her mind was racing as she remembered the seemingly deranged man in Berkeley. Now there was a firsthand account of another possible survivor, Arnie from Samoa. The man in Berkeley looked like a Samoan too. If they were both Pacific Islander's maybe there was something to Jill Barber's research. She slid the pad of paper back under the door of the office where Randall lay dead.

Jaime spent the next half hour gathering up a bunch of supplies including a huge amount of both dry and canned dog food. Brandy had been eating the same meals as Jaime and would probably welcome that change. A large pile of material formed just outside the main doors of the PX and luckily Jaime found a well-used hand truck in the grocery area. Piled high with supplies it took three trips to bring everything back to the small cove where she shuttled it out to the anchored JayJay in the small tender. It took another three trips to bring the fuel that she had siphoned from a large truck.

Jaime didn't really plan on it but she had spent three nights anchored in the little cove on Mare Island. Exhausted that first night she spent most of the first day organizing and stowing supplies but she did row over to the Catalina30 that was anchored nearby. Disappointed when she saw that it was partially stocked with naval supplies Jaime wondered if this was the boat that Randall talked about in his note. If that was the case, Arnie had not escaped. But that meant maybe he was still here. There was no sign of recent habitation on the boat but Jaime decided to wait a little while longer to see if Arnie would show up. Another few trips to the PX had filled JayJay to the brim with more food and other supplies and Brandy had now been given the opportunity to join Jamie on these little excursions. There was no doubt that this wasn't Brandy's first time on a boat but boy oh boy did she ever enjoy herself when she was back on land.

It had been bright and sunny since they had arrived on Mare Island and that seemed to take a little of the dampness away. Yesterday, Jaime heard what she thought might have been a gunshot but it had come from a long way away. From what she had witnessed herself and from what she had read from Randall, the world had become a much more dangerous place.

Jaime decided last night that she would leave the following morning. She had left a long note both on the Catalina and at the PX, hoping Arnie would find it. In the note she outlined what she had been through and that she was headed to Tofino, British Columbia and then, probably back to San Diego. JayJay was checked and double checked, fully provisioned and ready to go first thing in the morning.

As she often did once her chores were completed, Jaime reviewed her emails and notes about the virus, always searching, always looking for information or a clue. She knew she had to stay sharp and keep her mind active if she was ever to get to the bottom of this. Now looking through her personal laptop, she spotted a folder named Slinky. Giving herself a playful knock on the head she said, "Man, I completely forgot about this." Opening it, it appeared longer and much more detailed than a joke email and as soon as she started to read it she knew it wasn't a joke.

This was the fourth time Jaime had read it and the goose bumps were still there. Shocked could not describe her demeanor as she deliberately focused on each word and on each sentence, trying to pull it all together. The virus wasn't a natural phenomenon at all. It was something called LOCUST, a biological warfare agent developed by the Chinese government. The paper in front of her remained empty, the pen poised to make notes but nothing materialized. For the only time in her life, Jaime Jones was dumbstruck.

Jaime was transfixed about what Slinky knew and more importantly how he knew it. It was unfathomable that he could have been involved in such a thing. Like her father, Slinky was a man of true character. This wasn't making any sense at all. Slinkys typing was obviously rushed with a number of typos which was unusual for him so he was obviously in a hurry when he wrote this. Saying he was afraid his emails were monitored he would send this one page with more to follow, but just one page at a time. In the middle of explaining how the virus was manipulated with genetic material the note ended abruptly in mid-sentence. Regaining her wits Jamie searched both laptops for more emails from Slinky. There were none. This was it, one email and it looked unfinished. A feeling of dread swept over her as she realized if he was being monitored they may have stopped him or arrested him. He had obviously put himself in grave danger by sending this note but he said it was important that the world see what had happened. Checking the date she realized it was sent on the same day she was conscripted and moved to the university lab. If this email was sent one day earlier or if she had not been locked down while at the lab, they could have had their opportunity to stop what she now knew was called LOCUST.

Jaime went back to his email and read it all again. It was an almost unbelievable story. They used genetic markers to target a killer influenza virus on some of their own people in a plan to stop the democracy movement. Slinky and some other researcher named Dr. Bo feel that after it was released the virus somehow mutated into birds and then back into humans, losing its genetic component and becoming a completely lethal biological weapon. Purposefully designed to spread silently and quickly, mutating regularly to avoid being stopped by a vaccine, Slinky said he didn't think they could stop it. And obviously they didn't.

Her head was racing. She could feel a massive headache coming on but even though she now had some answers, she had even more questions. What about Jill Barbers work and that survivor on the pier in Berkeley? And what about Arnie from the naval base? She thought about Slinky, wondering if he was alive or dead and then she wondered about herself, why was she here?

Backing away from the table she threw herself onto the couch and buried her face into the pillows. Having this information had somehow made it all worse. Streaking pain swept behind her eyes and radiated out towards her temples as she lay there, too numb to even get up and take an aspirin.

A significantly choppy swell and an incoming tide made the trip under the Golden Gate a bumpy one as she left the protection of San Francisco Bay and headed back out into the Pacific. Jaime decided to sail hard today, getting every bit of speed out of JayJay to start the next leg of her voyage. She tacked aggressively, feeling the speed bleed off and then hearing the crack of the mainsail filling again with wind as they were thrust forward on their new heading.

We had done it to ourselves she thought, the wind whipping her hair across her face. For whatever reason, the Chinese government not only developed but unleashed a killer virus that has wiped out almost every human on the planet. Jaime was too angry to cry. She welcomed the physical work and the occasional spray in her face. It took her mind off of how mankind had finally, and completely, failed itself.

All day long JayJay performed flawlessly in the blustery wind of the northern California coast. It wasn't until the sun was just about to set that Jaime realized that she hadn't eaten since breakfast. She brought JayJay around up into the wind and reefed in the majority of the sails. As she slowly swung back into a quartering wind, Jaime set the autopilot and looked back to the east. Land was long out of sight. She headed into the galley to make dinner, followed expectantly by Brandy.

Jaime rarely drank alcohol, but she enjoyed it when she did. Later, she dropped the empty bottle of chardonnay before she was even close to the sink and it rolled noisily back towards the dining table.

"OK, well that's enough of that." Jaime said, realizing that a bottle of wine and one meal a day was nothing more than an invitation asking for trouble. Quickly preparing the boat for nighttime, she let Brandy out to do her business and fell asleep before she could turn out her bedside lamp.

It was light out when she awoke. Brandy was sitting quietly beside her bed, looking up at her. Jaime quickly looked at her watch and realized it was almost 9:00 o'clock. Her attempted jump out of bed quickly became a slow stroll as her stomach fluttered and her head started to pound. Taking a couple of aspirins and drinking two full glasses of water would help, she hoped. It wasn't her worst hangover but any hangover was uncomfortable, especially at sea.

After performing all her morning checks she charted their position and set a northerly course. Winds were following and light to moderate now but they would pick up during the day. They had drifted back south east in the north pacific current overnight which was normal but Jaime knew this wasn't a race.

The days easily rolled one into the other and it had now been seven days since she left San Francisco. They were making great time and JayJay had proven a very seaworthy running with the prevailing wind. The winds remained brisk this day as the sun set and as Jaime was following her daily routine, preparing for sleep, she checked the barometer. It was falling quickly. She decided to set the sea anchor just in case. It was a wise decision.

They had been riding the sea anchor, their bow facing the brunt of the storm for a full twenty four hours. It seemed that they were headed for another sleepless night as they were battered around in huge seas. Jaime had somehow managed to fall asleep when she was woken by a loud crash followed by a significant shuddering of JayJay as they heeled heavily over to starboard. She held on to the bed railing and then another loud crash as something slid across the deck above her. The sounds were both unmistakable and terrifying. Wood was splintering and there were the screeching sounds of breaking fibreglass. Her first thought was that they had run aground but she realized that wasn't possible. Something had hit them.

JayJay had now returned to level as Jaime ran to the rear cockpit. Her flashlight did little in the complete darkness but she could see a large piece of the cockpit railing had been torn away. Finding the rarely used light switch for the deck lights, she turned them on. Just a stone's throw away from JayJay was a partially submerged ship. It looked like some kind of fishing trawler and it was heeled over, floating on its side, battered by the huge waves and slowly getting pushed past them in the storm.

The parachute like sea anchor was luckily still holding JayJay's bow into the wind and it did not appear that they were entangled with the other ship. Jaime flicked off the outside lights to conserve their batteries when she heard the beep-beep of an alarm. Holding onto anything she could find as they rocked over yet another huge wave, she raced forward to the helm station and saw that the bilge pumps had come on. They were taking on water. A wave of panic swept over her but she knew she needed to remain calm and think all her decisions through. Jaime surveyed the damage inside first, a few small cracks and a few things knocked loose, that was all. She opened the hatch to the passageway to the engine room and saw no water there. Moving further down she opened the smaller hatch down into the bilge and couldn't see any water but she could hear the buzz of the pumps. Well we aren't sinking she thought to herself, not yet anyway.

There was little to do except hope that the pumps kept them afloat and wait till dawn. Not wanting to rely on battery power, Jaime started the generator and turned on all the lights to check for damage. The storm seemed to quickly blow itself out as dawn approached but the seas remained large and angry. The skies were heavy and grey with a low ceiling but once it was light enough out, Jaime wanted to have a look outside. She grabbed a life jacket, attached her safety line and stepped out into the cockpit.

The damage topside looked mostly superficial but JayJay had definitely taken a bit of a beating. She lost about thirty feet of railing on the starboard side and there was a big gash in the fibreglass decking amidships that had allowed the water to come in. Luckily there was no damage to the mast but she had lost some rigging. One of the automatic winches had also been partially knocked off its mount so she wasn't sure if it would work. The small wind turbine had been broken in half and their tender was missing. That wasn't good news but it could have been a lot worse. The morning was spent making repairs and Jaime was mostly pleased with the results. The only issue was she knew she needed to properly re-fibreglass the damage to make JayJay completely seaworthy again. The bilge alarm had stopped and that meant that there was no damage below the water line, which was her biggest fear. Whatever water that had entered JayJay had been from the rain or waves and had now been removed. Jaime remembered her father saying the only way to make a repair on a boat was properly so she knew she had to find a port where she could find the materials to make the appropriate repairs.

Later that afternoon the clouds parted and the seas continued to diminish and Jamie was able to come off the sea anchor and continue her journey. Having a long overdue meal, she literally gulped down a plate of spicy beans and rice as she wondered what kind of marine facilities were in Tofino. It was a coastal town and no doubt had a marina but she didn't want to chance that she wouldn't be able to find the material she needed to make the repairs.

Jaime decided to make sail towards Friday Harbour in the San Juan Islands. From her current position it was equidistant to both locations and she had visited Friday Harbour a couple of years ago as a guest of the University of Washington at their marine biology field station. The university had won the contract to do some venom research testing for Cleanetics and when they were touring her around town she recalled the large marina and also a number of boat building shops. Confident that Friday Harbour was the right call, she charted the course and set the autopilot. She should be there in less than a day.

29

The sun was just starting to set when Jaime nosed JayJay into the jetty beside the ferry terminal in Friday Harbour, San Juan Island, Washington. Before Jaime had even finished tying off the first knot Brandy had already jumped out and was sprinting up the jetty and onto land. Jaime finished and hustled up after her and found her sitting beside a bench in an overgrown scenic lookout chewing some sprigs of seeding grass.

"Well girl, happy again?" Brandy was filled with energy as she sniffed around the bench and Jaime thought this was as good a time as any to bring out the leash. Remembering San Francisco, Jaime wanted to keep Brandy close for both of their sakes.

With the sunlight fading, Jaime explored quickly around the ferry dock. There were a few vehicles in the parking lot, a concession stand and a small office took up the rest of the vast lot. An older blue minivan was parked at the front of the line and Jaime could see someone inside. She didn't get too close but she could see a decomposing corpse was seat belted into the driver's seat.

It was as usual deathly silent as Jaime went to the concession but the door was locked. She took her pike pole and broke the glass, reaching inside to unlock the door. Once inside she noticed that the counters and floors were covered in mouse droppings and the whole place smelled musty and dirty. A small candy stand was on the counter and she grabbed a bag of licorice, making sure it was intact, and a six-pack of diet Coke from under the counter. The day was rapidly turning into night when Jaime went back outside and off in the distance she heard what she thought was a wolf howl. It was quickly followed by another, much closer this time, in obvious answer to the first. Jaime knew there were some coastal wolves in British Columbia and probably Washington State too, but wolves or dogs, it didn't matter. She and Brandy quickly made their way back across the parking lot and down the jetty to JayJay.

The morning broke as a typical Pacific Northwest day with low undefined clouds and a steady drenching rain. Jaime was confident that she could repair the structural damage on JayJay and her temporary fix had eliminated them taking on much more water but you never knew in a rain like this. Leaving Brandy behind she headed over to the main marina to start her search for some supplies and material.

Friday Harbour was a beautiful little town, full of old homes from the 1940's and 50's, it oozed that moneyed seaside charm and character. In stark contrast to the hustle and bustle of her last visit, the only sounds now were of the pounding rain and the occasional cry of a seagull. She found it a little more serene than San Francisco but in a world that had been turned upside down, serenity was now judged on a different scale. Jaime knew she was still just in survival mode, somehow making it all work. Armed with her pepper spray and pike pole, she first visited the marina's office. A small service area led back to a larger than she imagined warehouse that was at first glance well stocked. Grateful that she remembered to being a flashlight, Jaime found almost everything she was looking for at the marina. She loaded up a wheelbarrow with high density foam, fibreglass cloth and a couple of gallons of resin as well as an armful of DVD movies.

The rain didn't look like it would end today so she wheeled her stash up and out of the marina onto the street and covered it with a tarp. Not absolutely sure in what direction the boatbuilding shops were it was just a short walk until she saw an old fibreglass speedboat mounted on the top of a small weathered building. The words 'Buds Boats' was painted on the hull in faded red block letters.

The doors were all locked so she had to smash a window to get in. Deep down, that still bothered her, she almost felt that she was violating a space that she shouldn't be in. Using her flashlight in the dim building she found the heavy grit sandpaper that she had been looking for and a long piece of galvanized chain to replace the broken side rail. In her mind she had some ideas on how to make the repairs but it would be trial and error at first. There were a number of tools in the fibreglass area of the shop that she had never seen before and she decided to take those also. Everything just fit into her packsack but the chain proved to be heavier than she anticipated so she looked around for something with wheels. The only thing she could find was an old office chair from the office up front and she piled that high with the chain and other supplies. As she was wheeling the chair outside she spotted a crab trap leaning against the side of the building. Throwing that on the top of the pile Jaime started to head back to JayJay.

Jaime had started to lose track of how many movies she had watched in the last two days. It had never stopped raining long enough to start her repairs and she was itching to get going. Even though she dried Brandy thoroughly after their last walk, the wet dog smell lingered in the cabin. Just at dusk last night she had again heard howling and had a plan to string up some chain link fencing across the ramp of the jetty to ensure they had no unwelcome visitors in the night.

The weather on her fourth day in Friday Harbour proved to be exactly the opposite of the previous days, it was beautifully sunny and fresh. Being a California girl she was not accustomed to the dampness and was thankful for the southerly wind that had broken up the clouds. The heat of the sun rapidly dried the hull and with her tools and supplies spread all around the jetty she started her repairs.

Knowing she would be able to top up her diesel tank here she had no qualms about using power tools run off of JayJay's generator. The days of rain had allowed her ample time to scavenge a number of intimidating looking tools from some of the local businesses. A large reciprocating saw made short work of the damaged fibreglass around the large gash in JayJay's deck. Jaime screwed and glued a number of wooden supports in and around the damage and packed the void with foam. Finally happy that there was some structural integrity beneath she started to lay on the fibreglass. Thankful for the breeze as the fumes from the resins were strong, the first part of the repair was finally done. When all that had dried, she would roughly sand the area again and then finish the fibreglass work and blend it as best she could into the rest of the deck. It didn't need to be pretty, just functional but as somewhat of a perfectionist, Jaime made it both. Repairing the broken railing stanchions proved to be much trickier but she did her best using copious amounts of fibreglass. She knew the railing wouldn't hold her full weight like it used to so she would need to be careful with that. After the fibreglass holding up the new stanchions had dried, she attached the chain with carabineers and that job was completed.

Taking advantage of a stretch of good weather, all the fibreglass work was done except for the cosmetic sanding and Jamie started to tackle the damaged winch. No matter how hard she tried, even with power tools, she could not loosen two of the bolts on the damaged winch bracket. It still worked but restricted the amount of mainsail she could put out to about 85%. Jaime had found a similar winch in one of the boatbuilding shops and stored it away on JayJay. Not being completely disappointed when she couldn't get the damaged one off, Jaime could manage with a diminished mainsail, it's not like she needed that extra knot of speed. The problem was if it ever completely failed, she would be in trouble.

Finding another tender proved to be her biggest challenge. Most of the ones on the yachts in the marina were too big and too heavy for her to handle. Her solution was to lash a ten foot inflatable to the mounts where her old tender sat. For good measure, she took another brand new ten foot inflatable still in its box from the marina warehouse. Now even if she lost this one, she had another.

Jaime and Brandy sat down to a meal of sweet and succulent Dungeness crab and quinoa salad. Against her better judgement Jaime had given Brandy a few pieces of the crabmeat and the crab proved to be a little too rich for Brandy's constitution. Although Jaime found dog flatulence amusing, it is not kind to the nose, especially in an enclosed space.

Another beautiful sunrise and an early start brought a quick end to the repairs. A final sanding on the deck repair, one additional layer of reinforcement to the railing stanchions and a quick coat of paint were all completed before lunch. Jaime had partially removed the damaged wind turbine and stored it below. It was quite heavily damaged and as it was custom built she didn't know if she could repair it. There were some manuals and instructions and she would need to do some reading up on that.

After San Francisco she promised herself to leave a message anywhere she landed so Jaime took a couple of hours to craft a long letter outlining what she knew and where she was going. It was left inside a waterproof bag hanging from the front door of the post office. Taking out a can of red spray paint, Jaime wrote *'message here'* in big block letters on the cedar siding and an arrow pointing to the bag. Afterwards, she felt bad for defacing the old wooden building but it needed to be done.

Back on JayJay, Jaime's spirits were as high as they had been for months. Opening a bottle of wine she toasted Friday Harbour and her fibreglass repair skills and sat out on the jetty throwing a ball for Brandy. Checking the crab trap, there were only four crabs and three of them were females. She knew you were not allowed to keep females and then she laughed.

"All the rules have changed girl," she said more to herself than Brandy, rolling the ball back down the jetty. "There aren't any rules or laws anymore. Survival of the fittest. Every woman for herself and you can do whatever you want." Laughing for the first time in a long time, she carefully extracted the female crabs from trap and dropped them back into the ocean, watching them quickly sink to the bottom. "Have fun girls," was all she said. The lone male could be heard scraping along the inside of her saucepan as she headed inside to make dinner.

After another delicious meal, Jaime was reflecting on her new reality. One of her biggest mental stumbling blocks was not knowing what happened to her dad. If Jill Barber was right, maybe her dad had the healthy gene too. The fact that she had been just a month away from seeing Jeremy ate at her as well. Jaime no longer cried herself to sleep or awoke each morning wondering if it was all a nightmare, this was now her life. Now realizing there were other survivors complicated her situation even more. With nothing but time on her hands it was easy to overthink her situation.

She would leave first thing in the morning for Tofino to see if she can find Tessa Henry. According to her old friend Jill Barber, the only other person with this so called healthy gene in almost 100,000 DNA samples she checked from around the world.

There had been a little more than seven billion people on the planet. Jaime was always good at math so she figured if two survived out of every 100,000 that would be about 140,000 survivors.

Jaime was accurate in her calculation but way off in her assumptions.

30

It had been an uneventful trip from Friday Harbour out the Strait of Juan de Fuca and up the west coast of Vancouver Island. Jaime slowly motored towards the dock in Tofino through an inquisitive group of harbour seals who had made a nearby floating gas dock their new home. They bobbed like corks, their eyes following Jamie's every move until with a silent roll they disappeared under the surface. Their forceful stares gave Jaime the feeling that they missed having people around.

As she reduced speed and was preparing to pull JayJay alongside the floating dock, she couldn't help but watch a large bald eagle carrying what looked like a small salmon. It was being harassed by a couple of ravens as it tried to gain some altitude, heading towards a stand of massive spruce and cedar trees at the water's edge. The ravens continually dove at the eagle, trying to make it release its catch but the eagle ignored them as it deftly landed on a snag, its screeching call echoing off the trees within the calm harbour. The ravens quickly disappeared and like everywhere else, the landscape was once again eerily quiet.

Being somewhat preoccupied with her docking procedure, she never saw it until the last second. Just as Jaime was jumping out of the rear cockpit onto the dock, a large black shape as shiny and dark as India ink rocketed across the dock towards her. Jaime screamed and fell back into the cockpit, tangled in her mooring rope. Leaping into the boat, it landed on top of the prone Jaime almost knocking the wind out of her. She tried to fend it off but she had little strength as she lay on her back, frozen in fear. The dog was crazily licking her hands and face while its tail drummed a furious beat on the cockpit wall. Jaime finally got a hold of its collar and she held it off as she scrambled to her feet. Brandy was inside the inner glass door scratching and madly barking to get out.

Retaining her grip on the dog's collar she tried to regain her senses after what had just happened. Her head was still ringing and she ever so gently ran her fingers over her scalp and felt a small lump forming on the back of her head. The dog was now rubbing its face up and down Jamie's pant leg its tail still drumming a beat against anything it touched. Finally looking outside the cockpit Jaime could see the docking process was now all messed up, the bow was now touching the dock but the stern was a good five feet away. Jaime let go of the dog and threw the mooring line out onto the dock and quickly ran forward, followed by this seemingly insanely happy dog. Jaime jumped down onto the dock, immediately followed by the dog and quickly tied off the bow. She then ran back down the dock to the stern, and pulled JayJay in tight against the fenders with the rope she had just thrown there, trying to properly tie her off while fighting off the affections of this dog.

As she caught a breath and composed herself the dog continued to do a little happy dance all around her, rubbing against her legs and licking anything it could. Jaime bent down and hugged the heavily muscled black lab, rubbing his ears and stroking his head. It was truly the happiest creature she had ever seen. Looking around she saw no other movement besides a few birds and the inquisitive seals who were all now fully engaged in silently watching the spectacle taking place in front of them.

Not wanting to aggravate Brandy any more than she already was she told the dog to stay on the dock as she climbed back aboard JayJay and grabbed the pike pole and her can of pepper spray. Introductions could come later she thought and she left the disappointed Brandy behind as she walked up the dock towards the ramp, closely followed by the big black lab.

Jaime could see some restaurants, a Canadian Coast Guard office and a few small shops. Just a block away looked like the start of a residential area. Tofino did not have the feel of money like Friday Harbour had, it was much more basic and functional, a true working man's town. The shadows were getting long so she knew there was little time for exploring so she picked up her pace and walked along the road fronting the harbour.

Jaime was amazed at how friendly this dog was compared to those that she had run across in San Francisco. It hopped and jumped in front of her like a puppy and she continually had to be careful not to step on it. It made walking at any pace quite difficult. Coming across a small stick she threw it out ahead of her and the dog immediately gave chase. Never slowing down, it scooped up the stick, ran at full speed back towards Jaime, dropped it at her feet and sat down.

"Well, you sure are a well-trained boy." The dog was now maniacally looking back and forth between Jaime and the stick, his bright pink tongue hanging out in such sharp contrast to his jet black coat.

Jaime picked up the stick and was about to throw it again when she froze. She was sure of it. The smell of wood smoke. There was no telling where it was coming from but Jaime had a plan. She hid the stick behind her back and the lab could barely contain himself as he shook with anticipation watching her like a hawk.

She looked the dog in the eyes and said, "Let's go home! Let's go home boy."

The dog immediately spun around and ran off up the street. It stopped at the corner to make sure Jaime was coming and then ran off again, up the side street and past a faded cedar planked cabin with window casings made of varnished driftwood. Jamie was running after him and when she rounded the corner, the dog was again stopped, a few houses ahead, waiting for her. Now confident that Jaime was following, the dog took off at a full run.

Just as Jaime started to move forward again a figure ran out between the two houses and that stopped Jamie in her tracks. It was a young girl wearing sweatpants and light woolen sweater, her long dark hair cascaded down her back.

The young girl called out, "Butch, Butch come back here, I've been looking all over for you."

Jaime was only about twenty feet behind her as the dog came sprinting back, sliding to a halt in front of the girl.

"Tessa?" Jaime said, maybe a bit louder than she had intended.

Tessa Henry jumped in the air and spun around, becoming entangled with Butch as she stumbled backwards, falling to the ground. Looking back towards Jaime, her brown eyes were as big as saucers.

T hey had been up all night and had already become the best of friends.

Tessa was eighteen and was initially not the only survivor in Tofino. Her grandfather Ben, hereditary chief of the Nuu-Chah-Nulth First Nation had died just a few days earlier. He was eighty four years old and had been healthy until last year when he had broken his hip. Multiple surgeries had left him in a much weakened state and he developed another infection at his surgery site. Tessa had been able to find the antibiotics he had been subscribed before in the local pharmacy but it didn't seem to help. Tessa had buried him, along with many others in the playing field at the local elementary school. Tessa's survival through what they now knew was LOCUST was very different than Jaime's experience. There was no violence and chaos here, like everywhere else the die off was rapid but all the people pulled together trying to help one another. Some took off on their boats or cars to the larger cities of Nanaimo and Victoria looking for help but most stayed. Almost all the First Nations people remained and they gathered each day in their ceremonial longhouse to chant and drum, hoping to invoke something, anything that could help. Eventually there were just two of them left, Tessa and her grandfather. Somehow Tessa had been able to hold her tears till just an hour ago when she opened up about how scared she had been.

All night long the conversation had gone back and forth with Tessa trying hard to understand some of the more complicated aspects of what Jaime had experienced since all this madness had started. Always a bit withdrawn and private, Tessa easily opened up to give Jaime a thorough rundown of her life since the event. Being of first nation's heritage she had been schooled on her people's ancient and innate connection to their land and surroundings. Tessa felt she had adapted well, all things considered, and was looking forward to showing her new friend what she had accomplished. The pain of recently losing her grandfather was significantly lessened by Jaime's arrival.

The sun had been up for over an hour when Tessa said, "I can't believe I'm not even tired." She was adding some fresh parsley and dried seaweed to the scrambled eggs she was making. Butch and Brandy, who had also quickly become best buddies, looked up expectantly, their noses not having to work hard to take in the aroma. Jaime stared intensely at the rapidly cooking eggs, the insides of her cheeks salivating with anticipation.

"I can't believe how much I talked." Jaime added, munching on another leafy sprig of parsley. "I've really missed anything fresh too."

"The most important meal of the day, that's what my grandmother used to say," said Tessa, putting a heaping plate of scrambled eggs and smoked salmon in front of Jaime.

"This is so good Tessa." Jaime hadn't had eggs in a long time and she loved how the dried seaweed added a salty crunch to the dish. They ate mostly in silence as the dogs noisily finished their portions. Sitting at the kitchen table, Jaime could see out through the window to the small houses that formed the neighbourhood. The vibrant green of the evergreens contrasted sharply against the weathered and faded grey of the cedar fences. Looking over at Tessa, Jamie saw her staring out the same window, her face was reflected ghostlike in the thin glass.

After breakfast they left the warm and cozy confines of Tessa's house and went for a walk, each chattering away, grateful for the companionship. As Jaime was toured around the house and neighbourhood she was shown all that Tessa and her grandfather had accomplished since they had been on their own. Jaime was continually amazed at the basic simplicity of these achievements. Tessa not only had running water courtesy of a local creek and a portable generator but had a significant cache of venison and both dried and smoked salmon in a buried shipping container. Excavated five feet down into the rich brown earth, it was the perfect cold storage room for this climate. Tessa had turned an empty lot on the block into a fabulous garden which was already growing well. The fiddleheads and early vegetables were already sprouting as it had been an easy winter. Tessa had explained that she had spent the last few summers at her father's logging camp so she was accustomed to working hard and using all kinds of heavy equipment. Her grandfather had most of the ideas and Tessa had provided the labour.

As they walked along the dogs were chasing each other, running in and out of the yards of the now vacant houses. The swing sets and abandoned children's toys was a shockingly grim reminder of what had happened, here and everywhere else. The population of Tofino was about two thousand Tessa had figured, with many more seasonal residents and tourists in the summer. Up ahead was the elementary school and Jaime could see hundreds of graves that had been dug in the large grass field. The still moist brown earth of one of the graves stood out as being recently dug.

"You buried all these people?" Jaime asked.

"I couldn't just let them rot in their houses," Tessa replied. "It would be disrespectful to their spirits."

Jaime could see that Tessa was completely serious and it was evident she was a very spiritual person. As her community had rapidly diminished around her, Tessa told Jamie that for the first time, sitting with all of her people in the longhouse, drumming and singing and smelling the sweetness of the burning cedar, that she felt personally connected to her ancestors. Up until then, I was just a teenager that happened to be native she had said. Now I am a native that happens to be a teenager.

Butch and Brandy were madly chasing each other, running around and around the two of them when there was a high pitched yipping sound from the forest behind the playing field. Both Tessa's and Butch's head spun around.

"Wolves," Tessa said.

During their all night chat, Tessa had told Jaime about the problem she had with the wolves. Trying to look after and feed all the dogs that were left in the village, Tessa had managed for a while. Slowly they then started disappearing and that's when she learned the wolves had started coming into the village at night. She surmised it was easier for them to catch semi-domesticated dogs than it was to run down deer in the forest. Butch, her family dog, was the only dog left. Tessa was normally armed when she left her house but this morning in all the excitement, she took neither her rifle nor the pistol that she took from the towns dead Mountie. The yipping started again, this time from behind them.

"Everybody in the backhoe," Tessa ordered as she grabbed Brandy and lifted her up into the cab. Jaime was the last one in and it was a very tight fit as there was only one seat but Tessa started the big machine up and expertly drove them back to her home. The wolves did not show themselves.

Later that day, they walked to the marina, this time with Tessa carrying her rifle. It was now Jaime's turn to host the tour.

"What a beautiful boat." Tessa was running her hands along the wooden casing of the cockpit door, admiring the craftsmanship. "This is so different from the other sailboats I have been on. I can't believe you can sail this all by yourself Jaime."

"Well it was actually designed for that purpose." Jaime had already told Tessa about her father and brother and the stories about how both JayJay and Unfinished Business came to be. Tessa continued to look around, admiring the finishes and commenting on how roomy it was.

After touring JayJay, Jaime showed Tessa the emails from Jill Barber and explained with a little more detail about the theory that the two of them may possess this ancient DNA that contains a healthy gene that somehow allowed them to survive the virus. Tessa listened intently. She was a high school graduate, but barely, struggling with both math and sciences. Jaime took the time to try and simply explain the scientific nuances and could see that Tessa was taking the time to think things through and ask questions so she could understand. Having just graduated from high school late last year, Tessa may not be tremendously book smart but she made up for it with her intuitiveness and a huge dose of common sense.

After going through the emails for a second time Tessa's head snapped up and she excitedly blurted out. "I have really never been sick Jaime. Almost everyone in my family has, or had, diabetes." Hesitating, her eyes were looking right through Jaime as she searched her memory. "Both my father and grandfather, they were always healthy too." Jaime just silently nodded her head, her mind methodically processing every new piece of information, trying to put all the puzzle pieces together.

While they relaxed in JayJay's well-appointed salon, they could hear the patter of rain above them. Brandy and Buck continued to rough-house, rolling around on the carpet play fighting. Jaime was going to spend the night at Tessa's place and this time the plan was to get some sleep. Jaime grabbed a few personal items from her stateroom and a few things from the galley, spotting her last bottle of wine. "Do you drink wine Tessa?"

"I guess I could try it but I have never had alcohol. It has been so bad for us." Tessa remembered a childhood of spousal abuse and very little money until her parents both had stopped drinking. Tessa knew that many of her relative's lives along with so many others in the community had been ruined by booze. Jaime too was well aware of how alcohol had brought many aboriginal and indigenous people around the world to the brink of despair. Somewhat embarrassingly, she put the bottle back into the cupboard. They packed up a few of Jaime's things and hurried back to the house through the raindrops, Tessa's rifle comfortably secured under her arm.

32

They were in their second day of exploring Clayoquot Sound when Jaime realized she could easily live here. The sheer natural beauty and the abundance of food and water were spread out like a set table before her. It was so different from California and just about any other place she had travelled to. The colours of everything, the trees and the water, the thousands of deep purple starfish clinging to the recently exposed rocks all shone through even in the flat light of mid-day. The air was crisp and seemed heavily oxygenated, the smells rich and lingering. The salty ripeness of the low tide, the fragrance of the cedars, the cool earthiness of the mossy forest floor, Jaime just couldn't help taking in deep breaths of everything.

Tessa had just shown Jaime a sacred spot on Flores Island where at low tide, rainwater that had slowly filtered through the thick moss of the forest spouted a small stream of water out of a crack in the cliff face and into the ocean. This water was used for the special ceremonies of the Nuu-Chah-Nulth First Nation. Jaime just couldn't get enough of it. The water from the desalination plant on JayJay had a slight metallic tang to it but this was the purest most delicious water she had ever tasted. It fit right in with everything else here, it was naturally perfect.

As they sat enjoying the mid-day sun Tessa explained that this was the time of year of the herring spawn. Hundreds of thousands of herring would congregate in the shallow bays and inlets, the females laying their eggs on kelp and anything else they could find. The males would be following close behind, fighting for their chance to reproduce and releasing their milt that would turn the water opaque.

"In ancient times, collecting the herring eggs was women's work." Tessa was looking out at a huge glassy mark in the bay, the surface calmed by the tens of thousands of herring just beneath the surface. "Pulling the kelp was hard and dangerous, many people drowned. Legend says that the ravens used to all laugh at our people until one day, there were so many ravens on a big cedar bough that they broke it off the tree and it fell into the ocean. Then all the herring spawned on the bough. All the women had to do then was to drag it onto the beach to harvest the eggs." She went on to explain how in ancient times the raven was known as a trickster or a joker, one to always keep your eyes on. But it was revered as well by all the natives along the coast, often taking top spot on their carved totems. "It was said that we cannot live without the raven and the raven cannot live without us. But looking around, they seem to be doing ok."

Jaime was transfixed listening to Tessa, often not knowing if she was trying to be funny or just poignant. Leaning back she just soaked up the spectacle in front of her. Sleek cormorants, gulls and little diving ducks all feasted on the herring and their eggs. Seals floated nearby, sunning themselves with their belly's protruding, unable to eat anymore. Ospreys dove, sometimes flying back to their nests with three or four struggling herring in their talons. It was nature at its finest.

Tessa continued, "After that, my people would just drop cedar boughs into the water and harvest the eggs that way."

It was hot for the first week of April and neither of them needed a jacket. The sun warmed not only their bodies but their souls. Tessa had taken the inflatable dinghy and rowed into the spawning masses of herring. She pulled up two huge pieces of kelp, cutting a portion out of each, gently dropping the remaining back into the ocean, ensuring both the kelp and the remaining eggs would survive. Proudly showing Jaime the two pieces, combined they were about the size of a standard piece of writing paper. The freshly laid eggs translucently glistened in the sunlight in stark contrast to the deep green of the kelp.

"I'll smoke these for us when we get back." Tessa carefully wrapped them in a seawater soaked towel. "Last year, a Japanese man came to Tofino and my uncle sold him twenty pounds of smoked eggs on kelp. He was paid a thousand dollars." Her face softened and after putting the kelp away she went forward and sat alone for a while, no doubt absorbing again what had happened. Jaime had already discovered that Tessa needed her alone time. That she deeply missed and loved her relatives, friends and elders was obvious but she like Jaime needed to decompress and somehow try to be normal in this most un-normal circumstance.

Later that afternoon they visited the small first nation village of Ahousat on Flores Island. There was bear scat everywhere and they kept both Butch and Brandy on a leash. Tessa had learned as a youngster that springtime was a dangerous time to run into a mother bear with a dog. More often than not the dog would start to chase the bear and then the mother bear would turn to attack the dog. The dog knew it couldn't win that fight so it would go running back to its owner, bringing the angry mother bear with it. Jamie shook her head in amazement at Tessa's knowledge of the things in her world.

Tessa was visibly shaken as she inspected a number of homes. Bears had broken in and had been feasting on what was left of the corpses of the villagers. It was not a pleasant scene. Tessa gripped her rifle a little tighter and hoped that the scent of the dog's would keep the bears out of sight. She knew she had to come back one day to bury the remains.

"Let's go Jaime, I'm not comfortable here." Tessa turned and walked back down the path, eyes alert, and ears primed for any noise.

After motoring for most of the day the water turned from a minor ripple to a small chop as they were finally able to catch some wind and sail back to Tofino.

Another week quickly passed and their friendship grew as they shared stories of their life experiences. As was her way, Tessa was quietly awed by what Jaime had accomplished but she couldn't help but voice her praise for Jaime's significant accomplishments. What Tessa didn't accept was how Jaime was even more impressed with what Tessa had done in eighteen short years. Generations of richness, culture and history passed down to her by the tribal elders and her experiences fishing, hunting and logging from an early age. Jaime had known a lot of environmentalists but none with the connection to the planet and all its creatures that Tessa had. Tessa's spirituality was profoundly functional and connected deeply to all of nature. Jaime couldn't help but wonder if there was some kind of genetic coding for all indigenous peoples that gave them that connection to the planet.

They had to keep Brandy tied on a long lead in the front yard as she tended to wander off if she was unsupervised and that was dangerous. Butch had all the street smarts he needed to be wary of the wolves but Brandy did not.

Jaime was reading a book on the porch while Tessa was enjoying a long luxurious soak in the bath. Although Tessa had running water, she didn't have hot water so she had rigged up a propane tiger torch to heat up a large galvanized tank that she filled with water. A bypass valve allowed her to then pump that water into her household system and fill up the bathtub. It was simple, smart and tremendously ingenious.

The dogs were again play fighting in the yard when Butch started barking. A high pitched rapid bark, unlike anything Jaime had ever heard. She looked up and saw the cause. Standing at the property line was a huge wolf. It's long grey and black fur tipped with silver. Its amber eyes unmoving, staring at its prey.

Butch advanced a few paces, barking. His hackles at full alert, his tail held high. This was his territory and he would defend it if he had to. Brandy didn't really seem to know what to do as Butch manoeuvered himself between Brandy and the wolf.

Jaime leapt out of the chair and as she approached the stairs started to yell for Brandy. Brandy ran back towards her just as the wolf made a short charge into the yard and stopped. Butch continued to hold his ground. He would be a fearsome adversary but in reality, he was no match for a wolf. His brave stand though had given Brandy the time to make it back to the stairs. Jaime yelled for Butch and he started to slowly retreat, never taking his eyes of the wolf in front of him. Jaime barely saw the silver blur come from the side of the house to her left.

Another wolf, this one even bigger than the first was onto Butch in the blink of an eye. The alpha male sunk his teeth into Butch's neck as they both hit the ground, rolling from the impact. The first wolf was now entering the fight when Tessa burst through the door. She was naked with water droplets flying from her as she screamed at Jaime to get out of the way.

Tessa brought her rifle up but couldn't fire into the rolling ball of fur without possibly hitting Butch. She fired one shot into the ground and that separated the three animals. She quickly ejected the spent shell and walking forward aimed and fired, the round quickly passing through the neck and shoulder of the alpha male who collapsed to the ground. The original wolf spun off to the side and darted away down towards the side of the house. All in one motion Tessa reloaded now sighting her rifle onto the fleeing wolf. Unable to get off a shot before it disappeared around the corner, Tessa still advancing, fired again into the prone wolf that lay beside Butch. Running now to Butch, she dropped the rifle and was cradling his head in her lap when Jaime arrived just a few seconds later.

Butch had a huge gash in his neck exposing pink muscle and tissue. A pool of dark red blood was forming on the ground and Jaime could see the blood spurting between Tessa's fingers as she tried to cover the wound. There was nothing they could do. Butch lifted up a paw and put it gently on Tessa's arm.

They buried him the next morning in the graveyard besides Tessa's grandfather.

Tessa had obviously been crying all night as her eyes were red and swollen. Jaime gave her the space she needed throughout the morning and decided before she cooked something for lunch she would go and drag the wolf carcass up and out of the yard. Tessa sat with an old blanket around her shoulders looking out the window as Jaime walked out the door and into the yard. Grabbing the wolf by its back legs she was amazed at its size and weight as she pulled it across the street. It was much bigger than she imagined wolves to be. Nervously looking around, she made her way back into the yard and into the house.

Later that day a light rain started to fall as Jaime watched Tessa cross the street and look at the wolf carcass. After a few minutes she came back in the house and sat down at the table opposite Jaime.

"I've never been off Vancouver Island," she said. "I don't think I can stay here right now. Can we go someplace else? Can we take JayJay and leave?"

Jaime reached out and held her hand. "Sure we can honey, sure we can."

It took less than four days to provision and stock JayJay with all the supplies they could carry. Tessa had even repaired and reinstalled the wind turbine that was damaged during the storm. They sailed out of Tofino into a blustery wind on the morning of April 15th. Tessa spent most of the time inside only coming out later in the day when the land was seemingly slowly sinking into the horizon. Looking back, Tessa sat down and quietly started singing a rhythmic song in a language that Jaime did not understand, Tessa's finger continually tapping a beat against the side rail.

When Tessa stopped singing, Jaime looked back to see her take a small leather pouch out of her pocket. She emptied the contents over the rail and started singing again, this time loudly and forcefully before placing the pouch back into her pocket and raising her hands above her head.

When she finished with a resounding thump of her foot against the deck, Tessa walked by Jamie on her way back inside and said, "That's just in case I don't come back."

33

Edgar Barnes opened his eyes and watched a small leaf spin lazily to the ground. Lying on a soiled foam mattress under a tree, his drug-addled brain was attempting to make sense of his surroundings. Slowly coming to a sitting position, his head hung lazily as he reached his arm out for balance. Finding nothing but the warm morning air he slumped slowly back to the ground and rolled onto his back. With deliberate purpose he turned over and rose to his hands and knees and then saw the prescription bottle sitting amongst a number of empty and crumpled beer cans. His brain was still trying to function as he crawled over and picked up the bottle. It was empty.

Rolling over again onto his back, Edgar looked up at the filtered sunlight as it streamed through the leaves and tried to focus. His eyelids seemed to be weighted as he struggled to keep them open and remain conscious. How long had it been he hazily thought? Three, four, six months? In a rare moment of lucidity he recalled that he was now out of drugs and let out a small groan.

Raiding every pharmacy within a fifty mile radius and breaking into hundreds and hundreds of homes, Edgar had found literally pounds of prescription drugs which he had been taking by the handful longer than he could remember. Just as another leaf started to fall he could feel himself drifting off and he knew it was coming. The reoccurring dream of what had happened and how he came to be here, barely alive, lying under a tree in Temecula California. It started as it normally did, like he was watching a movie and then his body seemed to split, joining into the scenes while part of him sat and just watched.

He was sitting in the Metropolitan Detention Centre in downtown Los Angeles awaiting his arraignment on attempted murder charges. Big deal, he was serving a life term already. He hated it here and just wished he could get all this over with and be sent back to Victorville, the high security prison that had been his home for the last ten years. So he stabbed a fellow rapist and murderer in the neck and almost killed him. Who cares? They are all going to die in prison anyways.

Edgar's mother was a heroin addicted prostitute originally from Tonga. He was taken away from his mother before his first birthday and had spent the next fifteen years bouncing from one foster home to the next. In trouble from a very early age, he had spent more than half of his life in jail.

Two weeks ago their TV had been cut off. Last week, all visitations had been stopped. The day before yesterday they stopped removing prisoners that were sick. Only one meal yesterday and that was an Army MRE or 'meals ready to eat'. The power went out yesterday afternoon and they had been on a backup generator until earlier this morning when that stopped. No guards were visible anywhere. The three remaining prisoners in the cell block had died. Edgar had planned on dying in prison, but not this way.

A long day without air conditioning turned into an even longer night. For the first time in a long time he cared about something. He cared about living. Every few minutes he had been kicking at the cellblock door and could hear the noise booming down the hallway, but no one came. Even picking up one of the plastic chairs and banging it against the tempered glass window did not bring a guard to investigate. Standing in the dark the only sound was his stomach growling as it had been more than a day since his last meal. He had seen riots in jail when a meal was even five minutes late, the seriousness of the situation was just hitting him. Edgar had only ever been scared a couple times in his life. The feeling was new to him and he didn't like it. His mouth dry, he went to the sink to get a drink of water and found the taps were dry. Not even having enough saliva to swallow, Edgar felt a chill as his entire body was instantly covered in a thin sheen of perspiration.

Edgar figured he could do nothing or do something, so he got to work. It had taken him over three hours to chisel a small hole through the cinder block wall using a broken table leg. The air was thick and stale and he was thinking at this rate he would be dead of dehydration before he would get out of the cell block, but he kept going as the beads of salty sweat ran into his eyes.

Having no idea how long it had been or what time it was, he just kept at it. Edgar finally squeezed out of the cell block in absolute darkness and lay on the warm cement floor of the hallway breathing heavily. Regaining his breath he started to feel his way along the floor towards the far hallway which led to the guard's station. Finding a door he tried the handle but it was locked. Further down the hallway he figured he must be at the guard's station by now and found another door. It too was locked. Moving slowly down the hallway by touch, he passed a few other doors, all were locked. A sense of panic set in and he sat down, his dust encrusted clothes still clung to his body, the air still and dank. Edgar had escaped one cell only to have entered another.

Standing up he continued down the hall, around a corner and then he came to a dead end and another locked door. He had had his eyes closed the whole time and when he finally opened them he saw a small flashing red light to his left.

It was coming from a box mounted on the wall beside the door. He couldn't find a way to open it but the front of it appeared to be glass and it broke as he pushed hard on it. Inside was a large rubber like button which he pushed.

A shrill alarm sounded, startling him. Trying the door again this time it opened. He stepped through the door and into some cooler and fresher air. Edgar held out his hands in front of him in the darkness, looking to find another wall. He took a step and felt himself falling. He reached out for something, anything to stop his fall as his other foot hit solid ground again but it was too late. After a hard landing on his shoulder he slid to a quick stop on the rough concrete stairs.

Edgar painstakingly felt his way down to the bottom of the stairwell and to his surprise and relief found a door that had been wedged open with what felt like a wadded up piece of paper. The area smelled of stale cigarette smoke. Using the walls as his guide he entered a carpeted area. Still feeling his way around he discovered the room was quite small with two doors, the one he came from and another one, this one locked. A small washroom was in one corner behind a carpeted partition and it contained a sink and a toilet.

It had been over a day since he had anything to drink and he quickly tried the sink, no water. The toilet was a real one, not the built in versions you find in prison. He lifted the lid off the tank and cupping his hands he was able to scoop out enough water to quench his immediate thirst. Exhausted and weakened by both thirst and hunger, Edgar lied down and almost immediately fell asleep. When he awoke a few hours later the room was lit from the outside via some small windows high up on the wall. Looking around, he was in some kind of holding room. The doors all seemed to be controlled electronically as they had no visible locks. The one door had a small Plexiglas window but all Edgar could see through that was a long hallway. An hour of yelling and banging on the door brought nothing. It appeared Edgar was again, trapped.

After sitting down on the floor with his back against the door for a couple of hours Edgar was startled by a voice. It was a woman's voice yelling in the hallway. Jumping up he looked through the little window and saw quite a hefty Latino woman yelling something in Spanish. Banging on the door, he got her attention.

The woman came to the window and Edgar was surprised at her appearance, red bloodshot eyes and a sweaty pall to her skin. She looked just like some of the others before they died.

"Hector! I'm looking for my Hector!" she screamed in heavily accented English.

Edgar could see that she had a small revolver in her hand.

"Is Hector there?" she asked.

Edgar responded before thinking. "No, I'm here by myself but can you open the door?"

The woman started to walk away.

Edgar yelled out. "Hector is upstairs, I saw him this morning. Let me out, I'll show you."

She stopped and came back to the window. "No tricks or I shoot you."

She tried the door but it didn't open. Edgar yelled through the door, "Is there a box on the wall beside the door?"

"Yes," she said.

"Break the glass and push the button inside that will open the door."

The woman held one hand against the wall to steady herself. Coughing, she spit a wad of mucous on the floor. Edgar couldn't see what she was doing but a moment later, he heard a click and then an alarm went off. The woman stepped back away from the door, using one of the walls to hold herself up.

Edgar grabbed the now open door as the woman unsteadily raised the pistol. Being a master manipulator his whole life, Edgar spoke easily and confidently, "Come here." He held the door partially open. "Hector is up the stairs, over there." Edgar was just pointing into the room.

She carefully started to enter the room, keeping her eyes and the gun on Edgar.

"Hector is right up those stairs," Edgar said, pointing, trying to look like he was being truthful. Like the hallway, the room was poorly lit and just when she turned her head to look, Edgar grabbed her wrist and twisted the gun out of her hand. She tried to fight but was so weak that she just crumpled to the ground.

Edgar kicked the gun through the open door and stepped out after it, closing the door behind him.

If he thought prison was hell, what he walked in to was a nightmare. Edgar walked out past the smashed front door of the Metropolitan Detention Centre and onto the street. It was eerily quiet. The only sounds were those of papers being blown by the wind.

As his eyes adjusted to the daylight he could see the damage. It looked like there had been a riot. Some windows had been smashed and abandoned cars were haphazardly strewn in the streets. He started walking and saw the first body. Then another and another until he lost count. Across the street he saw what appeared to be a teenage boy walk out of a delicatessen. The boy was trying to drink from a large water bottle but he continually vomited up whatever he drank.

Edgar walked over to him and saw he had a large pistol sticking out of his waistband. The tall skinny boy looked weak and exhausted as he sank down onto the sidewalk, leaning back against the building. Their eyes met as Edgar approached.

They stared at each other for a few moments and the boy asked in a dry raspy voice, "Why aren't you sick?"

Edgar didn't know what to say.

They stared at each other for another few moments and Edgar could now see his red crusty eyes start to squint with pain. There were small streams of sweat running down the sides of the boy's face. Edgar stepped back as he vomited again. The boy died right there in front of him. Edgar reached over and removed the pistol. Some blocks away he heard a car with its engine racing.

Edgar entered the delicatessen and saw his reflection in the mirror behind the counter. He still wore his county jail clothes and his dark curly hair was plastered down against his head. A large globule of sweat ran down his cheek and dripped onto his hand. The clamminess of his skin was unmistakeable and he felt a little light headed. He wondered if it was now his turn. Is he getting sick? Am I going to die like everyone else?

Edgar was no longer sweating and actually started to feel a little better after having something to eat. He had no idea why he was alive and everyone else wasn't. As a long term prison inmate you learn to make the best of your daily environment. Tomorrow is tomorrow. Today is today. Edgar loaded up a plastic bag with some food and water and walked back out onto the street.

The darkness came surprisingly quickly and Edgar spent the night at a small hotel. He had taken a pass key from the maid's room and after checking out a number of rooms he selected the penthouse suite. It had a set of sliding doors leading out to a large balcony which had a view to the south. A number of fires were burning off in the distance but the silence was the most disturbing thing. No cars, no sirens no hustle and bustle. He cracked open a beer from the fridge and took a long drink, not caring it was warm. Then he spotted the minibar. Not having had any alcohol since his incarceration he quickly made up for lost time and it took everything from his minibar and the minibar's in the adjoining rooms before he was satisfied.

The bed was luxurious and he was wrapped in real sheets for the first time in years when he woke with a start not knowing where he was. His head started to pound and his mouth was as dry as dirt. The hangover was exactly as he remembered them. Making his way downstairs he searched through the manager's office and found a bottle of aspirin and swallowed a handful. He sat in the lobby looking at magazines and trying to wrap his head around his situation. Looking outside he saw no one and heard nothing. Wondering if he was alive or dead, Edgar thought he might be in hell. Then he laughed as he quickly realized that it didn't really matter.

"Fuck you!" he yelled at the top of his lungs when he went outside onto the sidewalk. There was no response as he turned and looked at his ragged reflection in the window. He decided his first order of business today was to get some new clothes. Taking a walk down the street he located a men's clothing store and had no choice but to shoot his way in. The echo from the gunshot and the falling glass bounced through the neighbourhood but when it died out, it was replaced by the same unsettling silence. Nothing moved. It didn't take him long to find some new clothes and fashionable ones at that. Edgar continued walking to the east and found himself, according to the signage, approaching the USC Medical Centre.

The wind was luckily at his back as in the parking lot and the park area besides the medical centre, there were thousands of corpses. Some were placed in somewhat orderly rows but most seemed to have been thrown into piles around the building. It was an unsettling sight and Edgar kept well back. There were hundreds and hundreds of birds, mostly seagulls and crows, feasting on the dead bodies. A number of dogs were also roaming around, no doubt doing the same thing. It was a sight right out of a horror movie.

There were also a number of military vehicles here, including some armoured personnel carriers and large trucks. Some of the vehicles had been burnt out. A significant amount of barbed wire and other barricades were strung across the roads and open areas. The only movement came from the bids.

Besides that one moment yesterday in the deli, Edgar hadn't felt much of anything. His multiple diagnoses' in prison always came back to the same conclusion, he was a sociopath. In reality, he had no response to what was going on around him. There were no feelings of despair for what had happened to society. He had lived a life of basic survival since he was an infant and that would continue now. Just the playing field had changed.

A small motorhome was parked behind some of the traffic barricades and he approached it carefully. Looking inside he could see it was empty but he hoped it held some more food and water. Entering it slowly through the unlocked cab he went into the back. There was no food in the fridge but he did find some military rations in the tiny bedroom as well as three flats of bottled water. Looking outside Edgar saw two large dogs looking in at him through the window.

"Oh that's fucking perfect," he said.

There were no keys in the ignition and then he checked the visor. Bingo.

Edgar made his way through the empty streets to the Pomona Freeway and headed southeast. There were some fires burning in some of the residential areas but he saw no other people. Not living ones anyways. There were a number of abandoned cars and trucks but he was able to make it all the way to the interchange with Interstate 15 before he was stopped. A semi-trailer truck had jack-knifed and it looked like there had been a big accident. He couldn't get through so he took Interstate 15 south and stopped just outside of Temecula for the night.

Edgar explored Temecula for a number of days before setting up a small camp under a huge shade tree on the ninth fairway of a local golf course. He had stocked up on supplies from a couple of small grocery stores as well as from what he was able to find at the golf course. A small pharmacy just outside a seniors complex had caught his eye and although it had taken him hours he had broken into the locked cabinet and had taken over four hundred Oxycodone tablets along with a number of other drugs. That was a week ago and surprisingly he had not taken any as he remembered the ravages of addiction prior to his arrest and subsequent incarceration.

It was a blustery afternoon as Edgar waited for what he thought was the world's greatest creation to finish, microwaveable macaroni and cheese. Finishing a small can of cocktail wieners, he cracked another beer and was thinking about playing a round of golf tomorrow. Who gives a fuck if everyone else is dead, I don't care if I ever see another living person he thought. But deep down, he did care. As a high risk sex offender, Edgar had been locked up for twenty three hours a day. His one hour of yard time was the only time he was able to interact with anyone as even the guards that delivered their meals refused to speak with prisoners like Edgar. As the worst of the worst, he was accustomed to being alone, but even his warped mind recognized that this wasn't normal. That one hour a day was hugely important. Now even that was gone. His eyes kept going back to the big bag of prescription pills that sat on the small counter and being unable to process feelings or emotions, Edgar did what came naturally and he lashed out. Running outside he threw his now empty beer can at the tree and it bounced off and spun lazily to a stop in the hardened dirt.

His generator suddenly sputtered to a stop and he felt a strange emotion, he felt sorry for himself. There were multiple gas cans stockpiled just a few feet away and it would just take a few minutes for him to refuel the generator but he finally caved. His addiction that had been lurking in the shadows now showed itself. It had been waiting for an excuse and this was it. Re-entering the motorhome, Edgar ripped open the bag of pills and as it usually did at this time in his dream, every sound, every image and every action appeared in slow motion. He could see himself placing that first pill in his mouth and could again taste the slightly metallic flavour as he swallowed it and reached for another. His addiction, what he used to call his lover, was back. Awakening with a start, Edgar knew that there was only one thing that mattered and that was to satisfy his lover. He needed to find more drugs.

34

P rior to leaving Tofino, Tessa and Jaime debated whether they should first go to Vancouver or Seattle, looking for other survivors. Jaime was always hungry for knowledge, wanting to learn more about why they had survived and to try and learn more about the virus. More information was probably available in the larger centres but Tessa again proved mature beyond her years in pointing out if San Diego and San Francisco was essentially war zones, why would other large cities not be the same?

Tessa didn't say much but when she talked, Jaime soon learned she was one to be listened too. Thinking back she couldn't help but agree with Tessa's point that when she left the university and escaped in JayJay, she probably knew as much as anyone in the world about what had happened. Now that she had that information from Slinky she knew even more. It's not that Tessa didn't want to go to Vancouver, she did, but now didn't feel like the right time.

Jaime thought long and hard about their conversation, did she now really know all there was to know? Is there more information out there and if so, where? She couldn't access any mainframes or the CDC computer database and the internet had been down forever. Knowing the material on her laptops would be the most current and if there was anything more to discover, it was with what she already had.

"Are you sleeping any better Tessa?" Jaime was in the galley making a couple of salmon sandwiches.

"Ya, a little but I seem to feel every single movement when I lie down. It doesn't bother me during the day or when I stand up but I don't think I slept more than ten minutes straight." Tessa was struggling with a little nausea but had not yet been sick, to Jaime's knowledge anyways. Jaime knew how she was feeling as she felt the same way during her first sailing trip. Growing out of it, she had never again been seasick and hoped she never would.

Tessa was plotting their position on a chart and confirmed they were now off the coast of central Washington. The weather was perfect and the winds moderate, perfect for some aggressive sailing to put some miles behind them. Tessa was either a quick study or Jaime was a good instructor as by the time they reached southern California, Tessa could handle JayJay all by herself.

They sailed just offshore of Malibu so Tessa could see the palatial homes that she had previously seen on TV. As they continued to head south Tessa spotted the ferris wheel on the Santa Monica pier. Jaime brought JayJay in closer and as they slowly sailed by they both saw movement up on the deck of the pier.

Jaime luffed the sail as they watched a skinny redheaded man rollerblading, ducking in and out of various garbage cans and pieces of debris laid out on the deck. It looked like he was doing a slalom course as he came to the end of the pier, forcibly hitting the railing he looked at his watch and let out a scream, pumping his fist in the air.

They were now close enough to hear what he had said. "New record!"

With his chest still heaving and his aloha shirt plastered to his sweaty torso his eyes now quickly focused out at the sailboat that was now just off the end of the pier. He slightly tilted his head, seemingly questioning what he was seeing.

Jaime waved. He waved back.

"Are you real?" he called out.

Jaime had been watching their depth and with the wind and waves pushing them closer, she needed to head back out to deeper water. Jaime shouted out. "We'll be back," as she expertly manoeuvered JayJay back into the wind and tacked, bringing JayJay about and heading slightly offshore. They quickly dropped anchor in fifty feet of water and let the wind and waves push them far enough back for the anchor to take a deep bite into the sandy bottom. Jaime started to remove the inflatable and they both looked back at the pier. He was still there, his long red hair flapping in the breeze but they were too far away to see any expression on his face.

"What if he's dangerous, like that guy in San Francisco?" Tessa asked.

They both looked back at him again and he had barely moved. He was watching them intently, his only movement was brushing the hair out of his eyes. He wore a loud Hawaiian shirt and board shorts with bright orange socks. He sure didn't look dangerous.

Jaime hesitated but she knew they had to be careful. "Bring your rifle but hide it under a towel." Jamie was now very confident in Tessa's prowess with the gun. "We'll go talk to him and see what happens."

The inflatable was a little more unwieldy then her old tender and it was helpful to have another set of hands as they dropped it into the water. Jaime rowed while Tessa sat at the back, her foot resting on the hidden rifle. When they were close enough to converse with him she stopped and turned the little boat sideways, it rode high on the small swells beside the pier.

"You didn't answer my question," he called out.

Jaime looked up at him and replied, "Yes we are real. I am Jaime and this is Tessa."

"I'm Billy," he called back. "What do you need the gun for?"

Both Tessa and Jaime looked down at the rifle, it was still completely covered by the towel. They looked at each other quizzically.

"I'm in the army, or I used to be in the army," he said quickly. "I know a gun when I see one." Hesitating slightly he asked, "Do you want a root beer?" Tessa couldn't help but giggle at the question.

They spoke for another few minutes and made the decision to row to a small float that was connected up to the pier by a sloping ramp. As Jaime rowed to the float, Billy excitedly bladed back down the pier and started to head down the ramp.

They watched as he immediately picked up speed on his rollerblades. When he grabbed the railing that did little to slow him down but it did turn him around. Now coming down the ramp backwards he grabbed the railing once again, turning him this time forward just as he lost his balance. Two summersaults and a hard landing later, Billy had arrived on the float.

Both of them were still giggling as they slowly approached the float. Billy seemed no worse for wear but they could see multiple scrapes and scabs on his knees. This obviously wasn't his first fall.

"Hi, I'm Billy," he said again. They talked for an hour. It was one of the most interesting hours of Jaime's life.

35

J aime and Tessa had agreed to meet Billy back at the dock at noon tomorrow. He was very excited and wished the girls a good night sleep as he slowly made his way up the ramp and skated off down the pier.

Jaime had headed south and anchored behind the breakwater at the entrance to Marina Del Ray to spend the night. After a quick trip ashore to let Brandy stretch her legs, they returned to JayJay to start dinner. They had already gone through all the fresh vegetables that Tessa had brought and were now back to dried and processed foods. Jaime made a wonderful smoked salmon penne in a cream sauce and even though it came from a package, the sauce tasted great. Over dinner they had each admitted that they really didn't miss milk but what they both had a soft spot for, and what they missed most, was cheese. Staying up much later than normal, they chatted about a variety of things but the majority of the time they discussed Billy. Could he be trusted? Was he safe? Both were impressed by his story but neither of them was prepared to unequivocally say yes to him joining up with them.

Tessa had said, "Well if we choose not to, we should just sail away in the morning so we don't have to see him ever again. He seems like a really sweet guy and it would be hard to disappoint him."

Billy had told them everything about himself, especially his last ten years. He was a combat engineer for the Army Rangers and had served three terms in Afghanistan and Iraq. Three years ago his unit was ambushed by the Taliban after they had brought much needed food and medical supplies to a remote village. Pinned down and taking casualties, reinforcements were almost there when a rocket propelled grenade exploded nearby, killing another Ranger and severely wounding Billy.

After the Taliban turned tail when the odds weren't in their favour, a helicopter was able to medi-vac Billy back to the advanced surgical hospital in Kandahar where over the next ten days he underwent two lifesaving surgeries. Flown to Germany he underwent another surgery there before being flown back to the States. During another two surgeries at Walter Reed Army Medical Centre, Billy had a permanent titanium plate attached to his skull. Billy had little if any recollections of this time period and little memories for the next year as he was hospitalized and heavily sedated. His brain injury did affect his memory and in reality, that wasn't all bad considering some of the treatment he witnessed other wounded warriors receiving. Still carrying a dime sized piece of shrapnel in his brain, Billy had been initially warned by his surgeons to limit if not eliminate all physical activity. Not prepared for a life of inactivity, Billy had instantly rebelled and that started what he had explained as the worst time of his life.

Billy had told them that when he finally got his act together he realized that he was addicted to painkillers. The army doctor's solution to that was just to try and give him more and different drugs and Billy had vociferously rebelled. He had spent over a month being forcibly restrained before he was institutionalized, diagnosed with severe PTSD. Billy told an amazing story of how he weaned himself off the drugs and eventually winning his freedom from the hospital with the help of his local Congressman. Finally free from the army he was lucky enough to be placed in a new and ground breaking brain injury outpatient program at Cedars-Sinai in Los Angeles. Shortly thereafter, as he had put it, "the world crapped out."

It was Billy's honesty more than anything that impressed Jaime. He knew he had a brain injury and he knew it had forever changed him. Admitting to nightmares and debilitating headaches, he had refused painkillers and narcotics. Like everything else in his life, he would handle it his way. Billy said his brain injury in many ways had changed him for the better. The fact that he knew he had become addicted to drugs and was strong enough to do something to correct it, spoke a lot about his fortitude and character.

Tessa had asked him how had he changed and he said he was finally happy and didn't feel like he had to prove himself every day. He was still competitive which explained his rollerblading slalom exhibition but he now enjoyed the simple things in life. Simply put he was just happy in the moment. "I'm a lot simpler now than what I used to be. I never realized how beautiful a flower could be or took the time to marvel at the structure of a bird's feather. It all just feels right now," he had said.

Tessa finally supported Billy and was convinced he posed no threat but Jaime still had her doubts. She had seen firsthand in medical school doing rounds in the local hospital of the mood swings and potential for violence that some with brain injuries possessed. They finally agreed after a very long discussion to test him tomorrow.

Billy was waiting for them on the small dock adjacent to the pier. As they got closer and prepared to drop anchor they were finally able to make out what was on the dock with Billy. A small suitcase, a duffel bag and a long chrome clothes rack filled with what looked like a hundred Hawaiian aloha shirts. Tessa was already giggling as they started to row over.

According to the plan, they stayed about twenty feet off of the dock. Billy was drinking a root beer and looked rather perplexed when Jaime stopped rowing. The small bag beside Tessa's feet held her pistol. Although Jaime had insisted that they bring the weapon, Tessa disagreed but had eventually relented.

"What's with all the shirts Billy?" Jaime called out.

"Well, I know you don't have room for them all so I thought you could help me pick some out." He waved his arm towards the rack like a game show hostess, his face completely serious.

"Tessa and I have talked Billy and I'm afraid we don't like you and you won't be coming with us." Jaime studied him closely for a reaction.

Billy stared back but he couldn't keep the disappointment from creeping across his face. His body language softened and his shoulders sagged. He looked over at all his shirts and then back at the girls.

He spoke slowly, his words were measured and sincere. "Well, I guess I understand. I like the both of you but if you don't like me, well, then, I guess that's that."

Billy reached down for the duffel and reached inside. Jaime watched him intently and adjusted her legs so that Tessa could access the bag that held the pistol.

Standing back up, Billy held out a couple of cans of root beer. "Do you want a root beer?"

Jaime was still watching him, looking for any signs of aggression or upset.

"Do you know why we don't like you Billy?" Jaime was still testing him, pushing him a little harder. She wanted to see how he would react under more stress.

Billy looked back, still holding the root beer. "Well, I don't really know. I imagine you are afraid and are being careful and, I guess, that is smart. You guys know more about me than just about anyone else." The look of disappointment was evident now as he put the root beer down on the dock and started to pick up his things.

"I saw another guy about two weeks ago," Billy said over his shoulder, he was pointing towards the shore. "He never saw me but he was armed to the teeth and he looked mean, really mean. He was talking to himself and looked like he was spoiling for a fight, sort of all crazy. You girls will need to be careful."

Jaime was temporarily intrigued by the thoughts of more survivors. "Goodbye Billy". Jaime started to row away back to JayJay.

"I'll leave some root beer for you." Billy carefully placed the cans on the edge of the platform and then he waved, but not very enthusiastically. He didn't appear angry or upset and that's what Jaime was looking for. The look on his face though was heartbreaking. Picking up his suitcase and an armful of shirts he slowly headed up the walkway.

As Jaime continued to row away, Tessa was looking at her, not saying anything but her face belied her feelings. "I think he is fine Jaime," Tessa said, looking back over her shoulder at Billy. He was heading back down the ramp for another load.

Jaime said, "Let's just watch for a minute." They watched as Billy finally cleared the dock of his possessions, everything now up on the pier. He had left the two cans of root beer behind. They floated halfway between the dock and JayJay in the rising heat of the afternoon. Billy waved one last time, this time purposefully and started walking down the pier towards the beach. The wheeled rack of Hawaii shirts clattered noisily along behind him.

Jaime spun the little boat around and started rowing back towards the dock as Tessa broke out into a broad smile.

Billy was more than overjoyed when he was told he could join up with Jaime and Tessa. After a couple of somewhat uncomfortable hugs he did share how disappointed he was in their initial decision and how he thought that their denial was due to his injury. Jaime was completely upfront and honest with him about what they did and why and Billy showed no emotion at all throughout the somewhat lengthy explanation. Afterwards, given the same set of circumstances, he agreed he would have probably done the same. Jaime had given him the double bunked third stateroom on JayJay and Billy did not hesitate in loading his few supplies into it with military precision. Only half of the Hawaiian aloha shirts had made the trip off the dock.

Anchored just off of Santa Monica, they took the early part of afternoon to get to know one another and share their experiences. Billy's time had been as tumultuous and sometimes as dangerous as both Jaime and Tessa's as he was right in the middle of Los Angeles the entire time. Billy had a very straightforward, honest and simplistic approach to explaining things that Jaime really admired and she thought he would make a great teacher or instructor. His advanced military training and experiences no doubt had a lot to do with that. Billy did not come across as well educated, in an academic sense, but his intelligence was never in doubt as he described what he had experienced and witnessed. He spoke quietly about the people around him that had initially died and his voice became even softer when talking about the thousands and millions of deaths that followed. Death was nothing new to Billy, he had killed and had almost been killed. His demeanor was almost contrite and both Jaime and Tessa could tell that although he had the toolkit for violence, those days were now behind him.

Billy told them he came from a ranching background and Jaime recalled some of the things her father used to say about the farmers and ranchers that he had met. For the most part unencumbered by academic thinking, all they did was use common sense to properly care for the land and raise and grow the food we all ate. Smiling, she recalled him saying that if there was ever a catastrophic event and the only people that were left were academics, they wouldn't last a week. Somewhat apropos now she thought.

They had spent the rest of the afternoon walking in and around the Santa Monica area. Billy had spent most of the last few months here and had gotten to know the area quite well. Showing them a number of what he called safe houses, he had stashed food and supplies at each location, preparing for whatever happened next. The only unusual think was that each location had cases and cases of root beer. Tessa was teasingly questioning him about that and although the answers slightly changed the bottom line was simple. Billy just really liked root beer.

They had returned to JayJay and made the quick trip south to Long Beach harbour where they would anchor for the night. After dinner and while all three of them cleaned up Jaime had asked Billy, "What do you think our priorities are Billy?"

Billy was drying and putting away some dishes, seemingly opening every cupboard until he finally found their proper place. He was quick to point out he wasn't in charge here but added matter-of-factly, "Just like any survival situation, personal safety, water, food then shelter."

"We try and share the responsibilities so what areas do you want to handle Billy? What ones are you good at?"

"I'm good at all of those Jamie." Was the simple and honest reply but his sly smile gave it away. Billy knew that there were few people better equipped in any kind of survival situation than he was, brain injured or not.

Before it got too dark, Tessa showed Billy the small wind turbine that she had repaired and he inspected her handiwork from top to bottom. Looking over at Tessa, he gave her an approving nod and a thumbs up as he knew good work when he saw it.

They had spent a star filled night anchored in Long Beach and the plan was to check around the harbour for easy resources, specifically food and fuel and to, as always, look for other survivors. After a breakfast of smoked salmon, fresh cinnamon rolls and coffee, Billy asked, "Do you want the fuel and food brought back here or just marked and identified?"

"I don't think we need to start collecting things just yet and we'll be back in San Diego shortly so I'd call it just a scouting trip." Jaime handed Billy a crudely drawn map of the harbour. "Tessa and I will take this area here and Billy why don't you take this big container and dock facility here."

"Can I take Brandy with me?" Billy asked.

"After what happened to me in San Francisco Billy, I'm a little shy about wild dogs. I think it's best if she sits this one out."

Knowing if he armed himself, there would be no problems whatsoever but he preferred not to do that. After a lifetime spent handling and carrying weapons, he had little interest in them anymore and had no firearms in his possession. "Understood," Billy said. If there was only one thing that you learned in the army it was how to take an order.

Both Jaime and Tessa enjoyed their day exploring with one exception. What they didn't expect to encounter were all the rats, hundreds and hundreds of them, running around at will, basically now unafraid of humans. They came back a little earlier than planned and Jaime had rowed Tessa out to JayJay. When she was rowing back to shore she saw Billy approaching.

"What have you got there?" Jaime was just nudging into the small harbourmasters dock.

Billy was carrying a large navy duffel bag and he turned it over and spilled the contents out onto the weathered planking. She quickly saw a compass, a large military looking knife in a scabbard, a big can of pepper spray, a set of walkie talkies, a box of extra hot pepperoni and about a dozen cans of root beer.

Jamie said, "Walkie talkies, that's smart Billy. And that's a pretty mean looking knife."

"It's a knock off, probably crap because it's made in China," he said, putting his things back in the bag. "It'll do but I wish they would have let me keep my old knife."

During their trip back to San Diego, Jamie and Tessa put Billy through the paces of learning how to sail JayJay. He was a quick study as they had both anticipated but there were still a few things that they needed to repeat again and again. It was obvious that Billy had some sort of short term memory loss but it wasn't anything that they couldn't work through.

After arriving in San Diego they had pretty much settled into a standard daily routine within the first week. A quick breakfast just after dawn and they all got to the work at hand. Billy put even Tessa to shame with his work ethic and quite often almost single handily had completed their chores and tasks by lunchtime. It took a while for them to figure out what was going on but it soon became evident, Billy felt obligated to ensure all the work was done before he set out on his explorations. Most days Billy would be gone just after lunch and return late in the afternoon. It turned out he had stockpiled a huge amount of food and supplies in various locations both inside and outside of the marina where they were moored. Billy fessed up and then marked all the locations for the cached food and supplies on a local map. It took some doing but Jaime had convinced Billy that their situation was not dire and that he could tone it down a bit. Billy did just that and started exploring the areas around Mission Bay just for fun. Jaime and Tessa would occasionally catch sight of him off in the distance, peddling his mountain bike, his red hair streaming out behind him.

A few weeks after they had returned to San Diego, Tessa was scrubbing some clams that Billy had dug up earlier in the day when she heard the deep throbbing of engines outside. Running topside she saw Jaime helping to tie up what looked to be about a thirty six foot sport fisher with Billy at the wheel high up on the flying bridge.

"Wow. Where did you get that Billy?" Tessa was looking over the gleaming boat. It looked brand new.

"You know, a little birdy told me I should take it." Billy was now climbing down the stainless steel ladder and proudly jumped out onto the dock. "What do you think?"

"Very nice but a little overkill just for fishing don't you think?" Billy had never really fished before and once Tessa had shown him the basics, a day didn't go by that he didn't drop a line into the water. Tessa's intuition told her something else might be up but she let it pass as her and Jaime exchanged quizzical looks. Billy stood back admiring his new boat. He especially liked the name, it was written in big black script across the transom, *Gunslinger Two*.

Over dinner Billy solemnly told the girls that he had decided to move off of JayJay, so he could have his own space and they could too. He rambled on for a while, providing all the reasons why he thought he should have his own place not realizing that it didn't take that much convincing for the girls to agree. All thought that it was a smart thing to do.

A week later, after being back in San Diego for just a little over a month, Billy came back with a big surprise.

Billy figured he had either secured or located over two thousand gallons of diesel fuel and twice that much in gasoline just in Mission Bay so he had no qualms about taking Gunslinger for a spin every once in a while. He also knew there were millions of gallons of fuel in the area, especially with all the military facilities close by. Tessa had been right, his new boat was a little too big for fishing within the bay but he hoped to take it offshore to do some fishing later this summer. Today for his afternoon sojourn, Billy decided to take Gunslinger and go exploring from the water. Billy still liked to roller blade and ride his bike as he found the exercise and physical activity lessened the severity of his headaches, which he felt were now diminishing both in number and intensity.

It had been hot and sunny for a couple of days and Billy enjoyed the slightly cooler air washing over him as he sped along the calm waters of Mission Bay in Gunslinger. Always amazed at how much more you could see from the flying bridge, he was cruising around near the Sea World complex watching a small group of pelicans dive for fish. Billy didn't know why but he had always liked pelicans.

Looking like some ancient dinosaur they dove on the numerous schools of small baitfish in the bay. There were two things that had been unsettling for everyone in their new environment, one was how quiet everything had become and two was the lack of movement. There were no cars or trucks, no people and no airplanes. The only things that moved were the animals and the occasional plant that swayed in the breeze. It was the lack of noise though that stood out and Billy could hear the splashes of the pelicans from hundreds of feet away.

As Billy motored along enjoying the sound of the engine and how it reverberated off the nearby structures, his eyes were automatically drawn to some movement. He looked again as he thought his eyes might be deceiving him but there it was. A large white pickup truck with a camper was driving slowly over the Ingraham Street Bridge. Billy stared dumfounded and watched it for a few seconds before accelerating towards the bridge. He had caught up to the slow moving vehicle in no time and powered Gunslinger down to match the trucks speed. The truck started to slow, then it stopped and Billy promptly put his boat in neutral and it gently came down off of plane. He stared up at the bridge and raised both hands above his head and waved.

Sam Noappu hadn't seen another living person, except for his daughter Becca, since he had left the cruise ship. He just stared out the window at this skinny guy with long red hair and a crisp white t-shirt waving at him from the flying bridge of this boat that floated far below the bridge. Everything had run through Sam's mind since the killer flu had started and especially since they appeared to be the only survivors. Why had everyone else died except for him and his daughter? In a state of almost perpetual shock he had only been able to hold it together because of Becca.

Months and months travelling and they had only seen dead bodies, until now. Convincing himself that he wasn't imagining things, he placed his hand on the door handle.

"Stay here honey," Sam said to his daughter who was seated in the passenger seat, drawing on a small piece of cardboard.

Billy saw the driver's side door tentatively open and he manoeuvered Gunslinger just a little closer to the bridge. "Hey, Hello!" Billy yelled. The bridge towered over Billy and Gunslinger but with the world now an eerily quiet place, there wouldn't be any problem in being able to communicate.

Sam walked slowly over to the high guardrail and stepped up onto the curb as there were no sidewalks on this side of the bridge. Grabbing the rail he looked down at Billy. Having to literally force himself to speak he called out, "Hello to you." His normal beautiful tenor had been replaced with a raspy harshness.

"Hey, I'm Billy and we have a place over there." Billy pointed behind him back in the direction of De Anza Cove where they had set up their little camp. De Anza Cove was well protected from any weather coming in off the Pacific as it was on the shore side of Mission Bay. There was a big park with shade trees, lots of open spaces and there was even a small river that emptied into the bay close by.

Sam took a second to comprehend what he had just heard, clearing his throat he said, "Did you say we?"

"Yes." Billy replied, rapidly nodding his head.

Sam again hesitated, just trying to absorb what was a sudden bit of normalcy in a world that had gone mad. Sam just stared down at Billy waiting for more information. Billy just stared back up at him.

Sam finally shouted down. "How many are there?"

"Three of us," Billy called back. "Jaime, Tessa and me. Oh, and Brandy, she is a dog."

Sam continued to just try and process what was happening. The scenario of no other survivors and then there had to be other survivors had plagued him since the beginning. His only constant was Becca and now this. Being in show business since his teens, it wasn't very often that Sam Noappu was at a loss for words, but now was one of those times.

Billy reached down into an ice chest beside him and held up what looked like a can. "Would you like a root beer?"

The skin around Sam's eyes creased into multiple furrows as his mind tried to process what his ears just heard. Suddenly aware of his rapid heartbeat and shallow breaths Sam just held onto the railing almost feeling feint. It was a hot day and the afternoon sun was beating down against him and he could feel small droplets of sweat starting to move on his body. Suddenly feeling like he was in a vacuum, his head felt fuzzy and he had the impression that the world had suddenly slowed down.

Standing at the rail for another few minutes Sam continued to converse with Billy. Sam gripped the railing hard, still feeling weird, sort of like the first time he got stoned. It was like being a half beat behind the music and not being able to catch up. Even though he was sweating, Sam had goose bumps on his arms and a chill swept across his back. When Sam started to walk back to the truck he had to purposefully place one foot in front of the other.

Becca was now in the driver's seat looking out the window trying to see what was going on and she looked apprehensive. When he opened the door she lithely jumped over the console and he climbed in and started the big

Silverado. Surprisingly Becca never said a word as he drove down the bridge and took the off ramp and then stopped when he had reached ground level. Exiting the vehicle he opened the extended cab door behind him and grabbed a Glock handgun that he had found in another vehicle. Placing it in his waistband he covered it with his shirt and told Becca to stay in the truck. Gently shutting the door he started walking out across the overgrown grassy area to where Billy had nosed Gunslinger up onto shore and was waiting for him. While on the bridge Sam had agreed to walk down to meet Billy and now he wondered if he had made a mistake. He still didn't feel very good, his mouth was dry and his legs felt wobbly. Sam's only concern was for Becca and he felt a sense of panic set in like he had never felt before. Pressing on he approached Billy and stopped.

It was an awkward meeting, with long periods of silence as Billy's exuberance was parried by Sam's feelings of uncertainty. Sam sensed there might be something wrong with Billy, but under the circumstances that wouldn't be a surprise as he also felt something was wrong with him. Billy did everything to try and convince Sam to come in the boat and go back to meet Jaime and Tessa but that wasn't going to happen. Sam never mentioned anything about Becca and although he found Billy friendly and almost overly accommodating, he needed time to think about all this. Billy had explained to Sam down to the last detail where they had set up camp and although Sam was reluctant, he said he would drive over there later today. Billy was a little puzzled by all this but he remembered the girl's reaction when they first met him so he quickly put it out of his mind.

Billy returned to De Anza Cove and could hardly contain himself as he told Jaime and Tessa about Sam. They talked at length about the chance meeting and were both excited and a little concerned as Billy relayed Sam's standoffishness. It had been a couple of hours of waiting until they saw a big white truck and camper slowly driving along Mission Bay Drive just below the freeway. It stopped far across from the moorage and someone got out. "That's him," Billy said as he started to wave.

Tessa quickly grabbed the binoculars and had a look. "It's a man and he has binoculars too," Tessa said as they looked at each other from across the cove. Tessa raised her hand to wave and so did Jaime.

"There is someone else!" Tessa shouted. "A little girl, I think. Maybe five years old." That caused a minor flap as the three of them all wanted to have a look.

Sam put down the binoculars after a minute and helped Becca back into the truck. Having had a good look at the two women and Billy and even the dog, he looked in through the open door at his beautiful little girl. She had been through so much and had seen things that no child should ever even imagine and had done it with the maturity of someone much older.

"Were those were real people daddy?" Becca asked.

"Yes honey, they were real." Sam was conflicted. They had been alone since they left the ship in a world too horrible to describe. They had somehow survived and had now found other survivors but Sam was more hesitant than happy. His only concern was Becca. He would do anything for her, she was all he had. But what if something happened to him?

Sam took a deep breath and decided that Becca had a better chance with a larger group. The fact that two of them were women had sealed the deal.

"Are we going over there?" Becca asked expectantly.

Sam spoke softly, almost apprehensively. "Yes honey."

38

Becca had adjusted quicker to their new surroundings than Sam did. They spent their first night in the camper, parked just a short walk away from where the new group was moored but Sam finally relented to Becca's pleading and agreed to move into the stateroom on JayJay that Billy previously occupied. Becca loved her dad but missed her mother tremendously and the close company of Jaime and Tessa seemed to comfort her and she was much more talkative and vibrant, much more like the child she used to be.

Their story of survival was eerily similar to everyone else's. Sitting on blankets on the little beach adjacent to the marina, Sam told their story. He was a singer of traditional Hawaiian songs and had been working in a show on a cruise ship based in Los Angeles. Becca had flown over to join him from Hawaii with her aunt just before all travel was suspended due to the flu outbreak. Mahleah Noappu, Sam's wife was to join them but had not been able to fly out and had been trapped in Hawaii. Eventually losing contact with her as the situation worsened, Sam quietly recalled his last cell phone call with her and out of earshot of Becca, admitted that his wife was quite sick.

Sam solemnly recounted how they witnessed the event unfold from beginning to end on the cruise ship docked in Long Beach harbour. It was impossible for Sam to not become emotional when describing the desperation and violence they had witnessed both on the ship and ashore. Everyone could relate as no one had expected the depravity and violence that had occurred, especially in the larger cities. Tessa was quick to point out that like almost anything else, the good things would have been harder to spot than the bad, but all agreed the worst of the human race was saved for last.

Sam shyly admitted they had stayed on the ship for three full months after the last person onboard had died. Deathly afraid of taking Becca out into what he had witnessed, they had holed up with plenty of food and water. Showing little emotion now, he painted a vivid picture of the onshore destruction and violence that finally waned into nothing but silence. Finally finding the nerve to go ashore to what used to be Los Angeles, he described it as a complete hell hole. Billy quickly echoed that sentiment.

Numbed by what had happened and with Becca's safety his only priority Sam found a truck and camper and escaped. Travelling north by siphoning gas from other vehicles, they had made it all the way up the coast to Eureka California. They had stayed there a few weeks and then made their way from town to town in northern California before eventually heading for Lake Tahoe. Sam had performed there a few summers ago and thought it would be safer than the more heavily populated regions of California. Caught in a series of snowstorms in the mountains, they were trapped for almost a week and had run out of food and propane before a break in the weather and melting snow allowed them to escape. After that, they decided to stick to warmer climes and spent some time in the Palm Springs area before heading south. They had not seen anyone alive in all their travels until Billy spotted them on their tenth day in the San Diego area.

"It's been so hard on Becca but she has been a real trooper." Sam lovingly looked over at her as Billy was showing her how to fold a paper airplane. "She is all I have."

Jaime had shown Sam all the emails and had given him her theory's on what had happened. Recalling his heritage, he told Jaime that three of his four grandparents were of pure Hawaiian ancestry and he was considered seventy five percent Hawaiian. Being the most racially mixed state in the union, Hawaii had about one tenth of its population referring to themselves as Pacific Islanders. "There are only a few thousand pure Hawaiians left." Sam said he recalled reading that somewhere. "Less than ten thousand for sure."

Sam and Jamie talked late into the night about her thoughts and the so called healthy gene until Sam finally told her that he didn't really understand all the science stuff saying, "I do appreciate you sharing all this Jaime but I left home at sixteen and never finished high school, all this stuff is way over my head." Behind Jaime's back Tessa silently mouthed 'me too' which caused both Sam and her to start laughing. That caused Sam to take pause as he tried to think of the last time he had laughed. It was well past midnight when they gathered up their things and Sam carried the now sleeping Becca off to her bunk. As Sam kissed her cheek goodnight, he could see that her eyelids were rapidly twitching. I hope it's a good dream he thought to himself, the nightmare may now be over.

As the days passed their level of comfort with each other grew and it wasn't an exaggeration to say that this is the best all of them had felt since everything had started. Tessa and Sam often took some time after dinner to chat about their ancestry and heritage. Surprisingly, both cultures had legends and stories about the end of the world and how man would be punished if it didn't look after Mother Nature and the planet properly. There were many interesting discussions that circled back to that topic and the after dinner chats became a regular part of their routine.

Unlike Tessa who rarely spoke, but when she did it was always worth listening too, Billy spoke far too often. His thoughts and opinions were often rambling and somewhat scattered, he was far more coherent when he kept his speech and thought processes short and simple. However there were times, like when he spoke about the army, that his thought processes were crystal clear. Billy never came out and badmouthed the army but you knew it was always just right below the surface. He like so many other wounded veterans felt that they were abandoned when they needed help the most which is exactly the opposite of what any soldier is trained to do. It was the one topic that seemed to sort through the clutter in his mind. It was too bad they weren't able to tap into that side of him more often.

Billy and Sam quickly became friends and the group's routine solidified around their little camp at De Anza Cove, they all quickly became like a big family. Everyone doted on Becca and she loved them all but by far Becca's favourite was Brandy. Often napping together in the heat of the day in the shade, they soon became inseparable and where you found one, you found both.

Becca also started to monopolize a lot of Tessa's time. Wanting to dress like Tessa and help her with all her chores which as every parent knows, doesn't make things any easier but Tessa embraced the attention. They were the closest by age and Tessa was accustomed to being around a lot of children as she had had dozens of nieces and nephews. Tessa slowly started to communicate more openly as Becca routinely bombarded her with questions. Sometimes Sam just marvelled at the change in his daughter in just the few short weeks that they had been here. She was a little girl again. When Tessa taught Becca how to make bannock, which is a native pan bread, Becca demanded to be able to teach Tessa how to do something. In under a week in the warm waters of De Anza Cove, Becca taught Tessa how to swim.

39

Jaime just wasn't comfortable being around him anymore, he gave her the creeps. Sam wouldn't even talk to him and warned him to not go anywhere near Becca. Billy could barely tolerate him and became noticeably agitated whenever he was around. Edgar Barnes had in less than three weeks become somewhat of a pariah.

Edgar had appeared out of the blue one stormy afternoon almost three weeks ago and his first impression wasn't a good one. He had noticed their camp while driving on the freeway and haphazardly made his way over arriving drunk, unwashed and foul mouthed. His first words as he approached seeing them all standing out on the dock was, "Fuck ya, we have some ladies!"

Jaime noticed his condition right away and asked him if he was on drugs. His response didn't exactly enamour him to the group as he sarcastically replied that he had a prescription for everything that he took. Never invited to join them he nonetheless had been hanging around even though he wasn't exactly made to feel welcome. Some days he just sat under the awning of his motorhome in the parking lot of the marina, watching them. Other days he would drive off only to return in a day or two. The story he told of his own survival had so many holes in it that it was laughable and no one believed his story about being a landscaper at a golf course in Temecula. They all thought he was a letch and was trouble, and they were right.

Yesterday Tessa had been sitting alone outside on the dock cleaning and oiling her rifle when Edgar approached. He tried to make small talk but Tessa wasn't interested and she just continued to ignore him. Tessa was about to put her rifle into its lamb's wool case when Edgar challenged her to a shooting competition. The loser, naturally, having to do anything the winner wanted. It wasn't often that Tessa showed any emotion but she suddenly became angry and upset and unzipping a pocket in her gun case she rapidly loaded three cartridges into her magazine. Standing up, she raised her rifle and looked at Edgar's motorhome some eighty yards distant. A large skull and cross-bones flag flew from the raised satellite dish and she slammed a cartridge into the chamber and fired. A huge portion of the satellite dish exploded and Tessa expertly worked the bolt and fired two more shots. The flag now hung limply from the destroyed satellite dish that had slipped over the side of the motorhome connected only by its electrical cable. Tessa snapped the bolt back and the last cartridge ejected and landed at Edgar's feet, it spun wildly, slowly losing momentum as a small wisp of smoke curled from its open end. Not entirely by accident, Tessa swung the rifle around, the barrel missing Edgar's face by inches as his head recoiled from the acrid smell of the exploded gunpowder. Walking away Tessa stopped just as Edgar was about to say something. She turned around and in an unemotional tone told him to leave her alone. It was the first time that

Edgar didn't have the last word in a conversation. Tessa then deliberately walked down the dock towards JayJay.

The gunshots had naturally brought everyone immediately back to JayJay and after a quick meeting they reached a decision to move away from their current moorage. Billy had already found a suitable location which was the Bahia Resort Hotel Marina in Santa Barbara Cove on the other side of the bay. Hoping Edgar would get the message and leave them alone they decided to make the move the following morning.

It had taken the first part of the day to remove a number of existing boats and yachts to make room for both JayJay and Gunslinger at the new moorage. Just as the work moving the boats was complete and they were tying them off, Edgar came strolling down the dock from the hotel parking lot. To say they were disappointed was an understatement.

"You should see my new wheels man," Edgar said to Billy who really wasn't interested. "It's a Thor, forty footer with a big Cummins diesel. Took me all morning to hot wire it. Nicest motorhome I've ever seen man. Black and silver, go Raiders!"

Billy just ignored Edgar. He knew some people like him in the military, lazy, brutish oafs who couldn't be trusted with any task, no matter how small. Billy knew they all needed to work together and act like a team but Edgar wasn't part of their team and every day that went by he liked him less and less and it was starting to show, which he knew wasn't a good thing. For the first time since coming back from Afghanistan, Billy was tense and could feel the anger just below the surface. He didn't like feeling that way anymore.

"How about you sweetie? I know you want to see it?" Edgar said as he thrust his hips towards Jaime, his hand grasping his crotch.

Jaime was really tired of the nonstop sexual innuendo directed towards her and Tessa. She briefly stared at him, lips creased in anger, but ended up just silently turning and walking away.

"Your loss." He laughed. "Your loss."

Billy gave Edgar a long hard look and told the group he was going to check the hotel for supplies and would be back in an hour.

Jaime had previously asked Sam and Tessa to help her start unloading the storage lockers on JayJay. They had a good two days of work to remove everything and take a complete inventory. It was also decided it would be a good time to perform maintenance and do a top to bottom cleanup of their floating home. Lately their days had become a little lazy and Jaime didn't know if it was Edgar's influence or the fact that with Billy's daily exploratory sojourns, that they were completely organized and provisioned. More food and fuel than they could use in a year was stockpiled, neatly marked and protected from the weather. Tools, building supplies and wide assortment of just about anything you could think of was stored in empty semi-trailers, ready to be utilized or moved at a moment's notice. Jaime made a mental note to thank Billy and tell him how valuable his contributions are. Maybe I'll bake him a cake she thought.

Sam set up Becca at the end of the dock with a fishing rod and her water bottle. He wondered if she needed more sunscreen as all she was wearing was her little pink bikini. Sam reminded himself to bring out some sunscreen in a few minutes as the summer sun here was just as intense as

Hawaii. Becca immediately caught a small pile perch and was smiling and happy. Becca took fishing very seriously and was proud of the fact that she was not squeamish and could bait her own hook and handle bonking the fish. After having a short conversation with the brightly coloured perch she gently dropped it back into the water.

Sam had walked back to JayJay to help with the cleanup and Becca quickly moved down the dock of their new moorage following a school of small baitfish. She happened to look back toward the hotel and from this end of the dock she could now see a playground with swings and slides and a small castle with faded flags flying from the turrets. Squealing with delight she put down her fishing rod and ran back down the dock. As she passed JayJay she yelled out that she was going to the playground. Neither Sam, Jaime nor Tessa heard her.

Becca made her way up the ramp and out the gate and was running through the tall grass that used to be a lawn towards the far side of the hotel. As she rounded the corner she ran right into Edgar.

"Hey Becca, where are ya going?"

Becca almost breathlessly replied, "There is a playground with swings and a castle over there." She was pointing past the parking lot, a big smile showed her small perfectly white teeth.

Something clicked in Edgar. He hadn't felt it in many, many years. It was what almost constant therapy over the last ten years couldn't even begin to understand.

He held out his hand and said, "Show me."

Billy had found what he thought were some useful items in the hotel and was looking out the second story window of conference room when he saw Edgar holding Becca's hand walking through the parking lot. As Edgar approached what had to be his new motorhome, he turned around, looking quickly in each direction. He reached down and picked Becca up and opened the motorhomes door. Billy turned and ran for the stairs.

Billy was not the athlete and hardened Army Ranger he once was. His brain injury and repeated long hospital stays had diminished his once dominating physique into that of an average man. His training didn't dessert him though. He knew what was about to happen and he knew he had to stop it.

Becca struggled ferociously but Edgar had her pinned on the couch with his knee, one hand was across her mouth stifling her screams. The pain from her bites just enhanced his experience as his mind quickly flashed back to his previous rapes and he could barely contain himself, seeing each of them in order. Ripping off her bikini bottoms, he had just slid his pants down to his knees when the door burst open and Billy ran in.

Edgar barely had time to react before Billy's heel crashed into his chest, sending him flying. Edgar held up his arm in defence as he crouched down, groping at his pants for the big hunting knife he always carried. Billy grabbed his arm and severely twisted it up and back, spinning him back to the floor in front of the couch. Becca was frozen in fear, now standing on the couch with her back against the wall.

Billy quickly stepped across the now prone Edgar and applied the full weight of his own body to the arm. Edgars shoulder dislocated with a sickening pop just as his humerus snapped. Billy continued to twist sending the fractured bone through the skin, spraying Becca with blood.

Edgar's scream was more of a bellow as Billy dropped the now useless arm, raising his boot all in the same motion. He brought it down hard on the side of Edgar's face. Again and again and again, splattering brain matter everywhere. It was over in less than five seconds.

Becca leapt off the couch and ran for the door. She screamed long and loud, running as fast as she could back towards her father and JayJay.

40

"You are doing everything you can Sam. She is traumatized and it's going to take a little time." Jaime and Sam were sitting in the galley of JayJay discussing Becca's behaviour since the attempted rape.

Becca had withdrawn and had rarely spoken over the last five days. She clung to her father day and night and didn't want to be around Billy at all. Whether it was her own traumatic experience or if it was witnessing Billy personally carry out the death sentence that Edgar had carried for the last decade didn't matter. To try and make things easier on her, Billy had moved Gunslinger away, mooring it an adjacent marina to try and give Becca some more space. Billy had also moved the motorhome far inland to ensure Becca or anyone else never had to see it again. His initial plan was to light it on fire but it was summertime and there was always a wildfire risk so he just left the door open. Nature would look after the rest.

Jaime said, "I think she'll come back around soon but I think to help her we all need to try and get back into a normal routine." They had all been supporting Becca, holding her when she cried, being with her day and night. The thought process amongst them now was that they might not be helping her heal at all.

"My Grandmother used to say that kids will always adapt, it's the grownups that can't get over things." Tessa was putting out the last of the smoked salmon that she had brought from home.

"Last night all she kept saying is that she wanted to go home and see her mom. Over and over, she just wanted to go home," Sam said to no one in particular. They all knew that Sam's wife had been sick the last time they had spoken and there was little if any chance she survived. Sam couldn't bring himself to tell Becca and always just said that to keep her mom in her prayers and hopefully one day they will see each other again.

Becca had apparently finished her nap as she came out from their stateroom and climbed up onto Sam's lap, grabbing a piece of the salmon. That got everyone's attention as they had to almost force her to eat something even yesterday so this was a positive sign.

Becca looked directly at Jaime and said, "I want to go home."

"This is our home now Becca." Sam said stroking her long dark hair, he passed her the last piece of salmon and she delicately folded it and popped it into her mouth.

"I want to go back home, to Hawaii. I want to see my mommy and I don't want to be here anymore." The statement was said with considerable conviction and purpose and it made Becca sound much older than her six years.

Billy entered the main salon and stopped, looking nervously at Becca sitting on Sam's lap. After a hesitating, "Hi everybody," Billy gave a little wave.

Jaime was originally concerned that Billy might not understand Becca's reaction to him, but he understood completely and accepted it without complaint. They all knew what he had saved her from. To Billy, he was just doing what he was trained to do and asked everyone to forget about it.

"Umm, sorry, I just wanted to tell you that I'm going to catch the slack tide and go halibut fishing." Billy started to turn around to leave.

"Do you think we can all come?" Jaime asked, looking over at Becca to see her reaction as Becca loved to fish even more than Billy. For the first time since her trauma, Becca looked directly at Billy, her expression was neutral but she gave her head a slight nod yes.

Billy quickly said, "Sure that would be great."

The five of them spent the next four hours slowly drifting baits across a small but deep depression just inside the main channel of Mission Bay. Although the halibut eluded them this day they caught a number of medium sized sand bass. Becca's mood had improved significantly and they were all hoping that this was her first step back to her old self. On the way back to the marina Billy made a point of making some high speed swooping turns in the large skiff and Becca for the first time smiled. Tessa made a great dinner, carefully watched by Becca who had not immediately retreated to her room upon returning. Now both of them, helped by Sam had started in on the cleanup which didn't take long at all. Sam and Becca had gone outside and Tessa was now preparing the leftovers for use tomorrow when Jaime came into the galley and sat down.

"I've been thinking about what Becca said this morning." Jaime had learned that Tessa was never one for small talk and with her it was best to just get to the point.

Tessa was just finishing making the last of the fish cakes and said, "I don't remember her saying much of anything."

"She said she wanted to go home, back to Hawaii. I'm thinking that's not a bad idea." Jaime met Tessa's look as she was placing the fish cakes into the refrigerator.

Tessa sat down, drying her hands on a small towel. "Why Hawaii? What does it have that we don't have here?"

"I'm just recalling some of the information that my friend Jill Barber provided about that healthy gene and how it was more prevalent in pacific islanders than in other genetic groups. If that's why we survived, I wonder if there are more survivors there." Jaime was deep in thought, she was looking right through Tessa as her mind raced.

"Well Sam did say that he and his wife were almost full blooded Hawaiians." Tessa looked up as Sam walked back into the galley.

"Sam," Jaime was still deep in thought, not even looking at him when she spoke. "I am wondering if we should sail to Hawaii and see what is going on over there."

Sam was stunned. "I think Becca is doing much better now, she is outside watching Billy clean the barbeque."

Jaime said, "It's not her. Actually that didn't sound very nice, sorry. What I'm trying to say is that I am thinking that there is a much higher probability of larger groups of survivors there than here. Remember those emails I showed you about the healthy gene?"

"Ya, like I said I'm not very good with all the science stuff but this ancient DNA is supposed to be in more pacific islanders than in other people, right?" Sam asked.

"Right. And that one survivor I saw in San Francisco was a pacific islander and Edgar said his mother was from

Tonga." Jaime had looked around to ensure Becca wasn't within earshot.

"But that doesn't explain you and Billy and Tessa." Sam added.

"No it doesn't, that's what I need to try and understand. Tessa is aboriginal so a case could be made for some genetic transfer in the past. But for Billy and I . . ." Jaime's voice trailed off as for the first time in weeks she thought of her dad and her brother.

After a short hesitation she continued, "I need to be completely honest too, I want to try and find my dad. He was headed for New Guinea when Locust really took hold." Jaime was interrupted by Becca squealing as Billy chased her into the main salon with a small squirt gun. It appeared as things were well on their way to returning to normal.

Jaime was uncharacteristically quiet that night as they sat out on the dock after dinner. Everyone noticed it and it had started to become a little uncomfortable when Jaime excused herself. "Sorry guys, I just need some time to myself." As she made her way to her stateroom she said, "We'll all talk more tomorrow."

Jaime was up for most of the night. She reviewed Jill Barber's information for the umpteenth time and eventually fell asleep, fully dressed with papers strewn about the bed. Her dreams were vivid and she awoke with a start. She was dreaming of the last time she had seen Slinky. They were dancing and talking and laughing about his pirate story. Jaime's family history could be traced back to a doctor that served with Captain George Vancouver on his explorations of the south pacific. Maybe her ancestor took a wife and that's how her family inherited the healthy gene. Maybe her dad and her brother are alive too. What about Slinky and his story, his ancestors allegedly also explored the south pacific. He could have possibly inherited the gene as well. The light was bright around the curtains covering her window and she knew it was well past dawn. Jaime quickly tidied up her papers and washed her face and brushed her teeth before headed out to the galley.

Everyone had already finished eating breakfast as Jaime had slept in well past her normal get up time. Tessa handed her a cup of coffee and said. "Well sleepyhead, are we taking a tropical vacation?"

Still groggy but with her mind again racing, Jaime said, "Ya, I think we should."

Becca clapped her hands and smiled.

Jaime had been trying to get up the courage to return to Cleanetics as she wanted to try and get some of her previous research and the hard drives from their mainframe computers, not that she knew how to do that. Just the thoughts of walking into the building combined with all the thoughts of her dad were making her crazy. She wanted to go but she had been so much happier lately she was afraid that it may be too much. Planning this trip to Hawaii had given her the perfect excuse.

It was a unanimous decision and they had given themselves two weeks to organize and provision JayJay for the voyage. Provisioning took no time at all as Billy had more than ample supplies right at their fingertips. They performed as much maintenance as they could and JayJay was pronounced shipshape and seaworthy in only eight days. Seeing that as an auspicious sign, they motored out of Mission Bay that very next morning into a building breeze and began their 2500 mile journey to Hawaii.

41

Tessa was hoping to be the first to see their destination. She had first watch today and learned that visibility in the tropics was best just after sunrise. Waiting with a battered pair of binoculars hanging from her neck she checked their position and according to the GPS they had drifted slightly closer to landfall overnight. Checking the barometer, it was still holding steady, promising more good weather. Brandy had done her morning's business and sat leaning against Tessa's leg, her nose checking out the still unknown scents of the open ocean.

The island of Hawaii, their destination for the better part of a month was out there somewhere. Tessa scanned the eastern sky, looking for the first brightening on the horizon. Absentmindedly scratching Brandy's head she remembered watching television shows about Hawaii and how she always wanted to go there one day. Now that they were almost here Tessa was so glad they continued the journey after the disastrous first week at sea.

On the first day of their journey they had JayJay under full sail and in moderate to strong winds, they had quickly moved out of sight of land. The winds had continued to grow and by the fourth day they were being battered by gale force winds and monstrous waves. September was apparently one of the best months to sail from the mainland to Hawaii but you risked late summer storms and tropical depressions. All they could do was ride it out and hope that JayJay was built as well as Jaime said she was.

During the peak of the storm Billy had fallen in the cockpit dislocating his thumb and both Tessa and Becca were very seasick and were becoming dehydrated as they couldn't keep any fluids down. Both of the girls had received intravenous fluids administered by Jaime and finally felt better once the seas started to calm. Tessa could feel goose bumps on her arms as she remembered how awful she felt those few weeks ago.

This last week had been better than anyone expected for the open ocean. Twelve to fifteen foot swells with a moderate chop and strong steady winds had propelled them within a day or two of landfall. JayJay was designed and built for exactly this purpose and she had performed magnificently. Hearing a noise, Tessa thought a flying fish had jumped into the cockpit which had become a regular occurrence lately but she couldn't see anything in small circle of light cast by the single bulb above the steering console.

The door opened and Billy joined Tessa, trying to carry two cups of coffee out into the cockpit. Jaime had taped and bandaged his damaged thumb in such a way to make his hand almost impossible to use as he continually was re-injuring himself. Billy seemed to have a very high pain threshold, which based on his experience, wasn't surprising.

Tessa saw that the cups were only half full. "Thanks Billy. Good idea not to fill them up too." Tessa said.

"Well, that's not how they started out." Billy admitted, showing Tessa the coffee stains down the front of his clothes.

Tessa was really fond of Billy. He was a very hard worker and was always smiling, never confrontational or abrasive. He also respected her private space and never felt the need to talk just for the sake of talking. Tessa really appreciated that. The most important thing was that he made Tessa laugh, often for no reason. It was just the way he stood, or what he wore, or what he said. Tessa had finally convinced him to wear his hair in a ponytail and this morning he only gotten about half of it together. Tessa sat him down and fixed his hair, admiring how fine and colourful his red hair was. She never liked her own hair, it was thick and coarse, not exactly easy to manage for a teenage girl.

After sitting in silence for a few minutes Billy said, "The sun should pop in about fifteen minutes." He was looking at the brightening eastern sky.

Tessa looked back and felt a small gust of wind against her face. She breathed in the heavy salt air and it instantly reminded her of a summer's day on the beach in Tofino. For the first time in a long time she wondered if she would ever see her old home again.

A half hour later in the rosy post dawn light they both took turns with the binoculars as they looked at the massive volcano on the horizon, its summit surrounded by clumps of heavy white cloud. They didn't even hear Sam come out and he stood beside them at the repaired side rail of JayJay.

Sam had always been strong, mostly to support Becca, but he had changed since they were getting close to his home. Talking often about his friends and relatives, his emotions were quick to the surface. He had already resigned himself that his beautiful Mahleah probably didn't make it but what about his mother and two sisters?

Billy slapped him on his back and intuitively said, "We'll find out soon Sam."

Late in the afternoon they motored slowly into the Kona Kailua harbour, maneuvering carefully around the breakwater. There didn't appear to be a lot of good moorage or docking area so Jaime headed for a large charter company dock. Both Tessa and Billy were forward working with Jaime preparing to dock and Sam was scouring the area with the binoculars looking for any sign of life.

Off in the distance they heard an airhorn and then another.

Sam yelled out excitedly, "Someone's here!"

Jamie had aced the docking with JayJay barely nudging the big concrete pilings and she was quickly made secure. Brandy was one of the first onto land running around at a furious pace then falling to the ground to roll in the dirt. They all stood and stretched their sea legs, glad to be back on land safe and sound. Running and squealing with her arms extended like an airplane, Becca ran playfully up and down the dock and into the parking lot chased by Brandy. Sam had been here in Kona many times even though he was born in Hilo, across the island. Leaving the big island as a teenager and had tried to return to his home island at least once a year to see his friends and family. Working out of town, especially far away on the mainland had taken its toll on his traditionally close knit Hawaiian family. He stamped his feet and the earth felt solid. He was so happy to be home.

A battered pickup turned the corner into the parking lot and quickly stopped. A number of men, some of them armed and not looking very welcoming jumped out of the back of the truck. They approached, led by a delicate older woman holding a carved staff covered in beads and shells.

The woman raised her hand, pointing directly at Jaime and said with a croaking voice, "You are not welcome here."

Sam stepped forward. "I am Sam Noappu from Hilo. We just came from California. What do you mean we are not welcome?"

The woman spoke again. "I am called Mama Huna and I lead this group. We are Hawaiians. Hawaii is now for Hawaiians only. No haoles are welcome here. The whites are the causes of all Hawaii's problems and the gods have finally spoken and taken almost everyone away." She angrily banged the staff onto the pavement, looking as menacing as an elderly lady can.

"Sam Noappu from Hilo, you are welcome, as is the child." She was pointing at Becca. "You three", pointing at Jaime, Tessa and Billy, "Are not."

Sam talked to the Hawaiians for over an hour before he returned to the group now sitting on the dock beside JayJay. He explained that there were eighty eight survivors on the entire island, living in three different locations. Mama Huna as she called herself was their spiritual advisor and Sam felt that she exerted a lot of influence over everyone. He said it appeared to border on a cult. They did not know off hand all of the survivors names in Hilo but would bring him a list as well as some fresh food and water before nightfall. He was very embarrassed to say that they were adamant that only Sam and Becca could stay.

Sam was extremely nervous and paced back and forth along the dock as he waited for the list of names. Finally the pickup returned and there was another woman with them and she was carrying a binder. Looking at her face Sam knew that there were no Noappu's on the list. Hoping for the best since all this had started, he now knew in his heart that he and Becca were the only survivors from his family. The woman gently handed him the binder and patted him softly on the shoulder before walking away. Sitting down alone it didn't take him long to review the list of names. He slowly walked back, somewhat unsteady on his legs and handed the binder back to the woman. After a short and hushed conversation Sam walked down the dock and looked out to sea. Becca went to him and they sat down and talked for a few minutes. They hugged each other for a long time, rocking back and forth and then they slowly walked back. Becca immediately ran to Tessa who picked her up and held her in her arms. No one had to ask what they had just talked about.

Packets of still steaming food wrapped in banana leaves were dropped off at the dock as well as some large containers of water. No words were spoken by the men that dropped the supplies off but their hostility was evident. Even Jaime's thank you was met with cold silence. Sam was speaking to the men before they suddenly turned away, leaving him standing there. Slowly he walked back to JayJay.

"There is a colony on Lanai that they said would be best for us." Sam was visibly angry and swore under his breath. "JayJay has an hour to leave. They said we could anchor in the harbour for the night but we must leave in the morning."

The food had all been unwrapped and Sam like everyone else was famished and they each took huge platefuls of the steamed pork, fish and rice, all with fresh vegetables. No one spoke as they all ate in uncomfortable silence.

Finally Jaime asked, "Are you staying?"

"No." Sam's voice was loud and angry and he immediately apologized. "They have some crazy idea that everything was caused by the white people and that they should return to the old Hawaiian ways to placate the gods." Sam looked disgustedly out the window towards town. "That Mama Huna acts like she is a queen or something. There is nothing for us here." Becca held tightly onto Tessa fighting back the next round of tears. She had rarely seen her dad speak a word in anger and she didn't really know how to deal with his outburst and the news that her mother was probably dead.

It only took a few minutes to leave the dock and drop anchor in the middle of the harbour. There was not a lot of conversation as everyone digested in their own way what had just happened. Jaime was both angry and disappointed. To be shunned because of the colour of her skin hurt her in a way she had never felt before. She now knew what it felt like to be an unwanted minority and it was not a good feeling.

She selfishly hoped to get the list and to interview the survivors to try and understand more about their backgrounds. "Sam," Jaime asked. "Did she say anything about other white people? Were there non-Hawaiian survivors here or other people that had come and gone?"

"Yes, about two months ago a white man sailed here in a big yacht. She doesn't remember his name but she said he was a doctor. Even after telling him he wasn't welcome he still offered them medical assistance. He apparently leads the colony on Lanai." Sam was rubbing his temples, a stress headache radiating waves of pain across his forehead.

No one slept well that night except for Becca and Brandy. They left shortly after sunrise headed for Lanai.

42

S am was explaining to everyone that the main settlement on Lanai was Lanai City and it was not on the coast like most Hawaiian settlements but inland. Tessa giggled when Sam said that it's really just a small little town, not a city at all and that there were only a few paved roads and no traffic lights on the whole island. Even Tofino had traffic lights she thought.

Lanai wasn't anything like the other islands tourist-wise but there were a couple of high end tourist resorts built in the last few decades. Most did not know that 98% of the island was privately owned by some technology billionaire that bought it from the Dole pineapple company. Lanai was once the largest pineapple plantation in the world and Sam said it was like ancient Hawaii, a pristine paradise. Dominated by its single dormant volcano Lanaihale which rises to over 3300 feet in elevation, its fertile slopes were no longer farmed and it had few beaches. Most of the shoreline consisted of the land dropping off abruptly into the sea but there was one man made harbor at Kaumalapau along the western coast. Sam knew of one beautiful bay on the south side where there was an upscale

Four Seasons resort and he talked about how spectacular it was there. He had performed there as a teenager and that's where they were now headed, to Manele Bay.

They arrived just before dusk and after dropping their sails they slowly motored their way into Manele Bay. The bay wasn't that big and as they anchored Jaime calculated that JayJay's anchorage swing would just about fill the entire bay. Luckily there were no other boats anchored here. After dropping and setting the anchor in the crystalline water Jaime scanned the beach and saw a couple of kayaks and an outrigger canoe pulled up onto the sand. There was no other sign of life.

It took two trips on the small inflatable to get everyone to shore and as soon as Brandy's feet hit the ground she had taken off down the beach running at full speed and was just rejoining them now, panting heavily. Making their way up the beach and into the resort they could immediately see it was significantly overgrown but the grounds were still beautiful with flowering plants and trees everywhere. The sweet scented air mixing with the salty breeze was exactly what Tessa had hoped for. In her mind, this smelled like Hawaii. As they continued up the paths overgrown with vegetation it didn't take long to tell there were people here as they came across some laundry hung from a rope tied between two delicately sloping palm trees.

"Come out come out wherever you are." Billy called, which caused Tessa to start laughing.

They were now past the biggest section of gardens and walking through what looked like guest bungalows when a little boy turned a corner and appeared on the path riding a small bike with training wheels. He appeared to be about Becca's age and stopped and got off the bike and just stared at them slack jawed. Becca was now the one that was giggling as he wasn't wearing any clothes. The little boy stood unmoving and not saying a word when a small knot of laughing people emerged from around the same corner.

What happened next was exactly the opposite of their Kona experience. The greetings were loud and heartfelt with hugs, handshakes and even some tears. In just a few seconds all of the newcomers were made to feel very welcome and multiple conversations were all going on at the same time. Sam's emotions which had been close to the surface for a couple of days now burst through as he was warmly welcomed home by his Hawaiian brothers and sisters. It was the first time Becca had seen her father cry. They had moved to one of the poolside bars of the resort and were sitting in some wonderfully comfortable patio furniture when the story of their landing in Kona came up. Their new hosts even apologized for how they were treated and said that's not how it is here. "This is the real Hawaii." Sam had proudly said just as the last rays of the sun disappeared, sinking over the horizon.

The conversations were both serious and funny as the Lanai colonists all prepared a meal of grilled fish and some wonderful fresh vegetables for the new arrivals. Informally they each started to recount their stories and how they came to be here on Lanai. All the newcomers were surprised to hear how violent it was not only during the die off but after, amongst some of the survivors here in Hawaii. Jaime couldn't wait to delve into their history's and try to add to her knowledge of Locust and its survivors and had to force herself to be patient, she had lots of time. Just after dinner Jaime took about twenty minutes to provide the abridged version of what she learned from her emails about Locust. The colonists sat in stunned silence, asking few questions and almost unbelieving of how it had come to be. Starting to briefly touch on the theory of a healthy gene, Jamie could tell that now was not the time and told everyone she would be happy to fill in any of the blanks tomorrow, when they would travel to Lanai City and meet the rest of the Lanai colonists.

All twelve of the people that now lived here at Manele Bay had come to Lanai from other islands. There were another twenty people living in Lanai City and most of them were from other islands too.

"This is the place to be. On Oahu and Maui people are still living in the past and not embracing the future. And the people on the Big Island, well, you have already seen what they have become." There was an awkward silence and then he continued, "Word is out through the islands if you want to live peacefully and harmoniously and get back to the land, this is the place." Buck Pakollo was the second oldest settler here, sixty seven years old he had been a commercial diver on Oahu all his life. Trim and fit, with a full head of dark hair, he literally looked half his age. Tommy was the youngest settler at five and the one they first saw when the newcomers landed. Tommy was now fast asleep in a lounge chair beside Susan who had become his surrogate mother. Susan had found him alone and starving in Lahaina before they both came to Lanai. Susan was an artist and sculptor and she was twenty seven.

In the beginning there were apparently close to four hundred survivors scattered throughout the islands. Most were on Oahu but Buck had said that Honolulu had become a very dangerous place. A lot of people had fled to Maui and the Big Island. Some had come here with him. Fueled by drugs and alcohol, the survivors there were only living day to day, refusing to accept the new reality. He had heard that over forty survivors had been killed on Oahu since the event had taken place.

Jaime asked, "Have you seen any non-Hawaiian survivors Buck?"

"If you mean white people, sure. There is Glenn, he worked over in Maui as a golf pro, he was originally from New Zealand or Australia, I always get those accents mixed up. And Doc came here about the same time I did. I don't know if there were any other haolies out there."

Susan quickly added, "There was a lady from Hong Kong that was vacationing in Lahaina. She barely spoke any English and she was still there when I left."

The conversation carried on into the night and Jaime never really had the chance to ask about the one they called Doc. She had been dominating the conversation and asking a lot of questions so she decided tone it down a bit after Tessa had given her a bit of a sideways glance. Billy had excused himself earlier and with the help of one of the colonists had found accommodations in the hotel for the group. For the first time in a long time Jaime, Tessa, Billy, Sam and Becca would be sleeping on solid dry land. The one that appreciated it the most though was Brandy. After thanking their hosts the crew from JayJay retired to their luxurious rooms at the Four Seasons resort for a good night's sleep. It took Jaime a long time before she could sleep as she listened to the soft sounds of the breeze rustling through the palm fronds outside of her window thinking about all that had happened today. Trying not to get excited about possibly finding her father, she knew it was a one in a million chance. But it was still a chance. Finally, just a few hours before daybreak, Jaime fell into a deep and dream free sleep.

The next morning they all met again and sat in the courtyard overlooking the beach eating the most delicious fresh fruit that Tessa had ever tasted. Konala, one of the Manele Bay residents had already left on his bike to tell the others in town that they had some new arrivals. The conversations were much more subdued than those last night and in a lull Jaime asked Buck more about Doc. He didn't really say much except that he was probably in his late fifties, had dark hair and sailed in by himself shortly after the event on some huge yacht. Doc usually stayed in town but he was up at Kaumalapau where his boat was docked and was doing some big repair on his boat.

"Do you know his real name?" Jaime asked.

"Nope. We all just call him Doc." Buck replied.

"Is he really a doctor?"

Buck just held up his hands indicating he didn't know.

"Would you happen to know the name of his boat?" Jaime knew it was a long shot, probably the longest shot ever but she had to ask.

Buck was casually looking out into the bay and said, "Not a clue Jaime. Funny though, it's that same pretty green as yours."

Jaime's heart jumped into her throat as she involuntarily grabbed Buck's arm.

It took only two minutes to convince Buck to let Jaime take a vehicle to Kaumalapau Harbour as he had relented immediately when she said that the one they call Doc might be her father. Jaime was almost shaking in anticipation as Buck dug around in his bungalow for the keys. Coming out he dutifully explained to her that there was not an overabundance of gasoline left on the island and everyone guarded it jealously. Buck told Tessa she couldn't come as he was going to town first and there wouldn't be room for her as the plan was to he would find a couple of other people to go hunting in an area that was half way between town and the harbour. That way, they are killing two birds with one stone and not wasting any gas. Jaime couldn't argue with the logic but pleaded with Buck to get going and with a shout of good luck from Tessa, they headed off through the resort to the parking lot.

Buck had driven Jaime to Lanai City and after a few stops that had only taken half an hour, although it seemed ten times longer to Jaime, the small entourage was now headed towards Kaumalapau harbour. The small sedan was crammed with Buck, Jaime, two just recently turned eighteen year old twins Iki and Tonya and Sonny, the twins Rhodesian ridgeback. There were very few paved roads on Lanai, most were four wheel drive dirt tracks but thankfully, the road to the harbour was paved the entire way.

Buck explained the plan again as he wasn't sure Jaime had gotten it the first time. He and the twins were going to go hunting in a large ravine half way between Lanai City and the harbour. Jaime was to carry on alone to the harbour and find Doc. In three hours she was to return and pick them all up. With luck, they would feast on roast pork or maybe a deer tonight in a celebration that was planned on the beach at Manele to welcome the new arrivals.

There was only one road so there was no possibility of getting lost but still, Buck built a small cairn of rocks on the shoulder of the road next to the pull out where Jaime was to pick them up later that afternoon. It's not that Buck didn't trust her, he explained, but he could see how tense she was and wanted to make sure they didn't have the possibility of a long walk back into town.

"You know, I'm not getting any younger." The humour was completely lost on Jaime as she was just about to burst and she nervously dropped the keys that Buck had handed to her.

Running to the car she didn't even hear what he said next as she opened the door, hopped in and started the little Toyota. Jaime immediately stalled the vehicle as she tried to pull away and that brought a loud snicker from Iki who was holding the two hunting rifles. His sister punched him in the shoulder and told him to be quiet. Jaime restarted the car and riding the clutch a little bit, she pulled out onto the road and headed out on her ten minute journey to the harbour.

Oh my God Jaime thought, what are the chances? He was a doctor, about the right age and his boat was bigger and the same colour as JayJay. She tried to keep calm as she replayed the same thoughts over and over that had kept her awake for most of the night. Not having driven a vehicle since she left San Diego the sensation of driving felt strange as the small tress of the scrub forest flew by. A series of descending hairpin turns made her drive a little more purposefully along the surprisingly mountainous road, the intricacies of driving a standard and manually shifting were slowly coming back to her.

The road continued to descend and she dropped down through another ravine and a series of sweeping switchbacks as she passed a sign that read two miles to Kaumalapau harbour. Her view was still restricted by some small trees but the intense flashes of blue ocean were more and more frequent as she approached what must be the end of the road. Missing a downshift as she rounded a corner she broke hard and two wheels were momentarily on the gravel shoulder before she could correct and get back onto the pavement. Just a block away was a large somewhat derelict looking warehouse. Her view of the harbour was completely blocked by the big multi-story building and now turning the final corner she had a full view of the harbour.

Her sobs were audible as she saw the big beautiful steel hulled yacht tied up to the jetty, its name Unfinished Business in large sweeping letters across the stern.

She stalled the car again as she stopped. Quickly setting the emergency brake, she ran down the jetty. As she approached Jaime scanned the yacht, there was no one to be seen but she did see a short ladder leading down to the yacht deck which sat just a few feet lower than the heavy planking of the jetty.

"Dad, dad!" She yelled as she approached the ladder. She saw a head emerge from the aft storage hatch.

The man climbed out of the hatch and stood up to his full height looking up at her. He was in his fifties, with dark hair and was stripped down to the waist with streaks of dirt and grease covering his chest.

Jaime covered her mouth with her hands and felt the air rush out of her lungs. It was not her father.

Glenn was at a loss for words as he looked up at this pretty young woman. Jaime just stared down at him, her very soul crushed by what she saw. The tears now flowed as Jaime started to sob. She fell to her knees, her hands covering her face, her hand resting on the top of the ladder. All night long she had hoped and prayed for it to be him. Tormenting herself with both the chance of unexplainable joy and possibility of utter disappointment. Her chest tightened, her heart pounded and she felt like she was going to throw up with the taste of bile rising in her throat.

Glenn was holding a rag, wiping his hands still not knowing what to do or say. He stepped partially back into the hatch and leaned in. "Hey Doc, you better come out here."

Riley Jones, completely unaware of what was unfolding above him climbed the short ladder and emerged into the bright sunlight of the deck, holding his hand up to shield his eyes from the sun. Seeing someone he didn't really recognize, obviously distraught and on her knees at the top of the ladder he said, "Well who do we have here?"

Jaime heard the voice and her heart literally skipped a beat. Stunned and shocked, she slowly opened her hands, almost finger by finger and saw her father looking up at her.

Riley was up the ladder and in three strides as he picked his still unbelieving daughter up and wrapped his arms around her. Jamie couldn't catch her breath as she sobbed uncontrollably trying to get air into her lungs, gasping for every bit of oxygen. Riley started to shake and he could feel her tears on his bare skin. Neither of them was able to speak and even if they were, there was nothing really to be said. They both stood there, relishing the moment that neither of them truthfully believed would ever happen. It was like a dream, an unattainable wish that they both had, and somehow, standing there on a small island in the middle of the Pacific Ocean, it had just come true.

lenn was telling the story again for a small gathering of people sitting in the shade just outside the medical centre, his heavy New Zealand accent proving just as amusing as the story.

"They were like two seals on the beach, eh." Glenn was intertwining his hands for all to see. "I didn't know who she was or what was going on. They were standing at the top of the bloody ladder for fifteen minutes, and I couldn't get off the damned boat. I finally said the hell with it and went back to work."

Riley and Jamie's reunion had become the talk of the colony. It was an amazing reconnection that immediately brought hope to the other survivors that they might be able to find some of their loved ones still alive. Many of the colonists had watched Locust take their families and friends, one by one. Almost everyone had friends and relatives somewhere abroad, working or even marooned when all travel was ceased in an effort to stymie the spread of the virus. Although the atmosphere on Lanai had always been positive everyone just had a little more spring in their step now as that little bit of hope had crept back in.

Riley and Jamie had walked out of the recently refurbished medical centre and approached the group.

"Nifty little set up now eh Doc?" Glenn was obviously pleased with the work that they had done fixing up the centre to Riley's specifications and he knew Riley would like it too. "No pikers here, everyone got to work real quick and worked bloody hard." Glenn was gesturing to the colonists sitting around with him.

"It's perfect, fantastic actually." Riley was truly pleased with the renovation. "You can all take tomorrow off." That was met with a few laughs as Riley went around and shook everyone's hand thanking them.

It had been a hectic two weeks since Jaime and Riley had been reunited. The time had flown by for both of them and Jaime's head was still spinning. She had spent almost all her time with her father and hadn't seen anyone from her old crew in a couple of days. They had all taken up residence in the empty bungalows at Manele Bay and she had moved in with Riley here in town. Her new home was a cute little house just across the street from the small satellite campus of the University of Hawaii. It wasn't a large house, there were few of those on Lanai but it had a huge covered porch and was surrounded by flowering trees and shrubs. There was a second bedroom that fit Jaime's needs perfectly and even though it was smaller than the master stateroom on JayJay, she adapted just fine. Riley had put off the repairs of the generator on Unfinished Business to reconnect and spend time with Jaime. Never one to be idle, Glenn had been working on it whenever he could find a few hours and he had been pressuring Riley to get back to work with him on the rebuild as it was a big and complicated job.

Jaime was washing some salad greens for dinner in a large galvanized tub and Riley reminded her to keep that water so they could use it to wash the dishes afterwards. Riley drew most of his water from the rain barrels that he had connected to the downspouts of a few local homes. They had not been able to get the main water system working properly in town but they hoped to one day as it was a simple gravity fed system with a reservoir up on the hill. Jaime had already told Billy about it and he was anxious to tackle the problem.

As they often did during dinner, which tonight consisted of a hearty omelette and salad, they talked about Locust. Having already been through the shock and horror of what had happened there were truly few surprises left. They had all been steeled by their survival experiences and none more than Riley. When he had told his story of survival and escape from New Guinea to Jaime she could only shake her head. It had similar aspects to all the stories repeated by the survivors but with a really menacing and dangerous undertone. Riley had barely escaped alive from the main hospital in Port Moresby where he was attempting to help out during what they now call the Locust Event. His descriptions of various gangs of tribesmen from both the cities and the mountains descending upon each other in a fury he had never even imagined humanly possible. After Locust had run its course the killings just continued to escalate and tribal fighting raged amongst the survivors throughout the city. The only explanation was that the former head-hunters were settling the age old grievances and tribal disputes in the only way they knew how. Fueled by alcohol, the carnage raged and made it impossible for Riley to escape from his hiding place in the hospital. Jamie was sickened by the accounts of the severed heads of the vanquished being proudly displayed from the belts of the victors, just as it was done in the old times.

Riley finally was able to make it back to Unfinished Business as he moved through the city under the cover of darkness one rainy night. After cutting the mooring lines he had used a small fishing skiff to slowly pull Unfinished Business away from the dock right under the noses of a number of sleeping tribesmen. Once clear from the dock, he was able to start the engines and escape from Port Moresby.

Shortly after reuniting, Jaime shared all the emails with Riley and he was fascinated by the theory of the ancient Denisovan healthy gene. He dove into it but there was little if any research material available. Surprisingly he was able to find out more about Denisovans from the July 2013 edition of National Geographic magazine than he was from any other sources in the small Lanai library. It was exactly the kind of genetic mystery that Riley loved but it quickly came to an abrupt end.

Riley had said, "I think we have done all we can do here. We have been through everything; we need to access more material from some of the big university libraries."

Jamie had agreed but reminded him that there were other probably more pressing issues but she understood his need to know, she had been struggling with that since she left San Diego. What they both agreed on is that either the genetic coding had failed or like Slinky's friend Dr. Bo had warned, the virus could have mutated through probably an avian host and then back into humans.

Not wanting to dull her father's enthusiasm but they were now living in a completely different world. "I am as interested as you dad but I'd like to try and get my head fully around our new situation here."

The conversation this night went on till well after dark as they sat in the kitchen with their Coleman lantern projecting dancing shadows across the room. They were talking about the healthy gene and Denisovans and Slinkys note but the conversation kept returning to the present and their situation here on Lanai.

Jamie matter-of-factly stated, "Anything we discover or find will only benefit the next generation. I'm not saying that's unimportant, but we need to look after ourselves and make this colony successful."

"That makes perfect sense sweetie and we will do that. All I am saying is there will come a time when we all have our shelter, running water and enough food to last us forever and then what? I don't see me, or you, sitting in a lounge chair on the beach sipping mango punch for the rest of our lives."

"Of course not dad." Just being back on land after a difficult month at sea, Jamie knew where he was going with this and did not look forward to another adventure.

She smiled in that beautifully sly way that Riley remembered. It usually meant she knew something that he didn't. "I know what you are thinking."

"Do you now." He raised a barely discernible eyebrow in the semi darkness of the kitchen.

"Ya, I do. Unfinished Business isn't seaworthy and as JayJay belongs to me, you aren't going anywhere."

They both laughed, each thinking they were outsmarting the other but in reality, they could read each like a good book. Even in the dark.

Six weeks had now passed since Jaime had moved in with Riley and they had become almost like an old married couple, playfully nattering at each other at every opportunity. Jaime had learned that Riley had quickly organized the Lanai group after making landfall here. Although steadfastly refusing to be called their leader, in reality he was that and more. They were managing before but now, as she was told, everything is so much easier and a lot more gets done. All available food, fuel, medical supplies and a myriad of other essentials had all been identified, catalogued and moved to the school in Lanai City. The only school in town had been transformed into a series of classroom sized warehouses, its contents labelled and organized with the precision of someone with an obsessive compulsive disorder. Whenever someone needed something they could now easily find it. No one took more than what they needed and the system worked really well. Using a lot of the existing medical supplies as well as some from Unfinished Business, Riley had made the recently refurbished medical clinic almost state of the art. It was no doubt the best stocked and functioning medical clinic in the world.

The generator repairs on Unfinished Business had been delayed until the both Jaime and Riley had re-connected and decompressed from the emotion of their reconciliation. Glenn hadn't missed a day of work as he joined up with Billy and they quickly found the problem within the water system in town and now *'the townies'* as they were called had running water and functioning toilets. The two of them made an interesting pair with Glenn jokingly referring to Billy as his dag but never telling him what the slang meant. Billy seemed to retaliate by constantly trying to engage Glenn in one of his rambling diatribes which truthfully, Glenn would later admit, he quite enjoyed.

Unfinished Business was now repaired and she was fully functional again, her generator tested over and over again for the last week. When Riley had told Jamie that the generator failure was the only thing that had kept him in Hawaii as he had planned to sail to San Diego to look for her, it had melted her heart. She would have been long gone but they had both laughed at the possibility of running into each other in the middle of the ocean, waving as they sailed by in opposite directions.

What had started informally was now their first tradition, the entire colony would get together for Sunday feast at Manele Bay. The big resort there already had underground ovens and barbeque pits and they quickly adapted into a routine for what had become a much anticipated weekly event. Research into old Hawaiian recipes had yielded a treasure trove of readily available dishes and tonight they had all feasted on field salad greens with a papaya seed dressing, grilled mahi mahi and a huge batch of mango bread cooked in a traditional underground oven.

"You know, I have eaten in the finest restaurants in the world but this is by far the best meal I have ever had," Riley said, pushing himself back from the table, completely heartfelt in his praise. "A big thank you to our chefs."

Everyone applauded and many of the colonists felt the same way about their dinner, it was hardly roughing it and for almost all of them, they had never eaten healthier. With virtually no processed foods, little sugar or alcohol and an all-natural diet, they had all become a little leaner and much healthier. Sitting back in their chairs completely satiated they let the warm breezes wash over them as the brightest stars now started to twinkle lightly in the darkening sky. Sunday was their day of rest and no one was in too much of a hurry to start the cleanup duties.

Jaime leaned over to Tessa. "I think I've gained ten pounds since we arrived."

"I know," Tessa replied. "Me too, these Sunday feasts are just getting better and better."

After dinner in the waning light of day was when most of the colony's business was conducted and this Sunday was no different. Riley was always looked upon to lead these important discussions about colony life but he continually refused to accept that role. Constantly reminding people that they all needed to work together, they all needed to get along and they all needed to make consensus based decisions. Often telling the personalized war stories of his business career, Riley imparted a lot of humour but everything ultimately boiled down to mutual respect, something that had been tremendously lacking in both government and business prior to Locust. Sometimes he spoke for an hour, uninterrupted, about how he had grown to detest what had happened to the medical system. How it had become all about dollars and not about people. Riley knew how to work a crowd but this wasn't about pandering to the press or what he called peacocking for a photo op. His passion and honesty shone through as it always did for people of true character. Feeling a need to impart a sense of belonging and camaraderie to the colony, just like he did with his employees at Cleanetics, Riley never bypassed an opportunity to build the team. Purposefully not trying to lead, he was actually being an even more effective leader. Happy to just be *Doc* to most, Riley took immense pride in watching people grow and come together.

Among the many discussions this night was one about a possible trip to the Big Island. They had no beef on Lanai and Buck wanted to go to the Big Island to bring back a few animals to start a small herd. His cousin used to work at Parker Ranch and he knew they had close to 25,000 head of cattle just at that ranch alone. The grass grew all year long in Hawaii and those cows were no doubt prospering even without man's attention. Buck knew to keep the herds healthy they should be culled and with only limited harvesting now, they definitely ran the risk of quickly overpopulating their ranges or falling ill with disease. He was confident that that logic would be accepted by those on the Big Island. Buck like so many others was offended by that colony's racist stance towards non-Hawaiians, but they felt a trip to the Big Island was worth a try.

The following morning Buck, Glenn and Billy had headed off to Kaumalapau Harbour to try and get a handle on a problem with the small portable generator that had been brought to the harbour for Unfinished Business to use while her generator was down for repairs. They laughed as it appeared that no generators liked to work properly at the harbour. Heading off they were travelling in one of the solar powered golf carts that Billy had designed. Using scavenged solar panels and extra batteries Billy had adapted four golf carts to solar power. Although they weren't particularly quick, and only climbed the steep hills at a walking pace, they made travel between Manele Bay, Lanai City and the harbour much more efficient, saving their limited gasoline reserves.

As they rounded a corner they saw three strangers walking up the road and Billy brought the cart to a quick stop alongside the men.

The strangers ignored Billy and Glenn and spoke quickly to Buck. "Aloha bro, we need the doctor."

"The Doc is in town, what's the problem?" Buck asked.

"We are from Kona and our Mama Huna is very sick. She is in our boat back at the harbour and we need the doctor."

Buck had sent the men back to the harbour and they had turned around to head back to town to fetch Riley. They found Riley at his house and after hearing the story he quickly grabbed his medical bag and they all climbed into a small pickup truck to head back to the harbour.

Mama Huna was lying out on the dock, shaded by the men holding a tarp over her when Riley arrived. He quickly took her pulse and checked her vital signs.

"She has been in and out of consciousness for almost a week." One of the men said.

Riley could see she was extremely dehydrated and had some significant swelling in her abdomen. Her eyes were also cloudy and yellowed. "Looks like something is wrong with her liver but unless she gets some fluids, she isn't going to make it."

As gently as possible they carried her on the tarp into the pickup and raced back to the medical centre. Riley immediately hooked her up to an IV and sent Billy to go find Jaime. The second bag of fluids had just emptied when Jaime arrived. It was obvious to both of them that she was experiencing liver failure and that her situation was dire.

Riley was feeling around her abdomen and said to no one in particular. "We need to get some of this fluid out, its impeding her ability to breathe."

"I agree." Jaime replied. "What do you need me to do?"

"Swab her left side." Riley said, his directive surgeons tone was one that Jaime had not heard in a long time. Grabbing a large bore needle he rapidly explained the paracentesis procedure to the few others that had gathered in the medical centre.

Riley quickly screwed in a small hand pump to the back of the large needle and Jaime grabbed a bucket. In a little under an hour they had removed over five litres of foul odorous fluid from Mama Huna's abdominal cavity. Her breathing unfortunately remained shallow and ragged.

Continuing to try and hydrate the patient Riley gave her another bag of fluids and then went outside to speak to the men from Kona. He saw them across the street sitting in the shade of a large Jacaranda tree talking to Sam, Buck and Billy. They were all drinking root beer's.

Kini, one of the men from Kona saw Riley coming and stood up. "How is she Doctor?"

"Not good I'm afraid." Riley accepted a root beer from Billy's cooler. "I've drained the fluid from her abdomen and she is breathing a little easier but it appears she has advanced liver disease, possibly cancer."

Jaime had just joined the group and said, "It sure looks like it dad but that goes against what we know about the healthy gene." She saw the looks of bewilderment on the new men's faces but didn't bother to explain further.

"Ya, I know honey, I was thinking the same thing." Riley took a long swig of the root beer and looked back at Jaime. "It just could be old age, she looks to be at least eighty. If we all have this healthy gene, it doesn't mean we live forever."

"She is almost ninety," Kini said, still trying to understand what this healthy gene thing is.

Hesitating slightly, Riley replied, "It just might be her time." Riley finished the last of the root beer and flipped the bottle back to Billy. He and Jaime then headed back to the clinic.

Mama Huna never regained full consciousness but she did hang on for another three weeks. They placed her coffin in the small sloop that they had arrived in and as the men from Kona prepared to leave, Kini approached Riley.

"I just want to thank you for everything you did." Kini reached out and shook Riley's hand and then he hugged him, squeezing him hard, Hawaiian style. "We treated both you and your daughter poorly when you came to Hawaii but you always treated us with great kindness and respect. I am sorry."

"Thank you Kini. You may see me again sooner than you think." Riley was putting his final touches on a plan to take Unfinished Business on a tour of the islands, providing any needed medical or dental care to the survivors.

"I'll be back in a few months with some calves so you can start your own herd here on Lanai." Kini added, looking over towards Buck.

Buck smiled at that thought of fresh milk and having access to a steady supply of beef. They had all the fish and fruits and vegetables they could use. There were wild pigs and deer in the forest and they had goats and chickens roaming freely around Lanai City. They really had almost everything they needed food wise. Buck had always preferred Hawaiian beef to the grain fed fattier beef of the mainland. Envisioning a T-bone steak Hawaiian style, grilled hot and fast with pineapple and a little hot sauce made his mouth water. Helping untie the small sloop he gave them a big push away from the dock.

They all waved as Kini and his small crew caught the breeze and headed out of the harbour and back towards the Big Island. It was too early to tell if Mama Huna's death would change the attitude of the Big Island colonists but like everything else in their new reality, things would take time.

As the clock continued to tick, even with the traditional slowness of *Hawaiian time*, the colony was really starting to come together. People were starting to feel comfortable with their lives again, never forgetting their lost loves and families but just fundamentally recognizing that they must move forward. As Jaime and Riley walked back towards the golf carts for their trip back home they couldn't help but see Tessa and Iki walking ahead of them. They were close together, matching their strides, talking softly. Iki placed his arm around Tessa's shoulder and she placed hers around his waist.

Riley playfully elbowed Jaime in the ribs, leaned over and whispered, "And so it begins."

46

Jaime was watching Becca play ball with Brandy while Sam, Tessa and Billy were finishing the new pond. Her big sun hat was being buffeted by stronger than normal winds when Becca came back to sit with her in the shade. Brandy plopped down beside them, her pink tongue hanging out the side of her mouth, her head lying on the cool grass. Tessa was enlarging the excavation, manoeuvering the backhoe with the grace of a dancer, piling the rich black earth neatly in a pile beside her. Sam and Billy were using two small bobcats to move the dirt into what was to eventually become a taro and rice garden. Billy had recently gotten the idea of building a freshwater fishpond in Hulopo'e Park which adjoined the Four Seasons property in Manele Bay. He had been reading up on ancient Hawaiian practices and was fascinated by their mastery of aquaculture hundreds of years ago. Once Billy had an idea there was nothing stopping him and Jaime was amazed at the progress they were making.

Colony life for Jaime was easy to the point of boredom. Helping out whenever she could she often now looked after Becca most days when Sam was busy as Tessa was spending most of her time with Iki. Her only real job was being one of the cooks for Sunday feast. Swatting a fly away from Becca's bare back she could now see how the little girl had really sprouted from the first time Jaime had seen her back in San Diego. Her limbs were longer and she must have grown a couple of inches taller. Casually flipping a strand of hair behind Becca's ear she could see she would grow up to be a real beauty. Jaime was about to tell her that Brandy probably needed some water when Riley appeared, riding his bicycle.

"Wow, these guys don't waste any time." Riley was trying to be heard over the rumbling noise of the equipment. Billy waved at Riley then madly tried to regain control of the bobcat that turned hard right as soon as he lifted his hands off the controls.

"Tessa is actually the star." Jaime was looking over at her removing another bucket of dark earth. "She is amazing with that machine, so talented."

"No Iki today?" Riley was looking around the jobsite.

"He is up in town with some others collecting eggs and culling a few chickens. Those birds are starting to get a little out of control."

"Don't see them apart very much anymore, wonder what they do all the time?" Riley asked, although he was pretty confident he knew the answer.

Putting her finger on her chin, Jaime said, "Well, let's see. We have two constantly near naked hormonally charged teenagers spending day and night together in a Hawaiian paradise. What do you think they are doing?"

"Ya, thought so." Riley was smiling as he walked over to talk to Billy now that they had taken a break.

Riley had been back just a week from a month's long voyage to all the major islands providing medical and dental care to the survivors of Locust. Luckily, Marilyn Alonea was one of the original survivors to come to Lanai and she had been a dental hygienist prior to leaving work to raise her family the year before Locust had struck. Marilyn capably handled numerous fillings and the occasional extraction and Tonya excelled as her assistant and by the end of the voyage was handling all the teeth cleaning duties herself. It was good for Tonya to get away for a while as she had still not come to grips with Iki becoming romantically involved with Tessa. Her separation anxiety from her twin brother was now somewhat tempered as she had her own budding love interest.

Tonya had met Marco in Lahaina while he was waiting to see Riley about a partially torn off toenail. He wasn't very tall, about the same size as Tonya and his family was from the Marshall Islands in Micronesia and had been living in Hawaii for the last few years. It was obvious he was very shy and she had almost scared him off when she approached him on the dock and struck up a conversation. When he had started to walk away, Tonya had grabbed his hand and asked him to stay and that's when she first felt the spark. Tonya had never considered herself attractive and had only gone on one date prior to Locust, preferring to hang out with Iki and his friends. Marco's skin was the creamy colour of melted chocolate and his hands were strong but ever so soft in her hand. Tonya was pretty sure he got the message that she was sending and he said he would come to see her someday soon. She hoped he was telling the truth.

That night after dinner, Riley handed Jaime a small package in a brown paper bag that he had gotten from the pharmacy supplies at the school. Jaime peeked inside and saw three pregnancy test kits. Her look, a heavily raised eyebrow sort of said it all and Riley quickly said, "For Tessa." Jaime's looked softened as he patted her on the knee and the he went outside for his normal after dinner walk around town.

Another week had passed and the work on the pond had been completed. Billy waited until Sunday feast to flood the pond through a bypass he had set up from a small stream coming down from high off the mountain. After partially damming a ravine at the edge of the park Billy had diverted the beautifully fresh water using old irrigation pipes from the long closed Dole pineapple plantation. When he was ready to open the valve, a small crowd had formed to see Billy's latest achievement. Like a proud father he opened the valve on the three inch aluminum pipe and stood back. Nothing happened.

It took about twenty seconds for the water to force the air from the pipes but it soon came in a rush, pouring out onto the black plastic liner on the bottom of the oblong shaped pond. Billy had read that the ancient Hawaiians layered flat stones along the bottom of their ponds to diminish seepage. Even with nothing but time on his hands, Billy and the others felt that was far too much work.

Becca and the three other children clapped their hands and Marilyn placed a fragrant crown of flowers on Billy's head as some people applauded. Taking his time, Billy was explaining that the pond would provide the colony with easily obtainable fresh fish and prawns and also benefit the soon to be planted taro and rice garden. Overflow from the pond would be used to water and fertilize the crops. Ducks and geese would hopefully come and fertilize the pond, and ultimately the garden below it while eating most of the pests in both.

After listening to Billy's excellent and concise explanation Riley turned to Jamie and said, "If that's not the definition of organic, I don't know what is."

After dinner there was little new business to discuss. Most of the talk was social and the atmosphere was even more relaxed than normal. Buck stood up again to thank Billy and presented him with the last six-pack of root beer on the island that Jaime had hidden away some months before. The thing with Billy and root beer was never quite understood but Billy's gratitude was immediate and genuine. Charley announced that he had finally tweaked his smokehouse and successfully smoked some bacon and hams and that he would have them available for people tomorrow at his house in the city. The meat from the wild pigs of the island was much gamier and flavourful than the domesticated pork of the past. It was almost too gamey for some but with everyone now living off the land, no one could turn down a chance at some bacon. He then reminded people how much he liked beer and if anyone had any, he would appreciate them to bring it along. That brought a hearty round of laughter.

Jaime could see Tonya whispering and poking her brother. There was no doubt who was the boss amongst the twins and that was evident from when they were children. Now as young adults, nothing had changed. Iki finally stood up and that quieted the crowd as rarely did any of the younger people speak after Sunday feast. Tessa had covered her face with her hands and Iki reached down to help her stand up. He pulled Tessa's hands away from her face revealing a huge smile and he proudly announced to the colony that he and Tessa were having a baby.

A tremendous roar erupted from the crowd as people surged forward to congratulate the happy couple. Startled dogs scattered, barking loudly, adding to the noise from the cheering and applause. Even Tonya looked pleased, not that she had anything to do with it.

"And so it begins," Riley said again to Jaime as they both sat back down.

"Lanai colony's first birth." Jamie was proudly looking at Tessa as she continued to be mobbed with hugs and congratulations. "How many pregnancies did you come across in your travels dad?"

"There were eight all together but I suspected a few more. All but one were teenagers or very young adults. I think that age group could cope with the stresses a little better than the other women that were still of child bearing age that went through Locust." Riley hesitated for a second, looking out over the darkening beach. "I don't need to tell you how traumatic it has been for the survivors, losing their families, their parents, their children." Riley again hesitated a moment, thinking back to the utter destruction and despair described in almost every survivor's story. "Some of these other colonies are just a mess too. No coordination, everyman for himself. There are hygiene issues, violence, alcohol abuse, food hoarding." As he rose to go and congratulate Tessa and Iki, almost as an afterthought he added, "To rebuild, all women of child bearing age will have to produce offspring."

That comment resonated far too deep for Jaime and she pulled her knees up to her chest and wrapped her arms tight around them as if she was cold. Always wanting kids, she had decided to wait until her career was finished so she could stay at home and be a full time mother. She knew many successful career women had the same dream and most, if not all never accomplished it, ultimately, forsaking a family for their career. I didn't even have a boyfriend for Christ's sake she thought. Jaime had a tendency to be hard on herself and she now reflected on how she was actually part of the problem that she often complained about. Disgustedly she got up and walked away, not even noticing that Riley was now looking at her after he had congratulated the expecting couple. Just like her complaints to people about constantly sending emails, '*just phone me ok*' she used to say, she was as guilty as the rest. For some reason her decision to email Slinky instead of calling him when his mother was sick popped into her mind. I'm a hypocrite she thought to herself as she kicked a palm frond off the path and onto the grass.

Her mind started to race, like it used to when she was stumped by a big problem at work. She was thinking of everything and nothing all at the same time. A family had been the last thing on her mind but now, suddenly, it was front and centre.

Hearing footsteps behind her she stopped and Riley gently grabbed her elbow. "Everything ok?"

"Ya, I was just thinking and . . ."

Before she could finish Riley gently turned her around and pointed her back in the direction they had just come from. "I think Tessa would be pretty upset if you didn't congratulate her."

A look of horror crossed her face. "Jesus." She said to no one in particular and abruptly walked away from Riley leaving him standing on the path.

Hugging Iki and then Tessa, Jaime told her how happy she was for them and then for some reason she placed her hand on her belly. That caught Tessa a little off guard and she looked at Jaime whose mind was obviously somewhere else.

A pounding rain was lashing the metal roof and looking out the window, Jaime could see that the gutters were being overwhelmed, with water cascading over them like a miniature waterfall. Like most of their rainstorms, it would be over in just a few minutes but she continued to stare outside and could see a number of chickens trying to hide out under the leaves of a beautiful yellow ginger plant in the back yard. Jaime had never really taken an interest in the chickens but a number of hens liked to hang out around her house and in watching them, she noticed they always needed to maintain a little personal space around them. If another chicken came to close, there was a problem. Those rules seemed not to apply when it rained though as she couldn't even tell how many chickens were comfortably sitting in a large pile under the ginger plant, like a bunch of sleeping kittens, waiting for the rain to stop.

This was the third time she had started the conversation but had still been unable to get to the point. They had a great personal and professional relationship but he was still her dad and there were some things that were just really hard to talk about.

Riley patiently sipped his herbal tea, instinctively knowing that she needed to get whatever it was out on her own terms. There was no point in trying to draw it out of her. He surmised as to what the topic was but in this instance, especially if he was right, it was best to just shut up and let it happen.

As Jaime continued to look out the window she recalled seeing Tessa yesterday and could see her pregnancy was starting to show. When you are in a bikini most days there is no hiding it. The rain stopped almost as suddenly as it started and Jaime exhaled audibly and returned to the kitchen table. Stretching her arms out she took a deep breath, hoping to build her confidence. Exhaling again, it was now or never.

"I need you to help me have a baby." Jaime said looking directly at her father. The look of panic on her face was immediate.

"Sorry, what I mean is that I want to have a baby but by artificial insemination." Jaime could feel her face reddening from bottom to top. "Oh God, why is this so hard." Shaking her hands in front of her she purposefully looked away, over her father's shoulder and out the window again, her foot nervously tapping against the table leg.

Riley tried to hide his amusement as he hadn't seen her fumble with her words like that since she was a teenager. He had guessed what the topic was and could understand why it was a difficult one for her but he had to almost bite his lip to stop from laughing. He was a doctor, she was a doctor. There was nothing medically that they hadn't seen, studied or talked about.

"I'll help you with whatever you like honey and I know this isn't easy for you. It's a big decision, not to be taken lightly." His lips were drawn tight, more in an attempt not to snicker as opposed to trying to look serious.

They sat in silence for a few minutes, occasionally looking at each other for a few seconds before Jamie would look away, her face tingling and warm. Every fibre in her body was telling her to run away but she forced herself to stay. Riley had almost finished his tea and was wondering how long the uncomfortable silence would last when Jaime finally got up and started rummaging through some drawers. She came back and put a turkey baster on the table in front of him.

"I'm overthinking this. It's actually pretty simple isn't it?" Jaime could only imagine how red her face was now, the nerve endings in her cheeks were popping like water droplets in a hot frying pan. She couldn't bring herself to make eye contact.

"Well, not my instrument of choice but to answer your question, yes, it's pretty simple."

"Gawd! Sorry dad. I should know better. I'm sorry." Jaime was completely embarrassed and felt like an awkward teenager trying to talk to her dad about her period.

Trying to lighten the mood Riley said, "Well I guess you missed that class in med school." Riley rose from the table and gave her a big hug. "Don't be embarrassed honey. I understand what you are thinking and I can only imagine what you are feeling. I get it. If you need anything, just ask. You know I am here for you, ok?"

Jamie just nodded, hoping that the colour that she knew was there would soon leave her cheeks. Thinking this has to be the stupidest question I have asked him since I was a kid and asked why her brother had a pee-pee and she had a ya-ya. If there was any time in her life she just wanted to disappear, it was now.

It took another day before she could look Riley in the eye and he was glad it did. Although sworn to secrecy he really wanted to tell someone so he could have a good belly laugh about it. Using all his doctoral decorum, he somehow got through the next few days. Jamie had been deep in thought as who she could possibly ask to be the father. Already deciding that she wanted to raise the child on her own and knowing that she wasn't interested in having sex with anyone on the island precluded any typical type of relationship anyway.

She finally found the courage to discuss her dilemma with someone else as she sat beside the fish pond with Tessa one lazy morning. Not even getting near to the end of telling her story via a somewhat rehearsed presentation, Tessa who had been sitting open mouthed from the beginning broke into hysterical laughter.

"Ok, I'm sorry." Tessa was trying her hardest not to start laughing again, wiping her eyes with the back of her hand. "Ok, I sort of get the, don't want to have sex part." A smirk crept back over Tessa's face as she hesitated. "Well, not really, but whatever." Tessa turned away again, trying to be respectful but she buried her face into towel she was sitting on and was trying to muffle herself as her shoulders jerked spasmodically with laughter.

"C'mon Tessa, this is serious stuff." Jaime wasn't irritated. Knowing it was a touchy subject but she knew it should be a lot easier to talk to Tessa about it than her dad.

A smile was starting to creep across Jaime's face just as Tessa announced she had to go pee so they made their way back to the bungalows. Now sitting on the grass in the shade of a small flowering shrub beside the bungalow where Tessa and Iki now lived, Tessa apologized and asked Jaime to continue. In under a minute Tessa had rolled over onto her back and started laughing loudly and uncontrollably, her legs bicycle kicking up in the air. Jamie was laughing now too and was slapping Tessa's legs telling her to stop which only made her laugh harder.

48

Iki was sitting in the shade reading an old car magazine when Tessa came out of the medical clinic. He was glad he had brought her windbreaker as it looked like a rain squall was about to move across the island and a full on pelting rain couldn't be far behind.

"Everything's fine E." Tessa said. Tonya always called her brother E instead of Iki and Tessa was now doing the same. "Jamie said my weight is right on target although now that I'm starting my third trimester, I should start packing on the pounds."

Iki helped Tessa with her windbreaker. "No worries baby, us Hawaiians like 'em a bit chunky eh."

She playfully punched his shoulder as they climbed into the golf cart, preparing to head back home. Tessa was as happy as she had ever been and was deeply in love. Iki was kind and gentle, always smiling and didn't appear to have a mean bone in his body. He wasn't exactly a workaholic and usually needed a little extra motivation to get moving but Tessa knew that was just the Hawaiian way.

Almost everyone in the colony was out building or repairing fencing at the old riding stables today as a large catamaran had arrived late yesterday from the Big Island with six plump little calves. One of the little male steers had already escaped and was nowhere to be seen having run out of town as soon as they arrived. That left them with one remaining male and four little female heifers and they didn't want any more of them to get loose so it was all hands on deck to get a proper enclosure built. The paddocks and fenced compounds were in need of some significant reinforcement as the visitors from Kona had warned them that these cows were not accustomed to being fenced. Billy had hobbled the calves, folding one leg up and tying it off just like he had seen the Afghani's do with their camels. The little calves bellowed and cried unable to figure out how to stand up and rolled hopelessly from side to side. The work was going quickly and Billy was confident that they would be finished ahead of schedule and they could release the calves later today into what once were the grounds of the old riding stable. With its horses released into the wild by its owner when Locust hit, the corrals and pens had now become an overgrown lush pasture. Glenn was making jokes about sheep farmers in his homeland when one of the calves finally broke free and made a run for the hills. Billy got a hand on it but it ran right through a split rail fence and was gone from sight in no time. The visitors from the Big Island just laughed.

The rain intensified as Iki and Tessa approached Manele Bay and they ran into Buck on the side of the road. He had scavenged a bunch of metal roofing panels from the resort and was headed back to town when he had lost some from the back of his little pickup. Iki stopped to help and he was soon talked into heading back to town with Buck to help with the work party. Any extra motivation that Iki needed was supplied by thoughts of how good that first glass of milk would taste.

That night, over a dinner of spicy vegetable soup and fresh baked bread, Jaime could sense that something was up with Riley. He had been spending a great deal of time on Unfinished Business and making numerous lists and inventorying their medical supplies.

"What's going on dad?" Jaime asked. "Is there something happening that I should know about?"

"Boy, just like your mother. I can't get away with anything." Riley chuckled as he cleared away his dishes. He flicked on the solar powered lights that Billy had built for them and watched the small CFL bulb hanging from the ceiling come to life.

"Well honey." Sounding more serious than he had intended, "I'm basically getting itchy feet. My whole plan when I left Cleanetics was to travel and explore, to sail away on Unfinished Business into areas that may need medical or dental help. I didn't get a chance to do that."

Jaime just sat and listened but she instinctively knew by the tightness in her chest what was coming.

"I love it here. I think we have the best functioning colony in all of Hawaii and I am one of the few that have seen them all." Riley was now looking directly at Jaime. "I've talked to Marilyn and Tonya. Buck is chomping at the bit for an adventure. I think we are going to take Unfinished Business and do a circumnavigation of the Pacific."

Jaime knew it and she couldn't even remember the last time she had cried but she could feel the tears starting to well up.

Riley continued, "Japan, Hong Kong, hit a few places in the western pacific then head over to Alaska and then down the coast. I'd like to see San Diego again. There is a lot of information and research at Cleanetics that I was thinking of grabbing."

A single tear ran down Jaime's cheek and she quickly wiped it away.

"Sail down to Tahiti and Fiji and check out as many of the island groups as as we can. We are pretty confident that there are people there and if so, there are probably people in need of care. I think we could do it in twelve to eighteen months." Riley hesitated and could see that Jaime was upset. "I'm not really ready to retire and live the life of luxury here honey. I think I owe it to humanity or what's left of it, to do what I swore an oath to do and that's to help people, as many people as I can."

"I thought I lost you once." Jaime said, wiping another tear away. "I don't know if I'm up to another long journey." Jamie actually loved this place more than anywhere she had ever lived. The rocky shorelines and the few startling white beaches, the old pineapple fields and the scrub forests that lead up to the volcano. She had climbed it twice now and you could see the entire island laid out below you and even see over to Molokai and Maui.

"And I thought I lost you too. But I didn't." Not looking forward to what was coming, he hesitated. "You are more than capable of handling anything medically here." Riley was waiting for the question that he knew was coming.

Jamie was looking at him and she cocked her head. "You don't want me to come with you then?" Now the tears really started to flow and she made little attempt to hide them.

Riley took a deep breath, he was unsure but decided to just say what he felt. "Your journey here was one of the greatest adventures ever Jaime. You saw it all and conquered every obstacle in your path. This trip could be equally dangerous and I want you to live a long and happy life. I could go on and on and give you a hundred reasons but to answer your question, no. I think I need to do this myself." It was all true and he hoped she believed him as he still felt unfulfilled as his big plan for sailing away in Unfinished Business was sidetracked by Locust.

The thought of possibly losing him again was overwhelming but she remembered their initial talk in San Diego about him leaving Cleanetics and wanting to re-connect with Jeremy. Tired of the rat race, tired of corporate America and non-functioning government he just wanted to get back to the basics and return to just helping people. Building an amazing company, making so many discoveries, helping thousands of people but that wasn't what he was ultimately looking for and she knew it. Remembering the change in her father, how vibrant and young he looked when he decided to leave Cleanetics. Deep down she knew then, like she knows now, he needs more. The world had changed since then but the fundamentals were the same. She just couldn't stifle his enthusiasm for doing what every good doctor wants to do. Back then she didn't agree when he wanted to leave Cleanetics but knew deep down it needed to be done.

Silently she turned her head away and rose from the table, grabbing the remaining dishes. "I don't agree dad, but I understand. But that doesn't mean I have to be happy about it."

Since announcing his plan Jaime hadn't spent a lot of time with her father. She was still angry, still afraid and that just led her to be more disappointed in herself. For the better part of the last week Jaime had stayed nightly on JayJay, making up some phony excuses of what needed to be done there, knowing he didn't believe a word of it. Some people knew what she was going through and talking helped a little bit but it was her issue. Her closest confidant was Tessa and she may have given her the best advice of all; *'You can't make yourself happy by making someone else unhappy.'*

This would be their last Sunday feast before they left and spirits were high as dinner was finished and the tables cleared. There was no business this night as all the time was spent with wishes of safe travels and clear skies for the four adventurers. Unfinished Business was packed to the brim with supplies and a course was already charted for Midway Island. Deliciously cool champagne was served as Riley made the final toast.

"Every single one of you is to be commended for the richness of our lives here on Lanai. Our accomplishments are many and are needs are few. There are others though, out there, that will not have fared as well."

Riley took a moment and looked at the group. Each of them silently hung on his words, knowing that there was a deeper, more meaningful message yet to come.

"You all know my story, well actually, we all know each other's stories." His smile was now broad but his face belied the seriousness of what the message means to him. Riley quickly retold the events that led him to acquire Unfinished Business and how Locust had disrupted his plans. "I cannot in good conscience, be comfortable here knowing I have not completed what I had set out to do. I know I have disappointed my dear daughter and I hope she forgives me, again."

They were up past midnight clearing the air and when both Jaime and Riley went to sleep, they slept well. Eating a huge breakfast of bacon and eggs and fresh fruit, Riley and Jamie joined the procession to the harbour. Every member of the colony was there to wish them well and send them off. Leis of the most beautiful and fragrant flowers were given to the adventurers as they boarded and prepared to disembark. Jamie and Tessa stood together as Unfinished Business slowly pulled away from the dock.

Riley stood out on the stern and gave one final wave, his longish dark hair perfectly framed his smiling strong face. His shirt was open, revealing his lean tanned body which was in stark contrast to the delicate but brilliantly white flowers around his neck.

"Your dad is pretty hot for an old guy." Tessa said, straight-faced.

Jamie had really noticed how Tessa had blossomed here in Hawaii, no longer introspective and quiet. She didn't know if that was a good thing or not.

Now almost out of earshot, Jamie used her rusty American Sign Language to sign "I love you." Equally rusty, he signed it back and gave one final wave as he went forward to raise the mainsail as they cleared the mouth of the harbour. The huge sail filled with a crack and Unfinished Business heeled over ever so slightly as they set out into the unknown.

49

It seemed like it was a day of anniversaries for Jaime as she walked over to the medical clinic with a cup of coffee in her hand. It had been three months since Riley, Marilyn, Tonya and Buck had sailed away in Unfinished Business. It was also one month since baby Kanani had been born.

Tessa walked into the clinic carrying her little girl who was fast asleep in the sling against her mother's chest. Kanani started to wake and fuss a bit as she was placed on the examination table for her one month checkup, but that didn't last long. Jaime quickly checked her over and commented again on how beautiful she was and that they could not have thought of a better name, Kanani. Translated from old Hawaiian it meant *'beauty'*.

"You know Tessa, I'm still thinking of having a baby." Jaime was pinning the diaper back on, grateful that there hadn't been any accidents during her examination.

Kanani started to cry as she was passed back to Tessa who quickly sat down and opened her blouse. Baby Kanani was quickly quieted as she fed and Jaime pulled up another chair to sit beside Tessa.

Tessa simply said, "You should," as she stroked her baby's back. Tessa was initially a little afraid of the whole breastfeeding thing until she had talked to Marilyn who simply said that she can't really describe it but it's the most fundamental bond you can have with your baby. Marilyn told her, after the first time it'll never cross your mind again and she was right.

They talked for an hour and the conversation continually circled back to Jamie's dilemma. Although Tessa still couldn't quite understand it, Jaime was seemingly dead set on this artificial insemination thing. Tessa was teasing Jamie about that and trying to promote the virtues of their not so new anymore island life. "It's different now Jaime, the world has started over. I think you are still caught up in the past. We talked about this month's ago. When did you last have sex?"

"It's been so long, I can't even really remember." Jaime said, suddenly feeling somewhat embarrassed.

Tessa laughed at that although she wasn't really surprised. "Me too." She said with a sly smile.

That also brought a smile to Jamie's face as she could tell what Tessa was really asking. "I think you guys need to wait another couple of weeks. You need to take it very easy and let me know if there are any issues. Tell Iki to come get some condoms too."

They went outside the medical clinic and sat in the shade of a beautiful flowering white hibiscus tree. Jamie loved the subtle fragrance of this tree and she had taken a number of cuttings to plant around some of the more sterile looking areas of Manele Bay. They chatted while Kanani slept, discussing Jaime's plan and the discussion soon led to the attributes of the men in the colony. To

Tessa's surprise Jaime thought that one of the older men would make the perfect donor.

"The younger men will all no doubt produce offspring at some point. If I choose a father, or I guess a donor, that has a less likely chance of reproducing anyways, it'll add a little more genetic diversity into the mix for future generations."

Tessa rolled her eyes and wasn't buying the science argument. "Listen science girl that proves it. You really do need to have sex. You just need to think about you for once in your life. Geez."

Jamie looked back at Tessa with that little frown that showed her displeasure about being corrected or lectured. Tessa had seen it before and picked up on it right away. "Well if you want diversity, then . . . . I think it should be Billy."

Tessa looked away knowing she wouldn't be able to keep a straight face. Starting to laugh, she was afraid she would wake the baby. She loved Billy, everybody did and she didn't really mean to poke fun at his eccentricities. They had seen Billy a couple of days ago at the pond, shirtless, hands on his hips wearing a grass skirt and his work boots, his lightly tanned paleness covered with splotches of mud and dirt. Jamie had mentioned he looked like Mel Gibson in Braveheart and Tessa was still laughing about that one.

Jamie was trying to be serious which was increasingly hard to do with Tessa. "I think one red head in this climate is enough."

Tessa returned home later that afternoon and found a note from Iki. He was over at the fish pond helping Billy with something. She decided to walk over there to get some exercise. As most mothers are, Tessa was critical of her body post pregnancy. With a completely healthy and natural diet, including none of the old processed foods of her youth, her weight gain had been minimal. Still, in a climate where everyone was virtually naked, she wanted to get back to looking her best. She took Kanani from the car seat and put her into a stroller and headed out the door, setting a brisk pace for the pond.

Tessa had stopped wearing shoes just before she had given birth. Her feet had become so swollen she couldn't wear them anyways and now she just really enjoyed going barefoot. The grass of Hulopo'e Park was soft and luxurious on her feet and it felt even nicer as she approached the pond. Billy had designed and built some kind of pivoting fulcrum crane that dropped a baited net into the deepest part of the pond. Both he and Iki were now straining to lift the net out of the water and pivot it back to land. Tessa could see the net was filled with squirming masses of both prawns and fish.

"Great job guys." Tessa was watching them from the shade of a nearby tree.

Iki ran over and kissed both his girls as Billy was madly shoveling most of their catch back into the pond. He kept just a few of the smaller fish and a small bucket of prawns. Looking up from his knees Billy called out, "At least we know it works." No one was really listening.

Iki then gave him the classic Hawaiian Shaka hand sign which could mean anything from good job to just hang loose. Billy had never mastered the Shaka, his fist was always too tight and while he properly extended both his thumb and pinkie, he shook them too fast. That had always elicited howls of laughter from the native Hawaiians as he looked like he was being electrocuted or had some form of advanced Parkinson's disease.

A lone frigate bird floated high above them, seemingly motionless on the wind. His sharp eyes did not miss the fact that the pond was now full of fish. Two of Billy's newest fans also watched silently from the other side of the pond. A pair of Nene, the endangered Hawaiian goose, had found the pond last week and had rarely left the area. Breeding season was approaching and it appeared that this was going to be their chosen spot.

After doing some research in the library, Billy had discovered that there were fewer than a thousand Nene in all of Hawaii at the time Locust struck. Many of the native Hawaiians had never seen a Nene in the wild and almost the entire colony had come to look at the pair. It was considered by some as a fortuitous sign from the old Hawaiian gods that their colony was chosen by the most revered bird in all of the islands.

Billy couldn't agree more and had taken the pair under his wing so to speak. He was just finishing a large chicken wire enclosure on the far side of the pond that would keep any dogs away from the ground nesting birds. He had collected a wheelbarrow full of dried reeds and grasses from around the park and dumped them in the middle of the enclosure and was making his way out when the pair flew in.

He watched from outside the fence as both birds rooted around in the pile. It was apparently to their satisfaction as they then both stood tall flapping their wings and honking. It was the start of their mating ritual and Billy quietly left them alone as they noisily got to work.

50

Mulder and Scully flew in low over the pond and landed close to their enclosure. They were quickly followed by their four fully grown goslings that were just molting into their adult plumage. Only a few people in the colony understood the story behind Billy naming the geese after characters in his favourite old TV show. Most just chalked it up to Billy being Billy.

Last month Jamie had moved out of the little house in town and moved into one of the beach bungalows at Manele Bay. She felt she needed a change in scenery and was also hoping for a change in luck. Her third attempt at artificially inseminating herself had proved fruitless and each time she saw Kanani made her want a baby even more.

It was Sunday and it was raining quite hard. They had amazingly enough, never had it rain for Sunday feast. A number of people were trying to string up some tarps over the courtyard but most just sat under the trees to hopefully wait it out. This was Hawaii, when it rained, you got wet. When it stopped raining, then you got dry.

A light tap on her door startled Jaime and she started to stand up, the screen door opened and Tessa came in.

"Any news?" Her eyes were bright and her face hopeful.

"Negative again." Jaime picked up the pregnancy test stick and threw it into the trash. "I didn't think it would be this hard. You spend all of your twenties trying not to get pregnant and then when you want to, it doesn't work."

"Well, if you were with a man I'd just say keep trying but . . ." Tessa could see that perturbed look come across Jaime's face. "Maybe you need someone with some higher octane fuel?" Tessa giggled but quickly saw that Jaime didn't see the humour in it.

The colonies biggest secret was still who the donor was. No one would admit to it and Jaime wasn't saying anything. Numerous bets had been placed and someone had even painted a large sign in town with all the men's names and their odds of being the one. Not that the colony needed any comic relief but it kept everyone talking and laughing and it was a pleasant diversion from their normal chores. Everyone was on baby watch which probably added to the pressure Jaime was feeling.

Just a light drizzle now fell as the covering was slowly taken off the underground oven. The layers of leaves and wet burlap were removed and the steamy smell of the slow roasted pork and venison quickly filled the air. If there was one thing that had a routine in the colony, it was Sunday feast. Everyone had a job and tables were set, platters filled and chairs arranged with absolute precision. As if on cue, the clouds parted and beams of soft coloured light emerged from the setting sun. A little cheer went up as they all sat down to eat.

Just as the dishes were starting to be cleared away, Jaime decided to make her pre-emptive strike. Last

Sunday after feast, she had been teased and chided by almost everyone and although it was all done with good intentions, she didn't want to go through that again. Jaime was uncharacteristically sensitive about this issue.

"Can I have everyone's attention please?" Jaime asked, motioning those cleaning up to come back into the circle of tables and chairs.

There were giggles and laughter and a couple of off colour comments before Jaime started. The sun had now set and with the moon not yet up, the only light came from the oil filled tiki torches and table lanterns.

"I just want to say that I'm still trying and thanks for everyone's support." Jaime was interrupted by Kai Kaiwi who was the oldest member of the colony at seventy five.

"Is it my turn tonight?" Kai said to riotous laughter from most of the group.

Just as Jaime started to speak she heard running coming down the path from behind her. Everyone turned to see a man running towards them. As he entered the light they could see he had a big salt and pepper beard and was wearing cut off pants and a tattered shirt.

It took Jaime a second to recognize him, it was her father.

Cheers rose up from the group as Riley was mobbed by everyone. Jaime had her head buried in his shoulder hugging him tight as Buck, Marilyn and Tonya entered the fray. The conversations were both excited and deafening, all the dogs were barking at the excitement and it was like New Year's Eve in Times Square.

It took almost a minute before anyone took notice of the four others standing out on the path. As more heads turned to see the newcomers the noise quieted and Tonya's voice boomed out for everyone to be quiet.

"We have four new members of the colony everyone." Tonya beckoned them to come forward.

A lanky but well-muscled teenaged boy was the first to emerge, his huge afro and features indicated a Polynesian heritage. "This is Taylor." Tonya called out. Cries of welcome and aloha filled the air.

Next was a young girl of no more than ten who seemed rather shy. Her skin was jet black and she had the obvious features of an Australian aborigine, parts of her hair appeared bleached by the sun. "Come in Cassie." Tonya called out.

Calls of "Aloha Cassie," erupted from the crowd. A couple of the woman came forward to embrace her and make her feel welcome. It had been a long time since Cassie had seen this many people.

Everyone looked intently at the remaining two. One was much taller and the other was bald with a bandana or something covering his face. As they slowly made their way into the light it became obvious to everyone that the smaller man was blind as he held the elbow of the taller man. His face was also horribly disfigured, most of his nose was missing and he wore a double eye patch over a long welted red wound that stretched from temple to temple. He appeared to be in his twenties but it was hard to tell.

Most people were not looking at the taller man. He had long black hair that was pulled back into a ponytail, his skin was tanned a coppery light brown, his features were both soft and strong and he was obviously Oriental.

Riley was still holding Jamie, looking at her eyes as they moved from one man to the other until she slowly realized what she saw was real.

Jaime didn't hear Tonya introduce them as she pushed her way through the crowd and threw herself into Slinky's arms. He had known she was here and had seen her coming so he had the good sense to step slightly away as he absorbed Jaime's rush.

Her tears immediately stained his sun faded blue shirt as she tried to talk but no words would come out. Slinky held her tight and stroked her hair as she buried her face into his chest. Most of the crowd was now watching them, perplexed as to what was taking place. Their beautiful Jamie, a doctor, a leader and someone that was respected by all was blubbering into the chest of this tall Oriental stranger. They all fell silent as they tried to understand what they were seeing.

Jaime gently pushed away from him but kept a hold on his muscled forearms. Only Slinky could see the tracks of her tears glistening in the torchlight and the tremble in her bottom lip as she slowly ran her hands up his body. Her hands now on his cheeks she pulled Slinky's face down towards hers. Their kiss was long and passionate as the crowds silence quickly turned into hoots and hollers.

Tessa came to them both, tears also streaming down her cheeks. She knew how much Slinky really meant to Jaime, she had heard all the stories. Reaching out to hug them both as more people joined in, a large knot of people had now formed around the couple. Tonya quickly assisted Jun, the blind newcomer, out of the way and into a nearby chair.

Only a few people went home that night as the party moved to a large bonfire that was lit on the beach. Plates of leftover food and fruit were spread out on the tables and a couple of cases of wine were brought out of the now crumbling Four Season's bar.

Jun spoke very little English and Slinky routinely translated the goings on into Mandarin for him as they both sat passively in the sand next to each other. The explanations and adventures were spellbinding to those listening and everyone was mesmerized as Slinky recounted what had happened to them in China. How Jun, a Shao Lin monk had miraculously survived being shot in the face by General Han, the architect of Locust. Jun's injuries were severe and he would have surely died without Slinkys assistance. Once Jun was well enough to travel they tried to escape the coming winter and decided to move south to warmer weather and eventually made their way to Hong Kong. Almost everyone in attendance was appalled at Slinkys description of the environmental degradation across China. The huge industrial machine that was China's economy had come tumbling down with many cities and most river systems being ruined by releases of chemicals and toxins. Slinky appropriately pointed out that many rivers in China were already severely polluted but what had occurred after Locust was astonishing to everyone.

Using various vehicles and eventually even bicycles, both Slinky and Jun had eventually made it to Hong Kong. The colonists were in awe of Jun's abilities to ride a bicycle without being able to see and this was just the first instance of many for the impressive Jun.

After only a few days in Hong Kong they had found Cassie and Taylor living onboard a small floating restaurant in the harbour. Their struggles continued through the first few weeks as finding enough drinkable water had become a problem. Slinky respectfully patted Jun on the shoulder as he recanted how that problem was solved when Jun suggested they capture the ample rain water that fell almost daily. Their lives had just started to improve when Riley and the crew of Unfinished Business sailed into Hong Kong harbour.

Riley was asked about what had happened in the months prior to them arriving in Hong Kong and he tried to share those adventures but he soon tired and called an end to the proceedings by saying he needed some sleep. There was little argument from those that remained as the fire slowly burnt itself out in the growing light of dawn.

As the crowd dispersed, Riley wasn't the only one to notice Jamie and Slinky walking hand in hand back towards the bungalows.

51

The sun was now fully up and the light was streaming through the open windows of her bungalow. Jaime could see how tired Slinky was and she busied herself with shutting the blinds, slightly darkening both the sitting room and the bedroom. They hadn't spoken a lot since they had left the beach, just sitting on the small couch, fingers enter twined, enjoying each other's company.

Rising off the couch Jamie looked at him and said, "Time for bed. Just give me a minute." She pointed off at the bedroom and spun lightly away heading towards the small but well-appointed bathroom.

There was not enough water pressure for a proper shower in the bungalow so Jaime kept a large five gallon bucket of water in the shower enclosure. Quickly stripping off her clothes she started to sponge off, the cool water immediately brought out a series of goose bumps over her arms and legs. Looking down at her still full and shapely breasts, she was not unhappy with what she saw. Squeezing the sponge across her neck and chest, the water felt exhilarating on her skin which felt like it was charged with static electricity.

Refreshing the big sponge, she lifted her hair and squeezed it against the back of her neck, the water cascaded down her back and splattered noisily on the tile of the floor. Before she could dip the sponge a third time she felt his hand. Gently taking the sponge he dipped it back into the bucket and ever so slowly he rubbed it across the top of her back, the sponge barely touching her skin. The gentle waves of the cool water ran down her back, over her buttocks and down her legs to the floor, barely making a sound. Every goose bump now seemed bigger, intensified by everything that was happening. He did the same thing on her chest, the big sponge slowly releasing its water in gentle waves over her until there was no more. Unable to move, Jaime stood still feeling the last droplets of water falling from her breasts which tingled and ached, seemingly struggling to break free of some invisible restraint.

Reaching up behind her she ran her hands up his shoulders to his face and could feel the stubble on his chin which contrasted wonderfully to the silky smoothness of his cheeks. As she ran her fingers up into his hair and around his ears, he gently caressed her hip bones. Then painfully slowly, he ran his hands up her stomach and over her breasts which elicited a sharp intake of breath and an involuntary shudder of her entire body. Jamie was virtually paralyzed as that single touch had brought her right to the edge of ecstasy.

Lying on top of him in the big bed she kissed his face and then his neck as she slowly slid down his body. Placing her hands flat against his chest Jaime reared up slightly. Every nerve ending in her body came alive, a feeling of overall warmth enveloped her, a feeling she had never felt before. Slowly, ever so slowly, they moved together and it was like they had done it a thousand times before. Slinky was overwhelmed by sensations and feelings that he had never experienced, never even dreamed of.

Jaime's fingertips dug deeper into his chest as his hands squeezed her biceps a little tighter. Both their bodies had started to stiffen. Both now slack-jawed with anticipation, their minds joined as tightly as their bodies, they had become one organism, fulfilling its most fundamental genetic instruction. Each opening their eyes at the precise instant, they completely consummated their connection. Explosive was the only word she could later use to describe her orgasm. For as vivacious and attractive as Jaime was, she had only a handful of lovers, all more enthusiastic than talented. She now knew the difference between having sex and making love.

Falling onto his chest he enveloped her in his long arms and they lay there, both breathing deeply, in time with each other. Connected both body, mind and soul, sleep came quickly and it was the deepest most restful sleep either of them had ever had in a long, long time.

Tessa had walked by Jaime's bungalow twice later in the day and the blinds had been drawn both times. This time they were open but Jaime and Slinky were nowhere to be seen. Walking down to the beach she saw them splashing and frolicking in the small shore break of Manele Bay, Brandy was barking as her tennis ball rolled nearby in the surf, just out of her reach.

Tessa watched them from a distance for a few moments before realizing doing that was kind of creepy. Nonchalantly moving towards them, trying to act like their meeting was unplanned and failing badly at it, Tessa called out a greeting as she approached. Picking up the ball, Tessa threw it down the beach for Brandy as Slinky and Jaime came out of the water and grabbed their towels. Tessa noticed that Slinky had a serious farmer's tan going and that made her giggle a little bit as you don't see a lot of those in Hawaii. Looking at his long and lithe body, slim waist and wide swimmer-like shoulders she knew there was no reason for him to keep his shirt on.

As Slinky threw the ball again for Brandy, Jaime came over towards Tessa, flicking her wet hair forward as she towelled off. Wrapping the towel around her long raven coloured hair, Jaime stood back up, her eyes sparkled like diamonds and her smile told the story.

"Hey Tessa, what's up?"

Tessa had seen Jaime in a bikini hundreds of times but for some reason had never noticed how absolutely gorgeous she was, until now. Trying not to stare, Tessa blurted out, "Well, I had a question for you but I think you just answered it." Tessa's grin became a smile as she rubbed one index finger over the other. Tessa spun away to walk back up the beach, calling out over her shoulder, "Naughty, naughty girl."

52

All of the newcomers that had recently returned on Unfinished Business quickly adjusted to their new lives at Lanai colony. Cassie, no longer shy and withdrawn proved to be an adept storyteller. With quivering lips she initially recounted how their family had been in Hong Kong on a trade mission on behalf of the Australian government and how they had become trapped when Locust struck. Cassie's mother had actually survived the event but had drowned shortly after when she fell off the boat that they had taken shelter on in Hong Kong harbour. Cassie's confidence quickly grew and her ever so detailed stories and recollections of her cultural heritage were now told eloquently and emphatically, captivating both the children and adults and it was an eagerly anticipated new addition to the communal gatherings at Sunday feast.

Becca had become almost instantly infatuated with Cassie and the two young girls quickly became the best of friends. It soon became evident that they belonged together and Sam welcomed Cassie into his home like a second daughter. Shortly after their arrival all the newcomers were asked what they needed and how the colony could help them and Cassie's only request was to have someone teach her how to swim. Although the two young girls already had many things in common, Becca was enthralled to be able to do that for her. In just a few short days Cassie had lost her fear of the water and soon was able to swim almost as well as Becca's previous student Tessa.

Taylor had bonded very closely with Buck on their time sailing back to Hawaii on Unfinished Business and he moved in to Buck's small house in town. Buck had lost his only son in a diving accident many years ago, when he was about Taylor's age. They were a formidable force when it came to work parties as each tried to outdo the other, the young man versus the older man. Taylor was adopted and raised as a Mennonite, his faith powered his drive to work hard and to unselfishly help others. Taylor like Cassie was also trapped in Hong Kong where he was a delegate attending the World Youth Religions Conference. Adopted from his birthplace on a small atoll in the Solomon Islands as a baby, he had never before left his new home which was in a small farming community in southern Saskatchewan. When he had found Cassie in Hong Kong she was very sick, possibly from drinking polluted water and he had nursed her back to health. Just a month later, Slinky and Jun had arrived in Hong Kong and it wasn't too long after that that they saw Riley's majestic green yacht sail into the harbour one warm and sticky night. Taylor had little choice but to fully adapt to colony life as he was under the watchful gaze and guiding hand of Tonya who upon first setting eyes on him, knew he was now the one for her. Now away from the prying eyes of shipboard life, Tonya and Taylor spent more and more time together in the tropical paradise of Lanai and she soon forgot about the shy Marco from Maui, who had not kept his promise to visit.

Jun's story was both tragic and heroic. He was blinded and almost killed by the man responsible for developing the Locust virus and changing the world forever. Saved and nursed back to health by Slinky who also should have been dead was it not for General Han's gun jamming, they both had battled their way through many obstacles to finally reach the China coast and make their way south to Hong Kong. Jun had never wallowed in his disability and stoically accepted his horrific injuries as only a Shao Lin monk could. His quiet, calm and ever thoughtful demeanor helped cut through his ever diminishing language barrier as he adapted better than anyone, except himself, had anticipated.

Billy had immediately built a friendship with Jun, feeling they had a deep connection as both were warriors, both injured in battle and both now trying to survive in a strange land. For Billy, born and raised in the high plains of Montana and spending the better part of a decade in the harsh deserts of Iraq and Afghanistan, the tropical paradise of Hawaii was both a drastic change and welcome relief. Jun felt the same although he did say he would miss the seasons passing from one to the next as they did at the monastery in northern China. Jun worked hard every day to improve his language skills and he completely embraced his new home and the colonists who he referred to as his brothers and sisters. Quickly learning the idiosyncrasies of most of the colonist's footfalls, he could often greet them by name before they spoke. The children were befuddled by this ability and often tried to sneak up on Jun but they rarely could. His disability only seemed to heighten his already keen senses but it became quite the game and Jun enjoyed it as much as the children.

Jun had requested assistance in building a small shelter near the beach where he could live as it was evident even to a blind man that Slinky had found another roommate. Billy had a better idea and with Tessa's expert assistance with the backhoe, they had excavated a large shallow depression underneath one of the huge shade trees just on the edge of Manele Bay. Billy backed a small travel trailer into the depression, put it on blocks and then backfilled the hole. The trailer's door was now level with the ground and Jun had a small, safe and comfortable home that he could navigate in and around easily. His needs were few and being able to brew tea on his own, whenever he liked, made him very happy.

Quickly adapting to his new surroundings, Jun learned the pathways to the beach and back and forth through the resort despite his lack of sight. Billy found him every morning meditating, sitting on the same rock stoically still for hours, seemingly looking out into the bay. A broken tree limb was soon turned into a stout staff that he not only used to get around but to practice his martial arts. Later each morning after meditation, Jun would mark a large circle into the sand of Manele Bay with the staff and perform the ancient Shao Lin martial arts rituals. Those that watched were routinely amazed that he never stepped outside of the circle, not even once, despite not being able to see it.

What really impressed Billy though was how Jun not only interacted but blended in with nature, especially the animals. He would often see him stop and cock his head towards a tree and then Billy would hear the birdsong or see him stop at a flower only to see one of the rare

Hawaiian yellow faced bees fly silently away from it. The dogs followed him everywhere and he quickly learned their names, recognizing them as he did the colonists. The dogs that lived at Manele Bay all came to visit Jun at least once a day, often waiting silently and patiently for Jun to finish his morning rituals before they headed out on a walk together. Billy remembered the highly trained dogs of the Army Rangers and how they were always on edge, aggressively bristling with excitement and anticipation, awaiting their next dangerous assignment. Those dogs were soldiers after all, but he was sure that if they spent five minutes with Jun they would be as laid back and calm as the dogs of Manele Bay were.

Even Mulder and Scully weren't afraid of Jun and it wasn't just the tamer animals as just yesterday, Billy had seen Jun standing out in the bay in knee deep water. As he approached he saw a stingray slowly swimming around his feet. Crying out a warning, Billy rushed into the water only to see Jun dip his hand into the water and cradle the ray in both his hands. Turning it over, Jun caressed its stomach before releasing it, his hands gliding delicately over its slightly leathery skin. In heavily accented English Jun turned to Billy with a smile and had said, "No problem bro."

Slinky had rarely left Jaime's side during the last few weeks as they discussed all the details that had led up to the Locust event. Neither of them truthfully had ever saw anything in the cards more than a profound friendship between them and their love for each other was both sudden and shocking. It was obvious to everyone, except the two of them, that it was always meant to be.

Riley, Jamie and Slinky spent many long nights together talking of not only the past but the future. How man had failed itself and how they had somehow gotten a second chance. None of them were really happy with the way the world was going before Locust, they saw its danger and frailties. What they soon saw though was an opportunity to influence the future by learning from that very past. Each of them were born leaders and they each felt a deep obligation to do everything within their powers to set whatever is left of mankind off in the right direction.

Jun was often included in these conversations as not only did he have unique and thought provoking insights, it helped him immensely with his English studies. The most interesting discussions for all of them were about the practicalities of building a proper society in their new world. How to educate the young, how to care for the sick and how to govern what was hoped to be a just and caring society that would in all likelihood, quickly develop. It was just five hundred years between the industrial revolution and the space age but all the technology and knowledge was already here, there were just not enough people to make it work. It was agreed by all that mankind would quickly return to its dominant place on the planet. Unfortunately the discussion often circled back to how many generations would it take for the world to get fucked up again by the greed and selfishness seemingly inherent in the species.

Jun aptly put an end to that negativity once and for all with a comment that future generations would recall fondly; "You cannot stifle a man's drive to succeed. But you can help him understand what success really means."

53

The days turned to weeks and the months to years as the initial fight to survive was left far behind on Lanai. The colony was thriving, more successful than any of them ever dreamed. It was no surprise to any of them that they could find enough food and shelter here to live out their days but what set them apart from other Locust survivors was how quickly they adapted from a bunch of fearful and panicked individuals into a cohesive and functioning community.

Both settlements, Manele Bay and Lanai City, grew into small almost semi-autonomous enclaves that continued to meet every Sunday for feast. With a growing population, the Sunday get-togethers had become bigger and better and turned into an all-day event. The children showcased their singing and dancing skills while the adults took the time to catch up on each other's activities. Now that all the pre-Locust food was gone, Sunday feast also provided the opportunity for the colonists to barter. Although no one owned the chickens and goats or the vegetables and fruit, it took time and effort to capture, pick or prepare things. Bags of mangoes were traded for a freshly caught fish or fresh eggs bartered for someone's time to help fix a leaking roof. When you had extra of anything, it was brought to Sunday feast and it always found a home. Billy relished feast days as people would surround his wildly successful aquaculture experiment, waiting for him to lift his net that would be full of fish and prawns. Word spread far and wide through the islands and every available bottle or can of root beer eventually made its way to Lanai. Billy's taro and rice gardens were equally successful and more than enough to feed everyone on the island and both of those crops proved to be extremely valuable when they started to routinely trade with other colonies.

Those living in Lanai City were better suited to manage the livestock of the island and do any hunting that was needed as they were closer to the fertile slopes and forested ravines where the animals lived. Although managing might not be the best word to describe their experiment with the beef originally brought over from the Big Island. Only ever able to keep a couple of cows contained at one time, the ever expanding herd eventually all became wild and were hunted as needed as were the pigs and deer. There was always a supply of eggs and freshly butchered chickens but the surprising hit were the goats that happily lived in town. It became somewhat obvious to the colonists why goats were always in the forefront of what was referred to as third world or developing countries prior to Locust. The goats produced an endless supply of milk that produced incredible yogurts and cheese, they ate anything and were easy to care for, only asking for shade and water. Although animal protein was not in short supply, they occasionally culled the herd and they found the meat to be very tasty when cooked slowly in the underground ovens with garlic and the wild fragrant ginger that is found all over the island.

Inter-island trade had also become a regular occurrence with colonies on Oahu, Maui, Kauai and the Big Island interacting more and more. No one was ever found living on Molokai and it was amazing how quickly the jungle took back the towns and settlements there. In just a few years Molokai was returned to an almost natural state. Riley and sometimes Jaime made a point to go along on these short visits to the neighbouring islands once every few months or so to provide any needed medical care. Marilyn and Tonya did the same to look after the dental needs of the survivors.

The only thing that Lanai lacked for was fuel. Propane, gasoline and diesel were still relatively abundant on the other islands, especially Oahu with its big tank farms and military bases. What the other colonies wanted more than rice and taro seedlings or fresh meat was the amazing expertise of Billy, Glenn and Buck. Not only could they fix just about anything but they could design and build things like solar panels for homes, solar powered golf carts, water systems and the like. Not that Billy minded helping out but he preferred to show someone how to build their own rice paddy as opposed to supplying someone with the rice. It was a living breathing example of that old saying about give a man a fish and you feed him for a day. Teach a man to fish and you feed him for a lifetime. A small settlement in Makaha on Oahu was so appreciative of the work that Billy, Glenn and Buck did for them that they actually towed a barge loaded with three fuel tanker trucks to Lanai. That doubled the colonies fuel supply and it gave them an easy and operational method of refueling in the future.

As the old schoolhouse in town was slowly emptied of supplies it once again became a school, but unlike any other school that may have ever existed. A portion was reserved for mothers and infants, an easy place to all get together and socialize with everything they needed. Acting also as a day care it allowed parents to have their infants cared for while they worked to bring in a harvest or whatever other job urgently needed their attention. The other children of the colony were broken up into three groups depending upon their ages. School was in session four days a week from 8:00 a.m. to 2:00 p.m. Tuesday to Friday, or that was the plan. This was still Hawaii and sometimes schedules and times didn't mean a whole lot. With the colony functioning like clockwork it was easy to get volunteers to assist at the school. Volunteer teachers and assistants were found for the more traditional academic subjects and many more were found for what some may consider the unconventional, but functional subjects.

Jun taught a very demanding martial arts program twice a week that also included aspects of spiritualism and self-awareness. Every single child was taught not only how to swim but how to snorkel and surf. Traditional Hawaiian culture and beliefs were taught alongside the traditional world history classes. Animal husbandry, fishing, hunting and farming were all taught with equal importance. Singing, dancing, organized sports and even a study of world religions were included, all squeezed into a very tight teaching schedule. It was a challenge at first to refocus those that had been out of school and those that were now old enough to attend but somehow Jun was the one who made it all come together. A compassionate and gifted man, he also demanded respect and obedience and rarely had to correct anyone twice. The school soon became so successful that a few more families from other islands joined the Lanai colony specifically so their children could attend the school.

Although all the kids already loved Jun even before the school even opened, he wasn't the most popular teacher. By far the biggest hit for the students was Billy. Jaime originally took on the coordination role and with the many volunteer teachers they designed and prepared the learning plans and materials for each class but somehow Billy had managed to get his course, what he called *fundamental engineering,* approved without any plans whatsoever. The reason, as Billy explained in a way that only he could, was that each day brought adventures and challenges and that was what his course was about. Rarely if ever where they in the classroom and somehow Billy was able to weave an activity or point out a problem that needed to be solved and he guided the students, interactively and hands on, through to its resolution. Admittedly, some of these took a long time but he engaged and challenged everyone in such a way that they didn't even realize that they were learning until it had happened. From building palm frond windmills to charge your household batteries to designing and building a cabled walkway across a ravine, Billy's enthusiasm was contagious and his knowledge and ingenuity was ever so slowly passed from teacher to student. Most importantly the students learned to think critically, use common sense and work as a team. All three of those skills were necessities in this new world.

One rainy afternoon, Slinky, Jaime and Riley sat in the small library at the school and were discussing some aspects of Dr. Bo's book. The book was one of the few possessions that Slinky had brought with him from China. It was a little muggy inside the building today, the normal cooling trade winds replaced by today's un-typical wet and dreary weather.

"The work they did was amazing and I can see now why it was never published or shared within the scientific community." Jaime was referring to both the breakthroughs on genetic profiling and how General Han's team had been able to implant genetic material into a virus. "Just think of the possibilities of using these implanting techniques for curing disease. Too bad they thought it was better suited as a weapon."

"I was so angry when I learned my father knew of Locust. I still struggle with it." Slinky never spoke of his father and his face did nothing to betray his feelings. "I still want to believe it was the system that corrupted him. They were all reaching for the brass ring of power and control. Especially the old time communists in the military like Han, they used the fear of democracy to blackmail the government into killing their own people. That's how it all started. The Chinese government planned to use Locust to ensure not only Chinese survival but Chinese supremacy and then they unbelievably used it to destroy the world."

"Not just China, Shing." Riley could still not bring himself to call him Slinky. "It was the entire world that had started to go mad. Look at how crazy everything was becoming. I'm convinced most other governments would have done the same. How many times did dictators and governments use chemical weapons against their own people in the last few decades? Look what that sick bastard Assad did in Syria. Government, big business, even the environmental movement was corrupted by those seeking power. That's what made me want to leave Cleanetics, people just wanted the power. The more you have the more you want. I think it's just an inherent flaw in the human character."

Jaime hadn't spoken much the last hour or so. These discussions often brought her down and it was hard to go back to that place. "Not all humans dad. I have never witnessed you step on or over anyone."

Riley just smiled at her. "Well, when you look at what we have become here, I would hope that that flaw is being bred out of us."

"Ya, it's not exactly Lord of the Flies around here is it?" Slinky often commented about the serenity of their colony, amazed at the resiliency of the survivors, after what they had all been through. "Maybe there is something in the water?"

They talked until it was approaching dinnertime and then Dr. Bo's book was put back into its locked container.

Jaime could sense that something was up with her dad but when asked, he just said everything was fine. On his last trip to Oahu, Riley had brought back a huge cache of computer hard drives and reference books after spending a couple of days at the University of Hawaii. He was spending an inordinate amount of time studying or looking for something but she guessed he wasn't quite ready to talk about it yet. She knew something was going on though, a gift that Riley had always said was inherited from her mother.

Jaime and Slinky rode their bicycles back to their bungalow at Manele Bay as the late afternoon heat was starting to wane. They both thought it was the most enjoyable way to travel from town back home, especially since it was all downhill.

54

There were no seasons in Hawaii to help the colonists keep track of time and the warm breezy days blended seamlessly together as time comfortably marched on. Sunday was the only day of significance, for both those that worshipped and for the communal gatherings of Sunday feast. Monday to Saturday became irrelevant, those were just the days between Sunday's.

Lanai colony continued to prosper and slowly became a microcosm of what society was prior to Locust. Some people left the island and some people came. A few people had died while a few more had been born.

Tessa could tell this wasn't going to be a long labour, the baby was coming and there wasn't much she or anyone else could do about it, not that they wanted to. Her two previous pregnancies had gone well and she didn't expect this to be any different.

Jamie took her blood pressure and pulse and had a quick look under the sheet covering her legs as she lay on the examination table in the medical centre. "You're dilating quickly Tessa, shouldn't be long now."

Both of them could hear quite a commotion outside in the office area and suddenly the door burst open and Kimo, Jamie's four year old son ran into the room holding his twin sisters favourite doll. Caitlen was right behind him screaming to get it back.

"Out, both of you!" Jamie rarely raised her voice and that immediately stopped the twins in their tracks and they stood there, open mouthed, looking at their mom. Both Becca and Cassie, who were supposed to be babysitting the children, were nowhere to be seen.

Jaime immediately asked Iki who was here to help and support the birth, "Could you please take these children outside and find Cassie."

Iki looked down at Tessa and she just nodded to him as she suffered through another series of cramps. Tessa's family history was one of easy births and her first two were certainly not problematic but she couldn't help but wonder if this one would buck the odds. Never one to complain, Tessa handled the pain silently, knowing there was still much more to come. Another contraction immediately brought her mind back to the present and she went through her breathing ritual as Iki came back into the room. Their brown eyes locked as he walked over and again took her hand. There is nothing worse than to sit by and see your loved one in pain and there is nothing you can do about it Iki thought. Like every other expectant father, he supported the woman he loved as best he could, silently thankful that it was not men who gave birth.

Later that day Tessa, with a few minor complications, delivered a beautiful baby boy for which Iki was very grateful. He loved his two daughters but like most father's he really wanted a son. Iki's normally electric white smile was somehow brightened this day as he gently rocked the baby while Jamie looked after Tessa, who needed a few stitches. Standing by the open window he adjusted the small birthing blanket that covered everything except his new son's cherubic little face. Tessa called for him, "Let me see my little Iki." Iki walked over and placed the newborn on Tessa's chest. Not surprisingly, the name stuck and Little Iki happily enjoyed his first meal as the one hundredth member of Lanai colony.

Nine previous births from the original colonists had been supplemented by almost sixty new arrivals. Word had spread amongst the islands of the success and just the overall good vibe of Lanai. The biggest contingent had come from the Big Island two years after Mama Huna had died. Losing the leader of the movement, their irrational hatred and resentment of non-Hawaiians had appropriately lost its allure and twenty three mostly young survivors had arrived and sheepishly asked for forgiveness and sanctuary. They were welcomed, as was everyone on Lanai.

Jaime heard the clip-clop of hoof beats outside and knew that Jun had arrived. Billy had captured one of the old stable horses that were previously used to give tourists rides around Lanai City and the old mare quickly adjusted to its former life as a riding horse. Jun now used Willow to travel around the island and he no longer had to rely on others which was the way that he preferred to live his life. Willow acted as Jun's eyes and they bonded quickly as Jun seemed to do with all animals. Willow now called the area around Manele Bay her home and was only ever a whistle away when Jun needed her. She formed just another spoke in the symbiotic wheel of how Lanai colony existed as the lush grass of Hulopo'e Park and vegetable cuttings from the gardens sustained Willow. She provided Jun with transportation and provided Billy with ample manure to fertilize his gardens and the circle was complete.

Jun entered the clinic using his staff to get around the furniture and said in his improving but still fragmented English, "I have missed the birth but I still wish to give you my blessings."

"How does he always know what's going on." Iki whispered to Tessa, shaking his head in amazement. Like everyone, Iki liked and respected Jun but he had always been a little nervous around him due to his seemingly physic ways.

They all greeted Jun as he was guided over to the bed and he took Tessa'a hand and murmured some words they did not understand. Jun turned and reached out to Iki, shaking his hand and congratulating him on the birth of his son. Tessa just smiled as she held her baby to her chest as Iki again shook his head, continually dumbfounded by Jun's perceptions. No one had told him it was a boy.

Tessa had found spending time with Jun very enlightening and it reminded her of her youth, sitting with her tribal elders and hearing the stories and beliefs of their ancestors. Many other colonists also found Jun to be a very spiritual person and sought out his opinions and guidance. His grace and wisdom was to become a guiding force for future generations just as it had become a key element in Lanai colonies first official school.

Many credited Riley and now Jun for the continued success and harmony of their colony but it wasn't perfect. Those on Lanai were not besieged by the cancerous resentment of what had happened or alcohol and drug problems like some others were, but some tension was starting to creep into the fabric of their lives. Previously there was rarely a word spoken in anger but the discussions and debates after Sunday feast were starting to become somewhat feisty. There was still open communication and most discussions were purposeful and respectful but sometimes sides were taken and harsh words exchanged. The expectation of everyone always agreeing was not realistic but the more successful the colony became, the more the undesirable traits of our species started to bubble to the surface.

Some individuals had started to challenge the communal governance model that they operated under. What was occasionally referred to jokingly as 'Hawaiian communism' had obviously worked but now, things felt a little different. Somewhat regular trading between the colonies had already started but they were a long way off from returning to the capitalistic free market economy that some wanted. Although the idea of personal wealth was long forgotten by most of the colony, it was not forgotten by everyone.

As they usually did, Slinky, Jamie and their twins watched the sun set from the edge of Manele Bay. Their beach blanket was spread wide on the warm sand and was covered with the children's toys and books. Jun had masterfully built kites that looked like colourful birds for the children and they each stared skyward holding the strings and watching them swoop and flutter in the diminishing winds of yet another perfect sunset. Slinky and Jamie were so proud of the twins who seemed to be growing up way too fast. They were both tremendously smart, which was really no surprise and they both had such loving and giving personalities. Always smiling, always laughing, Caitlen and Kimo gave their parents nothing but joy. Slinky could just watch his kids for hours, fascinated by their games and antics, so grateful that he became what he thought he never would, a father.

They sat in silence for the longest time, listening to the laughter and squeals drown out the soft sounds of the surf. Jaime looked all around the bay, just drinking in the view and the sounds and colours, she was as content as a person could be. At one point in her life Jaime thought she could never leave the workforce, never be without the daily challenges and interactions of business. All the highs and the lows, the stresses and failures and the unbelievable adrenaline rush of the successes. Since becoming a mother, Jaime had rarely if ever even thought about her old world. Leaning her head on his shoulder, she asked, "Was this always meant to be?"

Slinky hesitated before trying to answer as he wasn't exactly sure what she meant.

"Sorry, not a good way to address a question to a scientist." Jaime laughed and held his hand tightly in hers. "The world was ultimately going to fail. We've talked all about that. Overpopulation, economic uncertainties, famine, war, it was inevitable our species would have been gone at one point. But here we sit. Look around, it is so beautiful, so peaceful and so perfect." Taking another second to breathe it all in she stared out at the sun as it just kissed the horizon and said, "But do you think we'll ever truly discover how and more importantly why our species got a second chance?"

The multi-hued rays of the setting sun reflected off of Slinky's tanned face as he pondered what appeared on the surface to be a very odd question, all things considered. Putting his arm around her and pulling her close he kissed the top of her head and deciding not to ruin the mood, he said, "Oh, I thought you were talking about us."

EPILOGUE

Although they like everyone else wondered why, Jamie, Riley and Slinky were never to get any closer to solving the riddle of their survival. But they had a clue; that newly discovered gene from an ancient hominid that once bred with the ancestors of modern man. Apparently Jaime and Tessa had it, but did everyone else? It would be many generations before that theory of the 'healthy gene' would be confirmed.

However there were other survivors of the Locust Event and they did not carry the gene. Remote Inuit villages in Canada's northern arctic, numerous small tribes of indigenous Indians in the Amazon basin and other small groups of remote peoples in the wildest places on the planet all survived. Also surviving were a few monks of various religions who had been on personal journeys of meditation and discovery, only to find that when they returned, it was civilization that had left them. Two scientific research stations in Antarctica also initially survived but all hands were eventually lost as there were no more supply ships or aircraft that arrived with life sustaining fuel and food. Two Russians and one Frenchman also perished in the

International Space Station, frozen forever in time orbiting the planet. The entire population of Pitcairn Island, descendants from the mutineers of the HMS Bounty and their Tahitian companions survived. None of them carried the healthy gene but they did live in the remotest settlement on earth, in the middle of the south Pacific, over 1300 miles from the nearest inhabited island.

Possibly the most intriguing group that survived the Locust Event were the aptly named survivalists or what some people called '*doomsday preppers*'. Almost a thousand people survived Locust around the world by being previously prepared for their personal version of Armageddon and removing themselves into an assortment of previously provisioned underground bunkers and remote caves. Stocked with food and supplies to survive a nuclear war, economic collapse or whatever it was that they had feared those that stayed hidden from society long enough survived. But they did not fare as well in what was eventually called The Renewal Period, the hundred years following Locust. Heavily armed, paranoid and angry, few survived long enough to contribute their genes to the next generation.

As had been discussed many times at Lanai colony, an event like Locust was inevitable. As man entered the twenty first century the worst traits of the species were being rewarded with wealth and power. Unsustainable corporate greed, unjust and corrupt governments, massive environmental degradation and a rapidly growing population, mostly in areas of the world that could barely feed themselves, would have eventually ended the world as we had known it. Locust just did it a little quicker.

It took two full decades for the earth to return to what some considered its natural state with man no longer dominating every aspect of the planet. Modern man's monuments and achievements were no match for nature's relentless march. Our massive infrastructure rarely aged gracefully and the record of man's small presence on the earth was now at the whim of space and time. The playing field had been temporarily leveled and nature, harnessed and abused for far too long, quickly fought back.

The mighty Columbia River in the Pacific Northwest was quickly returned to its natural course through a series of monumental dam failures. It started at the top of the watershed in British Columbia as dam after dam failed, emptying unbelievably huge reservoirs and unleashing floods of biblical proportions throughout what was Washington State. Billions of tons of water hurtled downstream in a seemingly never ending torrent, returning thousands of square miles to flood plain, as it was before man's intervention. The iconic Mississippi River never dammed but heavily regulated through diking and levees broke through and charted its own course to the Gulf of Mexico, as nature had always intended. Similar scenarios unfolded in watersheds throughout the developed world as what man called nature's most destructive force, water, struck the first blow.

The tall-grass prairie, an endangered ecosystem returned with wild abandon over the heavily farmed North American heartland. The Great Plains, once thought lost forever, returned farm by farm and town by town. Herds of buffalo prospered and multiplied, their hooves the only thing tilling the soil as per nature's original design. Many generations later, those few remaining survivors with Native American blood finally saw what their ancestors had seen, herds of buffalo that reached to the horizon. All around the world, species once considered endangered prospered once again, finally released from man's manipulations.

The great herds of herbivores performed their huge seasonal migrations across the plains of Africa, a continent now almost completely devoid of people. The animal populations quickly grew with many ungulate species breaking out of the reserves and returning to their traditional ranges, followed by the species that preyed on them. Fish returned in unfathomable numbers to the oceans, rivers and streams of the world. Species hunted and fished to the brink of extinction came roaring back unencumbered by nothing except natures abundance.

The world's cities became nothing more than glass and concrete ghost towns. Their few remaining inhabitants, including small bands of surviving humans, migrated to greener pastures or perished. These great cities were to some, once man's crowning achievements and they became void of all life until eventually being reclaimed by the very soils that they were built from.

Amazingly through all the chaos of the Locust Event, only one nuclear meltdown occurred which sterilized a large part of what was southern France. That dead zone would exist for hundreds of years.

Our species had been changed forever. The infinitesimally small chance that pieces of ancient and apparently random DNA could merge to form a healthy gene in some individuals was proven much later. That mysterious linking of DNA fragments from a recently discovered human ancestor that most had never heard of was to change how modern humans now developed. Immune to disease and viruses, accidents and old age were the only limitations to those that inherited the healthy gene.

The greatest pockets of Locust survivors were the indigenous peoples of Papua New Guinea and Australia as both of those ethnicities carried by far the most Denisovan DNA and therefore were more likely to inherit the lifesaving gene. Their darkly pigmented skin and heavy, chunky facial features were to become the new normal in both genetic makeup and appearance for what some considered the re-birth of modern humans. The paths of these two groups through the Renewal Period though were very, very different.

For many decades, New Guinea was nothing more than a war zone. Fully eighty percent of the Locust Event survivors succumbed to the hostility that closely mimicked the islands violent past. Not many generations removed from being active head-hunters, their warrior like culture was intensified after Locust and they quickly returned to a state of perpetual tribal warfare. Eventually they exhausted the supply of modern weapons and returned to the clubs and spears of their ancestors. That however did nothing to diminish the violence and savagery.

Conversely, the Australian Aboriginals prospered as they returned to their ancient beliefs of reverence for their land and unabashed respect and admiration for their elders. Populations from every corner of Australia quickly returned to their tribal lands, living peacefully and co-existing in harmony with their environment. Self-sufficient and only taking what nature could afford to give, they left only footprints. Ten years after the Locust Event, Australian Aborigines made up over sixty percent of the surviving humans on the planet. Australia was the last habitable continent colonized and populated by modern man. It was ironic that the simple yet sustaining Aboriginal belief system and their undying respect for nature and the environment was to eventually be exported and ingrained in all survivors of the Locust Event. Australians would lead modern man into its new future in a quirky turn of events, colonizing the world in the opposite direction from the first time.

Just like it had for thousands of years, man wanted to explore, to see what was out there and in this case, to see what was left. Like always it included the allure of adventure, treasure and wealth but in this case it wasn't gold, precious gems or spices. It was an opportunity to start over, to build a foundation of mutual respect for each other and the planet and to learn from the mistakes of our past.

The most significant voyage of re-discovery in the early Renewal Period was one that left Lanai colony on an aging sailboat named Unfinished Business twenty six years after the Locust event. A handful of explorers, mainly descendants of the colonies first generation set out to discover what their new world had become. It was a voyage fraught with danger as the inherent frailties of our species were both exposed and conquered.

Mahatma Gandhi once said, "A small body of determined spirits fired by an unquenchable faith in their mission can alter the course of history." And that's exactly what happened on the final voyage of Unfinished Business as it laid the foundation for the second iteration of Homo sapiens on planet earth.